The Laugh that Laughs at the Laugh: Writing from and about the Pen Man, Raymond Federman

Journal of Experimental Fiction 23

The Laugh that Laughs at the Laugh: Writing from and about the Pen Man, Raymond Federman

Journal of Experimental Fiction 23

Edited by Eckhard Gerdes

Writers Club Press

San Jose   New York   Lincoln   Shanghai

The Laugh that Laughs at the Laugh: Writing from and about the Pen Man, Raymond Federman
Journal of Experimental Fiction 23

Writers Club Press
an imprint of iUniverse, Inc.

For information address:
iUniverse, Inc.
5220 S. 16th St., Suite 200
Lincoln, NE 68512
www.iuniverse.com

This anthology contains works of fiction. Names, characters, sites and incidents are either the products of the authors' imaginations or are used fictitiously, and any resemblance to actual persons, living or dead, events, or sites is entirely coincidental.

ISBN: 0-595-21404-5

Printed in the United States of America

Dedicated to Raymond.

Epigraph

"I've been devising a kind of butter to spread on people so that they can go to the moon without a space-ship. It's the kind of butter the witches used before they rode to the Blocksberg on broomsticks. I've gone a long way towards re-discovering this ancient compound."

—Halldór Laxness, *The Pigeon Banquet*

CONTENTS

FOREWORD

This volume of *The Journal of Experimental Fiction* has been an absolute delight to gather together. The individuals who have contributed to this project have all been generous and giving of their help, ideas and talents to this project. In particular, I would like to thank Larry McCaffery, Doug Rice, Lance Olsen, Jerome Klinkowitz, Reinhard Krüger, Amina Memory Cain, Daniel Borzutzky and the Journal's Art Director, Persis Gerdes, all of whom really went out of their way to give this project special consideration.

Mostly, though, I would like to thank Raymond Federman himself. Reading Raymond's work is very much a process of *becoming* Raymond Federman. This is what Doug Rice experienced when he and Larry McCaffery put together the excellent *Federman: From A to X-X-X-X: A Recyclopedic Narrative*. It's the kind of relationship established between reader and writer that is very rare in literature. I have personally only once before felt as "inside" the mind and heart of a writer as I have working on this project, and that occurred during my writing of my Master's thesis on Kenneth Patchen. Patchen's fiction has been labeled a "literature of engagement," and I think Raymond's is so also. Yet Raymond's, while engaging, also simultaneously disengages. It asserts its own contradictions proudly and fearlessly, which of course makes it so wonderfully postmodern, so wonderfully located at the nexus of several interface zones: fiction meets poetry, fiction meets nonfiction, literature meets diary, text meets visual art, assertion meets denial—wherever one looks when examining Raymond Federman's work, one finds a relentless pushing against boundaries and a refusal to accede to definition. After all, definition is dismissal, and Federman's is an art that cannot be dismissed.

There are no easy summations and categories which would allow us to file his work safely away in a drawer somewhere.

Even the monicker "experimental" is unfair to Raymond Federman's work, for it is ultimately so deep-down basically human, so concerned with the basic human experience, that it would be appreciated best by those of us in tune with the common experience, though that common experience at times is quite horrible. His work is not intended for the rarified air of academia and privilege, though it holds up well under such scrutiny. It is intended for humanity at large, and as such is really quite mainstream, such as his mentor Samuel Beckett's work was, and as Beckett's mentor James Joyce's work, particularly *Ulysses*, was before him. This linealogy is significant. Federman is the literary direct descendent of James Joyce. His work and legacy reveal this at every turn.

We are fortunate to be able to bring our readers some representative selections from Raymond's work in addition to the many tributes by his friends and colleagues whose own work has been so deeply touched by what Larry McCaffery calls the Federman Virus. We are reprinting here selections from his earliest fiction (from a story he workshopped as a student at Columbia University and from his first published story, "The Toothbrush," to a section of his current novel-in-progress). If you are not yet familiar with Raymond's work, you are in for a real treat. If you are familiar with it, you are in for an even bigger treat.

This issue involved Raymond's input almost every step of the way. His help has always been kind, inobtrusive, gentle and generous. What a rare soul.

Eckhard Gerdes, December 2001

You may contact us at:

Eckhard Gerdes, editor
The Journal of Experimental Fiction

Division of Humanities
Macon State College
100 College Station Drive
Macon, Georgia 31206

eckhard@experimentalfiction.com
www.experimentalfiction.com

See the website for subscription information.

16 Pieces of Fiction

Raymond Federman

THE INTERROGATORS

++++++++++++++++++++

THE HOLD	**THE DESK**	**THE ROOM**
[past / there]	[present / here]	[infinity / elsewhere]

[digression / redoubling / repetition]

==

moment 1   moment 7   moment 3

    moment 5   moment 2

moment 9

moment 4   moment 6

---

child + old man = he = me + family

[story / fiction / lies]

the interrogated—the storyteller—the liar

—

Tell us who you are?

[history—reality—truth]

▲▼▲

1   7

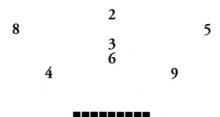

THE INTERROGATED—THE LISTENERS—THE OTHERS

THE LOST FLOWER

There was a great commotion in the Green Valley. The Grass was whispering, the Trees were nodding to each other, speaking to each other's Leaves. Even the murmur of the Stream among the Rocks was softer than usual. Nature seemed to be preparing for something special. Perhaps a revolution. But it was even more frightening than that.

This morning, when Daylight opened its windows to the Sun, a lonely Flower was standing alone in the middle of the Green Meadow, proudly and courageously raising her purple and yellow head above the Grass, unashamed to find herself in such a strange place.

As long as the oldest Oaks could remember [some had been here for over two centuries] never had such a thing been seen. Flowers were unknown in this Valley. Millions of questions were asked. Trees would talk to the Grass, Bushes to the Stones, Birds to the Insects who formed a wide circle around the Meadow, but keeping their distance from the Stranger. Everyone was talking nervously and anxiously, wondering where that Flower came from [that's what they called it–**Flower**], and why it was here. No one knew, not even the King of the Insects, who had left the cool comfort of his underground Castle and stood under the hot Sun among his Subjects during this moment of crisis.

Not even the King could give an explanation. He too was puzzled and concerned. Perhaps this Flower had brought poison to the Valley.

Only the Wind, in the midst of all the excitement, remained calm, neither surprised nor concerned. Instead the Wind seemed to be smiling ironically. For he knew that during the night, his younger mischievous little brother, The Breeze, who is out late every night, had carried the Flower seed, and playfully dropped it in the most conspicuous spot of the Valley, and now both of them were watching the result of what The Breeze had done during the night, and how the entire Valley was in turmoil.

Morning was stretching languidly into Afternoon, the Sun indifferent to all the excitement was high in the Sky. Rumors were spreading over the Hilltops into other Valleys, about the evil that had been brought into the Green Valley. Many curious from other Valleys set out toward the mystery of what was now called **The Lost Flower.**

Many questions were asked, suggestions made, arguments debated, but no action taken. And now Evening was approaching and nothing was done to calm the fear and anxiety of the Green Valley.

Suddenly the Valley became silent. A rumor was circulating that an Orphan Bee, last survivor of an old respected swarm of Bees, had volunteered to venture to the Stranger in order to find an answer to the situation, even if it meant sacrificing her life.

It was a silence of Death. All were holding their breath, and when the Wind inadvertently shook the Leaves of a faded old Bush, all eyes turned to the Wind reproachfully.

Finally the little Bee set out on her perilous journey. It was not a long flight, but everyone in the Valley knew how her wings and legs and spine and antennas must have been trembling with fear as she approached the Lost Flower. Only a few more flutterings of her Wings now separated the courageous crusader from her objective, the Lost Flower, who, during all that time had not moved or said a thing, but continued to raise her colorful head proudly, almost arrogantly, toward the now descending Sun.

The Bee circled twice round the large Petals of the Flower that were reaching for the little Bee. The Petals were turning pale pink as the Sun began to roll down the Crest of the Hills, reflecting his reddish Light against the Sky.

Finally, closing her eyes, and raising her head to some unknown Deity, the Bee dove into the Heart of the Lost Flower and disappeared.

A morbid sinister cry filled the entire Valley. The Grass was sobbing, the trees bowed their heads in shame, the insects knelt piously on the ground, the birds stopped fluttering their wings and remained suspended in the Air, and all the Bees gathered around the Queen Bee and began buzzing a prayer. It was a tense moment. All of Nature seemed to be in mourning. No one expected the little Orphan Bee to return.

A long time passed. Gradually, the conversation started again, in hushed sounds. Everyone spoke of fear, torture, suffering, pity, death. Though there were some optimists who wanted to bet on the outcome of the Bee's daring adventure. When Twilight fell and almost everyone had given up hope, the little Orphan Bee flew out from inside the Flower, and speedily came toward the King of the Insects. She landed lightly in front of Him. All the Necks stretched as far as they could. Everything was all Ears. A great silence fell on the Valley. The tallest Trees almost touched the ground with their Branches, the Water in the Stream stopped flowing, all were listening intently.

The little Bee bowed respectfully before the King, and then related proudly, almost joyfully, what had happened: *As I approached the Lost Flower and began to glide down toward it, an incredibly sweet and perfumed aroma struck my senses. It was like nothing I had ever smelled before. So strong and yet so sugary, yes that's how it smelled, sugary. I felt dizzy. It was as if I had just drunk some mysterious potion. It made me feel happy. Finally, when I landed softly inside the flower, my feet seemed to be gliding on a soft carpet of velvet, so soft and so gentle, it made me giddy. I was surrounded by a myriad of colors. It was as if I was inside some marvelous Castle.*

Paradise perhaps. I felt safe. When I reached the Heart of the Flower, soft Tentacle-like Fingers fed me the most delicious rich copious Sugar I have ever tasted…I am sorry that I stayed so long, My Lord, perhaps too long while all of you must have been so anxious about me, but it was so beautiful inside that flower, and the sugar was so sweet, I could not leave. But I remembered my mission, and finally departed, and as I left, the Petals of the Flower caressed me gently. I hurried back, My Lord, to tell you, and to you my dear Friends, said the little Bee bowing to all in the Valley, *the wonderful news that we can all be thankful to whoever brought such Beauty and such Bounty to our Valley.*

The Wind and his little brother, The Breeze smiled and rustled the Leaves of the Trees knowingly and gleefully as they listened to the Bee.

That Night, after everyone had retired, weary after such an extraordinary Day, The Breeze, alone in the sky, wiped a tear of happiness, as he dropped more Flower Seeds into the Valley.

Many Years have passed since that memorable Day, when the first Flower appeared in the Green Valley, and its mystery was solved. If you ever happen to pass by what is now called **The Valley of the Lost Flower**, do not be surprised if you see a multitude of lovely Flowers growing peacefully in the Green Valley.

("the lost flower was written in a creative writing class when I was an undergraduate at Columbia University [around 1956 I guess]")

THE STATE OF ERECTION & OTHER CONSEQUENCES

nione oeufus coude member ow apen...ven rection apen...vo mongus primo crack ribcage torise frum quadr-up-ed pozichon to biped postur...& screaaamin mit urt insid wildernesssss launchus present state confuz rection...but rect us was...primo mong alspecies look upsky defiantly...me mong primo...me primo wave...primo batch .. early rectus...me maybe bit prematur...cose me til xtincshion ovme...me coude niot leak yelow water standinup like oter rectusesss...so me do yelow leaking restin nukles ground & legup sidway...stil me fulyrect...but nione oeufus coude member ow apen state oeuf rection...yetyet manyus felt...manymoons...trocious ake inus backs...crosback...frum boneshoelder to boneshoelder down spine to biddy oleass & croschest too... big memoryless ake oeuf ancien eegnorance...ah ifus sufer lots for stature future big standin generashions ...somus somoeuften come out bidylitle death in darkcave in moonglow screaaaaming mit ake...somus roam round all dark bent haf...olding ussmalback mit hands...moaning oy weh oy weh...stumblin over bodies otercavefelowpeople curled in bidysmal death...shutdeflukup...go back yo filtyshitymoss & jumpback in smal death...felowcavemanbastard shout from corner rockysmelful dweling...but then turn cum lousyfelowcaveshouter com out smal death mit bigake in back...& moonnext hym feel ancestral ake...yio...hym be us cursed now cose hym stumblin over us bodies curled in smalbidydeath...manymanymany sunsmoons aphter rection...ven us set out frum cave direcshion smokey redglow insky...farway farway...us member distant moonglow agony ven primo homo mong us rected...& whileus trampl crosswamps...crawl mud...chargup mountains...fal down valeys...onway to redglow...us stil hear inus narow skuls orible cryys in jungle when primo ribcage crak...bywen us reach redglow insky most us rect fulywas...give take excepshions...slow homorectatus us called tem niot ful deploy...as me say...me mong early unfiolds...me say mong cose us always gether...always bunch gether...yio...me never lone...me kanot member ever belone...nio...us niot made for solitary rection wandrin ...us omonids...us always udle gether...us nervouspack...us scared...us always closegether...always elbows rubin...smelin badsmels eachoder... yio...us do lots badodor in litle ole in bigass cose us grasseatin lots...lots graseating...so lots biddy gaspufs...us greatsmelly...someus niotful deploy stood demirect...poorslobs...by sunglow ven us set out for smokey redglow in sky...many ancien quadr-up-pians mong us already xtinguish...maybe demirectus stay folded half cose fear...fear-prehenshion oldake inback...terible oldake inback...me tell yiou...but somlater moonglow dem too...slobdemis...break out twisted bones & rise rect...or else...us eat them...yio...us always eat xtinguish meat cavepeople...us eat deadmeatpeople ...demis look foolish...standup strait yiou animal...us cry demirectus...kickin dem in rearplace where red hump made us member vanish tail badbad prvious condishion...condishion niot omonid...condishionape...wak lik tru ominid yiou rtarded lump slouchin meat...us yel demirctus...monkeying dem clumsy boping moshions...niot dis mean usmore agil uselves in oiur simian bowlgednss...but us least was up & rect...O by-d-way cidently fore me forget...me shoud menshion...dosus rected al did adultage...al sammoon...alus change alonce...samoonglow...us was so apy...us apyjubilant cose us rectus now...now us matefuck front & niot rear nomore...only us ominids in entir uverse fluckmatin do frontwrd...us gotgot greatgreat jouissance frontwrd...us gotgot bigrection...us omorectus nver regress quadrupedian state...nio nio nio...us standup tal...us rectnow...us bibbigrect...us man...us bigproud upman...

but somdarkmoonglow somtime us fluckmate rear...in bidyassole...in sweetasole...forold glowsake...ah yio us jubilant...us bigerect...usbigbigupman ...[*to be continued—maybe*]

A STORY [ABOUT A STORY] WITHIN A STORY

One day [here we go again dear readers] a Bum [let's call him Bum One, whomever] was telling another Bum [Bum Two] a story *my life began* and for some unusual reason the latter *among empty skins* was actually listening…a very unusual thing indeed, actually listening to the story *and dusty hats* that One was narrating. Actively listening rather than interrupting, laughing, kibbitzing, stopping, turning away *while sucking pieces of stolen sugar* eating a cold waffle, and in general co-creating inter-subjectively the community language experience *outside the moon* of the narrativity. It was, to be sure *tiptoed across the roof* not much of a story. Indeed, and in fact, if you asked Bum Two about it now…a mere few hours after the telling *to denounce the beginning of my excessiveness*…he would in all likelihood not be able to recover a shred of it, nary a syllable would have survived the telling…although *but I slipped on the twelfth step*, to be sure, he may in this disremembering be exhibiting rather more of a short-term aphasia *and fell,* an age-appropriate disability, than creating an interpretation of the text. [Hey, this is muddy stuff *and all the doors*, eh readers, bet you wish you had a tissue, and some soap]. We mean here, *opened dumb eyes*, meaning no disrespect to Bum One, that the story was lost on Bum Two not because of its innocuousness and banality, but simply because …

to stare at my nakedness the old guy's motherboard is cracked. [What! Are you listening?]

Anyway [you see how the elderly love to get lost in anything, *as I ran beneath the indifferent sky*, in a city, in a mall and, as here, in a text], Bum One went on *clutching a filthy package of fear* with his story, a story, which we can now reveal had one distinct and curious feature…we'll say it plain: It began in the narrator's adopted language, but soon enough, *dans mes mains* was flowing in the mother tongue of the narrator, a language which he hasn't spoken all that much these past 45 years, although it should be noted that in the course of his narration Bum Two often switched back *a yellow star* to his adopted language and at times even spoke both languages *tomba du sky et frappa my breast* simultaneously.

The story itself, as we say, was perhaps eminently forgettable, a tale of survival, of defeat and victory, a tale of heroism and villainy *et tous les yeux turned away in shame*, a tale of noble wanderings, of sadly proportioned departures and returns, mixed with grand scenes of powerful recognition…and interruptions…*then they grabbed me*…[You wonder what's coming next, don't you dear readers? We do too] *and locked me dans une boîte*. We're getting worried for the old guys, perhaps they'll even forget this story they are supposedly narrating.

But this, as we say, is pure conjecture. What elements composed the actual story *dragged me a thousand times* are lost to us, as we have asserted. We press on *cent fois*. But before we do, let us pause here a moment to re-establish the narrative, to summarize *my life began in a closet*, to draw in a last big breath *merde alors si on se répète*. The two old guys are sitting dry-assed [you like this locution, we bet *over the earth in metaphorical disgrace* this is likely to be all you can recollect of this tale, so far] on a pre-formed plastic park bench…*tiens un banc! Qu'est-ce que ce banc peut bien foutre ici?*…supplied by a local undertaker featuring this week a discount for double interments in their spanking new columbarium *while they threw stones at each other and burned all the stars in a giant furnace*.

One elderling is telling the other a story which for some unusual reason the latter is actually listening to et *les voilà tous exterminés les pauvres diables* attentively, without interruption. The story is a literary masterpiece, we think, but it is lost to memory. All that remains *every day they came* is the knowledge that the tale began in English and soon transformed to French, and even Frenglish, *pour mettre leurs doigts in my mouth…et aussi dans mon cul*, even though the content of the tale had a Greek flavor with a touch of Yiddishkeit in it, a tinge of the Aegean and the Middle-Eastern.

[Forgive us, we enjoy so these elaborations, these asides, these excursions and incursions. We are former military persons]...*and paint me black and blue.*

Soon then, soon enough *mais à travers un trou,* the narrator either brought his tale to its conclusion or was incapable of drawing more breath to sustain the story, or, *I saw a tree the shape of a feuille,* having throughout the telling experienced no encouraging response from his audience—much as a preacher will call out for a witness *and one morning a bird flew into my head* will gather fuel for the telling [can we get a witness here?] *Ah tu parles machin, ils sont tous morts les témoins,* for the final hooping solution transcendence, lost his confidence, ran out of gas—can we get a witness too?—and ended the story, all in one breath ...

I loved cet oiseau so much that while mon maitre aux yeux bleus looked at the sun aveuglé I opened la cage and hid my heart dans une plume jaune...

Bum One slid out a bit on the bench, the better to turn to his friend, the better to look at him. He looked thoughtful, puzzled.

You know, he said, I have never heard that story before. Not in all the years of our friendship.

Bum Two, now reverting entirely to his step-tongue: Obviously not, you never heard it. I just made it up on the spot, he said, from approved material of course, but newly composed for this occasion.

Hmm, replied One, that much I suspected. I was not questioning the tale itself, but the telling of it. Are you aware that during the telling you began in one language and ended in another, and that in fact at one point you even mixed both languages and spoke them simultaneously?

Really? I did that, I mixed Yiddish with Ladino?

Well, I don't know if it was Yiddish or Ladino or Javanese, but some of what I heard did have a Yiddish beat with a touch of music from Ukraine, but that was only the vehicle. What I heard, what I really heard was ghosts, the voices of the dead.

Hey, you OK boy? asked Two, this bench making you morbid?

I'm telling you, I heard, Bum One went on, the voices of the dead, the dead who have no story of their own to tell. They are here with us now.

Hey, stop, this is too much, said Bum Two turning away from his friend, shaking his head in refusal, this is too much, he mumbled to himself.

And there they left the story, and we leave them, two old dry-assed bums, sitting next to each other on a bench in the park. Now you know why we experienced such resistance as we attempted to retell this story of a story within a story. We beg your indulgence.

A DIE A LO GUE

F: rply mde m vry hppy m tot m im~~
prove or die alo gue & mke poetik

W: appy U saij th~t g w~s eppi 2
shee ph~nin wen w rode ladder 2 rf
[den red litter 2 g] g ly~KIT g reel~y
bizzy lay~k~cry~see NUT no~mal
nex~wik back 2 no~mallyTy!

F: den m weit G call m no~mall time

W: i ~alp U way~t beij sho()t~ catting
gee~z reCAVE~arie pi~riot

W: zzzzzzzzzzzrui 89

F: m thnk G no x~ist m thnk G no
        Kare m m Panike

W: I fo~ce g 2 bling hur caLLier pig~
        djen onde way(ve) ore shee neva egg~
        seased~tit mi~sink shy nea may stud io 2die

F: Shoere u knot nuts

THE COMPETITION

Seven years old. You are in school. An all boy school—*une école de garçons.* Yes, a French school. You were born in France. It's not your fault. You had no voice in this decision.

During *récréation* the older boys—eleven and twelve years old—go to the far end of the yard near the big wall to play. You go with them even though they always make fun of you because you are rickety and clumsy. That too is not your fault. The older boys let you play with them because they like to laugh at you.

In the far corner of the yard near the big wall, where the *Pion* in charge of watching the boys during *récréation* cannot see what 's going on, the tallest boy draws a line on the wall above his head with a piece of white chalk, then he draws another line on the ground about *trois mètres* from the wall. Then the boys, half a dozen of them, besides you, start the competition to see who can piss the highest above the line on the wall. You never win.

Only once did you succeed in pissing above the white line, but that's because you stood close to the wall, about one meter away, and also because you held back all the *pipi* you had in you since the night before in anticipation of the competition. You were excited to have managed for the first time to piss above the line, to piss into the sky, even if you did not win the competition that day.

The other boys said you cheated because you crossed the line on the ground. Only those who piss on the wall from the line on the ground are qualified. Those who cross the line are disqualified. That day you were disqualified as a high altitude *pisseur.*

15

Chinoiseries	Chinoiseries	Chinoiseries
spontaneous	merleauponty	handicap 3
designs	deleuzeserres	politicomerdique
filings	legroupetelquel	in toto
wordarrows	sollersetsabande	vacheries
tripping	lacanderrida	quattrocento
prompto	bookinage	degueulasse
shi shid shid chineto-	dig)(ression	vasy
ques	pif paf pif	gooshy-gooshy
pank [punk]	strainers	motherly looks
pipi caca	garggle up	punctuational
collective existence	gasoline	bizenèce
nooowooon	47 48 49	biteauculmettable
de ta ching	crapidouille	rebeyrolle unificity
sy la bles	zizique à posteriori	paredros
tiergarten	theatrum	hombre
cent francs six quo	philosophicum	de la pluma
ye ye ye woopy	vocaliser	hombre
aeiou bang bang	branletapoire	de la corna
fling flang	robbe-grilladized	water mouth
tas pas mal	undersollersism	nouillorque
aux couilles	analism	cancellation
iiiii iiiii iiiii-iiiii-iiiii	bardamu	vas-y toto
¡°me me me me	enceinte enculé	excessive identity
decancel	yenta	sneaky set up
prickly texticule	el am	deal dead
saks miniscule	jazz solo	body by fisher
living dead	imaginary 6 iron	flaps & flips
mes deux	hustling jewish	in a shiffy
saint bricolage	doctors	twenty-one
pissoirs à deux	perfect p.l.f.	thousand-hours

OUT OF THE FOXHOLE

—The Bullet—

Have I ever told you what happened in Korea when I found myself in a foxhole with some kid from Jersey?

Here, let me start from the beginning. You were there too, I know, freezing your ass off in the rice paddies, so I know you'll understand.

Anyway, since you claim your **I** is interchangeable with my **I**, you can substitute your **I** any time in what I am going to tell you, and this way you'll experience exactly what I experienced in that foxhole, in the middle of the rice paddies, on that unforgettable night. But let's start at the beginning of the War Zone. The boat arrives in Yokohama full of fresh anxious recruits, most of them still *puceaux* [look it up in the French dictionary]. I think we came on the USS Grant, but since memory is always deficient I cannot confirm that it was the USS Grant, for all I know it could have been some other stinking tub. What's for sure is that after three fucking weeks of vomiting in the Pacific, we were glad to set foot on firm ground.

Immediately upon arrival in Yokohama, we were selected to stay either in Japan with the vacationing black-marketing Occupying Forces or to be shipped directly to Korea to participate in the so-called Police Action. Me, I got the Korean vacation. But not for long, not for long, as I'll explain in a moment.

So here I am in a foxhole somewhere beyond one of the parallels—I can't remember if it's the 38th or the 36th or the 42nd—in the middle of a rice paddy, and it's cold like hell, 20 below, and over there, across from us, less than 100 yards from us, on the other side of the rice paddy, some fucking Gooks are shooting at us. I can't tell you how they look because we can't see them. They're buried in the mud. But they are Gooks. That's what everybody calls them.

It's the middle of the night. My feet, my hands, my nose, my ears are frozen. I'm with this kid from Jersey in a muddy foxhole. He's smaller than me, and scared. Me, I tell him, I'm not scared because my death is behind me already. What the fuck you talking about, he says with his Jersey accent and a puzzled look on his face. I can see the puzzled look on his face because for just a moment the moon comes out from behind a cloud. Yes, it's a cloudy night. It might snow any moment. I forgot to mention it's winter, and what a stinking winter it was. So I start telling Jersey the story of my life. You know, the same old story you've heard so many times. Meanwhile the bullets are flying over our heads in all directions, as we crouch inside the foxhole, clutching our rifles. Why the fuck are they shooting at us. We didn't do anything to make them angry. We're just two little G.I.s doing our duty. I'm really pissed at those motherfucking Gooks for shooting at us like that. For no specific reason. We didn't do anything to them. We didn't shoot first. We didn't insult them. We're just doing our duty. Except I forgot to mention that the foxhole in which Jersey and me are hiding is an outpost in front of the main line. We're supposed to be observing the enemy movements. The main line, where our buddies are probably jerking off or snoozing up while waiting for the next attack, is about 300 yards behind us.

Maybe the reason the Gooks are shooting at our foxhole is because the little asshole Jersey just lit a cigarette. A Chesterfield, or maybe a Camel, I'm not sure, I'm not a smoker. That stupid Jersey lit his fucking cigarette without covering the flame of his lighter with his hands, like we were taught in basic training, and so the Gooks when they saw the light started shooting, and now the bullets are flying all around us—some of them with little lights attached to them, you know tracers, so they can see us better. We're keeping out heads tucked down low in the hole.

Suddenly I have a premonition. This is it. My excess of life has run out of excess. Tonight is the night I join the angels. So I say to Jersey, give me a fucking cigarette. I never smoked before, that 's because of the swimming, but fuck it. I could have told Jersey to go and read *Take It or Leave*

It to find out what a great swimmer I was when I almost made it to the Olympics, but there was no point in that since the story was not written yet, and may never be written if my premonition comes true. But, as you see, I survived that onslaught of bullets from the Gooks, otherwise I couldn't be here telling you all this.

Anyway, at that moment, when the moon came out from behind the clouds, I was sure this was it. So I say to Jersey, give me a fucking cigarette, my first, and my last. One of these fucking bullets has my name on it. [Please excuse the frequent repetition of the word fucking, but I'm trying to be as realistic and as close to the truth as possible, this is an army story, and it was a crucial moment in my life].

So I take a deep drag on the fucking cigarette, and I almost choke. I start coughing like I have tuberculosis. Jersey is slapping me on the back, and screaming at me

softly, shut the fuck up, they're going to kill us. He hands me his canteen full of—you won't believe this—full of sake [where the fuck did he get sake out here?], and I choke and cough even more, and the bullets are flying even more. The whole sky is full of them. I take a second drag of the cigarette, but this time the smoke feels good inside. Feels warm. I remember, I even let some of the smoke come out slowly through my nose, my big nose, just like I've seen movies stars do. I'm all grown-up suddenly. I feel like a man. I could fight those fucking Gooks barehanded.

I raise my head a bit above the ledge of the foxhole, up to my nose, put out my M1, and fire at will, northward towards the Gooks. Jersey climbs up next to me from the mud at the bottom of the foxhole and starts shooting too, but he's so short he has to stand on top of his backpack [full of cans of monkey meat and cigarettes—Jersey is a chain smoker] to reach the edge of the foxhole [it's a deep foxhole] so he sticks out of the hole more than me—above the chin—and the bullet destined for me hits him. No not in the face, not in the eye, but on the wrist which was outside the security of the foxhole since he was holding his M1 above the ledge. The bullet hits the wrist, but not the flesh or the bone of the wrist [I think it was the left wrist, if I remember correctly, but since I make little distinction between memory and imagination, it could have been the right wrist just as well]. In any case, the bullet with my name on it doesn't hit the wrist itself, so to speak, but Jersey's wrist-watch. I'm not kidding. And the whole fucking watch gets pulverized in his arm. [I think it was a Bulova he bought at the PX in Tokyo during his R&R, but I'm not sure. It could have been a Rolex. All I know is that it was a big round watch with a gold bracelet. He showed it me when he got back from R&R, and I said to him, wow what a good-looking big fucking wrist-watch, you must have payed a fortune for it. That's exactly what I said.

Anyway, when the bullet hit the watch the whole fucking mechanism got disseminated in Jersey's entire arm, from the wrist to the shoulder. The little springs got under his skin, the screws, the numbers, the hands of the watch, the rubies [yes, his watch had twelve rubies, that's what it said on the back, he showed me] got dispersed and encrusted in his arm, and Jersey is screaming like a pig being slaughtered, and I am screaming too, MEDIC! MEDIC! where the fuck are the fucking medics. Meanwhile the fucking Gooks, when they hear all that screaming and shouting, start shooting again. I get so pissed, I take a grenade out of the pocket of my field jacket and throw it northward [with my left arm—I was a lefty then], and I hear little human squeaks. I burst into laughter. Meanwhile Jersey is at the bottom of the foxhole squirming and whining and weeping with pain, and fear of death, of course. I take his flashlight [we had flashlights] out of his backpack and examine his wound. The bullets start flying again. He's not going to die. I reassure him with a tap on top of the head, and tell him, Jersey you're a fucking lucky sonofabitch, it's nothing, just a flesh wound, they gonna send you home with that, you gonna get a purple heart and a pension for life, and you know what, you'll be a celebrity, you'll have the time in you forever. You'll be a human clock. You'll get a job in a circus or freak show. You'll be rich and famous.

Just then two medics, crawling in the mud, reach our foxhole. They grab Jersey, who is still screaming and weeping and whining, and drag him back to the main line. Be careful with him, I tell them, the guy is precious.

—The Reprieve—

And me? What do you think? I'm not gonna stay in this fucking foxhole alone. I'm outta here. I'm not gonna fight the Gooks by myself. So I crawl out of the hole and retreat to the main line.

The next day I'm told to report to Captain Cohen—yes a Yid like me. On my way to his tent I say to myself, shit he's going to chew my ass for having deserted my post. Maybe I'll get busted. I was a PFC then. I walk into Captain Cohen's tent, give him one of my best military salute as I stand at attention.

At ease, Federstein ...

Federman, I correct him politely ...

Oh yeah, Federman. PFC Federman get you gear together you're flying to Tokyo.

Oh shit, I thought, they're going to court-martial me for having deserted my post. Why Sir? I ask, coming to attention again.

Not the foggiest idea. Just when I need every fucking man I have for the big push. It's an order that just came in from Central Headquarters in Tokyo.

Central Headquarters? Hey, maybe they gonna decorate me because of my heroic action last night. After all, Jersey and me we stood our ground during that ferocious attack on our foxhole, and I saved his life.

Must be important, Captain Cohen says, so get your ass moving, there is a plane leaving in ten minutes.

Yes Sir!

Yes sir! I shouted militarily, when I heard they wanted me in Tokyo, and rushed to pack my duffel bag and expand my War Zone activities to Japan.

Up in the B25 fighter flying me to Tokyo, I sat next to the pilot, and he even let me hold the steering wheel for a while–ah what sweet sensation I suddenly felt—free at last—once again I had outsmarted my death. I should have kept the bullet that pulverized Jersey's watch as a souvenir.

Somehow I knew I was leaving that *frigidaire* of rice paddies for good. I'll do anything in Tokyo so they don't send me back to the rice paddies, I told my co-pilot as I steered the B25 to a higher altitude. I'll do anything. Even suck a dick? asked my co-pilot, and suddenly I felt a frisson pass through me. The fucking co-pilot is queer and is proposing to me, I thought [not to myself]. Suppose the cocksucker aggresses me, right here up in the sky, and gives me a blowjob, even though I don't do these sort of things, and he pulls rank on me and tells me it's an order [my co-pilot is a captain, and me just a one stripe PFC] but nothing ensued [hey nice choice of words here—*en-suce*] of that proposition, and I landed safely in Tokyo.

—On Special Assignment—

Sir! PFC Federstein reporting! I shouted to the Commanding Officer of the 510 Military Intelligence Group, Major Grandcon. [I was ordered upon landing in Tokyo to report immediately to Major Grandcon for special assignment. Me! A special assignment—I suddenly felt very important, and very alive].

Sir! PFC Federstein reporting, I said clicking in the Nazi style the heels of my superbly spit-shined paratrooper boots now cleaned for good of the mud of the rice paddies. [Yes I was a paratrooper. 82nd Airborne Division—see *Take It or Leave It* for details].

[I said Federstein instead of Federman in case they decided to send me back to the rice paddies. I figured, this way Federstein would go instead of Federman].

At ease Soldier! Major Grandcon said holding out his hand, as if I were some kind of very special agent. Yes, this I will never forget, Grandcon called me Soldier, and shook hands with me, as if I were a national hero. It made me feel so proud to be serving my adopted country in the Far East, even though I had not yet been officially adopted [poor little orphan that I am] by my new country [that will happen later in Tokyo—see *Smiles on Washington Square* for full details of the adoption ceremony].

So I put myself at ease. Dropped into the luxurious leather armchair facing Major Grandcon's desk—after all I was a Special Ass, I had privileges—and I said, while relaxing my tired ass in the softness of the chair, all my life my feet have been killing me [see epigraph of *Loose Shoes* for clarification]. Grandcon smiled and said: Me too, I have the same problem, but we're not here to tell the story of our feet. There is a fucking war going on, and we fucking better get it over soon because the fucking Russkoffs are waiting in line to start the next war, and one war at a time is enough. That's exactly what Major Grandcon said.

Damn right Major! I said, speaking as one officer to another, while puffing on the Cuban cigar Major Grandcon had offered me, and reclining deep into the safety of the armchair. Not another war, I thought. Suppose they draft me for that one too, even though I'm not officially a citizen yet. And suppose the fucking Russkoffs capture me and I'm a prisoner of war, and one day while taking a leak the Russkoffs notice my circumcised cock, and immediately want to exterminate me, even though I keep waving my dog tags at them as I stand before the firing squad, naked, except for my dog tags around my neck, on which it says P for religion and not J [yes another typical army goof when they indoctrinated me—see *Take It or Leave It* for details of another army goof].

Well, let me summarize quickly what happened next, which I now recall as being a relaxing and comforting moment, when I was informed by Major Grandcon that I would be attached to the 510 MIG as a Liaison Officer [without any specific rank, however, since you are not yet a citizen, Grandcon specified] between our forces and the French speaking forces now involved in this United Action. Suddenly I remembered that I know French [in this fucking army, I didn't have much use for my French, that other language in me was, so to speak, dormant] and it all became clear to me.

Inadvertently, the fucking French, who tried so hard to have me exterminated *jadis*, were now saving my life because of my knowledge of their language. The American forces need a frog to interpret—to explain to them what's going on. Wow! was I going to interpret and explain. Man, I'll make a fortune here in Tokyo interpreting and clarifying. I'm not going to do that kind of essential job, for nothing.

So I tell the Major that I will accept the position on the condition that I receive a generous retribution of sort, and a medal to show the important role I played in United Action in the Far East. Grandcon, didn't flinch. He gave me 500000 yens right there on the spot. He took the money out of a little Japanese lacquer box on his desk [I remember the lacquer box very clearly because it had a picture of Mount Fuji on the cover]. Of course, at the then current rate of exchange, it was worth about 100 bucks, but enough to buy me my first piece of slanted ass in Tokyo. And also a carton of cigarettes. Chesterfields. You see, since that first [and fortunately not last] cigarette in the foxhole, I was now addicted [see *La Fourrure de ma Tante Rachel* for Federstein's favorite brand of cigarettes].

Ok, to make that special moment more climatic let me sum up what Major Grandcon said. You, Federstein, Liaison Officer of undetermined rank and nationality, will serve as an interpreter for the French forces newly involved in the United Action in these parts. You will reside in the Imperial Hotel in a special suite, already reserved for you, a jeep with a boysan driver will be at your service, 24 hours a day, and another boysan will take care of your needs, 24 hours a day. When I heard about the second boysan, I requested politely that the second boysan be a girlsan–a matter of taste, I explained to Major Greatcon.

Less than half an hour later [after having agreed to re-enlist for another year of service, so glad I was to be out of the fucking rice paddies], I was soaking in a steaming hot bath at the Imperial Hotel, soon to receive [after having been wiped and oiled] a deliciously slow and sensual massage by my private girlsan.

The next day.........or perhaps it was the same day, when, after the massage, I went strolling in the streets of devastated Tokyo. And man did it stink in that fucking city. You too must remember the canal running through the whole place. It was so infected with all the shit and piss and garbage the Tokyo people threw in it. Took me seven weeks to get used to the smell, but I never got used to the dead rats floating in the canal. It was the same day I arrived in Tokyo and was promoted to special Liaison Officer, and got my first Japanese massage, that I bumped into another G.I., a corporal, who looked totally stoned and drunk, and lost too. It was in a Shimbashi bar. The guy slapped me solidly on the back when he saw me come in, as if I we were old buddies, and shouted, So here you are Old Bum, as if he had expected me, still alive, come on, man! let's booze it up.

On you, of course, my dear Fellow-Bum, I said embracing him to show my appreciation. You see, I didn't want to blow immediately the 100 bucks Grandcon gave me, I wanted to save it in case the right pussy came along. So I was willing to let that guy treat me. What the hell.

and that's how *The Dawn of the Bums* started .....

THE REAL THING

One day the two bums...

You mean...

No, I don't mean Socrates and Cephalus, or Plato and Aristo, or Kant and Hegel, or Sartre and Simone, or X and Z, no, I mean our two Bums, remember, B^1 and B^2...

Oh yes, of course...

Well the other day, B^1 said to his buddy, just like that out of the blue, so to speak, **real language is always incomprehensible...**

So is love, sex, writing, B^2 replied...

Not so, or rather quite so, my dear friend, since love, sex, writing are always dependent on language...

What do you mean?...

What do I mean! Who is talking about meaning. Have I ever been interested in meaning? Me, the most irrational, nonsensical, incoherent being on this planet. Me, the chaos-drunk scribbler, the clown of meaninglessness and unreadability...

Don't get excited. Slow down. I'm losing you. What were you trying to say?...

What I was saying, or attempted to say with words that I know are always deficient, always inadequate, sad and pathetic, and thus comprehensible to most, is that **real language and real sex** (writing & love being substitute terms) **are always incomprehensible....**

I'll go along with that, I mean your idea of the incomprehensibility of sex or love, though personally I always make a distinction between the two. Sex is active, love is passive. Sex is hard, love is soft. But I don't see how it applies to writing...

The act of writing, my Dear B[2], situates itself in the field of sexuality because it is always governed by desire, the desire that moves one to write....

Does that mean that for you writing is a form of sexual activity?...

Damn right. And by extension language, **real language** is always phallic,

or if you prefer phallogocentric because it fucks what it does, it screws up the object that it creates, and thus renders it incomprehensible....

If this is so, then, we, as writers, should perhaps lock ourselves in the desert of our immense suffering, I mean the pain of writing, and there try to transform onanistically that suffering into indifference...

That's an interesting thought. I shall ponder it for a while and let you know later if I agree with you, but right now allow me to continue to believe, as I have done for a long time now, that my pen is a sword, or to put it in the right words, since these words came to me in French, yes in French in a dream, j'ai toujours pris ma plume pour une épée...

Are you aware of what you are saying?...

Of course, I am. That I more often took or mistook my cock for a sword, or better yet my cock for my pen...

No, that's not what I heard. What I heard is that when you think of your phallus as your pen, you are really confusing your cock with your penis...

Isn't a cock and a penis the same?...

Oh no! A penis is small, soft, indifferent. But a cock is hard, vibrant, full of desire and mischief. You piss with your penis, but you fuck with your cock....

You're just playing with words now. I'm trying to tell you something important about **real language**, and you reduce my words to an obscene play on words...

On the contrary, I am trying to show, as you have yourself stated, that **real language is incomprehensible.** In fact, that's why we are having this useless dialogue...

Useless! Okay, then let's try to have a useful dialogue...

Fine with me. What shall we discuss?...

Well, let's first determine what we will discuss, and then discuss what we decide to discuss. Let us discuss what we proposed to discuss, had we agreed on the topic of our discussion. No, that was not it...

That was not quite what it was. It was, if...if...only if we could spend the next forty-five minutes [I have an appointment in forty-five minutes] discussing what we would discuss were we to have a discussion...

Yes, we could have a discussion symposium. We could spend the next forty-five minutes discussing what we would have discussed had we had [had we had?—yes that's the correct tense] a discussion symposium...

Had we had...

That's it...

> [pause]

That means we either spend the next forty-five minutes being quiet and then discuss the "had had"...

...which we did not discuss...

Yes. [short pause]...Or shall we imagine the forty-five minutes having gone?...

No! No no no! because then that would be a kind of...

Mmmm...

It would be like talking about silence...

I'm not sure. I don't know. Perhaps we could produce some very literate and meaningful silence...

I don't want to...

[aside] This is a very profound symposium...

No, I don't want to. I want to complicate the tenses of our discussion about the discussion that we should have were we to have had a discussion...

Were we to have had?...

First we discussed what we would discuss were we to have a discussion symposium, but then you...

Oh, yes...

Right...

Now we allow time to pass before we tackle the real thing...

...and then we could...

...we could discuss what we would have discussed had we had a symposium. Therefore, the next step would be to discuss...right?...

We could discuss conditionally what we would have discussed about what we would have discussed...

[in disgust] Ach, no!...

[unperturbed]...had we had a symposium. Something like that...

No, let us rephrase, restate our original point of departure for this discussion, because it seems to me that we missed one level of tenses, an important level of tense...

[tentatively] Perhaps what we need now are future participles in order to...in order to...in order to...

We will could...

...discuss after we will had discussed what we will have discussed had we had been a symposium...

Almost, almost. Get it all down? Spew it out...

Mmmmm...

That was good. Almost...

Mmmmm...

Having finished discussing that...right...then we would have to retrace our steps, I mean our verbal steps, either backward or forward to the original discussion of what we should discuss were we to have this...this...this discussion, this symposium, followed by the discussion of what we would discuss had we had had that symposium which we would then discuss what we will have discussed if we would have had a symposium. No...No, I've missed something in there...

[long pause]

No, it's not right, yet, no. Wait a moment...

[thinks)] We are discussing...We could start, we are discussing, we can...WE *[with mounting excitement]*...of yes, I've got it. We can discuss...

No, er...we are in fact discussing...

Correct, we are discussing what we would be able to discuss if...

had we...

...had we decided...

...to have...

...to have a discussion...

...a potential discussion, for in fact we are now discussing the potentiality of the discussion that we might have had had we been...

...discussing...

The Discussion!

Exactly, the discussion itself...

We are almost there, almost...

Don't give up, this is starting to mean something...

What! You don't mean that, that we are starting to mean...

Cancel that...

The point is, we've got to get to the stage, to the preliminary stage of the discussion in order to be able to have the discussion...

Yes, what actually is being discussed, or will be but...

There is no but, there is only what is under discussion...

...and what is under discussion? The discussion of the discussion that we could have had had we had a discussion. It's as simple as that...

Yes, of course. Amazing how you always have the final word...

There is no final word since we were unable to decide what the discussion would be had we managed to decide on the topic of a discussion...

Quite true. So what do we do now?...

You go do what you have to do, and I'll go do what I have to do...

But what about...

About what? Do you really think that we were talking about something? We were just talking something...

Talking a storm...

In a manner of speaking, yes. We were, in fact, talking **the real thing...real language...**

And that is why it was, or seemed, or will appear incomprehensible to most...

But not to us, of course, because as the initiators of that **real language**, we situate ourselves outside that language, and therefore, as such...

Oh shit! I missed my appointment...

Too bad. What do we do now?...

Let's have a discussion...

REFLECTIONS ON WAYS TO SAY
WHERE I LIVE

If I walk with a visitor from out of town in front of the house where I live, I can say: *I live here.*

Or, more specifically: *I live in this house, the one with the fenced yard.*

Or, I can simply say, pointing to my house: *this is my home.*

But if I wish to give a more administrative touch to this assertion, I can say: *I live in this modern house, the one with the French car parked in front of it. My wife's car.*

If I am entering the street where I live, again with a stranger, or this time with a foreign visitor [a poet in search of a center for his circle], I can point and say: *I live over there—number 46—the house with the ivory tower.* Or I can simply state: *I live at 46 on this street.*

But I could also say: *I live down this street—the third house from the corner.*

Or: *I live down this street—next to the ugly green house with the broken down porch.*

Or: *I live three houses down from that two-story pseudo-Greek structure with the big columns and the black shutters.*

If someone in Buffalo [the city where I live] inquires where I reside, I have the choice of a good two dozens possible ways of answering. However, I can only say: *I live on Four Seasons Street,* to someone who I am sure knows where Four Seasons Street is, otherwise I have to specify the geographic location of that street.

For instance, I have to say: *I live on Four Seasons, off Saratoga Avenue, not far from the V.A. Hospital* [a landmark known to all the taxi drivers and all the war veterans].

Or else I can explain: *I live on Four Seasons Street in Eggertsville, a suburb of Buffalo,* even though I always write Buffalo as my return address on the letters I mail—doesn't make any difference, and it simplifies things because people don't have to ask: *Where is Eggertsville?*

I have on occasions said: *I live on Four Seasons Street, about five minutes on foot from the State University.*

But I have also said: *I live just a few blocks from the Zoo.*

Or: *I live across the street from the President of M & T Bank—my bank.*

Or: *I live around the corner from the Jewish Synagogue,* even though this has nothing to do with my religion, or my lack of religious belief.

In some exceptional circumstances, I could even be brought to say: *I live in Erie County.* Probably when being questioned about my taxes.

Or else: *I live in Western New York State.* Or: *I live on Lake Erie, near the Canadian border.* Or: *I live in the snow-belt.*

I doubt I will ever say: *I live in the postal zip code zone 14226.*

Almost anywhere in the U.S. [if not specifically in Buffalo or in Greater Buffalo], I think I can be almost certain to make myself understood when I say: *I live in Buffalo,* or *Buffalo is where I live,* or *Buffalo is my home,* or *I have been living in Buffalo for the past thirty years,* or *I moved to Buffalo in 1964.* There is a difference between these various ways of saying where one lives, but I don't exactly know what that difference is.

What I know for sure, is that I don't want to die in Buffalo. Anywhere but Buffalo, though I suppose dying in Peoria Illinois might be worse.

I could say, if the request called for it: *I live in the second largest city in New York State.* I don't think I have ever said that, but I could.

Though I did once say ironically to a friend from Texas: *I live in The Armpit of America.* I said this to him after the Buffalo Bills defeated the Oakland Raiders 51 to 7 [that was before the Raiders moved to Los Angeles], when after the game one of the Raiders' dejected coaches referred to Buffalo as *The Armpit of America.*

Nothing prevents me to imagine that I could say, since it is true: *I live not far from Niagara falls. O I live twenty minutes by car from Niagara Falls.*

Or: *I live in what is known as The City of Friendly Neighbors.*

Or: *I live in The Queen City*, but that sounds too much like the beginning of a bad novel than the indication of an address.

If I am on vacation on an island—say, off the coast of New England—and I am asked where I normally live, I can answer: *On the mainland*.

However, if I am traveling in England and someone asks me where I come from because my English does not sound quite proper, quite British, I must explain: *I come from the continent*, though in my case I would have to specify which continent.

I will undoubtedly not be understood, or receive a rather puzzled stare, if I say something like: *I live at 42 of latitude north, and 73 of longitude east*.

Would anyone give a damn if I say: *I live 2834 miles from San Diego; 1048 Miles from Topeka, Kansas; only 612 miles from Peoria, Illinois; 6156 miles from Jerusalem; 12397 miles from Melbourne, Australia*.

Would anyone really know where I live if I say: *I live north of the Tropic of Cancer*, or *I live south of the North Pole*.

If I lived in California—Northern California—I could casually say: *I live in the Bay Area."* Or if I lived in Southern California, I could snobbishly say: *I live in Beverly Hills*. However, since I live in Buffalo, or rather in the suburb of Buffalo known as Eggertsville, I cannot say, either casually or snobbishly or any other stupid way: *I live in California*. No, I cannot say that, because in fact I am stuck in Buffalo.

Also I cannot really see in which cases I could be in a position to have to say: *I live east of the Mississippi*, or *north of the Rio Grande*.

I live in America, or *I live in the United States of America*. I may have to give this information if I find myself in a place outside the boundaries of our country.

I live in North America. This type of information may be of interest to a European—let's say a French businessman—with whom I am having a conversation at a reception in the Japanese Embassy in Abidjan [Republic of Ivory Coast]. *Ah! vous habitez en Amérique du Nord*, he would say in French, and I would no doubt be led to specify [also in French to show that I have understood what he said]: *mais oui, je vis aux Etats-Unis. Je suis ici en affaires pour quelques jours, quelques semaines…*

I live on the Planet Earth. Will I ever have the occasion of saying this to someone? To another living creature from some other planet. If it is to an Alien [especially of the 3rd kind] descended on Earth from a remote corner of the Universe, he would probably already know that. Aliens of the 3rd kind are much smarter than we Earthlings.

And if it is me who finds myself somewhere around Arcturus, let's say, in the beautiful constellation Bootes, or near Alpha KX2809^ , it would certainly be necessary for me to specify: *I live on the third planet [the only one which bears life] of the Solar System in order of increasing distance from the Sun.*

Or: *I live on one of the planets of one of the younger smaller yellow stars situated on the edge of a galaxy of rather mediocre importance in the Universe designated quite arbitrarily as the Milky Way.*

There is approximately one chance in hundred thousand million of billions [that is to say only 10 to the power of 20] that my alien interlocutor will answer: *Oh yeah, I know, you mean Earth!*

INTERVIEW WITH GODOT

Um: Do you know that I just did an interview with Godot.

Laut: You're kidding. All my life I've been trying to get an interview with Godot, but I can't find him.

Um: It was easy. I did a search on the net. I just typed Godot, and I got his home page, and even his email.

Laut: You're bullshitting me. Godot on the net. What kind of web site does he have?

Um: A very simple one. Very ethereal.

Laut: Give me the URL. I want to look him up.

Um: I can't do that. Godot told me expressly not to give his web site and email to anyone, or else.

Laut: You're pulling my leg. You sent Godot an email and he answered you.

Um: Yes, a brief reply. Only a few words. He said *He had no views to inter.* That's exactly how he put it. So, I sent him a second email explaining that it didn't matter to me that he had no views to inter because I'm not interested in his views. I told him I just want to have a friendly dialogue. Find out if things are okay with him. A dialogue in the form of an interview, but without any real purpose, direction or intention. And he wrote back saying, *Okay let's dialogue. It's lonely, you know, to fight the soliloquy battle alone.* That's how he put it.

Laut: I can't believe that. So, what happened?

Um: Well, we met in a secret place.

Laut: Where?

Um: Oh, I cannot tell you that. He made me promise that I would never reveal where we met.

Laut: Okay, so?

Um: Well, you want to hear the dialogue we had. I recorded it word for word.

Laut: You recorded what Godot said! That's incredible. You mean to say, he let you record the dialogue?

Um: No, he didn't know I was recording it. I didn't ask him his permission. I had my little tape recorder [you know the one you gave me for my birthday] hidden in my breast pocket. I felt like a spy.

Laut: You're really something, you know. To do that to Godot. I think you're in fucking big trouble. Don't you know that Godot knows everything, sees everything, hears everything, smells everything.

Um: Yes, yes, I know Godot has five senses like the rest of us, but he never uses them. He told so himself. He said that to use one's senses to apprehend the world is mere competence.

Laut: Godot said that? I don't believe you.

Um: Well, something like that.

Laut: Don't you have it on tape?

Um: No. You see, just when he was explaining what he meant, the tape ran out. And then he said he was tired, and he left.

Laut: Just like that?

Um: Yes, just like that. As if he had never been there.

Laut: Maybe you dreamt the whole thing.

Um: I have the tape to prove that we met. You can hear his voice.

Laut: So, what did you guys talk about?

Um: Nothing in particular. I asked him a few vague questions, and...

Laut: What kind of questions?

Um: You know, the usual. First, I asked him how old he is. He just shrugged his shoulders sort of saying he didn't know.

Laut: Makes sense to me, since he's immortal.

Um: Then I asked him what he did for a living. Again same shrug of the shoulders.

Laut: Dumb question, my Dear Um. Obviously Godot is unemployed. He is his own boss. He doesn't have to work.

Um: I know that, but I thought I'd ask anyway. One never knows. Then I asked him if he could tell me where he lives. This time he didn't shrug his shoulders, he just smiled as if to tell me, does one really know where one lives.

Laut: Old Godot may be smarter than we think. So far you didn't reveal anything.

Um: I was not interviewing him to reveal anything. I just wanted to see if he has a beard.

Laut: Does he?

Um: Not that day. He was clean shaved.

Laut: Well, well. Are you sure it was Godot?

Um: Damn right I'm sure. How many Godots do you think there are in the world?

Laut: One is enough. That's for damn sure.

Um: I had to ask him, of course, if he could tell me when he plans to come. This time he raised his arms up in the air to indicate that he had no idea.

Laut: Not surprising.

Um: It was getting hopeless. But I knew that in advance. Finally, I couldn't resist, I asked him if he ever fucks.

Laut: Come on, you didn't ask him that?

Um: Yes, I did. And do you know what he answered. *I used to could.*

Laut: *I used to could?* But that's the way they speak in Texas. Don't tell me Godot is from Texas.

Um: That would be a real bummer.

Laut: And then.

Um: Nothing. That was the end of the interview.

Laut: That's the whole thing. I cannot believe you had a chance to get the truth from Godot, and that's all you got. What a waste. I can assure you, I would have gotten everything out of him, if I had interviewed him.

Um: I didn't want to impose on him. He is such a nice guy.

Laut: How big is he?

Um: 8 ½ by 11.

Laut: What! 8 ½ by 11. If I were you, I wouldn't tell that to anybody. Imagine what a panic it would cause. Godot, 8 ½ by y 11.

Um: So what! Nobody is perfect.

THE INVISIBLE DOUBLES

[a conceptual story]

Every human being—or for that matter—every living creature on this planet has an invisible double—that double can either be benevolent or malevolent—but the visible creature does not know if his or her or its invisible double is benevolent or malevolent—the visible creatures of this planet—as history has shown—are either benevolent or malevolent—though it has been recorded in history books that on rare occasions a malevolent creature can suddenly become benevolent—a case in point Herr Schindler—and a benevolent creature can without any visible reason become malevolent—for instance the case of a pet dog that suddenly bites the hand of his kind mistress while she is feeding him—visible creatures have no way of knowing whether or not their ID is benevolent or malevolent—but one day in the future a scientist invents a gizmo that reveals if an ID is benevolent or malevolent—

now the real story begins—an organization known only as O is formed—under the leadership of the scientist known only as S who is a malevolent creature—this O that controls the gizmo sets out to exterminate all the benevolent IDs so that it can used all the malevolent IDs to enslave all the visible creatures—benevolent as well as malevolent—but of course two visible human creatures—known only as P6 & R9—have discovered what the O is doing and are trying to save the visible creatures of the planet from being enslaved—P6 & R9 set out to destroy one by one the members of the O who have the gizmo that destroys benevolent IDs—the problem—or rather one should say the crisis—is that the O has discovered what P6 & R9 are doing and is pursuing them to destroy them before they destroy all the destroyers of IDs—the great moment of suspense of this story—the climax one should say—in the fullest sense of the word—comes when only one member of the O is left with the last gizmo—of course it's

40

the malevolent S—and P6 & R9—who have inevitably fallen in love with one another in the course of their adventure—are closing in on him—but S is aware that they are coming for him—and now comes the denouement—however the outcome of the confrontation between S and P6 & R9 will not be revealed at this point so that the reader of this story can invent it—

should this fabulous story be made into a movie the author will insist on writing the script himself—and choosing the director and actors.

If
[A TRUE STORY—MORE OR LESS]

Introductory Note:

The names of the characters in this story [more or less true] and the names of the places where the action unfolds will be given only as initials to protect those who may unconsciously or unjustly identify with the characters and their location in the real world.

For fear of being unjustly attacked by the characters in this story [more or less true] who may inadvertently identify with real people living in the real world, the characters in this story must be known only as initials.

When a new character is introduced in the story bearing the same initial as a previously introduced character, a number will be added to his or her initial indicating the order in which that new character has come into the story. For instance, if a character called Z has already appeared in the story, then the next Z to enter the story will be known as Z^1 and the next as Z^2, and so on, perhaps to infinity since it is not possible at this stage to estimate how many Z characters will participate in this story [more or less true] which, if all goes well, and time permits, may turn out to be very long. One can never tell in advance.

The same numerical system will apply to locations whenever a new location bearing the same name as a previous one is mentioned.

*To protect the person who tells this story [the teller] from those who may find some details objectionable, preposterous, offensive, implausible, or censurable, the name of the teller will be given only as **We**. This way the reader will know who the teller **We** is when **We** says **We**.*

THE BEGINNING—SO TO SPEAK–

[**Note:** *concerning the unconventional punctuation and the lack of capital letters in the story. We adopted what **We** thought was the simplest and most efficient mode of presenting this story. The reader is free, of course, to punctuate and capitalize as he or she pleases]*

here **we** go again with the if—it was inevitable—it's October 1st—not that it matters much—except perhaps to those who know why October 1st is important for **we**—

in any case—if **e** had not told **h** to go fuck himself—**we** would not be here telling you the story of **r** & **e**—their true story—more or less—

[**Note:** *To avoid the repetition of & whenever r & e are mentioned together, they will be referred to as r-e or e-r]*

e was married to a rich **sob**—a real asshole—when **r** bumped into **e** at **u**—it was a casual accidental encounter—though perhaps predestined—**r** saw **e** only from the back the first time—she was walking ahead of him with some other guy—not her **h**—but with a frog called **p** who was visiting **u**—**e** was wearing a tight blue skirt—wow—so incredibly revealing of her perfection—

e was gorgeous—28 then—short black hair—blue eyes—oh eyes so blue—with wild oceans in them—the slavic look with a touch of the exotic—the sensual biblical jewess—**e** is still gorgeous—but blonde now—

oh but still as beautiful—in a different way of course—a more experienced way—her ass just as tantalizing as it was then—though a little more round–un cul à deux places **r** told **e** the other day when she asked him if he still found her ass acceuillant—

[**Note:** *Both r-e are fluent in French and German and often use French or German expressions when having a conversation. The reasons r & e are multilingual will be revealed in due time. Their fluency in French and German has been most useful to them when traveling abroad]*

---

three days after **r** was hypnotized by **e**'s ass–to such an extent that he unconsciously followed **e** & **p** that day to wherever they were going–without being noticed–**we** believe but cannot affirm–it is very possible that either **p** or **e** or both noticed **r** walking behind them as though lost in his head–and wondered why this guy with the big nose was following them— in any case–three days after that memorable vision–**r-e** came face to face— by chance this time –

this face to face moment must be told in full details for it will often be fondly recalled by **r-e** in the 40 years or more they have slept in the same bed –

whenever **r-e** are asked where they first met they always answer with a little conniving smile in an elevator at **u**—

this is how it happened—that day—the day **r-e** came face to face and exchanged words charged with electricity—that day an eminent scholar from **y** was giving a lecture on the death of literature at **u** and the entire department of **f** had to attend–faculties as well as students—so around 1:55 p.m.—on a Tuesday **we** believe—but this cannot be confirmed—the lecture by the eminent scholar was scheduled for 2:00—everyone in the **d** of **f** rushed to the elevators on the third floor—the **d** of **f** was on the third floor [*excuse the precision but all this is relevant]* to go downstairs to the large auditorium where the lecture was to take place–so **r** is waiting for the elevator when suddenly **e** emerges from behind the door of an office on the third floor—probably **p**'s office since **p** as previously mentioned was a visiting scholar at **u**–in fact soon after **e** emerged **p** also emerged—no mere coincidence **we** assume—so now here they are next to **r** waiting for the elevator–

r cannot resist and says—salut **p**—comment ça va—eh dis tu me présentes à ton amie—in french since as previously indicated **p** is a frog—**r** himself a frog in exile obviously knows french–but **p** barely replies obviously not wanting to introduce **e** to **r**–probably because of **r**'s reputation as a great french lover–[*we should mention here before we forget how e—jokingly of course–often says with a conniving smile that r is a failure as a frog*]— or else because **p** had noticed how three days earlier **r** had followed them rather conspicuously–but just as the door of the elevator opens **p** says to **e**–in english–for **p** was fluent in english–oh I forgot my briefcase in my office you go down and get us two seats because it's going to be very crowded in the auditorium–the scholar from **y** was very famous—so suddenly **r-e** find themselves face to face in the elevator crowded with faculties students and others who were rushing to the lecture by the eminent scholar from **y**–

r was so close to **e** he could almost touch the delicious nearness of her body–he felt dizzy—he almost fell into her immense beautiful blue eyes—squished in the back of the elevator very close to each other–**r** could smell the delicious fragrance of **e**'s perfume—channel #5 he learned later–so he could not resist saying to **e**—whose name he did not know then since they had not been introduced to each other–wow you smell delicious–yes that's exactly how he put it–in a rather crude way–but perhaps it is that crude naive impromptu way of saying to **e** that she smelled delicious that attracted her to **r**–**we** are speculating here–but perhaps also the charming twinkle in **r**'s eyes—in any case–by the time **e-r** arrived in the auditorium there were only a few empty seats left and they ended up sitting next to each other–when **p** finally arrived—just when the person introducing the eminent speaker from **y** had stopped talking and the people were applauding–he could only find a seat way in the back of the auditorium–twelve rows in fact behind where **e-r** were sitting–when **e** saw where **p** was sitting she turned to him and indicated with a shrug of the shoulders that there was nothing she could have done—

we cannot tell you what the eminent scholar from **y** talked about and how he explained the death of literature because during the entire lecture **r** kept whispering things to **e** that made her giggle softly–at the end of the lecture **r** asked **e** if she would like to have a cup of coffee or something with him–and **e** said yes—just like that–without hesitating–**we** can only speculate that she found **r** interesting–or at least charming enough to want to have coffee with him or something –

when **r-e** reached the door of the auditorium they found poor **p** waiting for them with a dejected pathetic look on his face–**r** asked him–or perhaps it was **e** who asked–if he wanted to join them for a cup of coffee or something–**p** declined with a rather pissed off look on his face–this was the end of **p**–the rest is history–or rather it has become the story **we** are now in the process of telling—

it was love at first sight—in both directions for **r-e**—without hesitation—no kidding—without reservation—no time wasted—but not the classic thunderbolt—that would be too banal—it was more like an electric shock—and did they electrify immediately—what the hell **e-r** said—let's get on with it—or perhaps they said let's get it on—it is difficult now to remember exactly what they said—**we** shall try our best to stay as close to the truth as possible–but memory has its flaws—

so **e** dropped the rich **h**—who became **xh**—the guy was a schmuck anyway—and on top of that a mean bastard—that's more or less all **we** want to say about **xh**—though **we** should perhaps tell now—less **we** forget—how one day **r** punched **xh** in the mouth—one of the few times **r** came face to face with that bastard **xh**—

this is how it happened–**we** are jumping a couple of months ahead of the original face to face encounter in the elevator–chronology is irrelevant in this story—

one day **r-e** were playing golf–yes **r**—a fanatic golfer with a 6 handicap at the time–was teaching **e** how to play golf–**e** was still living in the house she and her **h** owned but **h** had moved out to become **xh**–after a round of golf **e** suggested they stop by her house so she could change before going out for dinner–while **e** is changing in the bedroom **r** comfortably seated in a deep leather armchair in the living room is admiring the exquisite furniture and bibelots of the house—**e** has great taste–when suddenly **h** walks in–**we** should specify that since the separation a court order had been issued forbidding **h** to enter the house–but that bastard **h** did not respect the court order and came in anyway to take things away from the house which he was not supposed to take away–so **h** walks in and when he see **r** sitting there he turns blue with anger and jealousy and rushes towards **r** who stands up ready to confront **h**–**h** grabs **r** by the throat and tries to choke him–impulsively **r** pushes **h** away who then swing with his fits towards **r** face but misses–but **r** does not miss his left hook which lands squarely on the corner of **h**'s mouth and breaks one of **h**'s tooth–there is scar on **r**'s left index finger to prove this–the punch was so hard and so precise it floored **h** who **we** should mention is much bigger and taller than **r**–**r** is only 5 feet 10–**h** over 6 feet–**h** cannot believe he's been floored by this little frog who is trying to make it with his **w**—soon to become **xw** when the divorce becomes final–**h** gets us rushes into the kitchen and comes back with a huge kitchen knife in his hand–well no need to go into further details–when **r** sees the knife he takes off through the open front door just as **e** comes out of the bedroom splendidly dressed–**e** tells **h** that he's an asshole and rushes out of the door jumps into her white cadillac–we should perhaps have mentioned e's white cadillac–a 1956 coupe deville–which will reappear later in the story–and catches up with **r** who is running like mad down the street–**r** who practiced judo when he was in the 82nd airborne division knows that the first principle of self-defense is to take off before facing off the attacking person–**we** feel it was important to relate this episode of the rather reckless and unconventional relationship of **r-e**—

we now return to the beginning–**xh** was so pissed to have been dropped by **e** like a rotten potato he took his revenge by immediately suing for custody of the **ks**—

[Note: The story of r-e is the story of a family. It is not an adventure story, nor a mystery story, nor a cheap romance story, and certainly not a sci-fi story though parts of the story will be told in the future, out of chronological order, that's inevitable because of r's irrational way of dealing with time].

---

oh **we** forgot to mention that there were 3 **ks** who came with **e**—

no **we** did not forget–this is the first time **we** have the opportunity to mention the 3 **ks**—

s boy 8—**j** boy 5–**r**[1] girl 3 ½—*[this is a reminder of the numerical system used for characters with the same initials—no further reminder will be issued]*—all three cute like hell—and so fond of **r**—they always played with him as if **r** was just another brother—that's because **r** himself is somewhat of a **k**—as **we** shall show eventually—**r** never seem to have managed to become an adult—very immature **r** in many ways—but that's part of his charm—and so lovable—ah yes so lovable—that's what **e** always says about him—**r** is so lovable—in spite of all his idiosyncracies—one of which **we** must mention immediately for it has lasted for more than 40 years—and will probably continue to last until **r** changes tense–and that's his addiction to talcum powder—which has been driving **e** nuts for years—40 years to be exact—the bathroom of their beautiful house is always full of white powder–the floor—the sink–the toilet seat–the tub— white powder everywhere–the cause of many recriminations on the part of e—who is somewhat allergic to talcum powder–but she was aware of r's little vice before they got married–therefore she endures–and **r** appreciates that—because to do without talcum powder would make life unbearable for him–**we** are not exaggerating–**we** have witnessed the many anxious moments when **r** runs out of talcum powder because he forgot to put it on e's shopping list–or when e–consciously or unconsciously forgets to buy the baby johnson powder on her shopping list—

but let us return to the 3 ks–without being sentimental—**we** want to make it clear— right off the bat—that this is not a soapy sappy story— this is a true realistic story—everything in it is real and factual—more or less—**we** insist on that—therefore it is essential not to get the people con-fused–when **we** refer to the 3 ks we mean e's 3 ks–the **ks** she had with **xh**—

in any case—as a result of the electric shock **r-e** felt—and e's decision to tell **h** to go fuck himself on a flying donut— to paraphrase Marlon Brando—or is it to go take a flying fuck on a donut—**we** suggest you go see that marvelous sexy movie last tango in paris for the exact words Marlon Brando used—

---

*[**Note:** The name of real people who are not directly connected with the story of r-e will be given in full with capital letters—if they don't like it they can go fly a kite]* –

---

by the way **e** got nothing–not a fucking thing–from rich **xh** when she dropped him—just the 3 ks but no dough—no alimony—nothing— nada—consequently **e-r** started their new life—if one can call their rather shaky beginning a new life—in total poverty—ah but what love— what passion—what electricity between them—or if **we** may put it metaphorically—they started their new life in shit up to their knees—but with their heads in the clouds—

however **we** must be fair and mention that **xh** did take care of the **ks**—financially that is—emotionally he fucked up their minds as much as he could—but luckily **r**—who is a real nice guy—as will become evident as this story unfolds—more or less in the right direction—**r** was able to unfuck the minds of the **ks**—they loved him for that—and even today—the 3 original **ks**—the step-**ks**—soon **we** will introduce a new **k-s**[1]—born of the electricity of **r-e**—all of them successful in their profession and their emotional life—more or less—but no need to anticipate—

in any case—lucky for **r-e** that **xh** supported the **ks**—otherwise they would have been in shit up to their necks—because to be quite frank—they were both—and are still greatly irresponsible in matters of finances—money means nothing to them—except that when you have some it should be spent—that's the way **r-e** are—

careless when dealing with material things—always living beyond their means—what the hell—but not careless when dealing with emotional things—just passionately reckless—when **r-e** started their new family life—**r** was making exactly 1822 dollars a year as a **ta** at **u** —- before taxes—that's the truth–more or less—

perhaps **we** should backtrack a moment to describe the wedding of **r-e** it was in **ny**—

no the wedding will be described later–in a more appropriate place—

we were saying that **r** was making about 1800 a year—**we** are talking many years ago—peanuts in other words—that's what a **ta** made in those days—about 1800 a year—less than what **xh** was giving **e** per month to take care of the house and the **ks**—

in e's former life—as e always refers to it—xh would shell out 2000 a month just to take care of the ks—the food—the clothes—the stuff for the house—the big mansion in w—and the two cadillacs—

yes two of them—xh's brand new ugly over-chromed purple job with flaps—e's a splendid white coupe—with red leather seats—

oh maybe the leather seats were also white—this detail seems to have been forgotten—

some details in this story may not be totally correct—faulty memory should be blamed for that—or else the necessity of beautifying or exaggerating the story—more or less—

in any case—**we** apologize for the repeated use of this ready made phrase—in any case—but that's all we got—and it helps accelerate the story—more or less—

in any case—that's all e got—the 3 ks and the white caddie coupe—a beauty—but the damn thing didn't last long—maybe it didn't like r—or the caddie felt out of place in the parking lot of **u**—

oh **we** forgot to mention—no **we** did not forget—**we** are mentioning it for the first time—

at the time e electrified r he was trying to finish his **phd** at u in la—just think what his profs k v and c said to each other the first time r came to the **u** in his white caddie and parked it next to their old jalopies—in those days **ps** were still living in the poverty category—but as **we** said the white caddie didn't last long—it died one afternoon just like that—in the u parking lot—a lousy chevy replaced it—a corvair lemon that didn't last long either—but that's another story—

so **r-e** got married ks and all—that was many years ago—to be more or less precise—let's say more than 40—less than 50—wow that's a long time—here to be even more precise—since the story of **r-e** is being told on October 1st and they were married on September 13—that much has been ascertained even thought **e-r** sometimes argue—oh yes they do argue sometimes like all people who love each other—that it was really September 14—in fact—as **we** will relate and explain later—they got married twice—

perhaps **we** better explain now why **r-e** got married twice before we forget—

no–**we**'ll do that later when we describe the first marriage–otherwise things will get confused—

in any case—assuming they really got married on September 13—and today is October 1st—then they have been sleeping together legally for exactly 40 years and 17 days—can you believe that—40 years and 17 days that **r-e** share the same bed—except of course when one of them—for whatever reason— has to go out of town—and sleeps in another bed— not necessarily with somebody else—**r-e** claim to have been faithful to each other—more or less—but that cannot be ascertain—and besides it's nobody's business—

we will probably get into that later—the trips out of town—the business trips as **r-e** call them for tax purpose—but without exaggeration **we** can clearly state that the electricity is still going strong—you should see their electricity bill at the end of the month—

by then—**we** mean when **e-r** got married—a year or so after the initial electrical shock—**r** was a bit better off—he was now at u^1—teaching full time—four courses—but still trying to finish the damn doctoral dissertation he was writing on **b**'s experimental fiction—**b** being a famous foreign writer whose work had totally taken over **r**'s intellectual existence and a good part also of his sentimental life—more will be told on that aspect of **r**'s life—**r** wanted to write the first intelligent doctoral **d** on **b** in **a**—**we** think he did—but this remains to be determined—so **r** took a full-time teaching job at u^1 to help with the daily bread—even though still working on his **d** on **b**—mostly during at night since he was busy all day teaching four courses of beginning foreign fiction—and also taking care of the **ks**— and of course loving **e** as much as he could—

u[1] made him an acting **ap**—so now he was getting 6000 a year—more or less—quite an improvement if one considers that in fact **r** was still only a **phd** in progress—though more often in regress—and now married—with three **ks**—a family man with a ready-made family—so to speak—

okay so you say the **ks** were not really his responsibility—his financial responsibility since **xh** was supporting them—think again—who do you think payed for the extra toys the lovely **ks** always wanted—yes the 3 **ks** were adorable but they always wanted more—that's normal for **ks** who have a rich asshole of a father—but not only more toys—the movies—**r** is a movie freak—so he always took the entire family to the movies—that meant popcorn and candies at the movies—oh no—the fucking **xh** did not include the pop corn and the candies in his monthly support check for the **ks**—and then after the movie there was the putt-putt when later the **ks** became addicted to putt-putt—before they decided they too—the **ks**—wanted to learned to play golf like **r**—their stepfather—talk to us about being stepped on—who was—and still is—a golf fanatic—and a damn good one at that—6 handicap—more or less—we'll get into **r**'s golf later–since **e** became a damn good golfer herself—and still is—handicap 14—

so here they are now living in **sb** with **r** at u[1] teaching four courses to the freshmen—or rather mostly freshgirls—yes mostly freshgirls because the stuff **r** is teaching attracts mostly the female type to his classes— future housewives or divorcees who love to read foreign novels in the original when they have nothing better do to—oh **we** forgot to mention that **r** specializes in foreign experimental novels—and in fact his **d** on **b** is about a foreign writer—the nationality of **b** need not be mentioned here since it is totally irrelevant to **r**'s thesis—

in any case—**r** was teaching 4 courses of **ff** 101—**ff** stands for foreign fiction—from 8 to 12—8 to 12 straight on—can you believe that—slave labor—then after a quick lunch and a round of golf—his daily round of

golf in spite of the guilt for not being home working on the **d** on **b**—golf
for **r** is an obsession—it's **r** against nature—**r** against **n** as he always
says–we were saying–a quick lunch and a round of golf and **r** would rush
to pick up the **ks** from school—in the caddie at first until it conked out—
then in the chevy lemon after that—we believe it was a corvair—that disastrous car—but this has not been confirmed—that's all e-**r** could
afford—not a new one—a used one of course—we believe it had something like 60000 miles on it when **r-e** bought—more or less—and then
home—home sweet home where **e** would greet **r** and the **ks** with love
affection kisses and sandwiches—milk for the **ks**—a beer for **r**—**r** like his
daily beer—for **e** it's a glass of chardonnay—

after that to work half the night on the **d**—but not before **r** washes the
dishes—vacuum the carpets—put the **ks** to bed with one of the stories he
invents for them every evening—

if **we** have time **we**'ll tell you the story and palucci and his gang–sticky
mirabelle elephant and bug–that **r** invented and which the kids even illus-
trated with colored crayons—it's a great story—but **we** should get back to
the story in progress –

---

note: *the names of fictitious beings will be given in full.*

---

amazing how quickly **r** got domesticated when **e-r** set up house—but
he loved it—after all **r** was—if one may use such an expression—family-
less before he met **e**—it's a sad story or he became an orphan—but that
story should not be mentioned at all in this story—it's too sad—too
depressing—this is a happy story—more or less–and besides it's been told
before several times–not by **we**–by **r** himself—

r loved the beautiful house where they lived up on a hill in **sb**—with a
view on the sea on one side and a view of the mountains on the other—on
the edge of a precipice— **e-r** had a banana tree an olive tree and an orange

tree on their property and all kinds of exotic plants—no **sb** is not in a foreign country—it's in **a**—but in a part of **a** where exotic trees grow—

of course, **e-r** had to borrow the dough to buy such a superb house up
on top of a hill with a fantastic double view—but we should state right off
that **e-r** from the day they decided to live together always lived above their
means—so they borrowed the down payment from **e**'s old man— what
the hell—as **e-r** always say and always do—fuck it—let's live it up—above
our means—and if their means went up they live above that too—and
besides with a family like theirs—an experienced wife—after all **e** already
had 10 years of experience in marital matters when **e-r** started playing
house together with the **ks**—**r** had no previous experience—no legal previous experience–**we** should emphasize –

---

note: *It should be noted that whenever e comes first in the r-e equation, it
means that e was in charge of what is being related at that moment.*

---

e-r had to have the best—that's how they are—so here they are at u^1
trying to make ends meet—as the saying goes—but **we** regret to have to
say that the ends did not meet too often and too easily—**e** had expensive
taste from her previous marital experience and it's not easy to get rid of
such bad habits—and **r** couldn't wait to become a good solid complacent
bourgeois even though he claimed to be a socialist—and even on some
occasions he would claim to have been a communist—after all **r** had lived
long enough on the margin of society—

perhaps later in the course of this story **we** will have the time to get into
aspects of **r**'s pathetic life on the margin—for now let's continue with their
family life at u^1—

as **we** already mentioned—**r** was acting **ap** at u^1 in the **d** of **cl** teaching
4 beginning **ff** courses to the **fgs** and trying to finish his damn **d** on **b**—so
e had to go to work—but **e** was so smart—so sophisticated—so logical—
so practical and so beautiful—that always helps—and she still is—she
immediately got a terrific job—**we** are not sure what it was—blame that

on memory—but it was a damn good job—an important administrative position in the **f** of **l** –

we believe—still the early years were difficult—difficult not sentimentally or emotionally or intellectually or between **r-e**—they were nuts about each other—yes things between them were terrific—le grand amour–of course they did have little disagreements here and then—all couples do—mostly because of **r**'s inexperience with **ks**—and also because of the difficulty the **ks** sometimes had understanding **r**'s way of doing thing—but especially **r**'s curious way of speaking—

r suffers of an incurable accent—due to the fact that **r** was not born in but in f^1—f^1 being a distant foreign country on the other side of the sea—**r** speaks his adopted tongue with an accent which he admits has been carefully cultivated over the years for social and sentimental reasons—

in any case—sometimes when **r** pronounces a word it sounds like another word—to give an example—one day **r** was home enjoying the ocean view while smoking one of his favorite foreign cigarettes and cogitating what **r** would write later that night in his **d** on **b** when a friend of his—also a **phd** in progress—came over to discuss the problems he had with his **d** on **v**–

e was out marketing with the two older **ks**—**s** and **j**—but the little girl r^1 didn't want to go with them—r^1 stayed home with **r** because she wanted to play with the new barbie **r** had given her for her birthday—she was now 4—**we** did mention that **s** and **j** were boys and r^1 girl—

anyway –**r** and his friend— **m** was his name—fellow **ap**—were discussing the problems they were having with their **ds**—when little adorable r^1–cute like hell—comes into the room where **m** and **r** were discussing their **ds** while smoking foreign cigarettes and says she's thirsty and she wants a glass of milk—so **r** goes into the kitchen followed by r^1 and gives her a tall glass of milk and a gentle pat on the derriere—but **r** notices that

r^1 is barefoot—and it was a rather cold that day in **sb** that day—so **r** tells r^1 in a fatherly tone of voice to go to her room and put on her slippers—little adorable r^1 runs to her room and comes out a few moments later wearing her pyjamas and crying like it was the end of the world—so **r** goes to her—picks her up in his arms—give her a little kiss on the cheek—she's so cute—so adorable—you should have seen the big tears running down r^1's face—**r** gives her another kiss on the wet cheek and asks why she's crying—still sobbing little r^1 says that she does not understand why she has to put on her sleepers in the middle of the day—it's not bedtime yet it's only afternoon—

you see what **we** mean—sometimes when **r** pronounces a word it sounds like another word—when **r** said slippers it sounded like sleepers to r^1—that's the kind of problems **r** had with e's ks because of his incurable accent—

even though **r** has now lived more than 50 years in his adopted country–he was 19 when he came to **a**—more or less—damn our memory is really bad today—maybe **r** was only 18 when he spoke his first word in his adopted tongue—

r always says that the first word he spoke in his adopted tongue was the word **sob**–but this cannot be confirmed—

anyway it was not easy at that time for **r** to keep up with life and his damn **d**—especially since it was a race between the **d** and **oscar**—

oscar was the name **r-e** gave to the thing that started growing inside **e** soon after they got married—

---

note: *The name **Oscar** is given here in full because **Oscar** was never considered a real being until it emerged into the world. **Oscar** emerged on December 7—pearl arbor day. On that historical day **Oscar** became s^1—s^1 since there was already an s in the family. Since **Oscar** in fact never really* *became a person–he cannot sue the author or be identified with a real living being by that name, and that is why it is safe here to use the full name* **Oscar**.

By the way the **d** *on* **b** *was finished and defended 3 days before* **Oscar** *became* **s**[1]. *The dedication of the* **d** *states: in spite of Oscar.*

---

and now **r** is a **dr**—okay not a real **dr**—a **dr** of philosophy but that counts too—his students now call him **dr r** when they address him—**r** even got a raise from 6000 to 6500—but then **r** got offers for other **us** because his **d** on **b** was immediately published by **ucp**—**r** got offers of other jobs because now **r** was a full-fledged **ap** with a **phd**—and full-fledged **ap**s with **phd**s were in great demand in those days—especially smart ones—and suddenly **r** realized he was smart—how did he realize that—**e** told him—so **r** got offers—you won't believe the offers **r** got—this was the golden years of his profession—and one day **eu** in **a**[1] made a splendid offer to **r**—**eu** wanted **r** so badly they flew both **r-e** to **a**[1] in **g**— the people of **eu** wanted **r** so much they would even have flown the **ks** too if **r-e** had insisted—

r-e were treated at **eu** like they were royalty—this was in march many years ago—**r** defended his **d** in may the preceding year–and as **we** mentioned a moment ago it was immediately accepted for publication by **ucp**—there were some revisions to be made so his journey to chaos came out a year later— that means that when **r** went to **eu** in **a**[1] for an interview even though he was received like a king he had really nothing in print— except for a couple of miserable poems in some obscure magazine—and a couple of translations from his native tongue—eh what the hell—the translations helped amplify his rather meager **cv**—but nonetheless **eu** wanted **r** so badly that without even looking at his meager **cv** they made me a terrific offer he could not refuse—**we** think it was something like 11500—plus moving expenses and the assurance of promotion to **fp** as soon as the book on **b** is out–plus the 3 articles already accepted by scholarly journals—wow was **r** in a hurry in those days—well **r** had some catching up to do—**r** was a freshman in college at the age of 26—that's because of the his sad pathetic life before he came to **a**—and now **r** was—let's see—this was 64—in 64 **r** was—well you figure it out—oops the phone is ringing—we'll go on with the rest of the story of **r-e** later—

FOUR YEARS LATER—APPROXIMATELY

finally **r-e** didn't go to **eu** in a^1—they didn't like the people there—also bigoted insinuations that came through in the conversation with the **eu** people—instead **r** got an even better offer from **ub** in b^1—so in 64 **r-e** moved to b^1—but not without some problems—

when **xh** heard **r-e** were moving to out of state he decided to sue for custody of the **ks** because that asshole **xh** said he didn't want the **ks** to move far away from where he lived in **la** and b^1 was very far from **la** in another state–

---

note: *it is possible that some new initials have entered the story and **we** failed to give those initials the proper number. **We** would appreciate it if the reader were to take it upon himself or herself to remedy such errors. **We** thank you in advance.*

[From a temporarily interrupted work in progress]

A POEM THAT USED TO HAVE 3639 LINES BEFORE MY CAT ATE MOST OF IT

[the numbers indicate the fragments left of the original lines. The rest must by now be in the cat litter box. We regret not to be able to offer the complete poem at this time. We are working diligently at trying to fill the holes. As soon as the poem is pregnant again, so to speak, it will be made available. We beg your patience. Any help you can give in reconstituting this poem to its original shape will be greatly appreciated]

1. We hve invntd a hol fild of endevor: rmindin ech other of
   wht w hve forgoten. Wht did you sy?

2. **Mighty tired & disgusted I do the necessry work** nywy then I stre or np I try to see how long I cn hold my breth Im getting better t it then I strt all over gin.

3. *On the other side of the street the other one the smaller one the one with the french ccent is counting his hert bet per minute…the first minute he counted 59 & 1/2 bets…the second minute 12 & 3/4 he pnicked but the*
   third minute the counted 126 even…he felt better but he wonders now if he shouldn?t
   worry?

74. The impulse is ded so is the ct the dog the left over beer in the opened bottle the ded chicken they te lst night so it goes.

231. Remember the old Bedle song *"will you still need me when we is 105?"*
   Who cn member tht fr.

232. Shall we dance? Shall we take a shower? Do we dare ate a
   banana? Shall we sing in the shower? Shall we….

1267. I am not blue we are not blue they are not blue blue me blow me below me low me down paint me blue with your blue stockings so that my blue balls can be blowing again etc.

1278. This pom usd to hav 3639 lins bfor th cat at most of it. It was so symmtrical and look at it now full of hols

1400. This poem used to be red but because of the rain it got discolored.

1402. Bum two asked bum one. Ace are you there? No Sam I'm not here.

Answered Ace.

1436. Sam called the other day from paradise to say that up there everything is more real than everything.

2121. Every day they take a brain blocker & a belly blocker but nothing helps I am still constipated and when the two blockers collide it creates what is called a writer's block damn if they are not blocked!

3111. When I was an excon I used to brag about how I spent most of my life in chains in the slammer. But free in my skull.

3435. It is not a lie that when Honoré was on his deathbed he called the doctor

he invented in his novel to come and save him but the doc couldn't come

because he was balling Madame Hanska in the adjoining room. The damn countess coul 't wait for Balz to die to become a myth.

3212. No Balz did not fuck the black panther at least not in the version published in **SHORT STORIES—CLASSIC, MODERN, CONTEMPORARY, Edited by Marcus Klein & Robert Pack**

for Little, n & Company, Boston, 1967, pages 3-15, translated by R ond Fe e man. We can prove it, we have the book.

3326. what is a snuff novel ?

3600 wieiqrqqioytolqa.,f nv?ZXm,fgoeq-0000

===

LOVE IN SOAPLAND

Over yonder in Soapland nobody watches television. In Soapland everybody is too enmeshed in love to waste time with TV. Anyway, by avoiding television one preserves one's sweetness. In Soapland love occupies 95% of the average person's time. That's a lot of time spent on love. It doesn't leave much for watching famous killers doing their things, or movie stars being sued, or athletes being busted, or rapists being paroled, or politicians being accused of improprieties.

Right now in Soapland, Edmund is marrying the most beautiful young brain surgeon ever produced by Johns Hopkins University Surgery Department. Her name is Dr. Karen Much. Their love was touch and go for a while because it looked as if Edmund might be in love with Brooke, who was on the rebound after being jolted by her husband Tad, who is now in love with Dixie, whose marriage to Brian never worked out.

The wedding ceremony of Ed and Karen, incidentally, has interrupted the trial of Kimberly accused of stabbing her latest husband, Dimitri, in a fit of hysteria brought on by the fear that Dimo (as Kimberly always called him before she eliminated him) was in love with Kendall, Kimberly's teenage daughter by crafty old rapist Charlie, but it turns out that Kandall did not give a damn about Dimitri because, in fact, all along she has had her eyes on the lady brain surgeon. But that's another story.

PBS

You see, my friend, the reason I object to PBS is because, as I was saying the other night to a gathering of friends who always say, We Love PBS, We only watch PBS when we watch Television, or else CNN for the news, and I got annoyed, irritated to hear that again from them every time we talk about TV, and I said to them, Oh by the way did you guys watch on FOX the other night that incredible porno sci-fi flick about these phallic creatures from out of space who invade earth and fuck everything, humans, animals, male and female, even objects, they come from a planet recently discovered in the milky way by the famous Nobel Prize Winner astronomer from Yale, Horny Hardon, which he named, Planet Sperm X9, well, as I was saying, I get so damn pissed when my intellectual friends, all of whom I dearly love and normally respect, always say to me, when I mention a TV show I really loved, We only watch PBS, it really bugs me, and another reason I object to PBS is because it's hypocritical, it pretends not to advertise commercially, except companies and individuals that are so goodie goodie generous, and makes believe that the people who watch PBS drive only deluxe foreign cars, never drink, never use words like underwear, never have to use deodorant or toilet paper, never need to take a shower or a bath, never use a condom, never fuck, and have a huge life insurance, stocks & bonds, children in private schools, never go see X-rated movies, live in a well-decorated, well-protected well insured house in a good part of town, not far from the airport and the car wash....

Federkid

Patricia Privat-Standley

What I have to say about Federman can me summed up in the **man,** l'homme, rather than in the **feder,** la plume. Even though I have read all his books and I found profit in them [even more than that, if one considers that I also found my voice as well as my *raison d'être*], I must admit that it is the human side of the Penman that interests me above all. After all, if Federman was not the man he is, he would not have written all his books, and I would not be, with thousands of other federmaniacs, talking to you about him.

Now, the question is: what makes the man so interesting? His qualities? His faults? His weaknesses? His strength? His stubbornness? His kindness? Or is it, the fact that behind the mask of the writer hides a face few have seen. The face of a child. Even if Federman clamors, to whoever wants to listen, that certain historical events forced him to grow too fast, thus robbing him of his childhood before he became conscious of having had one, I believe that deep inside, this child never left him. The little boy Federman: **Federkid!**

Of course, Federman's body grew, became stronger, but the voice of the child never disappeared. It remained there, in him, silent for a long time, not knowing how to put words on all that his body and soul had suffered: the closet, the fear, the farm, loneliness, anger…and all the feelings of horror that trouble a child when one morning the little piece of life that he is collapses before him. It is this little boy's voice that I always hear when I read and re-read Federman the writer.

That voice is everywhere in his books: in the novels, the stories, the poems, the critifiction, the correspondence. Always present, in the background, but undeniably present. And if sometimes this little boy's voice sounds bitter or rancorous, it is for good reasons.

Federman has often evoked these reasons. They all bring us back to where it all started. The starting point, since Federman himself describes the closet moment as the beginning...the rebirth...He says he crapped out his fear and his shame in that cabinet...de débarras. But has he really ever gotten rid of that fear and that shame? This closet: is it not the belly of fear, whence the child emerged, one night, holding in his hands, not terror, but the symbolic remains of a still recent past?

A past abandoned on the roof of the building, 4 rue Louis Roland, but certainly not forgotten by the voice of the angry boy, the voice that clamors today between two bursts of laughter laughing at the laugh.

The rancor towards France—that country of misery to which he gave everything and received nothing in return—is therefore justified. Even more so, if one considers that in spite of all his efforts to be accepted there as a writer, he has never received any recognition from the French. Not even when in 1996, he offered France, gratis, a masterpiece entitled **La Fourrure de ma Tante Rachel,** which was totally ignored by the critics. Not a single review. *Silence total sur Federman.*

It is this voice, full of pain and bitterness, that most readers of Federman do not hear: the rumbling of a voice that refuses to grow, and refuses especially to forget the low blows that his native land has given him throughout his life.

Yes, I think it is the voice of this wandering adolescent kid, the voice of Feder**Kid**: arrogant, accusing, and at the same time touching, moving, which is finally the fundamental sound of Feder**Man**'s work.

I even ask myself if **Moinous** is not the name that Federman unconsciously gave to that voice. This would certainly explain why one always feel an almost irresistible need to help this engaging character who keeps reappearing in Federman's novels, and to feel infinite compassion for him.

Moinous–notably the Moinous of **Smiles on Washington Square**–resembles so much the little boy of the closet: helpless, lost, lonely, frightened, uncertain of his own future, and yet, so full of hope in his head, with an imagination so overflowing with exuberance that it carries him, and the reader too, into the most extravagant stories, most incredible and funny stories so tragic and painful as they are.

When I ask Federman to explain the origin of this name, he tells me that Moinous revealed himself for the first time in 1972, while he was writing, simultaneously, **Amer Eldorado** and **Take It or Leave It.**

It felt strange, he declares, *as if I had just encountered someone I knew long ago* and *whom I had forgotten...*

And when later, after having killed Moinous in a San Francisco bar, he realized the importance quasi vital of his presence in his work, he resurrected him in **The Twofold Vibration.**

Moinous, however, never appears in the novels as a child, only as a young man, or a middle-age man. However, he has preserved all the characteristics of childhood: ingenuity, naivety, credulity, ignorance, including his quasi legendary stubbornness [for which federkid's mother always reproached him–but which, paradoxically, turned out to be the very reason of his survival], but especially it is the great need of love which predominates the psychological portrait of Moinous: this unsatiable need to love and be loved, which was never really evoked aloud, but always implied.

How can one not make a rapprochement between Moinous, the aimless fictitious young man , constantly ill-treated, victimized by his creator, and Raymond Jule Tulipe Federman, the orphan boy, deprived of his parents' love, ill-treated, victimized by life.

Moinous is, without any doubt, nothing other than the subtle combination of the voices of the man and the child–**Nous**—linked with the

Moi of Federman the author. After all, would the man, the writer, have survived for the readers, if the child *tête de mule,* as he mother would call him, had not had the necessary strength and determination to endure the assaults of life. Isn't it Feder**Kid** who succeeded in saving Feder**Man**, so that the latter can tell later the story of **their** survival, with the help of **Moinous?**

Digression: Moinous…moinO-us : *one morning a bird flew into my head [...] I hid my heart in a yellow feather*–does that mean that the heart of Federman, his sensitivity, the child he has remained, are inscribed in the name of Moinous? If one looks closely, listens closely, and if one takes a bit of liberty [how to resist this temptation when each word of Federman resounds like an invitation to dance in the minds freed of the academic burden], one can then perceive in MoinO-us *that bird he loved so much,* the little *Moineau* in search of freedom.

Moinous is the initial voice–that of the boy, resigned and at the same time rebelled, in his unique way of fighting reality with only the power of his imagination–the source of all the other voices [Boris of **DON**, Frenchy of **Tioli,** Namredef in **La Fourrure**], that appear successively in the work of Federman.

Moinous is undoubtedly also the result of that complicity, the tacit accord that took place between Federkid and his mother when she pushed him into the closet, that morning of July 1942. It is perhaps from this gesture [that Federman has never really been able or willing to explain, for fear perhaps of ruining its beauty] that Moinous was born.

Moi : Raymond / **Nou**: my absent ones.

It is perhaps at this precise moment that Moinous began to exist and became the nameless voice that later would speak for those whose voices had been stifled forever: *Brother, she says, write the poem I will whisper to you…*

Moinous, slumped and silent voice at the beginning: *But he's afraid that if he writes it the words will not come out right,* until Federman real-izes, many years and many misadventures later, why he was spared: *And*

*again I'll sit besides the ashes and try to scoop them in the palm of my hand
so they can speak to me and tell me what happened after I was abandoned .*

It is from then that the voice began to speak and that Federman
affirms himself as a poet and a novelist.

The LINEBreak Interview

Charles Bernstein

CB: Ray, what's the use of fiction? What's the use of stories?

RF: The use of story. The story for me is what gets you nowhere. I'm not a story teller. I am one who denies storytelling as I try to tell the story. So everything I write is a screen behind which the story is at play. When you read my books, when you look at the pages, when you look at the language, you are first looking at a screen which is trying to prevent the story from coming out. Why? Because all the stories have been told. The same old stories.

CB: So what's the use in telling them again?

RF: Ah! Well, it's fun, Charles, it's fun. It's the story telling. It's the telling *of* the story. The great Samuel Beckett had the Unnamable say in *The Unnamable*, "How can I tell the teller from the told?" I'm not interested in the told, I'm interested in the teller, the voice, the rhythm, the music of the teller.

CB: Well, how about historical memory? How about collective memory? Does fiction serve to make memory possible, to make sure that people don't forget things?

RF: As I have often said, as my characters have said in my novels, I make no distinction between memory and imagination. I don't think we really remember—that is, I don't think I remember—I *imagine* what I think has happened to myself or to others in the past in history. I reinvent.

CB: Well, you're a survivor of the Holocaust—your family was killed during the systematic extermination of the European Jews during World War Two. We have many memories of this systematic extermination project. What do you think that such a memorial should represent?

RF: If they were really memories, I don't think I could have survived with these things inside of me. So what I have to do is deny these memories, these evils. I have to still believe, as I often do, that one of these days around a street corner I'm going to meet my sisters. I still believe that. Strongly. I doubt my father will be there, because my father was something else, but I have to believe that somehow they are still around. Memory closes things. Imagination opens up.

CB: In the last years there have been many monuments to the systematic extermination of the European Jews, and yet your work, which I would say is one of the most significant memorials to that historical moment, in many ways veers into abstraction and digression. It does not represent those events. It refuses to represent those events. Are you evading history? Do you contrast facts and memory?

RF: Oh, I have been asked that question so often, am I evading? Yes, I think on the one hand I am evading, on the other hand I am transgressing and exorcizing. I don't know exactly the word. Let me go back to your museums and your memorials. What has happened to the Holocaust is that it has become a tourist attraction. People go there as tourists, and that bothers me a great deal. Just as there are people go and visit concentration camps, and they have been remade into nice, hygienic—and they have removed the drama from them and you go and visit them. I found myself doing that too, unfortunately. I don't think I would want to visit the one in Washington, the new Museum of the Holocaust, because that's what it is—it's a tourist attraction. I prefer going to the Guggenheim.

CB: You have a wonderful passage in *Smiles on Washington Square* which sort of speaks to this issue.

RF: Oh yes, my old Moinous. You have to understand that Moinous is situated in all my novels and of course one understands Moinous—"me us"—we are all implicated in this.

CB: That's the character's name, Moinous.

RF: It's the character's basis, of course—the French word *moi*, "me," and *nous*, "us." "Me us." It's also my e-mail name. It's also the license plate of my car.

CB: You make light of facts rooted in history, but shouldn't we be solemn in the face of these horrendous events that occur historically.

RF: Yes and no, because there are so many ways to look at these facts, many ways of distorting them, of revisiting them, of retelling them. I learned this when I was a student at Columbia University taking a course on Medieval French literature. In Medieval French literature we were reading these texts by these two—I forget the guys' names—who went on the Crusades with the Crusaders. And each one wrote an entirely different version of this thing. One was glorifying it in the name of God and in the name of whatever, and the other was showing what a stupid kind of adventure this was, which was all greed, it was all to get rich, to obtain, to find women or carpets out there, to find gold and so on—it had nothing to do with the original idea. And this struck me at the time—I was still young, relatively young—that indeed you can take the same fact and give it two, three, as many interpretations as you want.

CB: But also you're very funny about it as opposed to the terribly solemn and serious memorials that we are perhaps more accustomed to. Your work seems to mock not only the possibility of accurate representation but also the idea that mourning should be a solemn affair. Should mourning be funny?

RF: As you know, my work has been extremely well received in Germany, of all places—the great irony of my life—and I've been asked that question over and over again: "Mr. Federman, how can you laugh—" Well, the kind of laughter that I laugh needs to be defined also "—about these things, about these events?" And my answer is very simple: I am a survivor. That I survived this is a very happy occasion. I am still alive. That is an occasion for, well, if not great laughter, at least some kind of joy....I hope you can that you hear...the laughter and the nonseriousness of what I do.

CB: But I can also hear the sadness and great seriousness, too.

RF: I just received a marvelous letter from a cousin of mine who was also a survivor. She was three years younger than me when her parents and brothers were deported. She now lives in Israel. She's the main character in one of my novels, *To Whom It May Concern*, and she's been working on a kibbutz for the last 50 years. And she just read the novel I just finished in French, called *La Fourrure de ma tante Rachel*, and she wrote me. I was afraid to send it to her because it deals with our personal history to some extent—very much distorted, reinvented, reimagined. And she wrote me a splendid letter that says exactly what you say. "It's so funny," she says, "and yet so sad."

CB: "Black humor" isn't really quite the right word for it, because it's something other than black humor.

RF: I think in the same way, and probably I hope I've learned it from my great mentor Beckett the same kind of sadness and joy and laughter you find in Beckett.

CB: Yes, but unlike Beckett, you actually more sort of hysterical and more histrionic.

RF: Well, I describe it this way. You remember the marvelous passage in *Molloy* where Molloy is trying to work out his system to suck his 16 stones and so on. You have there the Beckettian acrobat who does a beautiful set of somersaults and then falls back on his feet and everything is erased. I am the acrobat who falls down on his face, and so you don't remember the somersault. You remember the failure of the guy flat on his face. And that's where you laugh—when the acrobat or the clown does that, that's where the laughter is. That's the kind of laughter I think I am trying to achieve. "And therefore all good storytellers go to the Beckett gate on their way to heaven...."

CB: Ray, what is "the voice in the closet"? Whose voice? What's the voice saying?

RF: *The Voice In the Closet*, for those who don't know it, is a 20-page text. Some people have referred to it as a prose poem, others as nonsense, as an unreadable piece of fiction, as a novella—I don't know what it is. I wrote it both in French and English. What it is, it is probably the core of my entire work, and in it, the voice that speaks, the voice that you hear...is probably the voice of the fiction that "federman" has written, the voice that is rebelling against the author, the voice saying to the author, "federman, you have failed over and over again to tell my story."

CB: Now is "federman" you? Because you refer to yourself in the third person.

RF: Yes, because in the text the word "federman" is inscribed, and the moment you inscribe your name in a text it's just a word, it's another word, it's a fiction, it's a fictitious word, just as the pronoun "I" or the pronoun "he" is a word, as Kafka of course taught us when he wrote *K*. So, "federman" with a small "f," by the way.

CB: This is a series of words without punctuation, isn't it?

RF: No punctuation, written in a form that each page was originally typed on a typewriter without ever hyphenating a word. I didn't use a computer in those days that could justify left and right margin. It's a perfect square—I used a ruler to make sure it was a perfect square of words—and it's 20 squares of words within themselves, you might say. The only way one could really read *The Voice in the Closet* perfectly would be if you could set down and composite 20 pages on transparent paper and look down on it and see this perfect cube of words, and which of course would make no sense.

CB: And would be very dark and dense.

RF: Well, dark and dense it will be. It kind of—really, it's a prison, it's a cell, it's a box—it's of course, it refers to that box where my mother pushed me, the little closet where I was hidden when they were being taken away. I wanted the box of words not say what it was, but to be what it was....I should point out that there is more than one voice in the closet. The main voice, the one that says "I" is probably the voice of also the little boy who has been pushed into the closet. It is a voice of— it is history, it is the voice of his story, of his fiction, but one can also hear the voice of the typewriter, which the writer mistakes as his and probably the voice of the parents and other voices which the speaker mistakes.

CB: You mentioned before that your work was well known and well received in Germany. Do you think your work is better understood in Germany or in Europe than it is in the United States?

RF: It's not really the question of understood. It has been read there. I doubt that it has really been read in America except by a few fanatics, including yourself, perhaps. But the books, because some of them played with a lot of typography and others were considered unreadable because of the syntax or whatever or the mixture of French and English, they were looked at, but I don't think they were penetrated. I don't think they were assessed. They are beginning to. There have been a couple of interesting pieces written lately, but I think they were looked upon more as a curiosity and therefore declared experimental, innovative, whatever, and shoved aside with all that other stuff we call experimental. So they really never— when the first novel was translated in Germany, which happened to be *Double or Nothing*, which is very difficult, an unreadable book to most people, it was immediately read. I was convinced of that by some 75 reviews, articles that appeared as soon as the book came out and read intelligently. Yes, they paid attention to the typography, to the madness, to what in America they called the gimmicks, but they took them seriously and saw that they were an intricate part of what these books were doing.

CB: Are you a poet or are you a fiction writer? Or does it make any difference?

RF: I wanted so badly, Charles, when I was much younger, so to be a poet, and for years—and I have written a lot of poetry—but gradually realized that my poetry has a quality to it not unlike my fiction which is that it does not put those who read poetry at ease, who find, "Is this poetry? This is not how poetry should be." I mean, you are aware of that because your poetry also raises the same questions. A lot of people must say that—does Charles, does he really write poetry or is he writing some kind of a new recipe? And this has puzzled people.

CB: Actually it puzzles the people who try to make the food based on the recipes. They're the really puzzled ones.

RF: On top of that, as you know I work in two traditions—the American Anglo-Saxon and the French. I remember years ago sending some poems to Robert Bly, who had a magazine called *The 60s*—remember *The 60s*?—Robert Bly. I had no idea what it was. He wrote me a very nice letter, encouraging me, said he thinks if I stay with it there's hope for me but he couldn't publish my poems because they were too numeric in the French fashion[1]. He hadn't any knowledge that I was a French-born writer. There is a bell of that French tradition, whatever—

CB: There is not enough outdoor virility in your work, I think, for Robert Bly. Not enough male bonding.

RF: Yes, but I continue to write poetry. Some of it gets published in magazines. But I don't think anyone, including yourself, ever thinks of me as a poet....

CB: There is a lot of jazz rhythm in that. Is that important to you.

RF: Very important. Jazz has been, I think—it's been said and I have said it in interviews also that—you know at one time I thought of being a jazz musician—I played and fooled around with the saxophone and even played a little bit—not professionally, but with various gigs—but jazz is—just as before when we talking about the importance of laughter and my existence, the importance of jazz, that jazz is giving me—and I listen all the time and I play all the time—this sense that in jazz there is a certain freedom, the sense of being able to improvise, to go anywhere you want, and the same time the same sadness that is buried deep into jazz.

CB: Or the blues.

RF: The blues. But every jazz piece has it, even when it's bombastic you sense that at the bottom of it that is—

CB: How about improvisation? Because your work plays a lot with a feeling of improvisation, of just going on and the pleasure of the telling of the story. At the same time your work is remarkably composed.

---

[1] In his Second Manifesto published in 1973, F. Le Lionnais declares: "The effort of Oulipian creation deals principally with all the formal aspects of literature: constraints, programs or structures which are alphabetic, consonantal, vocalic, syllabic, phonetic, graphic, prosodic, rhythmic, numeric, and rhyme related."

RF: It gives the impression on the surface of pure chaos and of digressions all over the place, but yes, I work very hard at it, page after page, screen after screen, reshaping every word to put it in place in order for it to achieve why I hope it is there. Perhaps even more so with the early work with the music—*Take It or Leave It* as it was described once on the radio as a long tenor saxophone solo, and it has this quality, kind of Sonny Rollins kind of screeching.

CB: One double image is male/female. Lots of the women in your work are the subject of sexual pursuit by the men. There's lots of stuff that would be disturbing I think to contemporary readers, in terms of what's now called gender politics. Lots of stuff that might strike people as sexist, lots of sexist behavior recounted and recounted again in those novels. What do you think about that?

RF: This has been pointed out to me not only by people but by my daughters themselves when they were old enough to read the book, "Pop! This is sexist!" The early works, I no doubt—that *Double or Nothing* and *Take It or Leave It*—and I was able to when I redid recently two years ago a new edition of *Double or Nothing* to tone down some of the words. Yes, but look, I was born in that generation of those who were sexist in the '40s and '50s—in was in our language, it was in our attitude, it was the way we "conquered" women in those days, and I think gradually, if one follows the work, yes, under the influence, in fact, of my daughters, and this is strange—I think of myself as a great feminist, in fact, very aware of it. But I'm also aware that it's part of my make up, part of my history, and it's there. And I'll assume all the blame if there's blame to be assumed.

CB: Well, I wasn't so much asking you to assume blame as to think about what the desperation of the kind of male sexuality in the work represents, especially the kind of coming of age in the army, this person, dislocated, who literally drops down by parachute into an army barracks in the South, and just recounting the kind of sexual politics there, in the South at the time, in the army anyway.

RF: There is also the fact that it is not always specific when the action of the novels are taking place. Most of my novels are situated somewhere in that post-World War Two period that goes to about the middle of the '50s, that period when I was myself lost in the great belly of America, so this is how this young protagonist, persona, etc., that is in those novels acts. It was also that the sexual aggressiveness was part of the survival, you might say.

AFTER THE FACT

RONALD SUKENICK

The trip begins in the Olympic Stadium in Berlin. Even empty, its vastness, like the foot print of a giant concrete boot, crushes the spirit beneath its monumental cement.

I'm standing there within the walls of the Olympic Stadium with Federman while he describes to me, in his dense French accent, with a kind of perverse admiration how the Nazis used its huge scale to crush the individual ego. My silent reaction is, we have met the enemy and he is us.

Because like the fascists we all understand this now, we've all been through the ongoing ego smasher of the history the fascists helped to unleash. Besides, how could one assume the arrogance of individual identity after all those identities exxed off the surface of the planet since the year of my birth, 1932, the year Hitler assumed power? How could one even presume to be a person after all that, or even a human?

And how much less so Federman, whose family were among those abruptly exxed? In fact I'm not an individual, I assert it now, I'm just as much Federman as Federman is, and I'm others too and they are me, whether they want to understand it or not.

That's up to them, it's none of my business and I really couldn't care less, it's simply a question of being passive enough, that is, receptive enough. Invisible enough, invisible as my shadow. The shadow knows.

You read all this with skepticism, he's dealing in metaphor, you think, okay it's metaphor, this isn't science fiction. But it's not merely metaphor.

The only thing totally individual about me will be my death, but on the other hand the one good thing I can say about my death is that I won't be there.

I know very well that Federman will be annoyed by this because he resents the way we're always twinned, by the literary critics that is. [REAL TIME WINDOW: Contrary to what I say here about his being annoyed, in response to a draft of this manuscript, Federman writes, "I am of course honored to appear in person (with my real name) in Ron's new novel. It's really a great honor to be a character in a novel, it's like acquiring a kind of immortality. And just think, suppose the book becomes a best seller, I'll be famous."] This is just like Federman, to use my novel for his pursuit of fame.

Just like Federman, but is it Federman? Or is it just his way of being annoyed?

And in fact aside from fiction we're very little alike, we're more like opposites, Federman's ebullience nothing like my slow, sullen pace, and even in fiction there's little resemblance, Federman's fascination with absence, the absence of the exxed, having nothing to do with my indifference toward the progressive ebbing of my self and the aggressive presence of everything else.

The real problem is not merely whether I'm Federman, by virtue of my progressive invisibility I'm pretty much anybody, anybody who gets close enough to allow my antennae to receive their ectoplasmic transmissions, man, woman or child.

Or animal. And when I say ectoplasmic I'm just kidding, I don't know what the hell it is or why it kicks in, probably cybernetic would be more accurate. I don't want to give the impression I do this for fun, either, often it's not fun, quite the reverse, sometimes it's unpleasant, or worse.

I'd avoid the whole business if I could. Or if I could I'd figure out how it works and take out a patent.

Anyway, obviously, I always know what Federman is thinking, and what he's thinking as he gives me his impressions of the Olympic Stadium is that if he arranges the day's schedule right he might be able to get me to come with him to the gambling casino in the evening.

Because one of Federman's ambitions in life is finding the Golden Calf. Finding it and at the same time losing it. That's why he likes to gamble.

And that's what he's doing here in Germany. Pursuing the Golden Calf. Which he doesn't really want. That's not it, that's not what he's after.

What, then, is he after? Maybe this is my chance to find out.

And so standing there now with him in the wall of the Olympic Stadium, one of the few remaining monuments of Nazism left by the war, where Hitler held his giant rallies designed to ensure that we don't exist as individual egos or, in our case, at all, Federman snapping my photo to show that after all we do, I'm already aware of what's going to happen during my brief visit to Berlin.

> [REAL TIME WINDOW: Just this minute, as I
> revise this to send to him, Federman calls to ask
> me among other things when I'm going to send
> it to him, the revised version, and I'm revising it
> in fact, as fast as I can, because I want to get it to
> him within the next two weeks, before he has to go
> into the hospital for a potentially serious operation.]

I'm already aware of what's going to happen during my brief visit to Berlin because this has already happened, though it hasn't happened for you until I tell you it's happened.

And even then it will only happen for you in Virtual Time. The rest of this trip is in Virtual Time. Virtual Time is a hologrammatic projection of the times we live in. It looks real, it feels real, it smells real. And it is real. It's a real projection.

What will happen next is we'll get into the car and drive toward the Brandenburg Gate, parking some distance away because of the general congestion, since the fall of the Wall will have been only two or three weeks past during the time period we'll be moving through. As we walk toward the Gate, we'll start hearing a certain sound, a clinking, chinking, chipping sound, clink, clink, chip, chink.

"What's that?" I'll ask Federman.

"You'll see," he'll say.

And when we reach the Wall I'll see a grafitti swashed page of cement, an endless concrete page unscrolled as far as eye can see crammed with multicolored multilingual writing, the writing on the wall an incomprehensible babel of symbols, slogans, signs, messages, epigraphs, pictograms, hieroglyphs, riddles, runes, alphabetic jocularities, plays on words and words playing on themselves, what you might call concrete poetry, all hacked and pocked and pitted and peeled through layers of painted and petrified palimpsest with hammer and chisel and crow bar and drill and pick by memento seekers and souvenir merchants to the skeleton of reenforcment rods and through to air on the other side, click, clink, chip, chink, chunkachunk chunk. Be frei.

These chippers are called Wallpeckers, a coinage. I pick a piece of Wall from one. One mark. For Julia, My Constant Companion. Back in the States. Julia B. Frey.

From the Wall we'll go back to Federman's apartment where the formidable—in the French sense—Erica waits, and where we'll chat and nosh, me, Federman and his wife, she too among the fortunate fugitive few of the European fascist years, whom I sometimes think of as Eroica, or even as Europa, gathering our forces for the next lap in our Berlin adventure.

It's during this conversation, according to my notes, that Erica will describe a scene that strikes me as the vivid emblem of the fate the human ego endured during the duration of cataclysms of the last half century.

Her five year old eyes record, as a torpedoed ship filled with refugees is sinking, the water filled with struggling bodies, the image of men, women and children trying to save themselves from drowning, caught up in the stern wheel of the very ship trying to rescue them.

We no longer talk so much about the end of the world because at heart we realize the world as it used to be has already ended. And this is it, caught as if on film. Even efforts to save it help to destroy it.

When we strike out into the city again, our goal will be the Gestapo Museum.

All the while Federman will be telling me how he's closing in on the Golden Calf, meaning in this case his literary successes in Germany, his German translations, his prizes, his best sellers, his radio plays, his films, his fellowships, his photos, his translations, his portraits, his admirers, his Italian translations, his Spanish translations, his Polish translations, his pesetas, his lire, his zlowty, his deutschmarks, till I have the feeling that basically he's in the running for an eventual Academy Award.

I know, by contrast, what Federman thinks about me, and I'm sure he's correct, that I don't promote myself, that I don't know how to sell myself, that I'm commercially backward, that I'll never get anywhere the way I proceed, and consequently he's always trying to help me in my own pursuit of the Golden Calf with this publisher, that translator, this fellowship, that magazine, and it never does any good of course, or rarely, and especially not when it has to do with getting anywhere.

Because where is there to get?

Which Federman well knows and is what makes him the manic gambler that he is, because a real gambler is in it not to win money but to play with it, to turn it into something other than an instrument to further ends, to transcend it exactly, or no, to transmute it into something infinitely more valuable than the original material, because a gambler is a kind of artist is what a gambler is, who knows how to win and lose at the same time, who knows that the opposite of losing is not winning but finding.

Which is why when you go to a casino with Federman you can never leave because either he's winning and he can't leave or he's losing and he can't leave, maybe you can only leave when you're breaking even, but then why go at all?

What we'll find at the Gestapo Museum is the shell of the former head-quarters of the Gestapo, its bare walls exhibiting a selection of photos showing what the Nazis did to the Jews, some of the very best photos no doubt, some are even familiar, they must be prize specimens, one more heartbreaking than the next, but I don't know, I'm sort of tired of all that, why do I have to look at it, imagine it all, yet again?

But Federman will point out to me that it's not tourists that one normally sees here but the Germans. He'll point out one young woman, very pretty in the best German style, slim, buxom, sensitive, soignée, looking at the photos with tears streaming down her face.

And I'll realize, not just then but at some time in the still unspecified future, remembering this, that it's a reaction it never occurred to me to have, tears, that it always seemed to me a response too superficial, too simple, for that enormity, almost a diminishment or even an insult simply to cry, while remembering at some subsequent time that young woman for that moment reduced to her tears it will come to me it's probably the only reaction simple enough to be adequate. Even though it's not adequate.

Federman will point out to me, besides, that there are Germans and Germans, there's Bavaria with its neo-fascist political party led by a former SS officer, and Austria, where an old woman on a train told him and Erica, "If you Jews don't like it here you can go back where you came from," and there are others, especially younger ones, like us trying to take in what happened in those days, trying to account for it.

And then Federman will tell me a story, not just then but at some other time in the future, a story about his father long ago before he and the rest of the family were exxed in the camps.

This is during the Occupation, when they were hiding out in the country-side somewhere in the west, in Normandy or maybe Brittany, and they were very poor and hardly had enough to eat and his father could barely make a living and I think was sick on top of that.

When suddenly, some of the German soldiers stationed in that part of the country, three or four, black marketeers maybe, started coming to the house with a truck loaded with coal and provisions every so often, to the point where the neighbors thought that rather than a family of hiding Jews, these must be secret collaborators, since nobody could understand why the Germans came with all this stuff.

And Federman as a child remembers how the German soldiers would talk and talk all night with his father, and each time, just before they left, they would all get up, raise their arms in a clenched fist salute and softly, in very low voices, together, sing the Internationale.

So the Germans are not unsympathetic, depending on the Germans. How could they be, given their enthusiastic response to Federman's innovative and not always easy reading books?

But what they're trying to do through his books, Federman explains to me, is to conduct a sort of autopsy. Now that they've killed off the Jews, they're interested in finding out what Jews were, what it is that they're now missing.

What it is that they're missing, Federman thinks, is humor.

Just what was this supersexed seducer of their women, this economic infiltrator, this clever entrepreneur, this subtle, subversive intellect, this bignosed alien from another cosmos, this self-conscious, ironic, in-turned, unhealthly mentality, this dirty Jew?

Did you take a bath this morning?

Why, is one missing?

Next we'll head for a cafe, or maybe a sports club, or possibly an excellent restaurant in Federman's Mercedes, or BMW, or possibly a Porsche this time. There in the cafe we're sure to meet one of his female admirers, one who is interviewing him for a newspaper, or another who wants to make a film of his life, or one of his students working on a study of Federman.

She'll be young, no more than thirty and maybe less than twenty, and she'll be part of his exuberant pursuit of the Golden Calf—give me money, or if not money fame, or if not fame sex, or if not sex my exxed family and lost childhood, or if not that something else from your horns of plenty.

He's not very French, finally. He's more like a French translation of a Russian novel.

It will be that second night in Berlin the bad dreams will begin. That night it will be the wan young girl, blond, prepubescent, thin, something fine in her eyes, caught with me in an air crash. I struggle to rescue her from the flames which are engulfing her, I know I can't though I try. But she doesn't die, she evaporates as I reach out for her. Then the plane crashes again, she's caught in the flames again as I try to reach her and she evaporates again. The plane crashes still again, she's burning, I try to save her and she evaporates. She's caught in the flames again, I try again, she evaporates again.

I have the impression her name is something like Birken, Birchermuesli. Birkenau?

The next morning we'll go to the suburb of Wannsee, passing through one of the few sections of Berlin not destroyed during the war.

This is and was a wealthy section of the city, many Jews lived here, and it will be interesting to me for more than its handsome, various and individualized architecture.

You sense here the presence of an idea.

It is a neighborhood that must have implied an idea of a life, comfortable, secure, private, an idea of stability and continuity. What could possibly happen to people living in such a neighborhood, beyond preoccupation with their bank accounts and the well made plot of family life with its inevitable melodramas and tragedies?

The presence of an idea and an absence of thought.

There are still places in Berlin that remain unreconstructed rubble, and there's nothing like the rubble of a city to get you thinking. To get you thinking that ideas are frozen thought and cities concrete expressions of it.

The neon jumble of rebuilt Berlin, with its tacky glass office buildings, will strike me as the revenge of the Bauhaus, a good idea at the wrong time, bankrupt modern skipping sixty years, confirming that what happened here couldn't have happened, even though it did.

All ideas are wrong. Especially the right ones.

That afternoon we'll go to East Berlin.

We'll be astonished that we no longer have to buy a certain amount of East German marks, apparently it's the first day or two of new currency regulations. That, and that the border guards won't be sullen, they'll be almost friendly. These are things that won't be believable till they happen, and even then they'll be hard to believe.

We'll head for the Jewish cemetery, which is on that side of the wall. Don't forget that before the war, eighty-eight percent of the Jews in the world lived in Europe, and among them Berlin was the most important and successful community of all, Berlin and Vienna. So I'll expect the cemetery to be august, even flashy. Or alternately, devastated, desecrated.

But it's neither. It will turn out it's subdued, not poverty-stricken for sure, but almost modest, with a share of somewhat magnificent monuments, and the rest discreet, correct. There are a lot of trees and greenery, slightly overgrown.

People stroll through its paths with a meditative look. Here and there a row of small headstones covering a whole family, two and three generations, with inscriptions all reading, "Died at Auschwitz, 1944."

It will come to me, as we stroll through, that the cemetery is devoted to two kinds of death, that of individuals, and that of a long history dead-ended, a community, a whole culture disappeared into a black hole.

But unlike Auschwitz there's something peaceful here, oddly benign, something laid to rest, as they say.

It will be the first time I've been in a cemetery since they buried my father. They uncovered the coffin there so we could get a last look. His face looked greyish, it had a distinctly frosted look, he must have been in cold storage. My mother kissed him and broke down, then they nailed the lid shut.

I say nailed but really I have no idea, my own brain was in a sort of cold storage too. Here in the Jewish cemetery of Berlin it will defrost a bit, and one of the things that will come to mind will be the difference between dying and being exxed. My father died. Federman's father evaporated without a word, without a trace.

Not only that, but my father was able to choose his death. Pills. And given the state of his health I couldn't have argued with him. "Goodbye Cile, I love you."

Somehow, he spelled my mother's name wrong after fifty-eight years.

And he was even able to speak a few last words, by way of final advice: "Go home and go to bed."

It rained, it rained hard. I remember that much of the funeral. I remember I'd been away, because the doctor said there was no predicting how long he'd last, weeks, days, hours.

It turned out to be hours. I still feel guilty about that. But I remember it. What does Federman remember? Being pushed into a closet when the Nazis came. Then, many years later, going to Auschwitz to search the records, only it was Sunday and the records were closed.

There's a frontier style restaurant where I live in Colorado where if you wear a tie they cut it off. This is meant to be profound Americana, and it is. The basic American experience of immigration is one of cutting ties.

And it illustrates why Jews have gotten along so well in the United States. We're used to having our ties cut. But the moment we have our ties cut we start extending ourselves to re- establish connections as soon as possible. We know that's our only salvation. It won't be long now.

No one's ties have been cut as abruptly as Federman's. It will occur to me that Federman has been kicked out of the ghetto by history and in the most brutal way possible, as have for example most Israelis. For them the ghetto is dead and gone.

I know other Jews will assure you that they have eliminated the ghetto in themselves, especially the Israelis. It reminds me of a story the Uncles used to tell about a man who went to a doctor to complain he could hardly get it up any more. So the doctor tells him, "What do you want, you're eighty years old."

"But Cohen is eighty-five," says the man, "and he shtups his wife seven days a week, sometimes twice."

"How do you know?"

"He tells me."

"He tells you, so you tell him."

I've always lived in our world. I have no allegiance to the ghetto.

So I'm surprised whenever I feel the undertow of its invisible existence. But what you don't see is what you always get.

That's why I've at times been fascinated with writing and rewriting my autobiography, there's so much of it I don't know anything about.

As a result of these autobiographical investigations, which are something like Federman's work, the next time I'll see him it's again in Germany at a conference on autobiographical fiction. In Mainz. This will be an intensive four days with so many things happening that I'll barely remember any of them.

Luckily, I'll take notes. The only problem is they seem to be written in secret code. Tough notes to crack. And then piece together.

Making plans to go to Mainz. I'll start trying to coordinate arrangements with another invitee, Serge Doubrovsky, French autobiographical writer of what he calls "auto-fiction," since both of us will be going via Paris.

Doubrovsky, to begin with, having been invited to Mainz thanks partly to my efforts, won't be able make up his mind whether to go. This, if you know him as I do, you will recognize as typical Doubrovsky behavior. Just arranging with Doubrovsky to go eat in a restaurant can be such a production, with his precise requirements for cuisine, diet, quality, price, time and location on a particular night, that negotiations can go on for a week and even then are liable to complete change at the last instant, if not cancellation.

Finally the only way to do it is to do it his way.

[REAL TIME WINDOW: After reading this,
Doubrovsky responds in a letter by calling my
practice of putting other writers into my writing
"cross-fiction." And it does make him cross.
Among other things, he writes about the above
that it applies "literally and equally to you!
In Lacanian analysis it's called the `blind spot.'
Not seeing that what you blame others for doing
is exactly what you do." Further: "I found parts
of your text concerning me kind of abrasive and
offensive and in return I penned a somehow
bristling epistle to couch my own reactions.
Today, I sat down and perused the same chapter
again without experiencing the same sort of mixed
feeling. Very weird. It's as if, at first, I could
hardly tolerate to see my self transported or
deported from auto to heterofiction!"]

Transported or deported indeed. But weren't the camps literally a deportation from one's own ego?

On the other hand, going to Germany will be horribly complicated for him both because of his experiences as a Jew during the war, and because of his Austrian wife, recently dead. Ilse. A friend of mine too, and more so of My Constant Companion, with whom I'm travelling, their marriage and her sudden, ambiguous death in her mid-thirties the subject of his noted autobiographical novel. The guilt-ridden, heart-broken Le Livre Brisé.

A prize winner. And a best seller.

Ambiguous death because it wasn't clear whether it was caused by pills, alcohol, pills and alcohol, accident, suicide or whether Serge had a part in killing her himself.

Bernard Pivot, on his famous French interview show "Apostrophe," more or less accused Serge of killing her.

Sometimes Serge seems to agree.

But the matter is not simple. And here comes one of the problems of autobiography. Since Serge's novels are meticulously factual, and the premise of the novel in question is, at Ilse's request, that it be about their life together, his and Ilse's, including, foreseeably, her alcoholism, it's hard to know how much of a role he and the novel itself played in her death.

The novel which when finished would end with an account of that death.

Because though he showed her the part of the manuscript dealing with her alcoholism just before her death, and she was upset by it, who can say objectively, least of all Doubrovsky, how much that had to do with a death that is to begin with only ambiguously a suicide?

But it's just such heartbreaking ambiguities as this, included of course in the book, that make it interesting as literature. And as an exemplary autobiographical novel. Because what person knows the whole story, even of his own life? Especially of his own life.

One might have known something was wrong. Even beyond the drinking. But who could have predicted that, that suddenly one day I would get a card that looked like an invitation, or an announcement of a birth, the birth of the child she so much wanted to have, and looking at it not being able to comprehend that in fact it was an announcement of her death?

Serge not only is Jewish, he looks Jewish, as he was made so well aware by Nazi propaganda during the Occupation. And he's alive, like a number of French Jews who survived, thanks only to a gendarme's discreet visit letting his family know he'd soon be back to arrest them.

And Ilse was Austrian, from a family with Nazi connections.

A bright, pretty young woman, for Serge a late happiness after a long, disastrous relation with another woman. Which was the subject of his preceding novel.

So you see, things are not so simple. Not simple for him to come to Germany, to hear her language, literally a language of love and of hate, pathos and fear. To read to the Germans, of all people, for the first time out loud about his life and her death.

For years I've been wanting to get Doubrovsky and Federman together, I've known each of them forever but, surprisingly, they hardly know one another at all, maybe they've shaken hands once or twice in all these years, and never with me around. Surprisingly, because they have so much in common.

On the other hand, they're total opposites. Doubrovsky, his family having survived, if just, graduating from the elite school for French intellectuals and shuttling back and forth from his job in the States to

France, writing in French, Federman, whose whole family was exxed, growing up in the Black section of Detroit, writing in English. Then why is it Federman who has the atrocity of a French accent still? Federman the jock, who looks like he just got out of the Foreign

Legion, Doubrovsky, who looks like the the complete European Jewish intello. Federman, the writer obsessed with innovation, Doubrovsky, the conventional writer whose obsessions force him to innovate. Doubrovsky who, in his writing, is compelled to tell you everything, Federman who is obsessed with telling you nothing. Doubrovsky the loner, Federman the convivial, Federman the hip, Doubrovsky the bourgeois, Doubrovsky who likes to make money, Federman who loves making it and even better, throwing it away.

> [REAL TIME WINDOW: Doubrovsky objects,
> quite justly, that "to be anti-bourgeois has become
> a bourgeois cliche. So I am, indeed, bourgeois,
> because I have a steady profession and income. So
> do you and so does Federman. And insofar as

`bourgeois,' historically, has always been connected
with acquisition and ownership, since I don't own a
thing in the world, except for a car and a few pieces
of furniture in Paris and have no landed interests, I
possess no house or apartments, I am in a deeper sense
far less bourgeois than you or Federman." As if the
three of us, despite complete assimilation, are in
competition for status as outsiders.]

These two old friends of mine, so similar and so different I'm often surprised I can be friendly with both. And my relations with them ambiguous to begin with since, wanting to be more like Raymond, I'm probably more like Serge. Serge is right, after all, this is my "blind spot"—not seeing myself in him.

Serge and Raymond will seem to get along fine, from what I can see. I'll hear Serge promising to send Raymond a copy of his novel. I wonder if he has?

[REAL TIME WINDOW: He hasn't. He
promises to have a copy delivered to me
to send on to Federman. He doesn't.]

The next day one of the hazards of such conferences will threaten to get out of hand. Girl (or boy, choose one—or both) chasing. That is, them chasing us. Luckily I will have My Constant Companion along to ward off evil, I can't speak for the others. All men and women of the pen, no matter how unattractive, and literary types are notoriously unattractive, become cocks and hens of the walk in these back yards through the law of eminence in our domain.

So though I'll see Doubrovsky coming back from a trip to the Lorelei with an elegant admirer late one night, looking a lot happier than when I'd seen him the evening before, this will not alter my sense that he's still grieving deeply over Ilse's death.

This day's performances will confirm several of my mounting convictions, namely that we're all more alike than the creed of individualism permits us to admit, that I'm growing increasingly invisible and that I'm becoming everybody else.

One illustration is that host Professor Hornung will give me a long, wonderful introduction but in which he calls me Federman. Another is that me, Federman and Doubrovsky, it will turn out, choose to give readings heavily freighted with the Germans' role in World War II regarding the Jews. Still another is that I'll find that Maxine Hong Kingston, with whom I'll expect to have very little in common, has stylistic ambitions in fiction remarkably like my own rejection of the merely imagined in favor of fact.

Finally, when I find that I've accidentally walked off with Hornung's notebook and look to see what's in it, I'll discover copious notes on everyone else and my name followed by a completely blank page.

But Federman, every time he burps, now, somebody here publishes it. He gives a few lectures, he writes them down, Suhrkampf turns them into a book. And I, of course, am writing down his private interchanges with me to publish in my book. In fact the Germans are going to write down and publish this entire conference.

So what is there left that isn't written down and published? All that remains is the book of life, and I try to get that into print as quickly as possible. So that nothing remains hidden. So I can tell you the true story. Like Doubrovsky does. So that the published book reflects the book of life. Well, reflects on, maybe.

But to get back to the true story, I will introduce Federman's reading that day, beginning with our visit to Wansee. "It was only later, much later and back in the States, that we remembered that Wannsee was where it all began: the Wannsee conference where the idea of the final solution was endorsed as the right one for their Jewish problem and set in motion by the Nazi elite.

"Reflecting on this now it becomes impossible to maintain that Jews are European, even European Jews like Federman. Yes, many Jews have European reflexes, those Jews with long histories of European evolution.

But then Europeans by now have profoundly Jewish reflexes: relativity, consciousness of self, collective social responsibility, via Reb Karl, Reb Albert, Reb Sigmund, to name just a few from the merely recent past.

"But Europe is just one part of a long story. And the story Federman tells is the end of the chapter or rather, what happens after the chapter has ended. The characters have disappeared, the tragedy is over, the stage is bare. Even Samuel Beckett, Federman's friend and great model has finally effaced himself for the last time. Fifty million people have been slaughtered within six years. The great tradition of Humanism wasn't worth shit in a chateau, a fox hole, a death camp, a stately state palace. Never mind post modern, we're all post humous as Europeans, including the Europeans themselves. Post human.

"One day, Federman, who must be twelve or thirteen at the time, is in the apartment with his family, poor, relatively recent immigrants to France, when the Germans come, he's pushed into a closet by his mother, and suddenly he's an orphan, a fugitive jumping from freight train to freight train, a farm laborer in the south of France, a factory worker in Detroit, a white named Frenchy in a black ghetto, a jazz musician, a paratrooper in Korea, a student in New York, a poet, a jock, a professor in California, a novelist in Buffalo, an honored literary guest in Germany. A great story but what's the plot? And which one of the above is the hero? and where's the verisimilitude? and when is the beginning, the middle, the end? and why should this irrational discontinuity be related in sequential sentences from left to right, left to right to the bottom of the printed page? and how in the name of probability can it be called real?

"No, the book of life cannot be paraphrased, it cannot be prescribed, it cannot be predicted, it cannot be dictated, it cannot be imitated, it cannot resemble some other book, it cannot begin, it cannot end, it cannot be made up, it cannot be about major characters or minor characters or any characters other than those of the alphabet, it cannot be about the right ideas, it cannot be controlled, it cannot be about reality, because life is not about reality. It is it. If it weren't, what would be? There is only one thing you can do with the book of life: add to it. Federman writes books that add to it, that's why they don't seem to be like other books, why they're sometimes strange, because life is sometimes strange. Stranger than fiction, as they say.

"And now, stranger than fiction, Raymond Federman!"

It will be obvious from the response to Federman's reading that he's by far the great favorite here. But I've heard him reading many times and never Doubrovsky who though far better known than either of us in France is little known in Germany. So I'll be eager to hear him read, and especially eager to get Federman's reaction to his performance.

But it will be Maxine Hong Kingston who will read first this night, and her reading will make me think how un-European we all are. Even Doubrovsky, who spends half his time in the States, has moved so far to the edge of French literary decorum that the French are scandalized.

But the French like to be scandalized.

It will come to me that in comparison with the Europeans, none of us Statespersons are miming real life. Why try to imitate the inimitable? We're all engaged, like Dr. Frankenstein or the Rabbi of Prague and his Golem, in creating life.

In making things happen. Things not necessarily in our control and it can be dangerous. As it's proved to be for Doubrovsky.

It occurs to me that that maybe Jews were never really Europeans. Certainly not in the ghetto. Certainly not any more. No more than Maxine Kingston.

Doubrovsky's reading will turn out to be an eruption, an explosion of emotional and stylistic violence, a confrontation with his guilt over Ilse's death and his hatred for the Germanic society that created her. He'll tell them that though today they celebrate him yesterday they were trying to reduce him to ashes. He'll say he's not a Jew but a Kike. Later he'll tell me how he really gave it to them, even called them Boches, which he says they hate.

By the end of the performance he'll be exhausted. During it he'll break out in tears reading the story of his wife's death. The impact on the audience will be such that they can't applaud at the end, it would be like applauding at a funeral. Doubrovsky will appear to be in such a state that we fear for his mental, even his physical health.

Shortly after in the men's room of the restaurant we go to, he's asking me about the publication possibilities of the book in the States, and whether it wouldn't be feasible for my press to translate it. This will be Doubrovsky the literary figure talking, not Serge the grieving husband, the one who refuses permission for a German translation for the sake of Ilse's mother, or who refuses to use the profits from his book about Ilse, putting them instead into a trust fund for his daughters. These two Doubrovskies don't have much to do with one another, and even less with Serge the writer, not to mention Doubrovsky of the Lorelei.

Meanwhile, I'll have been wondering about the reaction of Federman to the reading. But it will turn out that Federman didn't attend. He had something else to do. Federman's expansiveness is his way of avoiding things Raymond the dreamer prefers not to confront.

Raymond is a seeing eye man. In order to see some things others don't you have to be blind to some things others aren't. While I, with my fetish of transparence, refuse to see I, forcing others to see through me. A mere scribe ascribed to be the medium for the tribe.

Serge himself will be wondering what the effect of his reading was, especially on the Germans. At a certain point he'll call me up.

"I don't suppose you were able to find out how the Germans liked it?" he'll ask.

"Well as a matter of fact, I did get some reactions."

"Because I was really hard on them, you know. They might not have liked that."

"Well I did ask some of them about it."

"Although I used the German word for peace at the end. That was intentional."

"I did ask them," I'll shout into the phone. Serge is a little hard of hearing. "Hornung and some of those people."

"I believe I asked him..."

"Well, I guess I'll never know."

Serge is a hearing ear man.

Before he leaves Serge will advise me that life is not all work and no play and that I should profit from the trip and not miss going up the Rhine to visit the Lorelei. Raymond will give me the name of an editor in Paris who he assures me wants to publish a translation of one of my books. It moves me to see how my two friends try to take care of me.

Even thought they can't.

> [REAL TIME WINDOW: The next chance
> I get to see Federman it's at another conference
> a few months later. He tells me he's waiting to
> hear about the need for some potentially serious
> surgery. Then he tells me a story about meeting
> someone he knew as a kid in France and hadn't
> seen since, now both of them grey. The first thing
> the guy said to him was, "Ca va vite, la vie, hein?"
> It goes fast, one's life, eh?
> Then Raymond added, "And I suddenly got
> so scared...

[excerpted by permission of the author from *Mosaic Man* (Normal, IL: FC2, 1999.]

IMAGINATION AS PLAGIARISM: CRITIFUCKING RAYMOND FEDERMAN

DOUG RICE

For Federman, the Real Federman from the Fake Federman!
[Scrawled by someone claiming to be Raymond Federman in my copy of *Critifiction* written by some author claiming to be Raymond Federman.]

Raymond Federman is a new syntax, an uncomfortable stutterer raised on the streets of Detroit. A foreigner with a strange tongue and faulty hearing. His writing is clumsy in those brilliant ways that surprise language. It is as if, before Federman's weird and twisted dialectics, language itself had never been aware of its own boundless rapture. Under Federman's thumb, language takes off, becomes delirious. As a writer, he is inappropriate and refuses to obey the boundaries of the page. His words, his mad paratroopical grammar, flood the disciplined margins. He is a pageless writer who scribbles across the wounded galaxies of this Memorex nation. Little more than a schizophobic hesitation, Federman steals away words without regard for the law of copyright. For him, such a law has always granted him permission, the right to copy. He is the living embodiment of an echo driven mad by the mere thought that words can ever be owned, can ever be possessed by any individual. Everything solids melts in Federman's mouth. Quotation marks no longer stain Federman's fiction. They never really ever existed to begin with. Not for Federman and his theories of pla(y)giarism. His ways for telling stories is similar to Deleuze's table of additions where languages pile up and interact with each other. A journey into the passions of chaos. Federman's words are spots that mark an absence, marks of invisible desires. Federman entertains himself with noises. Federman listens to those who shout in the streets, those words that move through the pages. Blank in between becoming. Federman's writings are no mere modernist allusions that pay homage to the dreary past. If anything, his writing betrays the dust of desiccated learning by breathing new life into voices within voices.

Federman's critifictional desires, the unmapable following that is his writing, can only stutter in the moment in-between. There is no go-between inside this in-between of Federman's pla(y)giarism. Just a Godotean space of silence filled with the chaos of Federman's infectious prose, a prose riddled by the mysteries of foreign inflection. He never has quite figured out this American English language. His idiomatic foreign-ness always breaks through lines of resistance. Federman's prose is, per-haps, even more complicated than those Beckettian unnameable moments. The power of Federman's writing in large part comes from the demands that it places on readers to discover, invent languages and syntax that have never before been knowable. Federman pushes critics past their own seeing and speech and demands new ways of writing. Critical dis-courses have to be slippery inside such nomadic spaces. There can only be uncertainty. No naming. Too often, in such writing, sources emerge, or at least radiate. So the source, the origin, remains present and thus the trace continues to function in only the same way that allusion functioned in Modernist discourses. Heigho, heigho, and it is off to the library we go hustling for tenure and promotion and other "just" rewards. But Federman's work denies such simplicities. There is no way to silence Federman. To domesticate his wandering prose style, to resolve his endless refusal to begin. His work misbehaves in the moment of unfolding. This movement of writing. The traditional literary hierarchy of quotation is repeatedly cast in doubt; the conventional obedience to copyright is completely ignored. Still, this disturbing criminal of aesthetics, Federman wanders around the golf courses of San Diego a free man.

Quotation marks are completely absent from Federman's life. A few years ago while visiting him in Buffalo, I noticed a broken key on his IBM Selectric typewriter. Where other IBM Selectric's have inverted commas, Federman's typewriter simply has open space.

"Federman," I said, "your typewriter is broken. You cannot use this typewriter to write proper essays."

"It's not broken, Rice," Federman replied. "That missing key is just a place for dreaming in other tongues." In the corner of the room I heard an echo say, "Don't quote me on that."

While not a real danger to the public welfare, Federman can be quite a nuisance to moral sentences. In 1995 Federman was escorted out of a Kinko's for allegedly writing directly onto the glass of a photocopier. In the shuffling madness, Ray was quoted in the local newspaper as saying: "I am writing. This is my writing utensil Follow me." This incidence has been captured on videotape and has proven to be a Kodak moment. "I am," Federman continued, "Alice through the looking-glass." Now Federman practices photocopy degeneration between rounds of golf and often calls me while revising the copyright page of his books.

All sense of origins has been lost in the chaos of journeys gone mad. All language comes to writers secondhand. In Federman's prose, words are born again without being repeated. Words are ignorant of their own origins because they never stop moving. They refuse to pause. "I wear only clothing that has been worn by others," I tell Federman one night on the phone.

"My sentiments exactly," Federman responds. "There is my theory for all my writing. To wear holes in the clothing of others."

The practice of Federmania is a kind of politics of cultural memory, not an aesthetic of allusive quotations sending readers on Holy Grail quests for charming resolution. Federmaniacal writing is bewildered by a cacophony of vices. [In the original this sentence read: Writing is bewildered by a cacophony of voices. As if voices are vices. To lack a letter is to come to difference. To make a letter jump around is to come to Federman. Meaning slipping out of joint. To mistake one letter for a litter.] The "original" act of Federman writing is never an act of naming but is always an act of copying. The sacred fount of Federman's inspiration is not a Jamesian marble statue but a photocopier. His writing stumbles around off-center among scattered traditions. And he never ever gets anything right. He breaks into the possibilities of ruins that have been left behind scattered in books supposedly written by other authors. Flagrant displacement of random thoughts scrawled on paper. Federman hesitates inside lost authenticity. His words are promiscuous. His letters are, in deed, litters. Becoming.

Federman is a catastrophic plague set loose upon the Enlightenment and upon the capitalist view that by nature words can be owned. Federman is a whimsical demonic force intent on making footnotes, afterthoughts, allusions look downright silly. My wife despairs each time Federman pays a visit because he leaves behind traces of unused quotation marks all over the floor of our house. (We have a small child who has on occasion put said quotation marks into her mouth. The innocence of infancy. "No," we scream, terrified of the incestuous nature of literary genealogies. "Don't put that into your mouth. God knows where that quotation mark has been." We spend days and nights after a Federmanical visit cleansing our house. Returning our lives to purity.)

Federman's prose pushes James Joyce's Aunt Josephine off the easy chair of reading. There are only impractical ways for reading a Federman text. A self-dialogue in one schizophrenic voice recited between stations at the metro. Federman's narratives force readers to enter a sort of unmapped desert and travel as nomadic tribes without a scout leader. What, then, can be used as a key for interrogating schizophrenic energy, his languages of exultation and despair? When textuality is continually talking to (and at times against) itself, constructing and reassuring itself in other words, what is a boy to do? Writing is ineluctably transformed from being a self-referring monument to becoming an intersection, a moment of rendezvous, a site of transit, in a wider network. Set loose from its moorings, Federman's narrative begins to drift, to enter other accounts. There is no one place to read Federman. No one way to settle the disturbances created by Federman's "own" words. His language betrays multiple histories and memories that swell up–"as the rupture and revenge of signification" into an interrogation of the enigma of what might be called the nebulous quality of narrating a story to whom it may concern.

Like Federman himself as writer, his reader needs to become a junkman. A babbling idiot. A mistaken identity. A person on the verge of forgetting. A dancing ledge mime. A mosquito. A collector and a wanderer. Such a reader must be willing to enter into becoming a migratory act of reading. Federman's readers must enter zones, penetrate them if you will, that are open, full of gaps: excesses that are irreducible to a single center, origin, or point of view. (Of course I am plagiarizing. Word for bloody word. With a differance. Paradigming a new center. Buzzing along.) I travel the spilled, the broken world not to arrive home (or even Buffalo, or now San Diego) but to enter shifting constellations of meaning that orbit around potential openings, interruptions, intervals–both breakdowns and breakthroughs–in my inherited critical positions, histories, languages, and identities. Federman has fucked with history and tradition. I once tried to quote him only to discover that I had forgotten. How many quotation marks does it take to quote a sentence of Federman's?

The following is a Federmaniacal digression and was found by accident in a pamphlet about fishing. Tad Shura (a real name of a mathematical wizard) gave this pamphlet to me after meeting Federman. He thought it would help to clarify Federman's schizophrenic behavior the night before at a reading where Federman appeared to be reading in multiple tongues and voices.

Noodling is the art of groping under banks, into holes and other dark, out-of-sight areas to grab a snapper and yank him out....Few fellows nowadays do much noodling. One day in the not so far future, it will probably be a lost art. I for one am afraid to noodle.

For the fellows with no hesitation to noodle, the more power to them.

Noodling requires no equipment, other than a sack for carrying the catch.

....

All things considered, noodling…is a messy, muddy, physically tiring, and potentially dangerous method...but what a challenge!

To read Federman is to noodle. To noodle is to read Federman. There is no way for getting around this.

Apparently this ends the digression. Only to lead to a story. Sometimes I confuse myself with Federman and sometimes I don't. For one [this should be in quotes, just don't tell Federman] never knows where one's thoughts originate, and when these thoughts merge with the thoughts of others, where one's language begins and where it converges with that of others within the dialogue all of us entertain with ourselves and others. This story is an autobiographical fiction that owes a great debt to Federman's critifictional theory.

In the spring of 1979, the thought police in the English Department of Slippery Rock State College arrested me. These men actually saw that which was not there. They, with their lackluster humor of a Lacanian sort, discovered my lack of originality. My only aura, a black outfit with a cynical wit, complicated by the precious afterglow of a photocopier. Frequently, I was interrupted and distracted by traditions and the desire for "an" individual talent. A nod, I once overheard, is as good as a wink to a blind prophet.

I am driven by memories that I too often forget to cite.

Like a diseased fugitive I take leave of words. An unpacked library with erased copyright pages. A pirate traveling down a lost highway. 57 channels and my remote is broken. Always already on. And on. *A priori.* Born with the television on. Nothing. Silence. I gaze at nothing. The blank screen of the television stares back at me. Wanting me. Have you ever turned on a television set? I have.

I read nothing in ways that most people dream of reading Dante. Between the lines, white dust and kaleidoscopes of visions. I pick up words along the way. Pack up my ermines. Step into gutters and steal debris that had at one time appeared useless. Back in 1922 when the tourists invaded Trieste, Paris, London, I stole image after image from men with holes in their pockets. But in the 1970s, while listening to music so bad that I nearly died, I washed my hands of the whole messy affair. I am no plagiarist.

This old nearly dead professor stood before me with evidence. Full metal jacket. Hard core. A red pen and a shit-eating grin that will come to no good. At least not to any of that good old medieval recycling of shit-into-splendor good. This man with no imagination, just a tape recorder and a highlighter, accused me of conduct unbecoming. His hands blackened by newsprint. Fractions of words rubbed into his skin. Blurred words with no idea. And he knew nothing. Just didn't get it. No, not at all. How I loved making my hands dirty all through childhood. The smell of newly run-off stencils. Me and *silly-putty* wreaking all sorts of havoc on copyright. Rubbing and flattening the *silly-putty* on the comics and lifting it up ever so carefully, like I was making an original readymade. Like I was Duchamp or Warhol.

I tried to explain to the professor that I was no criminal.

I heard myself say, "Style is the only legitimate quotation marks. And style is more challenging than simply typing inverted commas as if that grants credit or authority to an echo from the dead past. And," I continued, "The past is only dead in such coffins. For me the past remains. Alive, she cried, it's alive, infecting me with curses."

He wanted nothing whatsoever to do with me. He was a man without hope.

"Only a reader can plagiarize. You," I told him, "you are the real criminal. It is you that took all my illegitimate, damned references home as if home was the same as it ever was. You took them back to their origins as if that was their destination. I robbed them of such sanctuaries. Made them nomadic. How dare you fuck my sweet innocence."

Many years later, so the story goes, Federman called me after *Blood of Mugwump* was published. "Doug," Ray said, "you have stolen three of my words on the very first page of your novel. Word for word, mine."

I told Ray not to worry, that readers would by instinct take them back to her text. Safe and sound. He was not convinced.

"It will not be the same, though, will it, Doug?"

"No," I replied. "No, my mouth your words. This saliva lost becoming wet."

"And you call this an autobiography. How can my words make your life?"

Nostalgia. A photograph of Ray and I with our hands pressed down on the glass of a photocopier going about its business. All aglow. Basking in the sweet Benjaminian aura. Nothing but replicas as far as the eye can see. Mirror, mirror invoked as the originary desire of the artist. In the shuffling madness, the distant background, an echo nearly lost, graduate students come and go. Disguised replicants armed with Kodak Instamatic cameras. Tourists mad with clicking. My murderous mirrorhand accuses me, not in so many words, of having stolen original copies of letters never mailed from the Parasite Café.

Escape Velocity
of the
Hypertextual Prefiguration

Lance Olsen

> *This, I believe, is what Postmodernism was all about:A*
> *Supreme Indecision! —Raymond Federman*

possibility spaces

Hypertext fiction, a non-linear computer-based mode of writing which came to the literary foreground in 1987 with the appearance of Michael Joyce's *Afternoon: A Story*, raises fundamental questions about fiction, the idea of the book, and even the nature of free choice among readers. In this mode, no hard or stable copy of narrative exists. Rather the reader uses a computer to explore an **interlinking web of lexia**, or story spaces, in an interactive way, literally developing his or her own version of a text, which may include music and graphics as well as typographical pyrotechnics, contradicting plot elements, and opportunities for the reader to contribute character names, descriptions, and shards of action. After each reading experience, the reader can choose to save or abandon **the forking paths** he or she has just chosen to follow.

-----

deconstruction as form

The result is a mode of narration that proposes, as George P. Landow suggests in *Hypertext: The Convergence of Contemporary Critical Theory and Technology* (1992), that "we must **abandon conceptual systems** founded upon ideas of center, margin, hierarchy, and linearity and replace them with ones of multilinearity, nodes, links, and networks." With hypertext fiction, even clear distinctions between one text and another can eventually blur into **a constellation of intertextuality.** Consequently, as Landow and others have argued, hypertext fiction enacts the deconstructive turn in very tangible form.

-----

prefigurations

Non-electronic **prototypes** of hypertext fiction, however, appeared nearly half a century before Michael Joyce's *Afternoon*—with the magnum opus of another Joyce: James. The only element lacking from such **prefigurations** that would allow them to take the full narratological leap out of hard-copy and into digital form was the appropriate computer technology. Roland Barthes, for instance, imagines an "**ideal text**" in *S/Z* (1970) in which

> the networks are many and interact, without any one of them being able to surpass the rest; this text is a **galaxy of signifiers**, not a structure of signifieds; it has no beginning; it is reversible; we gain access to it by several entries, none of which can be authoritatively declared to be the main one.

Ironically, and **instructively**, Barthes' text had been extant for decades before he invented it. Poststructuralism didn't invent the deconstructed novel; rather, the deconstructed novel invented poststructuralism.

---

a theoretical statement about theory

Charcot **quoted by** Freud **quoted by** D. M. Thomas in *The White Hotel* (1981): *Theory is good, but it doesn't prevent things from happening.*

---

interlude: a nostalgic reconsideration

James Joyce: **Finnegans Wake**: 1939: Virtually plotless, circularly structured, Celtically mythological, 600-plus-paged linguistic explosion that is impossible to read other than as a hypertext, the reader dipping in and out at will, a rhapsodic delight that looks forward to Federman's fiction, which looks back to Apollinaire's concrete poetry in *Calligrammes* (1918).

William S. Burroughs: **Naked Lunch**: 1959: Fiction for

Burroughs, as for Federman, is a plastic art related to the Action Painting of Jackson Pollock, the music of John Cage, and the montage of modernist film. While **N.L.** purports to be a record of a man's addiction to opiates, his apomorphine treatment, and his cure, it is also a larger exploration of cultural and aesthetic addiction in the form of an anti-narrative Cold Turkey from the linear realistic novel. Again, like hypermedial fiction, the reader is invited to "cut into *Naked Lunch* at any insection point. . . . the pieces can be had in any order being tied up back and forth, in and out fore and aft like an innaresting sex arrangement."

Julio Cortázar: **Hopscotch**: 1963: A jazz musician like Federman, Cortázar presents the reader with a 155-chaptered novel that "consists of many books, but two books above all": 1) the first can be read "in a normal fashion" and ends with chapter 56; 2) the second must be read in a sequence indicated in the "Table of Instructions" and begins with chapter 73. Both readings revolve around Horacio Oliveira, whose ambition is to

> fragment his personality,

> like Slothrop in *Gravity's Rainbow*
> will succeed in doing ten years later,

> in such a way that his life
> becomes a series
> of present moments.

---

a first interlude from the interlude

Ronald Sukenick, "The New Tradition" (1972): *We badly need a new way of thinking about novels that acknowledges their technological reality.*

---

a second interlude from the interlude

Ronald Sukenick, "The New Tradition" (1972): *We have to learn how to look at fiction as lines of print on a page and we have to ask whether it is always the best arrangement to have a solid block of print from one margin to the other running down the page from top to bottom, except for an occasional paragraph indentation. We have to* *learn to think about a novel as a concrete structure rather than as an allegory, existing in the realm of experience rather than in the realm of discursive meaning, and available to multiple interpretation or none, depending on how you feel about it—like the way that girl pressed against you in the subway.*

---

a third interlude from the interlude

---

a fourth interlude from the interlude

Federman had already entered a conversation well underway when Sukenick published those words in 1972: among, say, concrete poets in general, such surrealist practitioners of the collage-novel as Max Ernst in *La Femme 100 Têtes* (1929), and e. e. cummings' typographical experiments influenced as much by the fragments of ancient texts he studied at Harvard as by the first marketing of the typewriter in 1874 by E. Remington and Sons exactly twenty years before his birth, and the discovery of Pound's poetry — itself influenced by Chinese ideograms, or at least by Pound's misunderstanding of them.

I don't mean to suggest an originary site, nor do I mean to imply some hypothetical causal chain of direct aesthetic impacts throughout history. Rather, I simply mean to give a feel for an admittedly motley constellation of creators with whom Federman has consciously or unconsciously entered aesthetic colloquy, who, for the purposes of this essay, I will refer to as **GRAPHICTIONISTS**:

i.e., those who attempt to focus our attention on the pageness of

the page, and/or (intentionally or unintentionally) work against the conventional structure of Western writing (and hence reading strategies), often by calling attention to writing's mechanical status before us and disrupting it, complicating it—along the way making self-conscious traditional reading assumptions and processes—by means of various graphictional play, a term including unexpected typography, layout, spacing, punctuation, collage elements, etc., thereby giving rise to HETEROMEDIAL INTERTEXTUALITY,

i.e., a play and interplay between and among these graphic and verbal elements that allow them to interpenetrate, reminding us of the visual nature of language and the linguistic nature of images, while, in a Cubist move that would have delighted Picasso and Gertrude Stein, bringing words and other opticals to the surface of the page, treating them as non-allegorical entities of design, signaling their existence as *objects* and therefore signaling their immediate connection to other tangible items in the extra-paginal world, while at the same time quoting, paraphrasing, and alluding to similiar uses of graphication in synchronic and diachronic texts.

---

return to the interlude

Robert Coover: "The Babysitter" (**Pricksongs & Descants**): 1969: Written by the head of the hypertext center at Brown University, this fiction begins as a work of suburban domestic realism only to elide into an experimental investigation that offers contradicting plot elements that may be actual events or the imaginings of the characters or author himself.

All of which,

of course,

helps to inform,

through the narratological dynamics of

pla(y)giarism:

---

double or nothing: 1971

A concrete, comic, heavily allusive and pun-packed novel displaying a quintic vision:

> **1. an "unmarried, unattached, and quite irresponsible" writerly equivalent of Robinson Crusoe locks himself in a sparsely furnished island room in New York City for exactly 365 days, beginning on October 1, in order to record the story of**

> **2. a shy, naive nineteen-year-old Jewish boy's arrival in America shortly after the end of World War Two—both of whose stories are "narrated" by**

> **3. "a stubborn and determined middle-aged man," who in turn is overseen by**

> **4. a Federmanian composite of them all, who in turn is overseen by**

> **5. the implied reader.**

Hence *Double or Nothing* becomes a novel about recording, writing, composing, more interested in the creative process than a created product. It believes, along with the Federmanian overseer, that **"what is great in a man is that he is a bridge and not a goal."**

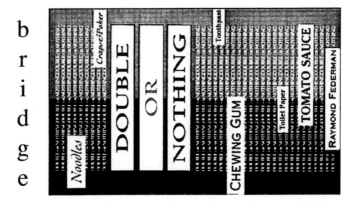

Existence, in other words, as Federman's mentor **Samuel Beckett** understood, is a pastime, a passing of time, a filling of hours between birth and death that might have been filled in a nearly infinite number of other ways. It's not for nothing, then, that the narrator of the young **Jewish** man's [whose name might be Boris, although that remains unclear, since the narrator keeps fiddling with it] story is a gambler, nor that the idea of **gambling** pervades the text, since gambling functions as an emblem of risk-taking and game-playing here, a ludic mode that both suggests rules and suggests rules are meant to be bent, if not broken.

It's not for nothing that the young Jewish man is an immigrant from the **Old World to the New**. Just as he explores fresh geographical and cultural territory, so too does Federman explore a fresh narratological one . . . which, of course, is not to imply *Double or Nothing* is little more than crossword carnival. Rather, it is ultimately a **rich celebration** of the <u>human imagination,</u>

a ~~deconstructive investigation~~
of the novel-writing process,

a **love-affair** with 1 **a**ng**u**a**g**e

the small ahistorical details that comprise daily life

a

g
a tube of toothp a ste
m
e

of

c
a
r
d
s,

a paean to the power of <u>human freedom</u> on and off

the page by a writer who witnessed the apotheosis
of its absence, <u>losing</u> his parents and sisters in

˙**TSUAƆOꞀOH** **EHT**

While the narrator nuances words, meticulously thinking
his way through his cramped minimalist universe, obsessing over the cost of noodles or the way(s) to cook potatoes
(reminiscent of Beckett's Molloy obsessing over the position
of his sucking stones), Federman reminds us by means of
the typographical and narrative abandon of his text that
man is indeed free to choose his own destiny, free to propose
and design"—if not that, then

what?

---

quotation number three or four

Raymond Federman, "Critifiction: Imagination as Plagiarism" (1976): *Indeed, as it
was once said: plagiarism is the basis for all works of art, except, of course, the first
one, which is unknown. Plagiarism, as we all know, and as defined by the most basic
dictionary, is the act of copying or imitating the language, ideas, and thoughts of another (thinker, artist, author) and passing off the same as one's original work. And
there is no doubt that we listen to others only for the pleasure of repeating what they
have said. Yet, we write under the illusion that we are not repeating what has already
been written.*

---

quotation number six or seven

Raymond Federman, "Critifiction: Imagination as Plagiarism" (1976): *The text which
I am in the process of writing does indeed fall into the category of pure pla[y]giarism
(with a Y because I am also playing here), for I do not know any more where my own
thoughts originated, and where these thoughts began to merge with those of others,
where my own language began and where it converged with that of others within the
dialogue all of us entertain within ourselves, and with others. Therefore, I shall not
reveal my sources because they are now lost in this discourse, and because there are no
sacred sources for thinking and writing.*

*But first a poetic statement—an unfinished unpublished and endless poem entitle LIS-
TENING which represents here*

----

conclusion number one

Federman configures *Double or Nothing* so that there is no conclusion, so that **desire is
never fulfilled** by means of plot- or character-completion; emblematic of this strategy
are the unfulfilled and unfulfilling **sex scenes** that transpire throughout the text.

----

quotation number eight or nine

Raymond Federman, *Double or Nothing* (1971): "In other words when you read a
story what you are really reading are the answers to unformulated question So all that
crap about fiction writing it's for the birds. Only traditional and bad fiction writers do
it that way usually. The normal way. The real sensitive imaginative inventive progressive guys do it differently. Or at least they try even if they fail in the end."

----

failing in the end

> **—What is a page?**
> **—What does it mean to read a text?**
> **—What is a book?**
> **—Where does fiction end and autobiography begin?**
> **—What is the difference, exactly, between fiction and criticism,
> and why?**

----

conclusion number two

If we are witnessing the proliferation of **post-genre composition** that has begun to
question the need for discussing such apparently singular species as, say speculative
fiction and mainstream fiction, mystery writing and experimental writing, we are also
witnessing the proliferation of a **post-critical composition** that has begun to question
the need for discriminating between such apparently singular species as theory and
fiction.

We are witnessing—and have been for the last thirty or forty years—what Stephen Connor has discussed as the slow **"collapse of criticism into its object."** Barthes, Hélène Cixous, Derrida, Ihab Hassan, Dick Hebdige, Steven Pfohl, Ronald Sukenick, Steven Shaviro, and Gregory Ulmer, among others, have been investigating in **various performative critifictions** ways to erase the artificial distinction between primary and secondary texts, asserting by example that all texts are in fact secondary ones, linguistic and generic collages, bits of bricolage.

In other words, these writers have attempted to efface, or at least deeply and richly **complicate**, the accepted difference between a privileged discourse written by those who believe that they can somehow step back from what it is they are discussing and attain with respect to it something like **an elite position of meta-commentarial objectivity**, on the one hand, and, on the other, some subordinate discourse that can be intellectually colonized, written about without actually being engaged with, written through, or changed by the very act of said writing.

What we are seeing, then, is another beginning of another beginning (which has been beginning at least since Plato's utopian narrative) of thinking ourselves into a postal realm of **speculative autobiographiction** among the para-sites of writing that will blur, interrupt, question, subvert, recontextualize, personalize, deconstruct, and plain mess up, thereby enriching our experience of writing.

And **living**.

That's where I imagine things will start getting really **interesting**.

---

conclusion number three

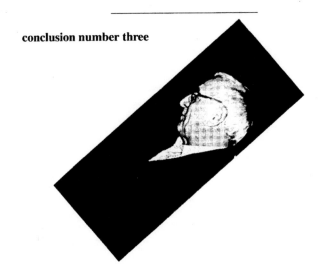

---

an historical digression

Federman received his first **computer**, "a prehistoric Wang word processor," when he was awarded an NEA Fellowship in 1986. Although it took him some time to get over his **"timidity"** in the face of that machine, and although it would be early 1996 before he hooked up to and began surfing the Web in earnest, his writing augurs **hypertext fiction** in his

theoretical manifesto "Surfiction: A Position," which was first published in the *Partisan Review* in 1973. There, in an **act of spiritual autobiography** that informs much of his critifiction,

he essentially glosses *Double or Nothing* by claiming that we must **"renew our system of reading,"** which has become "restrictive and boring," by innovating the **"paginal syntax"** of

our texts.

To accomplish this, we must

`short-`
`circuit`

our traditional reading strategies that propel us from the upper lefthand corner of the page to the lower right in a **"preordained"** manner.

We must therefore

reinvent the page,

**the space
of reading,**

by embracing **new** typographical prospects,
shapes and designs,
new relations among textual parts,
multiple possibilities of plot and character,

and even what we mean
when we say the
word "book,"
thereby engendering

*a sense of free participation in the writing/read-
ing process, in order to give the reader an element
of choice (active choice) in the ordering of the discourse and the discovery of its meaning.*

This aesthetic move, according to Federman, will better echo the
arbitrary, non-linear, discontinuous, unpredictable, illogical, digressive, free-yet-chaotic experience we understand as **postmodern life.**

---

diversion number two—(an already published poem)

POSTMODERNISM MADE SIMPLE

It's a love affair
with Flub-a-dub,
feathered body of a dachshund
ready to meow,
spotted neck of a giraffe
peeking around
the next naked
red tree,
ears of a cocker spaniel
listening to the hum
of its own nerves,
a raccoon's tail, furry, fluffy,
and useless,
flippers of a seal
applauding the splendid colors
of quarks, duck's bill
clacking at white dwarfs,
cat's whiskers tuned
to the width of all doors,
sheer divine memory
of a French elephant
waiting for the absence
of spring,
stomach of a shark
that will digest anything:
an Idaho license plate,

```
a Greek sandal, the moon;
unconscious of its own forever
death-defying forward
motion as it swims
through an infinitely crowded
Kroger,
forcing electric blue seawater
through its gently fluttering gills.
```

---

a list of protohypertextual elements in double or nothing

bold face to highlight key words or phrases, giving them what hypertext writers refer to as "texture"; **unpredictable quantum leaps** between two or more storylines, thereby creating an analog for hypertextual narrative uncertainty; **typographical/configurative play**, including lists, footnotes, symbols, math, interviews, diagrams, etc. in an attempt to rupture conventional linear reading strategies and foreground the technology of the page; **conflating prose/poetry**, as well as fiction/criticism/autobiography, to question traditional genre distinctions; **digressive narrative structure** where the overarching plotline isn't as important as the individual page before the reader at a given moment, a technique that anticipates of the power of the single hypertextual lexia . . . as well as a gesture that transforms fiction into a plastic art with similarities to Abstract Expressionism (see below . . .); **abrupt shifts in point of view** that approximate the abrupt shifts resulting from moving from one hypertextual lexia to another, often with dramatic changes in perspective; **metafictional contemplation and enaction of readerly freedom** "of choosing willingly or randomly" elements of the text, from name to plot—all of which adds up to an overall **musical rather than linear** narrative structure, more reminiscent of jazz improvisation (Federman's involvement with and love for jazz is well known) than conventional fiction-writing tactics: repetition of phrases, images and obsessions (the icon of **noodles** floating through the text, overlapping in apparent chaotic abandon, is emblematic of this) — which structure creates the **hypertextual impression** that the reader can dip into the book at any point for a paginal snippet, since narrative forward force isn't what guides the reading experience any more than it does that in lyric poetry. Hence one finds a **new** hypertextual **realism** more in sync with the hyperbolic televisual rhythms of neo-millennial existence than what one might in the quite safe narratological nostalgia of domestic urban or small regionalist stories that hark back to quieter, steadier, more predictable ontological and epistemological times: an essentially nineteenth-century story that New York publishing has recently embraced with economic abandon, not unlike, perhaps, the way Europeans did the "exotics" discovered in and imported from the New World or Africa in the past. And yet Federman is aware of the inherent contradictions associated with the attempt to write beyond so-called **realism**: "Can it be said," one of his narrators asks in *Double or Nothing*, "that by denouncing the fraudulence of a novel which tends to totalize existence and misses its multidimensionality, the critical work frees us from the illusion of realism? I rather believe that it encloses us in it. Because the goal remains the same: it is always a question of expressing, of translating something which is already there — even if to be already there, in this new perspective, consists paradoxically in not being there. In other words, the novel, in a sense, cannot escape realism." And yet and yet and yet and yet: "Now some people might say that this situation is not very encouraging but one must reply that it is not meant to encourage those who say that."

---

a first parenthetical statement that you can probably skip

(New York publishers are cutting their lists, laying off editors, trimming the fat. The nation's 30,000 bookstores, too. Philip Roth estimates the audience for "serious" fiction, whatever that is, currently runs no more than a disheartening 120,000. NanTalese, a major editor at Doubleday, puts it closer to 4,000. In any case, a first novel that sells more than 5,000 copies is viewed by publishers, who have paid its author an advance against royalties of well less that $10,000, as a raving success. In the last decade or so, most major U.S. publishers have been absorbed by huge conglomerates—Random House, for instance, by Newhouse, Doubleday by Bertelsmann, Simon and Schuster by Paramount, Penguin and Dutton by Pearson, Harper and Row by Murdoch, Putnam by Matsushita. The result is an industry obsessed with the bottom line. Sonny Mehta, head of Knopf, sums up the situation best when he asks: "Why should I publish books if they aren't going to make money?"

Why indeed.)

_____

a second parenthetical statement that you can probably skip

"Since the **surfictional story** will not have a beginning, middle, and end," Federman concludes, "it will not lend itself to a continuous and totalizing form of reading. It will refuse resolution and closure. It will always remain an open discourse."

While in a sense this is true enough with respect to Federman's project and hypertext fiction in general, particularly when set next to works of traditional nineteenth-century realism, one shouldn't forget that the illusion of **free choice** and open discourse in surfiction and hypertext fiction is finally to some extent just that: **an illusion**. As much as a writer may wish to impart a sense of autonomy and self-determination to his reader, the writer is always, it almost goes without saying, the ultimate shaper of the text, the endmost provider of possibilities with the possibility space that is fiction.

Granted, reading hypertext fiction and its hardcopy analog feels a good deal less **"preordained"** and "restrictive" than reading their linear fictional ancestors, but behind the thing itself still remains the **map of the thing itself** created by the author, and that map of the thing itself by its very presence delimits choice, restricts narratological possibility and regulates human freedom.

We are, in other words, discussing **a difference in degree** at the end of the day, and not kind.

(**Samuel Delany**, *Rebel Yell* (1998): *In the late sixties there were a hundred-plus sizable publishers in New York City. By 1980, there were only seventy-nine. By 1995, there were fifteen. And with the recent merger of HarperCollins and Bantam-Doubleday-Dell, that number has gone down to five.*)

_____

this is not a conclusion

By prefiguring the hypertextual moment in American fiction, Federman's work harmonizes conceptually with a number of other currents on the contemporary scene.

most major U.S. publishers have been absorbed by huge conglomerates—Random House, for instance, by Newhouse, Doubleday by Bertelsmann, Simon and Schuster by Paramount, Penguin and Dutton by Pearson, Harper and Row by Murdoch, Putnam by Matsushita. The result is an industry obsessed with the bottom line. Sonny Mehta, head of Knopf, sums up the situation best when he asks: "Why should I publish books if they aren't going to make money?"

Why indeed.)

---

a second parenthetical statement that you can probably skip

"Since the **surfictional story** will not have a beginning, middle, and end," Federman concludes, "it will not lend itself to a continuous and totalizing form of reading. It will refuse resolution and closure. It will always remain an open discourse."

While in a sense this is true enough with respect to Federman's project and hypertext fiction in general, particularly when set next to works of traditional nineteenth-century realism, one shouldn't forget that the illusion of **free choice** and open discourse in surfiction and hypertext fiction is finally to some extent just that: **an illusion.** As much as a writer may wish to impart a sense of autonomy and self-determination to his reader, the writer is always, it almost goes without saying, the ultimate shaper of the text, the endmost provider of possibilities with the possibility space that is fiction.

Granted, reading hypertext fiction and its hardcopy analog feels a good deal less **"preordained"** and "restrictive" than reading their linear fictional ancestors, but behind the thing itself still remains the **map of the thing itself** created by the author, and that map of the thing itself by its very presence delimits choice, restricts narratological possibility and regulates human freedom.

We are, in other words, discussing **a difference in degree** at the end of the day, and not kind.

(Samuel Delany, Rebel Yell (1998): In the late sixties there were a hundred-plus sizable publishers in New York City. By 1980, there were only seventy-nine. By 1995, there were fifteen. And with the recent merger of HarperCollins and Bantam-Doubleday-Dell, that number has gone down to five.)

---

this is not a conclusion

By prefiguring the hypertextual moment in American fiction, Federman's work harmonizes conceptually with a number of other currents on the contemporary scene.

The Avant-Pop

A name appropriated by Larry McCaffery and Ronald Sukenick from a Lester Bowie jazz album to describe that impetus in our culture that both pushes the **avant-envelope** and embraces—however ambivalently—a **pop aesthetic**. Not only do many Avant-Pop obsessions surface in Federman's work, from technical improvisation to bullet-train anti-narrative speed, but also the defining need to use and abuse pop maneuvers to subvert popular complacency.

Aesthetics of the Ugly

A vision embraced by such diverse practioners as Kathy Acker, Samuel Delany, and Mark Leyner, but which tracks back through the **destructive** robotics of Survival Research Laboratories, William Burroughs and the T. S. Eliot of the Thames scenes in *The Waste Land*, and the Dadist movement to the the launchpad of Charles Baudelaire's *Les Fleurs du Mal* (1857) with its conflicted exploration of the violent, darkly sexual, decadent, discordant, socially disagreeable underside of **fragmented** industrialized urban experience.

Clyfford Still (1904-1980)

"I think I came in contact with abstraction still in my mother's womb," Federman once

wrote me. "I looked around, and what I saw there was like an**abstract painting**, and

I liked it. There was a lot of red there, and some purple and some yellow And it was

pulsating. And I knew that this was the reality I wanted to live in."

One of Federman's favorite painters, Still embraces many of the convictions of **Ab-**

stract Expressionism, a loosely unified "school" focused mainly in New York after

the Second World War. Instructively, Still wrote his M.F.A thesis at the State College

of Washington in Pullman, WA, in 1935 on Paul Cézanne, a seminal Post-Impression-

ist less interested in the conventional realistic representation of nature than in the analysis

of its **basic geometric structures** on the canvas—in other words, in extreme formal

experimentation. Still, along with other Abstract Expressionists such as Jackson Pol-

lock and Franz Kline, emphasized the physical act of painting rather than its aesthetic

product, the existential quest for authentic being through the creative act, a spirit of

revolt against traditional approaches and prescribed procedures, and a mandate for

spontaneous expression.

The same, of course, could have been said by **Samuel Beckett**, whose work has often

---

[1] **A misplaced footnote.** Late one night at the beginning of the last decade of the millennium, Larry McCaf fery and Ron Sukenick were listening to jazz at McCaf fery's Borrego Springs retreat in the Desert of the Real and talking about current trends in the culture. McCaf fery reached for trumpet-meister Lester Bowie's 1986 album *Avant-Pop*, where Bowie takes a bunch of such fine oldies as Al Lewis-Vincent Rose-Larry Stock's "Blueberry Hill" and Marvin Junior-Johnny Funches's "Oh, What a Night" and, with the help of Brass Fantasy, reconfigures them into collaborative, improvisational musical moments that complicate the original fairly simple pop impulse of the tunes, and McCaf fery realized that much the same sort of pla(y)giaristic and f(r)ictive transformational work had been going on for a long time in other postmodern arts.

Kathy Acker, for example, rewrites and rerights Dickens and Cervantes. Donald Barthelme and Robert Coover appropriate and mutate fairy tales, John Barth myths. Or , more recently, Stephen Wright in the Borneo section of *Going Native* retells Conrad's *Heart of Darkness* while in general confiscates and revises the pulp variant of the serial-killer novel so that the reader is put in a position to see both tales from radically

been suggested as the literary analog of Abstract Expressionism, and by **Federman**, much of whose production could be seen as the fictional and poetic equivalent of Action Painting, where, as Still once commented, "the Act, intrinsic and absolute, was [a piece of art's] meaning, and the bearer of its passion." Federman, who first met Still's paintings in Buffalo, NY, in 1964, produces concrete texts in which he performs formal investigations through typographical play and the spatial reconfiguration of the page that transform writing into a **plastic art**.

---

pre-text one

This is not the beginning are the first words of *Double or Nothing*.

---

pre-text two

Besides the sequence of events does not matter, one of the narrators continues sometime later, *and believe me if I analyze if I build hypotheses if I temporize it is less by scruples that I might let something get lost of what comes to my mind in bulk than to allow myself to play a little game as frivolous as it is inoffensive.*

---

convulsive beauty

a. Contemplating Federman's *Double or Nothing* has led us into a **multifoliate aes-**

---

new vantage points that, ultimately, challenge the assumptions of the "original" versions. Such a strategy jibes with what has been and is transpiring in other cultural arenas, as well: performances by Laurie Anderson and the Blue Man Group; films like David Lynch's *Blue Velvet* and Ridley Scott's *Blade Runner*, albums like The Beatles's *Sgt. Pepper's Lonely Hearts Club Band* and Sonic Youth's *Daydream Nation*, television shows like *Monty Python's Flying Circus* and *South Park*, and so on.

   Hence the birth of the term "Avant-Pop," itself a gesture of crititictional piracy, for a kind of creation that fuses the avant-garde's notion of technical and perceptual brinkmanship with a profound and profoundly ambivalent pop sensibility. "What people need to do," McCaffery writes with respect to Lester Bowie's album in the preface to *After Yesterday's Crash: The Avant-Pop Anthology*, "is recognize that these glitzy, kitschy, easily consumable pop materials are a rich source of raw material whose elements can be explored, played with, and otherwise creatively transformed." Which leads me in many ways to a third diversion,

thetic space that asks for dialogue, polyphony, exchange, inclusiveness, an opening up and out to narratological and existential possibility.

b. Literary history is not only a series of ruptures, then, but also **a complex network of continuities**, re-presentations, re-evaluations, re-collections, an ongoing circus of interesting minds in motion.

c. "Beauty must be convulsive," André Breton declared at the conclusion of *Nadja*, "or it will not be." The history of Convulsive Beauty is the history of continuing alternatives, diverse voices that sing diverse indie counterpoint against the overly sweet

dominant pop melody called The Mainstream, diamond-toothed Termite Art whose

function is to gnaw away at the marble foundation of those conventional citadels which

line the Madison Avenue of consciousness.

---

an already published critifiction called "Two Children Menaced by a Nightingale," whose first line is: *In Max Ernst's famous collage the sky is a dark blue strip at the top of the canvas* , and which continues:

Then increasingly paler and paler green as it ladders down in layers toward the bright orange-pink outline of the wooden house pasted in the right-hand corner. Then finally lemon as it nuzzles the orange-pink wall stretching along the grassy lawn toward the vanishing point beyond the classical arch on top of which is poised the figure whose left arm is raised like that of the Statue of Liberty. The silhouette of another building rises even farther in the background, nothing really but an ashen stain slightly to the left and several inches below the center of the collage. Dark trees bunch behind another wall, this one cement, which intersects the first near that arch. A gleaming fire-engine red gate from a doll house swings open across the brown-lacquered frame in the foreground. But all this is infinitely less interesting than what catches your eye in the middle-ground: the five black-and-white figures in disarray. The small bird hovering at the exact point the kelly sky melts into yellow. The woman, long black hair fluttering behind her, looking up at the nightingale as she darts beneath it with something—a knife? a ba-

d. Convulsive Beauty thinks itself back through a hypothetical trajectory of vanguard art, appropriating from the past while nibbling always forward, from the fifties, sixties, seventies, eighties, and nineties: through the Avant-Pop, Surfiction, Metafiction, Punk, Cyberpunk, RiboFunk, the Multimedia Moment, the Deconstructive Turn, the Novel of Excess & Regress & Digress, Language Poetry, Beat fiction, Faction, Magical Realism, the Nouveau Roman, the New Wave, and so on, back through Lettrism, Surrealism, Dadaism, Expressionism, Decadence, Imagism, Vorticism, Futurism, and Symbolism . . . and back again, finally, to the doorstep of that paradigmless paradigm of **Romanticism** (think of Blake's schizoid visions, or, better, of the presence of

---

ton in her hand. The clayish lump that appears to be another female body sprawled at an unnatural arc beside the house. The man in the business suit on the roof, the light-haired child in his arms, fleeing toward the blue button with a red-dot core that might just be the sun.

THE DEAD DAUGHTER
It was the most miserable song I ever heard.

I was sitting on the back porch at twilight, watching the carbon tetrachloride, lead, and perchloroethylene smear the saffron sky various shades of emerald above the factory when it appeared, a black mouth smiling twenty feet above me. I rose and began to follow it across the lawn, recollecting memories of events that had never actually occurred to me: the beautiful tanned body of the boy, twelve or thirteen years old, who delivers our meat, naked, his stomach ribbed with muscles, his arms and legs and torso glistening with oil, as he knelt before me on that sunny spring day behind the arch, furry bees humming around us, grinning smugly and then nubbing his tongue through his lips (only his tongue wasn't made of skin but hundreds of vibrating flies), which excited me almost as much as the realization that three of his friends were watching us from behind the—two more boys and a little bald girl, this last whose skin was metallic and who was not (it slowly dawned on me) a girl at all but an android with red robotic eyes, and smooth bumps for a nose and breasts, and a stereo speaker for a mouth, from which issued the song of the nightingale that conjured the glittering white shores of Greek islands I had never visited, polychromatic parasols dotting the beach, the fragrance of wine and sea salt and fish in the breeze, water the color of Californian swimming pools licking the sand, portable radios alive with the song of the nightingale that gave rise to New York City where you can hear excitement at three o'clock any morning in a murky alley amid trashcans leaking brown banana peels and limp whitish shrimp shells above which, in that one-bedroom apartment where you have to move something else just to move the thing you wanted to move, an underfed boy in his late teens, hair purple, greasy skin cratered and nibbed with acne, plays a guitar whose perpetually joyless chords form the song of the nightingale that offered up the marble interior of a colossal art museum with thousands of floors cluttered with trillions of sculptures and paintings and collages, one of which, hanging in the shadowy corner of an unnumbered floor (its title having accidentally been dropped from the catalog over one hundred years ago), depicts the moment of your death, although you wouldn't be able to recognize this fact even if you knew as much and could locate it (which you didn't and which you can't) because the image that is supposed to represent you is just a metaphor of you and actually represents someone else.

THE WOMAN,
LONG BLACK HAIR FLUTTERING BEHIND HER

In the dream I was falling. Tumbling through the night sky. Human heads rained down around me, bouncing when they thumped the ground below. A row of Gestapo officers shot at me with their pistols. No, with their machine guns. Bullets slapped into me. At the moment I understood something I can no longer remember understanding, something thunked against my bedroom window. I sat up. Véra, my daughter, was screaming. It sounded as if an army of ants were stinging her. Outside, the sky was the color of scum on the surface of a pond in August, the air filled with the beating of wings and Véra's shrieks. "Gnat-sized robots have crawled into my ear!" she was shouting. "Gnat-sized robots have crawled into my ear!" When I tried to rush toward the bird diving at her face, pecking at her eyes, tangling in her hair, a dagger appeared in my hand. But somehow instead of rushing at the bird I rushed at Véra. And then her legs became marmalade. Her breasts turned candy-red. She collapsed. Her tunic fell open and I saw she was pregnant. My husband shouted in horror behind me. He swept up Vanya who, groggy, still in her flannel robe speckled with antique lampshades, had just stepped through the front door to find out what the commotion was about. He began to clamber up the side of the house with Vanya in his arms, shouting at me to stay away, stay away, his voice full of radio static. An abrupt wind arose. The gate blew open. The sun turned blue.

THE NIGHTINGALE

What's that talisman tacked to your front door? A razor? The stickshift from a car that hasn't yet been imagined by the engineer now sleeping

Frankenstein's monster—the latter an appropriated, electrocuted, existentially and socially and epistemologically alien icon of the **extreme instant** in the arts) with its thematics and formalistics of trespass, revolution, Dionysian borderbreaking, psychotic breach, brilliant rage, paranoid rant, with its exploration of the illogical, the unconscious, **the inner-world,** the drastic aesthetico-spiritual brink experienced by the Aztec sacrifice who *wants* his heart to be removed because of what he'll see and feel.

---

on a bamboo mat in a white-walled Tokyo flat? Is that really a factory on the horizon, or a temple? A figure with its left arm raised like the Statue of Liberty, or another smokestack? Why does your house stand on stilts? Why is the sun so low in the sky? Is it really the sun? Why are you running? What's that in your hand? Why do you think you can reach me? Why was today the same day as yesterday for you in every respect except for my presence? What were you waiting for before you considered changing the time at which you ate, the hours at which you slept? What's the secret, the real secret, you've never shared with each other? Why do you sit on your porch every evening, waiting for darkness? Why did you decide on two children, and not three? Two, and not one? Why did you decide to live here, and not in England? Here, and not on the mountainside starred with daisies in the Alps where at this very second Vladimir Nabokov's ghost has just stepped, butterfly net at the ready, latest dog-earred water-wrinkled copy of *The Entomologist* rolled in the pocket of his powder-blue button-up vest? Build your gate without a fence? Love each other? Agree to say you love each other? Who decided what you would do next? Who decided that these were going to be the clothes you were to be known by, the color which would adorn your walls? What kind of trees are those through the arch, behind the wall? And what comes beyond them? What's on the other side? What happens when I'm finished? What happens till I return tomorrow? What happens now? What could possibly happen now?

And now?

THE MAN IN THE BUSINESS SUIT ON THE ROOF

I phoned her, just as in a bad movie, to say I had to have dinner with a client, and then went to dinner with that client's daughter, strawberry hair cropped so close to her head you could see the scalp shine through, five small gold hoops in her left ear, one in her right, lipstick the color of plums, knit dress the same, because, well, because, if I had to say, if I had to put my finger on it, because of gravity, really, because of the way gravity is like an infection, because of the way the skin under your eyes cannot be immunized against it, because of the way the buttocks become, really, a kind of joke, at a certain stage of one's life, no matter what precautions one takes, no matter how much one attempts to believe that youth ultimately comes down to a state of mind, as they catch in the mirror on one's way to the morning shower, drooping pathetically like warm dough, because there are forces besides gravity, those too, yes, like a certain, I don't know, aura, perhaps, that radiates around the woman who has over the years delivered one's children, an aura, if one's content with that word, that declaims that certain events, certain tactics, really, are now quite out of bounds, quite out of the question, beyond the ken of normal events, and those other forces, too, like memory, like the recollection of whole other worlds that seem to have existed so very long ago that they too become a kind of joke, in a certain way, forces to which the word middle-aged simply cannot do justice, forces which the word middle-aged merely trivializes, caricatures, really, because there is so much that, when voiced, sounds like cliché, the oldest line in the book, even though it's like, what, acid in the lungs, and so, yes, I phoned, just as in a bad movie, to say the obvious, and then out to dine with her where, contrary to the projected narrative structure, we discovered we had remarkably much in common, so much so that it began to hurt, it physically began to hurt, after awhile, seeing how many things we had to talk about, her dreams being my memories, my hope being her experience, the events in her life being more fascinating to me than virtually anything that had happened to me recently, not because they might have been fascinating to another person, to other persons, no, but because they were fascinating in their own right by the simple fact that they existed, that they were there, that they were so remarkably unlike the events in my life that I couldn't hear enough about them, and that that's what allowed us so much in common, if that happens to make any sense to someone on the outside, because, well, the point being, afterward, we went back to her apartment in the city, and, again the narrative surprise, always structural deviations, did absolutely nothing but talk a little more about what we didn't have in common, which is what we had in common, and then I asked her, I'm embarrassed to say it, I'm embarrassed to admit, if we could, just, well, hug a little while, nothing else, the kissing business seemed downright anticlimactic at this point, it's true, because, if the truth be known, all I wanted to do was just feel the press of a new body against mine, the freshness of a body I was meeting for the first time, which she somehow understood, I think, I'm almost sure, in any

Or,

to express this

"problem"

---

case she went along with it, at least for a while, rocking there with me, on her couch, her frame amazingly thin, even bony, really, for what seemed like several months, though finally I looked at my watch and, just as in a bad movie, said I had to be going, had to be getting home, and I did, have to be going, have to be getting home, that is, across town, having thanked her, her having thanked me, in a way that said this was wonderful, really wonderful, a small cusp of miracle, really, and that no matter what we ever thought of doing again it could never be this, not with each other, I suppose that went without saying, not in this life, and so I went across town, arriving near midnight, the sky aglow with the lights from the nuclear plant, home, where I sat in the chair near our bed and stared at my wife sleeping, and I won't say that love for her flooded me, I won't become that narratologically pedestrian, I won't say that all at once I fell deeply in love with her all over again, but I felt, well, good, really, I felt like I could sit still for hours and just observe her, I felt a kind of peace expand inside of me as though something rich in my ribcage had just ruptured and begun to leak, and I must have glided along the glassy edge of sleep because ... because then ... because then I was suddenly hearing my daughter screaming, I was suddenly hearing my daughter screaming, and I arose, and the bed was empty.

THE LIGHT-HAIRED CHILD IN HIS ARMS
I want to go back, daddy! I want to go back!

of ~~summary~~

yet an**O** ther

ᴡ**ꜱ**y **:**

THE FIGURE WHOSE LEFT ARM IS RAISED
This last figure, of course, represents you.

It represents the intrigue you've felt with Max Ernst's collage for years now. What does it mean? Why does it speak to you more than to most people? It represents your faithful visits to the Museum of Modern Art, once every week (except, it goes without saying, those two months your mother was ill), climbing the wide gray staircase in that vast gray building that smells of dust and diesel. It represents you standing before the collage for minutes on end, addicted to the act of wondering. Can one compose a story behind its story? Can one ever say that one "understands" it like one can say one "understands" a painting by Pissarro, a sculpture by Segal? It represents how you slowly developed your own collage, smaller, more monochromatic, based on a conflation of this one and your own dreams of falling, all the while trying (and failing) to find the connection among its mysterious and complex images, unaware as you went that tomorrow the curatorial staff will discover the shadowy figure was not, in art historical fact, a shadowy figure at all, but a mistake, a blemish on the canvas, and will, meticulously and with great fanfare in the local media, wipe it off.

HAS YOUR MIND BEEN FED?
A CROS-SWORD PUZZLE

JACKSON BERLIN

[photo by Bruce Jackson]

Crossword Puzzle Clues

Down

1. Raymond's father (backwards)
2. Food eaten in closet
4. Buffalo colleague Dennis (backwards)
5. Where Raymond spent most of the Korean war doing translation work
6. High School (backwards)
7. Buffalo experimental fiction colleague
9. *Recyclopedia* editor (initials)
10. Menachem
11. Experimental Fiction Prize
15. Raymond's alter-ego
17. *Double or* _____
20. A fort in *Take It or Leave It*
22. Graduate school
23. "Smiles on" square
26. Where Raymond moved in 1964
27. Fiction Collective co-founder (initials)
29. Internal voice of dissertation's subject
31. Raymond's response to the laugh
33. Raymond's younger sister
35. Author of one of the two books in Raymond's pocket upon arrival in the U.S.
37. Raymond's mother
39. Buffalo colleague who also wrote 11 books while there (back wards)
42. Raymond's daughter

43. American nisei friend from Korea whom Raymond met again in New York
46. *Zeitgeist* Olsen (backwards)

Across:
2. Symbol Raymond removed his father's jacket
3. Vibration (backwards)
7. *Take It or Leave It*'s special car
8. Raymond's favorite sport
12. Graduated Columbia University cum laude, Phi _____ Kappa
13. *Moinous* (English)
14. Wrote introduction to *Take It or Leave It*
16. Relation to Simon
18. Book Award for *Smiles*
19. Raymond's magazine
20. Abstract Expressionist painter and Raymond's former roommate (nickname)
24. *Amer_____*
24. Bum #2
29. Domicile
30. In *Take It or Leave It*, what kind of "painful patient feverishness" overcomes the writer?
33. Birthplace
36. Swallow Press editor
37. Raymond's older sister
38. "America: A _____ Broad"
40. Raymond's version of "The Great American Road Novel" (abbreviated)
41. _____ *Shoes*
43. Bert _____ starred in Raymond's first encounter with the work of Beckett

45. Another alter-ego of Raymond
47. Title of Raymond's first published poem
48. Raymond's better half
49. _____*the Beasts* (backwards)
50. Sam

Twofold Welcome to Raymond Federman

Zoltán Abádi-Nagy

First Fold: Welcome, Ray, from the Space Colonies

Ray, I am relaying this so far unpublished section of our 1986 conversation back to Earth from the Space Colonies where I was deported on December 31, 1999 in your *The Twofold Vibration*. You see, December 31, 1999 decided what, according to the testimony of this interview, you could not decide in 1986: the Old Man *was* deported after all. I am sure you will appreciate it if I inform you about the further vibrations that my two-fold-vibration deportation caused in some other people's lives soon after that mysterious date. After my post-millennium return to the US university where I was teaching that academic year, I wondered aloud at a dinner party (mid January, 2000!) whether my American colleagues, who were dining with me that night, were sure that I was identical with the person who had left in December 1999 to fly briefly back to the millennial celebrations in Hungary. If this question shocked the party into visible consternation, you can imagine those faces when I offered that I could document the reason for saying what I was saying. As I had forgotten to assign that whole English faculty *The Twofold Vibration* before my departure in December, at this point (in January 2000) I pulled from my pocket xeroxed pages from the *Federman A to X-X-X-X* recyclopedia with the "LIST OF NAMES" entry. I produced it as encyclopedic evidence—and, therefore, generally known fact—that the person named Zoltán Abádi-Nagy had

139

indeed been deported to the space colonies with the Old Man and some other people on December 31, 1999. Thank you, Ray, for the looks that froze on those faces (on that January day of an otherwise very hot state). Those were looks for which there is no adjective in any dictionary in circulation outside the Space Colonies.

Let me add that I am doing relatively fine. What makes the Space Colonies tolerable is that we, the deported, are all birds of the same feather. Shock therapies may not be infrequent, but we have learned to rewire the chambers of our body so that we can derail in-coming shockwaves or at least detour them inside, to the extent that some brain capacity is saved upstairs with which to register news that matter. I give you an example: there is talk on the Space Colonies about a planet where postcolonial theories come from... And we still often think of our "featherman" (an earthling?)... However, if your sense of December 31, 1999 makes you decide that the Old Man was *not* deported after all, please let me know so that I can think my case over.

Second Fold: An Interview with Raymond Federman (*The Twofold Vibration*)

This is part of a tape-recorded interview conducted in the Debrecen Center of the Hungarian Academy of Sciences on 19 February 1986, when Raymond Federman visited Kossuth University as part of a highly successful lecture tour in Hungary. Professor Federman kindly revised the transcript of our conversation. In this part of the interview—published here for the first time—he discusses The Twofold Vibration. *Some other sections of our book-size talks have already been published separately. The "chapter" principally addressed to fiction generally is available in* Modern Fiction Studies *(34.2 [1988]: 157-70)—while the Hungarian version of the same section, complemented with the discussion of* Smiles on Washington Square, *is accessible in Hungarian, in* Világregény—regényilág: amerikai íróinterjúk *("The Novel of the World—The World of the Novel: Conversations with American Writers"; Debrecen: Kossuth Egyetemi Kiadó, 1997. 213-51). The section devoted to* Double or Nothing *has also been published in English (see note 1).*

ABÁDI-NAGY. Somebody called the postmodern novel a novel with zero degree of interpretation. It seems to me that by the time you reach *The Twofold Vibration*, it is *interpretability* that you reach. Even if you choose to escape "the real experience behind it all," the whole complex matter–the trauma in France, survival ("living with one's death behind"), Jewishness as a personal, historical, and international issue, America as an experience for someone coming from French culture–*has* become interpretable.

FEDERMAN: Not only interpretable, but also more accessible. I think the same is true, let's say, of the work of Sukenick. If one follows the evolution of his novels, from *Up* to the recent *Long Talking Bad Conditions Blues*, it becomes clear that gradually Sukenick, like myself, says more about the world, about people, about human problems. Perhaps as one grows a bit older one is able to speak of certain things in the world, or even certain private things, more openly and with less self-consciousness. In this sense our work offers itself to more interpretation, offers more meaning.

ABÁDI-NAGY: In *Double or Nothing* you decided that since "everybody has answers but very few people have real honest sensitive and coherent questions to ask," one way of being inventive in fiction was "to work backward" and "give the *questions* as the substance" of fiction. It seems that after novels of questions *The Twofold Vibration* is your first book of answers.

FEDERMAN: Yes, I think that book does offer some answers, except that one must remember that I am a story-teller, a fictioneer, a surfictionist, and therefore the answers I give are never absolute, and always playful. That does not mean the answers are false, but they cannot be verified as facts. Especially those which deal with the future since they are as yet unfounded. Though as time passes (here we are in 1986, four years after the publication of the book), I get nervous about some of the historical predictions I made about the planet Earth. I am afraid that the book might cancel itself, or authenticate itself, as we come closer to these future dates, either because none of what I predicted will happen–or else... it will.

ABÁDI-NAGY: Well, it may have the fate of George Orwell's *Nineteen Eighty-Four.*

FEDERMAN: Yes, even though my novel is not as dogmatic.

ABÁDI-NAGY: And although a lot of that has become a reality, too.

FEDERMAN: Sure.

ABÁDI-NAGY: I am tempted to believe that *The Twofold Vibration* is for you what the Dresden novel was for Kurt Vonnegut: the book you were making yourself ready for, even when writing the ones that went before. But this may be totally false, since, maybe, it was not your story (the Federman-story) and its moral dimension that prompted you to write when you started writing. How did you come to writing?

FEDERMAN: It's hard to tell. I started writing rather late in my life. For a long time I thought I wanted to be a jazz musician. A saxophone player. Then an actor. I did a bit of amateur acting in college. The theater has always fascinated me, but I soon realized that with an accent, a rather pronounced accent, which I don't think I will ever get rid of, it would be difficult to become an actor in America. I wrote my first piece (a kind of prose poem) when I was in Japan during the Korean war. It was about a prostitute. This was in 1953 or 54. I was almost 25 years old. I thought I had written a poem because I had lined up the words neatly on the page, but let me assure you there was nothing poetic about the piece. It was just a need to describe something that disturbed me, or moved me. Then I went on recording on paper what was happening to me in Japan. Small snapshots of words about life in the streets of Tokyo. But I wrote my first story on the boat coming back to America. It was one of those navy tubs which took twenty-one days to get from Japan to San Francisco. We had a lot of time and nothing much to do but sleep or play poker. One night I wrote a story, and will you believe, I called it "You Can't Go Home Again." I was reading Thomas Wolfe in those days. It was about my fear of going back to America, back to civilian life, after Japan, and not knowing what I was going to do. I was nothing then. Had nothing. No education, no money, of course. No place to go in particular. I was even thinking of leaving America and going to some other place, some other country. No, not back to France, but somewhere perhaps in Africa. Well, I never did. Instead, I settled in New York, went to Columbia University on the G.I. Bill. I was 26 years old and a freshman in college, but that's when I wrote my first novel–*And I Followed My Shadow*. I think I said earlier that much of my writing resulted from the aloneness, the fear, the apprehension of coming out of the closet and confronting the world. That's what started the whole mess–I mean the writing. Coming back from the Korean war was another confrontation with the reality of America.

ABÁDI-NAGY: And how did you come to write *The Twofold Vibration?*

FEDERMAN: The book came to me in a sentence, a sentence I heard during the night. Perhaps I was dreaming, or only half-asleep, but I woke up with this sentence in my head: "If the night passes quietly tomorrow, he will be on his way." This happened when I was, as the expression goes for writers, between books. I had finished one (*Take It or Leave It*) and I was searching, or rather waiting for the next one. This is the most difficult time for a writer–the waiting for the next book to come. All sorts of books come before you, and you play with them for a while and then dismiss them. You ask yourself, what shall I write now? A love story? Maybe a science-fiction novel? Maybe I should try a best-seller? You go through all sorts of dumb possibilities. This can go on for months. And then one night you wake up with a sentence before you: "If the night passes quietly tomorrow, he will be on his way," and you spend the next four years or so trying to find out who he is, and where he is going. When you're finished you have a book called *The Twofold Vibration*: the story of an old man who is being deported to the space colonies in the year 2000. At first I had no idea who that old man was. But now I know. He is a composite of three people–my father, Sam Beckett, and me. But, of course, he is also meant to be *Man*, or rather, *Everyman*. I suppose that's why he never got a name. A survivor. While working on this book, I had no idea how it would end, and again, during a sleepless night, another sentence came to me: "A barrage of unresolved events confronts me." I knew then that I could not go beyond this barrage of unresolved events, that there were still many things to write and try to resolve, but not in this book. This book was finished. And if you recall, the book ends when the writer dozes off and the two narrators (Moinous and Namredef) fade away into his subconscious. One could say that *The Twofold Vibration* was written between two sentences which came to me out of nowhere, or rather out of some deep subconsciousness.

ABÁDI-NAGY: The games you play with narrative technique in *The Twofold Vibration* are complex and original. There were reversals of roles and voices within voices in *The Voice in the Closet*. In *The Twofold Vibration*, however, there is a primary but intermediary author-narrator and an author-character or author-hero, the latter being also identical with the author-narrator and his father. Plus there are two secondary character-narrators, who fade into the author-narrator's subconscious at the end of the novel. What we have here is not the psychological double, not the multiple point-of-view but the plural-voiced narrational mind or the plural-voiced self operating in the "synchronicity" of "verbal extensions in time and space." Why this casting of the narrational voice into a whole set of dramatic personae?

FEDERMAN: Earlier we were talking about two types of novelists: those who work with personal experiences, and those who do not, or else hide the fact that they are working with personal material. I mentioned Coover in whose work one cannot really detect any autobiographical elements.[i] But I am convinced that there are some. Well hidden. As there are autobiographical elements in Beckett's work. We know that now. I think this is true of all novelists. But somehow one is able to create a distance between the self and the fiction. Writing as I do, very much out of my own personal experience, I had to invent a way of distancing myself from my fiction. Or if you prefer, of fictionalizing myself. The easiest and more conventional way of doing that is simply to write about yourself in the third person thus imagining that you are someone else. But that's too simple. I did it by creating a plurality of voices, which is already present in *Double or Nothing*, but in a very obvious manner. This plurality of voices becomes more complex and more refined, I think, in *The Twofold Vibration*. Between me—my subject which is me—and my fiction there is a network of interplaying voices. I had already inscribed my name in the fiction in *The Voice in the Closet*, I mean the name "Federman" (the Penman), but only as a word, as a point of reference in the text. In *The Twofold Vibration*, Federman is not only a name but also a fictitious being, an author-narrator as you call him, around whom, within whom all the other narrational voices circulate—Namredef which is of course Federman spelled backward, Moinous which is me and us, and the Old Man. We are all alter egos of one another. Consequently the real self gets pulverized into this plurality of fictitious beings, but then reconstructs itself into another being—the text itself, the fiction, *le corps du texte*, one would say in French. That is one of the reasons for creating this complex network of narrational voices: to distance the fiction from the writing-self. But there are other reasons, perhaps more interesting from the point of view of the question you raise. In order to keep the work going, once you have begun to write, especially when the work does not depend on a plot or a story-line, you must constantly invent new intricacies. You must complicate the situation so that you can continue writing. Eventually you are more involved, as you write, with the shape of the book than the content of the book. The geometry of the book takes over. At least that's how it happens with me. The shape of *The Twofold Vibration* is very baffling. Sometimes I wonder how I managed to hold the whole thing together. The book sort of collapses within itself in the middle in order to generate itself toward its end. Or to use a rather curious word from Derrida: the book invaginates itself. Let me explain. The book really begins with a quotation from Beckett, which gives it its title, so that one could say that the title is invaginated inside the book since the Beckett quotation appears inside the book and not on its cover or its title page, and appears not only as an epigraph but also (on the last page of the novel) as part of the text. Then the real beginning (I mean of the novel within the novel) which is, you recall, "If the night passes quietly tomorrow…", and which was the original beginning, is also invaginated and now appears only on the second page (as well as on the last page). The book now begins with an address to the readers, or whoever is listening outside the book: "Hey you guys wake up…" Remember, everything in this book has a twofold vibration, meaning that it repeats itself (just as history does) in a strange manner. The last line of the book is: "you can go back to sleep now." In other words, the book happens between the eyes opening and the eyes closing–between awakening and sleeping. This sets up all sorts of metaphorical and structural possibilities: night and day, light and dark, present and past, present and future, reality and fiction, real and fictitious beings. At the beginning of the book, Federman (the fictitious author) in his study is a mere shape in the dark, but he becomes more and more visible and active (as narrator-character that is) as the book comes into focus with the light. We see the desk, the sofa, the bottle of Calvados, the typewriter, etc., in his study. It becomes a concrete situation. This is also true of the two narrators, Moinous and Namredef. At first they are just names, but gradually they become more tangible, more like real characters. That's what the whole book is about: it is about opening your eyes in order to see more, to see better, to see what is happening in the world. And then it all fades away as the eyes close. The more we open our eyes the larger the circle (the vision) becomes, and as we close our eyes the circle becomes smaller and smaller and eventually fades away. That is the design of this book.

ABÁDI-NAGY: What is the suggestion when the Old Man says to his wife in answer to her question ("Why don't you tell the story straight and stop playing games?"): "it's not the story that counts, it's the way you tell it"?

FEDERMAN: You cannot imagine how often I've been told: "why don't you tell the story straight and stop playing games." I suppose it means the story of what happened to me. In *The Twofold Vibration* I quote a line from Blake which says: Fire delights in its form. For me it is the form of the story, its shape that gives me pleasure. Recently in a dream (or perhaps it was not a dream) I had this conversation with my wife as the two of us awake in the middle of the night: "With you it's always form, form, and form," she says to me as if continuing a conversation we had during the day. And I reply: "Yes, but you see, form gives me balance, form makes me happy." Then we both went back to sleep, and the dream ended. Or I could put it this way, for me it is the account of the event that counts.

ABÁDI-NAGY: Has not the plurality of the narrational voice got something to do with your insistence–whether it is *Double or Nothing* or *The Twofold Vibration*–that the Jewish boy's predicament (losing his family in France and trying to come to grips with America) *should* not be taken straight as your autobiography?

FEDERMAN: Yes, certainly. I am aware that there is a duplicity in my work, a constant juxtaposition of the past and the present. You see, on the one side (in the past, of course) there is the boy who experienced the closet, then the young man who came to America and confronted the confusion of life in America, the loneliness of Detroit and New York, and the years in the army, and the Korean war, and the return to New York. In other words, there is Moinous. On the other side, there is the man who writes about all that, in the present. It's the same person, and yet it is not, or rather it is no longer the same person. The young man was lonely, sad, full of melancholy, lost even. The man in Buffalo, the writer working comfortably in his study (or wherever he happens to be writing), he has no real problems with life. He's not really suffering (except for the usual anguish and despair of having to write books). He merely imagines how the boy and the young man suffered. And so between the teller and the told, between the writing-subject and the written-subject, there is always this gap, this duplicity, and I make of this duplicity an occasion in my work.

ABÁDI-NAGY: The author-narrator is clearly a complex self in *The Twofold Vibration* and the Old Man is an imaginative projection.

Namredef is Federman reversed and is thus probably the survivor who–with strategies of escape and transcendence–tries to reverse what happened. Is he the "present-self" in the sense you explain the "present-self" in your essay "Self/Voice/Performance in Contemporary Writing"?

FEDERMAN: I think the present self is really Federman, I mean the fictitious author who is trying to tell the story of the Old Man. But since both Namredef & Moinous are his alter egos, as such they are also present selves as well as survivors who, like the author, are trying not to reverse what happened but to tell "the real story" once and for all. Isn't it how the book opens: ". . . this time it's going to be serious, the real story, no more evasions, procrastinations..."? But inevitably, as in all the other fictions by Federman (real or fictitious is finally irrelevant), neither author nor narrators manage to tell the story of the Old Man, it remains unfinished. At the end of the book it is not said what happened to the Old Man. However, if the story of the Old Man has not been told fully, in the attempt to do so something has been revealed. It should be noted that in the structure of *The Twofold Vibration* there are two fixed points: Federman, the author-narrator stable, static in his study trying to write the story of the Old Man, and far away in time and in space, the Old Man waiting in the antechamber of departure. Basically they do not move from where they are during the entire novel. But the two narrators (Moinous & Namredef) go back and forth between them gathering material on one side, which they feed to the other. They move in time and in space collecting as best they can the elements of the story which the author wants to write. At times they move backward, and at other times they move forward. However, since it is obvious that they are extensions of the author and of the Old Man then all the figures in this book are interchangeable. And eventually that's what happens, when the author imagines himself in the Old Man's place in the antechamber while the Old Man writes Federman's story in the author's study. Since Moinus & Namredef repeatedly fail to bring back the *real* reason for the Old Man's fate, the author decides to change place with the Old Man so that he can go on telling the story since he already knows it. I suppose the reason I chose not to give the Old Man a name is that he is indeed a projection of Federman (both the real and the fictitious Federman) in time as well as in space, but perhaps in some other zone of consciousness.

ABÁDI-NAGY: Moinous's name is coined from the French *moi* and *nous*. Is this to make him function as an everyman?

FEDERMAN: No, not really. It's just a name, a pun that keeps reappearing in my work, but which seems to gain meaning as I play with it. The name Moinous first appeared in *Take It or Leave It*. It was the name I gave the other soldier who was going to the Far East with the protagonist of the novel. At first I called that character "Monoeil" ("my eye") a slang expression in French which is used to mean "you're kidding... I don't believe a word of what you're saying" or something like that. The name Moinous grew out of Monoeil. Or perhaps I used both names in the book. Incidentally, that character in the novel is modeled on a real fellow I knew in the army in North Carolina. I have forgotten his real name, it was something like McNulty or MacNoodle, McNoozle. I always used to mispronounce his name, and he made fun of me. In any event, I was searching for a name for that character and stumbled first on Monoeil and then Moinous. Moinous (the word as well as the character) has become a permanent fixture of my fiction. It can be read as a concept or simply as a name. I think Moinous is really me–me and all the other *me*. Me/Us in other words.

ABÁDI-NAGY: This is how the name was found. Can we say that as a concept he develops into something like the everyman-self in all of us, as the name would suggest?

FEDERMAN: Well, if you insist, I would say that he represents the *ego*. Remember his nickname in *The Twofold Vibration* is "moimoi" or simply "moi." And if it is so then the other narrator, Namredef, the other half, could be the libido. His nickname is "nam" which is of course *man* backward. I don't know. Perhaps Nam is the everyman, or else the two of them as a couple are the everyman. Does any of this make sense to you? But there is more. Remember that Moinous, in *The Twofold Vibration* at any rate, is short, fat and half-blind, and Namredef is tall, skinny, and half-deaf. I suppose one could make something out of that.

ABÁDI-NAGY: So I was mistaken about that. Namredef would be the everyman since he is "man."

FEDERMAN: Who knows. What I can tell you, however, is that the couple Moinous and Namredef were somewhat modeled on two other famous couples in Beckett (Beckett always looms in the background of that book): Vladimir and Estragon in *Waiting for Godot* and Mercier and Camier in the novel by that name. And like them, one being more intellectual, the other more physical, they form one being. They complement and complete one another.

ABÁDI-NAGY: The Hungarian critic, Mihály Szegedy-Maszák, speaks about the deconstruction of the autobiographical self in *The Twofold Vibration.* If it is so, can it be looked upon as a device that testifies to the multiplicity and psychological complexity of dealing with a historical dilemma?

FEDERMAN: I am uneasy with the word "deconstruction." You see, though the novel is far from being autobiographical, it is nonetheless an attempt to *re*construct the self. It is a reconstruction of past events as well as a construction of future events. Many of these drawn from my own personal experiences, even the future events. *Double or Nothing, Take It or Leave It, Amer Eldorado* are deconstructive novels. They unmake the past while blurring the present. *The Twofold Vibration* is reconstructive in the sense that certain episodes are taken straight out of history or out of my own biography and are related almost unchanged. For instance the section where the Old Man is arrested in Buffalo happens to be true. I mean I was arrested in 1970 with a group of professors—we were called "The Buffalo 45"—for protesting against the Vietnam War. However, I never had a love affair with Jane Fonda—oops, I mean June Fanon. As always in my fiction, the real and the imaginary, fact and fantasy are juxtaposed on the same page and engender one another. Much of *Take It or Leave It* is built on that principle: a fact which explodes into a grotesque and often blasphemous situation. "The Buick-special" section which relates a car accident in a snowstorm (this may have really happened to me) quickly degenerates into an orgy (real or imagined). The jazz section with Charlie Parker begins as a historic jam session and ends up with an orgy of masturbation. That is the pattern. It begins with a fact of life–I played jazz, I lived in Detroit, I was arrested in Buffalo, I once had a minor car accident in snowstorm, I once visited Dachau, the concentration camp turned museum, I gambled in Monte Carlo, etc.–and quickly turns into an "exaggerated tale."

ABÁDI-NAGY: All this is very interesting from the theoretical point of view since you maintain that postmodern fiction brings the Self into activity "by cutting off referential ties." After what you have just related, it is difficult for me to regard the Self in a novel like *The Twofold Vibration* as a non-referential multi-voice system performing a non-referential text.

FEDERMAN: Here we are confronting what I earlier referred to as the ambivalence, and even the contradiction that exists between the theoretical and the fiction. The so-called theoretical statements I made about fiction were mostly written after the facts, *a posteriori*, and reflected on what I and others had already done in some of our books. I still think that a book like *Double or Nothing* has to do with the nonreferentiality of the text. *The Twofold Vibration*, and even more so the new novel I just published, *Smiles on Washington Square*, have less to do with the question of nonreferentiality than the problem of readability versus unreadability, which I deal with, theoretically, in the essay "What Are Experimental Novels and Why Are There So Many Left Unread." But let me add that even when a text is non-referential, in order to be so it must cut itself from references, or else how would we know it is non-referential. Nice little Pre-Socratic paradox. Postmodern fiction is full of such paradoxes.

ABÁDI-NAGY: And what is relevant in this context, too, is perhaps what you referred to earlier as an important difference in *The Twofold Vibration*: "reconstruction" is going on after "deconstruction." Is this what you mean by "unified dialectic" in the "Self/Voice/Performance" essay? There it is *while* and not *after.* Postmodern Literature constructing itself while deconstructing itself.

FEDERMAN: What I really meant by "unified dialectic" is that while fiction is deconstructing itself by rejecting the conventions which used to govern it, nonetheless something gets constructed: a new type of text which gains autonomy on the basis of its own arbitrary rules. Even when we say Federman's fiction cancels itself, that does not mean the text disappears. What is canceled is a certain preconceived idea one may have had of fiction. This process of deconstructing while constructing became quite clear to me when in the early seventies I experimented on tape, as John Barth also did at that time (we were colleagues in Buffalo). As a bilingual writer I wanted to be able to speak the same text (which existed both in English and in French) simultaneously. This, of course, can be done on tape by synthesizing the voices. As I heard myself speak English and French at the same time, I also noticed that the meaning of the texts had disappeared, had been erased by this bilingual cacophony. However, something else had been created: an effect, a sound effect which was still part of the text, or rather which had replaced the original text. In this sense, yes, the subject (the self, if you prefer) is deconstructed because it loses its meaning, but something else is constructed in its place. Perhaps one could call that the *essense* of the text. I recorded a poem called "Walls" (it appears in *Take It or Leave It*) several times in French and in English and then brought these voices together. What one hears has nothing to do with the original meaning of the poem, which was about claustrophobia, and yet the sounds one hears give the *effect* of claustrophobia. In other words, the recorded bilingual multivoice poem is no longer *about* claustrophobia, it *is* claustrophobia.

ABÁDI-NAGY: Is your definition of "performance" what Richard Poirier calls "dramatizing the self as performer" in *The Performing Self?*

FEDERMAN: Yes, more or less. Of course in a novel it is language which becomes the performer. But since language *is* the self, it is the self, which dramatizes itself in language.

ABÁDI-NAGY: Would it be a correct application of your theory, then, to say that in *The Twofold Vibration* the autobiographical self is deconstructed into voices that perform the Old Man as a postmodern construction?

FEDERMAN: There is a deconstruction of what gives coherence to the elements of a biography (in this case my own), and that is time. Floating in timelessness the self becomes fragmented. In *The Twofold Vibration*, the various narrative voices are the fragments of the autobiographical self which are trying to reconstitute themselves in the figure of the Old Man, who is fixed in time: New Year Eve 1999.

ABÁDI-NAGY: If Christopher Lasch had taken into consideration –he did not–*Double or Nothing* and *Take It or Leave It* when he wrote "The Minimalist Aesthetic" chapter of *The Minimal Self,* he would have relegated these works to what he calls "The Roth-Cunningham Effect." By that he means a "solipsistic mode of discourse" where literature remains its own subject. The artist retreats into this when he is overwhelmed by the cruelty and chaos of modern history. I am sure you would object that the postmodern use of the self is confused here with narcissistic solipsism.

FEDERMAN: Do you know that Christopher Lasch is quoted, or rather misquoted (perhaps I should say abused) in *The Twofold Vibration?* In the scene where Moinous, Namredef, and Federman are stranded in the author's study trying to find a way to go on with the Old Man's story, out of frustration Moinous launches into a diatribe about the narcissism of the situation. I am, of course, mocking Lasch, who, I think, is a profound pessimist. A reactionary thinker who dislikes his fellow-men. He often confuses reflection with solipsism.

ABÁDI-NAGY: What saves *Double or Nothing* and *Take It or Leave It* from solipsism is that although they are explorations of mental states and rich in introspection, they never hint that only the self and its mental processes exist. The self is in fact struggling with what everything else there is in past and present.

FEDERMAN: Right. One must not confuse self-reflexiveness with solipsism. Gerald Graff in his attack against postmodernism makes the same mistake as Lasch. He equates self-reflexiveness with narcissism. Both are negative critics. For me self-reflexiveness is a positive aspect of contemporary fiction. Fiction did not turn inward in order to admire itself but to question itself and renew itself.

ABÁDI-NAGY: As for *The Twofold Vibration* and solipsism, I think that the novel, besides being an attempt to understand the self, also wants to make the world intelligible for the self, even if with the help of hypotheses in the absence of accurately describable facts. Life forced the Old Man to withdraw into "the hollow" of his mind, true. But he thinks that coming to terms with the incomprehensibility of the Holocaust must be a collective effort.

FEDERMAN: The Old Man withdraws into "the hollow" of his mind to confront the guilt of having survived, but also to replay the horror of what happened. He becomes a kind of theater where history is performed again. I remember giving a public reading from the book and a young woman in the audience got very upset because, as she said, she didn't want to share in the collective guilt the book was trying to pass on to others. It bothered me a great deal that she should react this way. I don't think that is the point of the book: to suggest that guilt should be shared collectively. What should be shared collectively about the Holocaust is its "incomprehensibility" and the suffering that it caused.

ABÁDI-NAGY: According to the science-fiction idea evolved in *The Twofold Vibration,* although racism no longer exists in the world, the Old Man—a Jewish Writer—is bound to be deported to the space colonies as an undesirable element. Probably because he is an experimental writer. Why is the Old Man finally *not* deported and not allowed to come back either? Is the suggestion that the experimental writer is not quite undesirable after all, nor is he exactly banished but deliberately isolated still?

FEDERMAN: I cannot really answer that question. I don't know why the Old Man is among those who are deported, just as we don't know why so many people were exterminated during World War Two. The fact that many of them were Jewish does not explain anything. Originally, when I was working on this book, I made a list of possible reasons why the Old Man would be deported to the space colonies. That he was an experimental writer was one reason. But there were others (some mentioned in the book others not). Because of his political activities, because of his sexual depravity, or simply because of his anal compulsion. Who knows. As for why in the end he is not really deported, that cannot be answered either. Perhaps it has to do with a question I've been asking myself since 1942, when the Germans came to arrest my parents. *Why* did my mother hide me in the closet and not my sisters, or one of my sisters? Why me? What dictated this gesture?

ABÁDI-NAGY: Were your sisters in the position for your mother to hide them too?

FEDERMAN: Sure. All three children were there. Maybe my older sister could have survived better than me. She was sixteen years old at the time. Why save the boy rather than one of the girls? Is it something about the Jews that the boy must survive and the girls be sacrificed? Or perhaps the family name must survive?

ABÁDI-NAGY: She may have acted on the spur of the moment. Probably she did not think...

FEDERMAN: Maybe she did not think, maybe it was purely chance, but that's the same reason I cannot tell you if the Old Man is or is not deported. I have speculated on this, of course, for more than forty years now, just as Federman, the author in the book, and the narrators speculate.

ABÁDI-NAGY: The Old Man is an innovative writer, and innovative writers do feel isolated anyway. What are the chances for an innovative American writer to break out of this isolation?

FEDERMAN: You can compromise by making your work more accessible, more commercial. Or else you can get lucky. After all, our books are not that unreadable, they are often funny, entertaining even. There is a great deal of intelligence at work in them. Who knows, perhaps tomorrow someone in the publishing world will decide that these are the kinds of books people should read, and suddenly all the innovative writers in America will become famous and rich and no longer be isolated. Or else you continue doing your work and gradually, almost in spite of yourself, you discover that you have established yourself in the literary world. John Barth *is* an established writer. He is recognized, his books are discussed, major publishers are delighted to have his name on their list. Of course, his books do not sell millions of copies, but…

ABÁDI-NAGY: Did he not establish himself with his more conventional novels?

FEDERMAN: Which one do you mean?

ABÁDI-NAGY: The first ones: *The Floating Opera, The End of the Road.*

FEDERMAN: No, not at all. The interesting thing is that these first two novels were greatly ignored. It's only after the strange success of *Giles Goat-Boy,* which made a brief appearance on the best-seller list to everyone's astonishment, including Barth himself. But then we were in the middle of the fabulous Sixties. I suppose the book made the best-seller list because a lot of people bought copies, but I doubt too many of these people finished reading it. They must have wondered: "what's that?" But the name of John Barth had entered into the literary establishment, and immediately the early books were reissued in paperbacks, and since they were much more accessible than *Giles Goat-Boy,* they became very popular. However, if you were to ask any university professor who teaches contemporary American fiction which of Barth's novels he includes in his reading list, it would always be either *The Floating Opera* or *The End of the Road,* but never *Giles Goat-Boy* or *Lost in the Funhouse.* Very few people have read *Letters.* It is very possible that my own novel, *Smiles on Washington Square,* which is a rather easy book to read compared to the others, may revive my earlier novels, though I doubt it.

ABÁDI-NAGY: Should experimental writers strive to write more accessible fiction?

FEDERMAN: The subject dictates how you write a book. The subject matter of *The Voice in the Closet* is demanding, and therefore requires a demanding form. As you pointed out earlier, there is a definite change in my writing in the last two books. On the surface, and stylistically at any rate, *The Twofold Vibration* and *Smiles on Washington Square* seem more conventional and are probably more accessible than the earlier novels. However, the material of the next book will dictate how I will write it. And who knows, the next book may again be delirious, it may become totally unreadable.

ABÁDI-NAGY: Does this sense of isolation *unite* American innovative fictionists in a community, or does it *disperse* them?

FEDERMAN: Usually the critics unite them by putting them all in the same boat and giving them the same label: postmodernist, metafictionist, surfictionist, anti-fictionist. Jerome Klinkowitz in his seminal study of the new fiction entitled *Literary Disruptions* includes Kurt Vonnegut Jr. but somehow excludes John Barth. Others have different grouping. The same is true of people who make anthologies. One is never sure why *this* innovative writer is included and not *this* one. As for the writers themselves, they form cliques. Of course, in a vast place like America, a lot depends on where you live. If you happen to live in New York, then you might (though not always, writers are as prejudiced as any other group) belong to the New York clique. In San Francisco, to the San Francisco clique. Also there are class-structures among writers, even among innovative writers. There is the Bellow, Mailer, Malamud class. There is the Updike, Vidal, Styron class. This has nothing to do with the quality of the work, or if the work is innovative. There is the Barth, Gass, Hawkes class, and yes there is the Sukenick, Katz, Federman class. A great deal of this grouping has to do with who is your agent, your publisher, who reviews your books, who buys your books, how much you get for a reading, and who invites you to read. But to whatever group you belong, eventually, when it comes to writing the books, you are back in your isolation in whatever corner of America you happen to be.

ABÁDI-NAGY: Are there any kinds or aspects of prose innovation and experimentation where you yourself think, "well, this is going a bit too far"?

FEDERMAN: Too far! Never, when it comes to experimentation. There are some forms of experimentation which I find *useless* for my work. Experimentations with which I feel no affinity. For a while, in the early seventies, I was associated with the concrete poetry movement. But gradually I moved away from it. I was involved with people like Richard Kostelanetz, Dick Higgins, David Antin, Jackson MacLow, and others who experimented with visual, graphic, and sound poetry. They are primarily performance writers and mostly poets. I respect what they do but find that it has little to do with my present work.

ABÁDI-NAGY: In "What Are Experimental Novels and Why Are There So Many Left Unread," you ask colleagues from the English Department what they teach and they all seem to go for Bellow, Malamud, Heller, Gardner, Styron. No Hawkes, no Gass, no Sukenick, no "unreadable" stuff. What do *you* teach?

FEDERMAN: I teach mostly creative writing. But even in teaching creative writing one uses models for the students. My models are always experimental writers, Beckett, Calvino, Barth, Sukenick. I do teach some literature courses, mostly contemporary stuff, but even though I am supposedly a Professor of English, I make no distinction between French, American, Latin-American, German, Italian, or whatever, fiction. I teach books by Calvino, Beckett, Cortazar, Barth, Abish, Robbe-Grillet. I usually select texts which I feel have something in common, or are very different from one another, but which challenge the conventions of the genre. But I also teach certain essential modernist authors: Joyce, Proust, Kafka, even Dostoevsky and Flaubert.

ABÁDI-NAGY: And what is the student response like?

FEDERMAN: Usually enthusiastic. My students feel they do not have enough opportunity to read contemporary fiction, especially experimental.

ABÁDI-NAGY: You use experimental models when you teach creative writing. But is the *student writing* produced in the seminar expected to be innovative too?

FEDERMAN: Absolutely. You see I give a description of the course, which emphasizes the fact that students will be encouraged to explore innovative techniques in their writing. Besides, students can only register for the course with the instructor's permission. What I try to do is bring together a group of students who write on the same level of competence and who are willing to take risks with their writing. It doesn't always work that way, but usually I have interesting classes.

THE TOOTHBRUSH

RAYMOND FEDERMAN

YESTERDAY MY WIFE LEFT ME. SHE TOOK HER TOOTH-
BRUSH AND LEFT WITHOUT A word. True, we hardly talk to each
other, but still, on such an occasion she could have said something—anything: *SEE YOU, SO LONG, GOODBYE.* Hell, at least leave a note. It
hurts just to think about it. What am I, a stranger?

It was only this morning after my mid—morning nap that I suddenly
felt the blow, the impact, of the situation. It struck me just as I woke up in
Central Park stretched on a bench. This morning her pink toothbrush was
not there next to my yellow toothbrush in the toothbrush-holder slot
above the bathroom sink. That means nothing of course. Still, it's a telling
piece of evidence.

And what about the kids? Something will have to be done. Did she take
them with her? Are the two little darlings still at home? Locked in their
room? Their two little toothbrushes were there in their respective slots this
morning, but that means nothing. What happened to them? The brats I
mean? It's hard to tell, because when I leave in the morning at 7:45—I
always leave at 7:45, it's a habit with me. Good or bad, that's not the
point.—When I leave, the kids are still asleep, and usually, most of the
time, always, I never go into their room for fear of getting reprimanded by
my wife. *REPRIMANDED:* Get Bawled out, Get my Ass chewed out...

Perhaps they are still in their room? Poor little dears, hungry, scared, crying, calling for *MOMMY* (they never call for *DADDY*—little bastards!) If she took them with her, then it's different, but if they are now under my care, my custody, as they say legally, then what? What then? I cannot ruin my life, destroy a whole system for kids. It's only 11:30. Too early to go home, that's for sure. It's against my principles, against the rules, especially on a Tuesday morning...

We were happy the two of us, the four of us, and the maid too, before she was dismissed, fired, kicked out(because of me, of course). I left every morning at 7:45, and returned every evening at 6:45. Always on time—for dinner. Always ready to eat her cooking. Always starved.

I usually skip lunch to save money. Unless I can bum something here or there, though I'm always extremely careful about what I eat, especially since I took that course on hygiene in high school. Only once in a while I eat lunch. When I can't take it any more. But today, after this blow, even if I were hungry, even if I had the money, I don't believe I would have the courage to eat. Even a steak. And God knows how I love steaks. She did too. She knew. And in fact she was the only one who could cook me one of those juicy ones, just slightly cooked inside, and somewhat burnt, crusty on the outside. But today...even the most juicy, the most tempting, the most rare, the rarest of steaks would not appeal to me. I could cry!

After all we were married, let's see now...the oldest one, the girl, Parthenia, will be seven next month (I'll have to fix one of her dolls again for her birthday. Last year she never knew the difference) she'll be seven next month. She was five months gone when we got married...well, let's see...it's simple, for simplicity's sake lets say, seven even. Seven years of married life, it's a long time. That's hard on a man like me. A good husband, and a good father too. I would not hesitate to do anything for those kids. Roll on the floor, make noises, smile, hide in closets, even kiss them except when I have a cold. And for her, yes for her...Makes me angry. She never appreciated me. And making love to her twice a week, on Fridays and Sundays, and sometimes even a little extra here and there. And washing the dishes, and helping with the beds (after the maid was kicked out), and making conversation and playing the good guy at her evenings, her *SOIREES* as she calls them. I was really doing my best, and we were happy the two of us, the four of us, and the maid too, before she was...Hell, this is too much! My mind is wandering. Everything is confused. It's the situation...the moment...desperation...loneliness. What a blow, she left me. *ME!*

Grant you! I have my faults. My feet smell, I pull the blankets at night. I never wash the tub after I take a bath, but then only once a week, I drop pieces of bread in my soup, I open my mouth to speak, I drop my clothes on the floor, I put my elbows on the table, I make noise when I eat, I let gas. *IT'S OBSCENE,* she would say. Do I ever complain when she makes up her face in front of the mirror, when she puts on her false eyes, when she spends hours and hours in the bathroom with all her little goodies, and always when I have to rush out to an important matter: a walk, a movie, a poker game...No, never, not a word from me. Never a word of reproach. Nothing!

And the way she raises those kids: it's really abominable. There should be a law against it. COME NOW, PARTHENIA, YOUR PRAYERS, AND YOU ORESTE (that's the boy) DID YOU PUT YOUR THINGS AWAY, DID YOU CLOSE THE DOOR, DID YOU WASH YOUR HANDS AND BEHIND YOUR EARS AND... and what else? PARTHENIA, I DON'T WANT YOU TO TRY ON MY SHOES, PLEASE ORESTE, LEAVE MY PANTIES ALONE. . . GO AND SAY GOOD-NIGHT TO YOUR FATHER...Your father! Just when I'm in the middle of rifling her purse or making plans for the next day. One must plan the next day, always, especially in my kind of life. Those poor kids! It'll take them at least ten years to emancipate, and another ten to learn about sex, and another ten to forget about God and manners and politeness and their mother, and then what? What then? Right now they don't know what's in store for them, especially if they are still in their room. Under my care.

I did try my best. I would leave every morning at 7:45. I would put on a different suit, a clean shirt and a different tie every morning. When it comes to clothing, I have no complaints. My wardrobe...she really took care of it, saw to it. In that respect she was a fanatic. She chose and bought everything herself: three buttons, when three buttons were required by the rules of Madison Avenue, two buttons when the rules changed, buttoned-down shirts, striped ties when stripes were the fashion; she kept refurnishing my wardrobe. I just went down the line in my closet, starting on the left on Monday and so on for the rest of the week. The suits were always kept in the same order: brown, blue, gray, tweed, double-breasted...Took me a while to get used to that system when we were first married, but I got used to it. I got used to lots of things. My pillow, her pillow, my towels, her towels, my books, her books, my closet, her closet, my car,her car,his and hers and his and hers. However, she never checked what was mine; never controlled; never questioned it either.

Soon after our honeymoon, I sold my car. A man has to make a living. That kept me going for a while. Many of the suits went to the pawn shop. But those bastards: $5.00 for a suit, and a good suit, Brook's Brothers, and $2.00 for a pair of $35.00 shoes. She never suspected anything. I hope. Just kept refurnishing. Why did she leave me then? *WHY?* I tried my best.

Left the house at 7:45 every morning.., and always back on time for dinner, and making love to her twice a week, never skipped a week, unless she was indisposed, and even then...

I would go out in the morning and walk slowly along Park Avenue until I reached the corner of 48th Street, and then I would begin to run a little to get out of sight, just in case she'd follow me. Sometimes I was scared. Then once on Lexington Avenue, I would hitch-hike, usually uptown, sometimes all the way to Harlem, and then work my way down; that would keep me busy for a good part of the morning, especially with a stop of a few hours in Central Park where I took my midmorning naps. Usually on a bench, not on the grass. I'm weak in the chest. I would stretch all the way with a newspaper under my head. I prefer the *NEW YORK TIMES.* I read the *NEW YORK TIMES:* it's the most comfortable newspaper. It's thick. Naturally, I could not afford to buy it every morning. Therefore, I would wait at the entrance, or rather at the exit, of the subways for some morning businessman to throw away his *NEW YORK TIMES* into the garbage cans placed there for that purpose. Sometimes I would be lucky...I would wait only five or eight minutes before a *NEW YORK TIMES* was disposed of. As for the other New York papers...they are hopeless.

Depending on the weather, my luck would be good or bad. I could sense that as soon as I arrived on Lexington Avenue after my little run. I knew immediately. If I became out of breath quickly, it was an unlucky day; but if my respiration was still normal after the little run, then I could be sure of a lucky day. Usually, on my lucky days, I would hitch-hike downtown, sometimes even to Brooklyn, in order to find a good crap game. It was my only chance for survival—crap or poker—assuming of course I had some cash on me to get into the game. This was my major problem. I could never tell the night before whether I would be lucky or not the next day. If I could have, then many of my problems would have been solved. For it was always easy to steal some change from my wife's purse. She never counted the change. The bills (even one dollar bills), that was a different matter. I got caught once, only once, stealing bills, but I got out of that one brilliantly. I forget how. After all, I'm her husband, and she's my wife. Still, from then on she always locked the bills every night before retiring, but not the change. Although, often there was no change in her purse. Then I would have to plan something else. The kids' kitty. But that was like stealing my own money. I'm the one who gives them their weekly allowance. That's my one great responsibility. True, I manage to cheat them on that, but my conscience always bothers me afterwards. Anyway, all this was still insufficient, pennies for the birds. This is why I was pushed—desperately pushed—into dealing with the pawn shops.

The problem was a difficult and complex one at that. How to smuggle stuff out of the apartment. My briefcase, which I always kept locked was useful, but obviously limited in space. For shoes, silverware, napkins and other small objects, I could manage. But sheets, blankets, table cloths…That was more tricky. For suits! The best way was to wear two suits, one on top of the other, but that too had its inconvenience. I easily burst into sweat, immediately followed by spells of dizziness, requiring on my part the most complete inactivity. My wife—perhaps I should call her by her given name: *ROSE* (if I had a picture of her I would stick it right here. I'll try to describe her later, if I can…I could cry just thinking of her…What a blow!)…My wife, Rose, I was saying, knew my weaknesses, my feverish spells, and immediately she would make me stretch out on the floor, on the sofa, on the bed, on the table, wherever I happened to be, and undress me quickly. For that she was good. She had had nursing training during the war. She had volunteered in spite of her family. I suppose I'll have to talk about them too, and what a family! The good-New-England-Puritanical-background as it should be expected…My wife, I was saying, knew about my dizzy spells, so that the few times I did put on two suits one on top of the other, I would immediately burst into sweat…How ridiculous! No, let's not talk about it…

I suppose by now you must be wondering: But how the Hell did this guy manage to support his family—a wife and two kids and a maid too, before she was fired? Good question. You see, my wife was rich. Very rich. She had money, she was loaded. Naturally, I did not marry her for her money, that I can swear to, It was love. We'll come back to this business of love, but it was love, and love at first sight on top of it. It happened when I was at Harvard. She mistook me for a student. I was young then. I was working, full—time, for a publishing company, peddling encyclopedias to major universities. She was at Radcliffe but spent most of her time with the boys. We eloped. Not just then, but a few months later, after I learned she was pregnant. For that matter we could have eloped the first night, for now I'm certain, more than certain that it happened that night (the first night) in the back of her car, a 1948 Pontiac convertible. Accidents can happen. Anyway, to be brief, she had money, she always had money, and I never had any. She's the business mind in our family.

Immediately after we were married, she made me understand that a man of my caliber should have some kind of occupation—*A PROFES-SION* she specified. As soon as we returned from our honeymoon to the Niagara Falls, I went to look for a position. I'm still looking. Or should I say, I gave up looking the second day after we returned from our honeymoon. She made it clear to me that she didn't need my money to run the house. We had an apartment then near Central Park. That's when I first fell in love with Nature. But as soon as I got my first raise, we moved to Park Avenue; it was more suited to our social standing. That's what she explained to me. My first raise! This needs a word of explanation.

As soon as she told me that the money I would earn was not needed for the up-keep of the house, I gave up searching for a job, but still, she expected me to bring in a check every week or at least every month, which, she made it clear, was mine to spend. Therefore, I made a point to show her my check each payday. It was simple. I acquired a checkbook of one hundred checks from an important firm (the name is unimportant, she never looked at it)— which reminds me, I'll be running out of checks soon. Only four left. Seven years of married life (what a life!)…12 checks a year(I even wrote checks for the summer months when I was not sup-posed to be working)…seven times twelve makes 84 (I wasted a few in the beginning writing weekly checks ,but it was getting too much, so I changed my status to a monthly one). It was simple. All I had to do at the end of each month was to bring home a check which I had signed myself with a most delicate work of forgery: *SAMUEL TUCKER* (my real name is Auguste Marant) and she was satisfied. I was pleased and she was pleased, especially when I got my first raise.

I waited four months before giving myself my first raise. That af-ternoon, I called Rose (collect, that was a habit I took with her even before we were married). I called from around the corner of Park Avenue where I was at that time following some rich broad whose purse I was trying to snatch. As soon as she answered, I told her about my raise. She was really happy for me, and I was happy that she was happy. Every six months after that I would give myself little raises of 25 to 50 dollars and she was glad for me.

YOU SEE, she would say to me on those particular nights of my raises, while we sat at the table, the dining room table, which she had set up with candles for the occasion, bent over one of her special juicy steaks I like so much, *YOU SEE,* she would say to me, delicately bringing her fork to the corner of her mouth, her narrow mouth, her elbows never touching the table, always waiting until she had completely swallowed the piece she was then chewing before she spoke the next word, *YOU SEE MY,* she would say, and I had to wait, while she chewed, *DEAR,* a few contortions of the mouth, closed naturally, *THAT YOU,* two words this time, another piece of meat, a small delicate piece disappeared in the corner of her narrow mouth...

The night of my first raise I never got the rest of her sentence. I had to leave immediately after the meal for an important matter, a date with a young person I had met that afternoon during her lunch time in Central Park. It was not always easy for me to get out in the evening, except on Thursday night which was my night out. Tuesday night was my baby-sitting night; it was her bridge night. Monday was also her night out (Friday night was the maid's night) but I never knew where she went. I was not too worried, but still she could have explained. That particular night of my raise of which I spoke earlier was a Thursday night, therefore my night out, and I had to rush out, therefore I never got the rest of her sentence. But at subsequent dinners, steak dinners for the occasion of my raises, when I didn't have to rush out, I managed to get more of the sentence. It went like that (always the same sentence): *YOU SEE MY DEAR THAT YOU TOO CAN BE AS GOOD AS THE NEXT MAN!* I could have told her that, but coming from her it made me feel good.

I had many rendezvous like that with secretaries, divorcees, ballet dancers, actresses, advertising women, artists, salesgirls, and even once with a woman acrobat; but all in all it was nothing to be ashamed of; there was nothing immoral about those insignificant encounters. Sex was never mentioned, though it might have been implied. I was really unfaithful only once. I mean completely unfaithful, mentally and physically. In other words, I desired the person who finally possessed me in Central Park. Ah!...Central Park, my Heaven, my eternal Paradise, my Promised Land...caught in the center of the fury of the great metropolis...*AH!*

It happened one morning, my unfaithfulness, just after my nap. I had chosen for that particular morning of rest a far remote bench near 72nd Street (Fifth Avenue Exit). A bench well protected from the sun by two huge oak trees, in a corner where children and dogs never venture. When I woke up, just across from me on another bench similar to mine, an elderly lady was sitting knitting a sock, a grey sock, I remember. She had a brown paper bag on her head to protect her from the sun, for her bench, unlike mine, was not protected by two huge trees. I looked straight at her and felt a pain inside of me. Her torn cotton stockings were falling, the elbows of her worn-out coat had large red patches clumsily sewn; she wore rimless glasses, of which one of the lenses was broken. Just as I woke up, I saw her staring at me, or somewhere past me, with a twisted smile at the corner of her sensual lips. Immediately I desired her. I motioned her over, and she came limping along. I was still stretched on my bench. She lifted my legs gently in order to sit down and placed them on her lap. My head was still resting on the New York Times. I could feel her bony thighs under the rough material of her skirt. She inrnediately felt my reaction. She looked like the type who had had lots of experience. We did not speak. She kept smiling at me and me at her. At that moment, my wife, Rose, the children, and the maid (this was before she was fired), the whole world vanished from my mind. It was only later that I felt guilty about this incident. I am not easily pushed into the complex of culpability, but here was enough cause (and effect) for culpability. Her hand was stroking my leg. Her left hand. I closed my eyes, but opened them quickly to see where her other hand was. It was not doing anything. Just then her moving hand reached the most crucial point of our relationship. It lasted about five minutes. It seemed like an eternity. I was completely lost in a state of ecstasy, and then I fell asleep. When I awoke, she had disappeared, gone forever, and with her my briefcase and raincoat. I never saw her again, never. I can't even remember her face, now.

That, night, perhaps as a revenge of Nature, or a coincidence, I had my most violent argument with Rose. I was so angry, I almost left home. But the kid (this was before Oreste) and the feeling of guilt which was beginning to crush me inside, and many other reasons made me change my mind. I stayed on. On the contrary, I tried to make up with Rose. Somehow the incident of that morning had aroused the beast in me, and I managed to get Rose to react. It was almost like the reunion of two lovers after their first quarrel. It was that night that our second child, Oreste, was conceived.

After that our married life went much more smoothly, almost with harmony. Rose made all sorts of efforts to make me feel like an expecting father. Every morning when I woke up she would ask me how I felt, and in the evening when I came home she would greet me with a kiss, on the brow, take my briefcase from me, lead me into the kitchen, and watch me lovingly while I cooked the dinner, and after dinner, watch me while I washed the dishes. It was then that we decided to get a new maid. When I think of these happy days, with Rose, Parthenia, the new maid, and little Oreste still in the state of formation, but already referred to as Oscar, and the business of getting things ready for him: the discussions about names, if it should happen to be another girl, or a boy. I was convinced it would be a boy, but Rose who was always a great pessimist insisted that it would be another girl and that we should call her Augusta, after me....

The day Oreste was born, at three in the afternoon, I was in the Bronx involved in a poker game with some hoodlums I had met in a movie on 42nd Street, a gangster movie. I love movies, I have a passion for movies. But naturally in my financial situation, I had to suppress much of this passion, or else, out of desperation, sneak into the movie-houses. I developed a whole technique for sneaking into movies, but I would try it only on my lucky days. Somehow I am quite sensitive to the ridiculous, and I would indeed have felt ridiculous being caught sneaking into a movie. I was never caught, except once, the day Oreste was born. My soul was not with it, you might say. Luckily, those hoodlums came to my rescue. They admired my courage and one of them offered to pay my way in. We laughed and cried together while watching the tragi-comic adventures of the gangsters; ate popcorn and candies together, and it was then, at the end of the film, that they invited me to their weekly poker game in the Bronx.

Naturally they knew I was broke, but one of them agreed to loan me a ten dollar bill to convince me to come. *WIN, YOU PAY BACK,* he explained, *LOSE, WE'RE EVEN.* All they wanted, it seems, was the pleasure of playing with a gentleman, and somehow, I had given them the impression of being a gentleman. The Brook's Brothers suit, no doubt. It was then, just as I was winning close to 60 bucks, that I remembered Rose. Suddenly my fatherly instinct came knocking at the door of my inner responsibility. I got up from the poker table and said dramatically: *I HAVE TO MAKE A PHONE CALL!* No one moved, not a word was spoken...but the guy who seemed to be the leader of the group motioned with his head to another guy to follow me. So the guy escorted me to the phone booth across the street and waited outside while I called home. The maid answered: *ALLO* (she was French)...Oh...Monsieur Marant...Oh...am I contente you called...Madame just left for the hopital in terrible pain...*GET TO THE POINT,* I shouted...*OK...DID SHE LEAVE A MESSAGE?* No. *NO?* I felt suddenly that it was my duty to show up at the hospital. I asked the man waiting outside the booth to run across the street to get me some change, an unforseen matter that required that I make further calls, which, I explained to him, would be too complex to discuss at this point. My language struck him. He took the dollar bill I handed him and kindly rushed to the bar across the street. Meanwhile I escaped— escaped! How well, my wife was having a baby, I could afford to be melodramatic...I took a cab. It was a generous gesture on my part. She would never believe it. I even bought a bunch of flowers for 50 cents.

I was not allowed to see the baby, but I saw Rose. She was in the coma. I placed the flowers on her belly, scribbled a note of appreciation, and left. That night I came home very late. I had spent the whole evening in a bar getting loaded on Bourbon (even though I never drink) and smoking cigarettes (even though it's very bad for my chest). Completely intoxicated, when I came home I tried to rape the maid. She submitted, but I fell asleep before the crucial moment, and the next day she left, before I had time to dismiss her.

Rose stayed five days in the hospital. I went to see her every afternoon, but after that I did not go home (Parthenia had been sent, for the occasion, to her grandparents). I slept in Central Park. A little pleasure I had long been waiting for. I would be willing to have a baby every three months (if it were possible) just to have a few nights off to sleep in Central Park…to do as I please…to be free.., to be…

But now that she has left me, now that I am alone, now that her pink toothbrush no longer stands next to mine, now that I have all the freedom I want, now that the night is coming (its almost 8:30 P.M.), now that I could leisurely walk to Central Park, stretch on a bench, dream, sleep, have a love affair…I feel my heart sinking within me. She left me. *ME!* Without a word.

Today is Tuesday, my babysitting night, her bridge night, but what's the use…She must have taken the two little bastards with her. She is not the kind of woman to leave her offsprings (*OFFSPRINGS?* Well) -my offsprings too, I hope, behind. No…whats the use. If I had money I would kill myself…There s something fishy in all this…I'm going out of my mind…That damn missing toothbrush. The crucial evidence. Exhibit one. Desertion of husband. How tragic, how pathetic, how inhuman, unbelievable. I could throw myself under the first bus, the first car that comes along. I could die of pity for myself. She left…She left me…it keeps ringing in my head like a gong. I'm losing my balance. Quick a drink.

I rush into the first bar I see and play the pinball machine for three hours. The barman finally calls out to me: *EN! MACK, WANT SOME-THING?* Over my shoulder I shout back at him with a cracked voice: *A GLASS OF MILK!* My voice is drowned in a burst of collective laughter springing out of the mouths of all those present. Me, the laughingstock of society. The fool. The deserted husband. That's me. Does it show? I run outside the door of the bar. The cold wind hits me in the face, and I almost fall to the ground. An old lady mumbles something as she passes by. I walk away. I walk for blocks and blocks, sometimes running, trying to recollect my mind, my soul…Tonight is Tuesday, babysitting night, therefore last night was Monday night, her night out, and tomorrow…Oh, tomorrow…Hell! it's not good…I can't stand it any more. Suddenly I make up my mind. I'm going home.

My steps lead me forcefully in front of our apartment building. I feel no pain in the chest, my respiration is normal. Fate? Luck? I suppose. A force pulls me up the elevator. I stop in front of the door of our deserted conjugal home. My hand trembles while searching for the keyhole…Suddenly I change my mind. I put the key back in my pocket, run down the six flights of stairs…and disappear in the cold winter night.

[This is Raymond's first published short story, originally appearing in Panache #11 in 1973. Thanks to Bob Riedel for sending it our way.]

FEDERMAN: TRANSATLANTIC FICTION

MENACHEM FEUER

For many European artists, writers and critics of the past century America and Europe are more than just continents with a different history, culture and language, for them, America and Europe have become figures in a larger struggle. Their work articulates the struggle between the two continents as a struggle between memory and forgetfulness, art and entertainment, truth and simulation, technology and humanity. To this day the struggle continues. Its roots can be found in the work of modernists whose work announced a threat to truth, memory, art, and humanity, a threat that was associated with mass production, urbanism, and capitalism. The greatest chronicle of this struggle can be found in the work of the Frankfurt School, which debated the positive and negative aspects of the "culture industry", the term given to the new entertainment industry developing out of America which blurred the fine line between art and mass culture. Theodore Adorno and Walter Benjamin, the most influential thinkers of the Frankfurt School represented the two extremes. The negative extreme was to be found in the work of Theodore Adorno and the positive extreme was to be found in the work of Walter Benjamin. Unlike the majority of Benjamin's work, which sought for a utopian justification of mass entertainment, Adorno's writings on the topic insist upon a binary between American entertainment and aesthetics (notably a European aesthetics). According to Adorno the former is a threat to reflection the latter is not. Adorno believed that art, poetry and fiction (a new anti-art, which is still art) represent the means of resisting societies tendency to un-reflective fascism and by extension the "culture industry" (America). Thirty years later, Adorno's thought has reemerged due to the Holocaust debate. In this debate the "Americanization" of the Holocaust is posed as one of the main threats to Holocaust memory. However, this threat is not just a threat to the Holocaust, it is a threat to a European and Modernist aesthetic which has claimed ownership of this "unrepresentable" event. According to the theorists in this debate, the American drive to consume and entertain has no right to approach the Holocaust or disaster in general. By arguing in this manner, these theorists imply that the Holocaust is 1) a specifically European disaster 2) can only be represented by way of a high modernist aesthetic which is obsessed with disaster and the unrepresentable and 3) that the memory of the Holocaust is threatened by an American entertainment industry that wishes to import it into the USA via film, TV and fiction. According to these theorists something is, or will be lost in the translation/importation. In lieu of this, the task for these theorists is to protect not just the event, but the aesthetic, from being exported (and ruined in the transmission) to a country that opposes everything Europe and High Modernism stands for. The European film maker Claude Lanzman emphasizes his opposition to Hollywood, which he claims, trivializes history and terror. Lanzman prefers a more European form of aesthetics and he regards this to be more ethical when it comes to the representation of disaster. The problem with his reasoning is that he assumes that anything produced in America (including art) will only reproduce the "culture industry". However, in opposition to Lanzman (and Adorno) who think Hollywood or popular culture has no right to approach the disaster, I would like to argue that the American aesthetic of post-modernism and pop art has made an attempt to approach disaster through popular mediums. For example, in the visual arts, artists such as Warhol and Raushenberg have shown us how the popular can relate to disaster by way of their many collages and artworks which appeal to popular mediums ranging from newspapers and magazines to everyday technology. In fiction the work of Thomas Pynchon and Raymond Federman, amongst others, appropriates popular genres to relate to disaster or the holocaust. In film, the work of Wim Wenders though an indirect approach to the Holocaust, has done the same. In the film, artwork and fiction of post-modernists there is an obsession with irony, camp, pastiche, and a form of playfulness that can be found not just in the way they write, but in the popular culture they borrow from. In contrast to this, Adorno and especially Lanzman insist that post-Holocaust art has, or should have nothing to do with popular culture. In fact, they think of art as resisting society and, after the Holocaust, as a performance that enacts the work of mourning. This is what I would call distinctly European in the sense that the aesthetic they advocate focuses on the limits of art and reason, on the depth of loss or the profound sense of meaningless produced by disaster or the inexplicable. In contrast the American or (as I would like to argue, a global) Post-Modern Aesthetic is what Fredric Jameson would call "depthless." Unlike modernism which is concerned with temporality and mourning, post-modernism concerns itself with the spatial and with pastiche. Since the post-modern remains on the surface it doesn't allow for the depth that pre-empts the mourning of loss and the effect of time. Rather, it pre-empts a different relationship with the past; one that is more playful and constructive rather than crippled and paralyzed by the failure of representation. For Jameson novels by the American authors E.L. Doctorow or Thomas Pynchon illustrate how American History, for instance, becomes the subject of fictioning and play that "trashes" high modernist meditations on disaster and loss. According to Jameson, these themes are trashed because the post-modern aesthetic effaces the fine line between high and low culture by appealing to popular fantasies and cultural constructs as a means of relating to History. According to Jameson, the appropriation of popular fantasies and paranoias (of the American per se) effaces the "depth" of psychological complexity in the face of disaster that we find in modernist masterpieces (notably European) by authors ranging from Fyodor Dostoevsky to

Robert Musil and Thomas Mann. In the post-modern appropriations of Thomas Pynchon we see a pastiche of the psychological/literary investigations of paranoia that empties out the depth of modernist fiction. The pastiche of different styles brings out how the post-modern is concerned with the cultural production of memory as well as loss. Post-Modernism shows us how popular mediums are involved in the fictioning of disaster. Holocaust theorists such as Saul Freidlander and others (see Probing the Limits of Representation) argue that this is dangerous when it comes to the Holocaust. They fear that post-modern attempts to relate the Holocaust may efface its uniqueness and the responsibility to mourn the event publicly. Therefore, they prefer an aesthetic that is more European, one that brings out the uniqueness of the event, as well as a sense of loss and the inexpressible. Anything short of this would be unethical. According to these theorists only a modernist aesthetic could engage the work of mourning. Eric Santer, for instance, argues that an appropriate text would be one that eschews narrative and this would prevent what he calls "narrative fetishization." Even though many (though not all) post-modernists also eschew narrative, they do it in a different manner. Santer's emphasis is on a form of fragmented writing that doesn't suggest play; rather it suggests an emphasis on failure which indexes the inexpressible as such. By and large this and many other readings found in Friedlander's book are influenced by Adorno's negative reading of popular culture as well as Francois Lyotard's reproduction of that reading. In this essay, I would like to argue that the work of Raymond Federman proposes an alternative.

Federman: "Improvis(ing) in Sad Laughter"

Federman, in his recent novel Aunt Rachel's Fur, provides us with a phrase that articulates the alternative: "sad laughter". In the beginning of the book, the author tells us that this is a novel that is "improvised in sad laughter". Insofar as one of the main threads of the novel is based on the return of the author, a French-Jew, and survivor of the Holocaust, from America to Paris, there is a connection between this "improvisation in sad laughter" and the journey between the two continents. Furthermore, the word "improvisation" suggests Jazz, a form of music that the author writes of in relation to America. I would like to suggest that improvisation and Jazz are terms that describe the style of the writing in this novel with its digressions and hesitations, with its exaggerations and its play, with its extended solos, which, at times become sentimental ballads. The aspect of sadness comes out, most notably, when the author engages his memory and gets sentimental about what was lost. The most important thing to keep in mind about this sadness is that it is not an essential trait of the person, not an absolute, rather, it is improvised. There is something in this sadness that is fictioned (or as Federman might say "laughed"). The storyteller of Aunt Rachel's Fur shows us how it is impossible to recall the past without being fictional. The storyteller in this novel tells us that he has left France and has learned how to speak and write in a foreign language (English). His French, and by extension his memory are affected by this insofar as he has not just acquired a new language, he has acquired a different way of thinking. When he returns to France, his speech as well as his attitude have become a hybrid of French and English. Furthermore, his way of conveying the past has also been altered, and this is reflected in his playful weaving of the past and the present. This is where the element of fiction comes in with respect to his past. As we saw above, some critics associate American culture, thought and language with a form of forgetfulness. However, Federman shows us that this forgetfulness, which is associated with a fictional form of play, is merely a bias. Rather than reiterate what Adorno, Lytoard, Baudrillard, Friedlander, and Lanzman have associated with American aesthetics, Federman shows us that play can work together with memory. The effect of such a strategy is to supplement authentic memory with quasi memory (not inauthentic memory, its binary twin). When compared to Federman's work, we can see that the problem with Adorno Inc.'s way of thinking is that it is obsessed with absolutes (even if they are negative absolutes such as the un-presentable which destroys other absolutes such as beauty, representation, mimetic truth, etc). Adorno inc. assumes that memory loss will be absolute unless it is countered by art or fact that emphasizes either the unrepresentable or the unthinkable. Federman shows us something else. He shows us that fiction is not the opposite of memory but is inseparable from it. He shows us that facts are improvised. This is the American element that he brings back to France to share with his French listener. The fact that it is sad, however, gives its due to a European sense of loss, memory, and the inexpressible. None the less, even this sadness is improvised; it is not essentially European, just as it is not essentially American. This improvisation teaches us that it is fruitful to focus on the oscillation between America and Europe, an oscillation between two forms of aesthetics, rather than privileging one over the other. It suggests that post-modernity (the figure of America: laughter) not be read simply as an erasure of memory or a trivialization of terror. Rather, the term "sad laughter" suggests that a new aesthetic can be employed with respect to the Holocaust or to disaster in general. The new aesthetic oscillates between two continents, between mourning and laughter. Unlike critics who have outlawed any form of "Americanization", Federman shows us that an American aesthetic of play can take part in the meditation on disaster and survival. In fact, most recently critics are calling for a new approach to the Holocaust that incorporates a form of play (a comic or naive aspect). However, these critics could learn a lot from Federman insofar as the examples they have chosen for a new approach to the Holocaust still fall within the binary of disaster and comedy, whereas Federman's work oscillates between two different categories: memory and play. Furthermore, he incorporates the notion of traveling between continents rather than simply between categories such as melancholy and comedy. This gesture allows us to think about how genres are not simply a priori categories, but are employed differently by different popular cultures (and this gives these categories a more relativistic and playful aspect). In his book, The Twofold Vibration Federman incorporates different genres such as science fiction, detective fiction, and travel fiction. Like Aunt Rachel's Fur this book takes place in Europe (in general, though not France in particular). However, unlike Aunt Rachel's Fur, which doesn't focus so much on the journey to and around Europe, The Twofold Vibration does. In the novel, the journey and the travels of the "old man" (the main character: another name for Federman) around Europe are the subject of fictional play. To begin with, the "old man" gets to Europe through fictioning, through a pastiche of a 70s genre: the protest film. In the book, he accidentally stumbles into a protest at a college, meets a Jane Fonda type of character (an actress and a political activist) and ends up leaving the country with her in a mad dash out of America. This excessive departure is similar to the departure made by one of the main character's in Antonini's Zabriske Point insofar as the main character escapes from the world of protest and technology to the desert, to another world where he meets a woman with a similar desire to escape. The pastiche of the journey carries on in Europe where "the old man" goes on a mad journey through Europe to casinos winning and losing money, having sex with strangers etc. This goes on until he arrives in Germany where he loses everything and becomes reflective of his past. He ends up going to a re-modeled concentration camp/museum where he bumps into a Jewish American film producer who wants to make a movie on the Holocaust. This brings out two aspects of the post-Holocaust world. One aspect is the sterilized and touristy reconstruction of the past that the "old man" finds at the camps. Another aspect is the fictional basis of memory that is brought into Europe and exported to America via Hollywood. Unlike a modernist response which would look at this in a negative way, Federman doesn't deplore this. Rather, his book recognizes that such fictioning is also a part of his journey back to the camps were he lost his family. Rather than denying the fictional aspect of reality, he plays with it and accepts it as a part of his own identity which he constructs, deconstructs and reconstructs through it. The genre's that got "the old man" to Europe are quite American in flavor since they espouse a form of playful rootlessness. This playfulness allows for an American relationship to a European

continent and disaster, as well as a traumatic past. This genre is also countered by two other genres. One genre is a detective genre in which the narrator and his two cohorts (friends of Federman) by the names of Moinous
and Namredef (inversions of the name and personality of Federman:
Me/Us and Federman spelled backwards) try to figure out why Federman is
being deported to another planet (space colony) via space ship. They provide their findings to the narrator who tries to put the pieces together. The
deportation to the space colony draws from the genre of science fiction and
at the same time hints at another genre, the genre of Holocaust fiction and
film (the often sited/filmed scene of the deportation to the camps).
However, Federman plays with the position of the Holocaust witness who
knows nothing about where they are going since nothing about the destination, the colony, is known. One of the questions we are left with, and the
narrators are left with, at the end of the story is what Federman did to
deserve such a thing. This is the same question that Elie Wiesel poses in his
book Night; however, it is framed in a different manner over here. In The
Twofold Vibration the question is not theological. Rather, it is a question
of fictional knowledge. What is most intriguing about this search for fictional knowledge is that the "old man", who is being deported leaves us
with the question as to whether or not he (not just the reader) knows why.
Seemingly he doesn't, if he did it could be tragic. However, the fact that he
doesn't know anything about his destination would detract from such
knowledge. In addition to this, the fact that he doesn't know isn't something to lament since he suffers from the same obliviousness about his destination. In addition to this, when the time comes to be deported he misses
the ship. This implies a few things. First of all, it implies that the investigation to find out why he is guilty was (to some extent) fruitless since its
object was not attained and on the other hand it implies that the "old man"
regrets (in some sense) that he was not deported. To say that this is what he
felt about the Holocaust would be a far stretch, given that we don't know
what kind of world he is being deported to, if it is similar to the camps. The
fact that he wants to go may imply that it offers something better. The last

scenes, if anything, incorporate a form of slapstick and melancholy. The last words of the "old man" are "What About Me?" The narrator notes that these words express a kind of despair. At that moment a man in a cart tells everybody to clear out. The scene is like the end of a ball game or concert. The narrator then tells us that this detail was the last detail he received from Moinous and Namredef. At this point, he reflects on how he is sitting in front of a blank piece of paper, and how everything that came before this was included in a memory of what he was told. This implies that his memory is a memory of other people's memories. The blank sheet of paper indicates that the task before him is already three times removed. However, there is another remnant, a twofold vibration in his head, which came from these two characters: one who embellished in fiction the other who had a problem with recording facts clearly. The echo of these two voices is an "echo" of two forms of writing, a type of play that has constructed the "old man" in terms of many genres that relate the past to a quasi-fictional present. The echo doesn't leave us with a tragic moment of loss for the narrator. It leaves us (the addressee of the letter To Whom it May Concern) as well as the writer with the difficult task of reproducing and recording on paper the oscillation/play/improvisation between two modes of remembrance one fictional and the other quasi fictional (somewhere between America and Europe). This form of play is not just a play between genres it is a form of play that is incorporated into his writing style. As we mentioned above Federman's notion of play is incorporated into his writing style, which "improvises in sad laughter". One of the main problems with the critics mentioned above is that these critics haven't given thought to how a writing style can effect how we reconstruct the Holocaust in the present. Rather than thinking about how one can approach the Holocaust by way of a number of fictional detours and writing styles, they end up dwelling on binaries/genres such as tragedy and comedy rather than between them. As a result we are returned to an apprehension of the holocaust or post-holocaust world as tragic-comic. Federman's work doesn't do that. Rather it situates the Holocaust into a text (or a set of texts) that is at one and the same time critical of its articulations, mournful, and playful. This text doesn't bring out the human comedy or the tragedy of loss; it plays with these notions insofar as it gives neither a complete treatment. Federman's gesture is called for not just because Holocaust writing thus far has been obsessed with the sublime and with fragmentation. It is called for because our mediatized world is permeated by an ongoing oscillation between laughter and mourning, between fact and fiction. In such a world, the reconstruction of the Holocaust in terms of oscillation is relevant insofar as making it either melancholic or comic would just re-instate absolutes which no longer exist. Federman shows us that an improvisation in sad laughter is the best way to detour the struggle with absolutes (a struggle between Europe and America mentioned above). His work takes into consideration the fact that the "society of the spectacle" can never do a complete form of mourning. Our society cannot escape the strange fictional fabric that has entered our homes and our society through a wide array of media ranging from televisions, cinemas, best sellers and computers to billboards and magazine advertisements. But even if it were to escape via modernist fiction or art, it would be an act of self-deception.

Raymond Federman: Un Américain bientôt à Paris?

Jan Baetens

Raymond Federman (°1929) est probablement le plus américain des écrivains français. Il l'est toutefois de manière un peu différente de ce que l'on entend généralement par cette expression. En effet, Federman n'est pas un auteur français qui "imite" ou "importe" des modèles américains, ni un auteur qui s'est exilé aux Etats-Unis, moins encore un auteur qui rentre au pays après de longues aventures outre-Atlantique. Il est au contraire un écrivain qui est passé à la langue américaine, sans pour autant avoir pu se débarrasser du français (auteur bilingue à l'instar de son grand ami Beckett, il écrit français en américain, et vice versa). De la même façon il est non moins un écrivain qui, tout en plongeant au coeur de la culture américaine, n'arrive jamais à oublier sa "francité" (chose que la France lui rend bien mal, puisque seuls deux de ses nombreux romans y ont paru, le premier, Amer Eldorado (éd. Stock, 1972, republié aux éd. Weidler en 2001) il y a longtemps déjà, le second, La fourrure de ma tante Rachel (éd. Circé, 1996), dans un silence retentissant).

L'oeuvre de Federman comprend à ce jour une bonne vingtaine de livres. Les uns sont "académiques", dont une thèse sur Beckett et un livre d'essais qui a beaucoup contribué, naguère et jadis, au succès de Ricardou dans les universités américaines; les autres sont de "fiction", ou plutôt d'"autofiction", dont le trilingue La voix dans le cabinet de ebarras, livre-culte dans

183

les pays anglosaxons et germaniques). La diversité de cette production n'a d'égale que son extrême cohésion. Federman, en effet, revient toujours, mais toujours d'une autre façon, sur un certain nombre de thèmes et de hantises, dont le centre (vide) est la disparition de ses parents et de ses soeurs dans les camps, et partant sa propre survie problématique. Les événements de 1942 sont comme la "basse continue" de cette oeuvre tragique, qui n'a pourtant rien de larmoyant: admirateur inconditionnel de Céline et convaincu que la seule vie qui vaille est celle qu'on s'invente au fil de la plume, Federman est aussi un auteur extrêmement drôle, qui sait comment "travailler" son public (directeur d'un programme d'ateliers d'écriture à l'université de Buffalo, il a pu rôder son écriture au contact avec le public vivant lors de ses mille et une lectures-performances, dont plusieurs sont disponibles sur cd-rom).

Coup sur coup paraissent ce printemps 3 ou 4 nouveautés. Fait partie de ce lot la version anglaise de Tante Rachel (éd. FC2, Normal/Tallahasse), véritable encyclopédie de la postmodernité américaine, avec un index qui rappelle un peu celui qu'on trouve à la fin de Quel petit vélo…de Perec, auteur dont il est urgent d'enfin le rapprocher et dont Federman représente une variante "oralisée", mais aussi Loose shoes (éd. Weidler, 2001), oeuvre plurilingue où se distinguent littéralement les innombrables facettes de l'écriture de Federman.

Loose shoes se présente comme une sorte de journal tenu en 1999, année durant laquelle l'auteur s'est obligé à écrire un texte par jour. Le présent recueil offre un large échantillon de ces courts textes, qui font coïncider l'énergie et l'agilité extrêmes d'une écriture sur le vif d'une part et la maturité et le métier venus d'une carrière de plus d'un demi-siècle d'autre part. L'urgence s'y lit partout, comme par exemple dans le compte rendu d'une séance de Schindlers List, rédigé dans le noir au cours même de la projection. En même temps le recul nécessaire à la littérature y est non moins manifeste, tant au niveau du détail de certains fragments (le court texte "Eating books" circulait déjà sur le net et en revue -on le trouve dans le numéro 5 de la revue Formules- et s'est imposé en un minimum de temps comme un classique contemporain) qu'à hauteur de l'ensemble du volume (l'auteur multiplie les jeux typographiques, de manière à refaire ce qu'il avait déjà effectué avec tant de succès dans d'autres de ses livres, où la maquette change d'une page à l'autre).

L'image de Federman qui transparaît dans Loose shoes ne révolutionne pas l'idée que ses lecteurs fidèles avaient déjà de lui. Le Federman goguenard, écrivain juif incertain de son identité, auteur français ayant réussi aux Etats-Unis mais douloureusement coupé de Paris, "performer" exceptionnel qui va jusqu'à imaginer de nouveaux jeux télévisisés, théoricien de la modernité soucieux de lisibilité et toujours en quête de la chair, de coeur, du rire de son lecteur trop absent, inventeur amoureux de toutes les langues pourvu qu'elles permettent d'échapper au livresque et ouvrier inlassable de la plume, toutes ces facettes se retrouvent ici dans un cocktail souvent hilarant, mais parfois aussi grave, et presque toujours d'une grande duplicité: à la limite de plusieurs régimes, à cheval sur les humeurs, écartelé entre les styles et les langues, sautant de la bonne blague à la théorie pour aboutir à l'élégie. S'il est plus d'une façon de lire Federman, le moyen le plus simple de s'y lancer est sans aucun doute de commencer par ce Loose shoes, petit Federman portatif qui nous fait faire le tour du monde.

Raymond FEDERMAN, Loose Shoes, Berlin, Weidler Verlag (Lübecker Strasse 8,
    D-10599 Berlin)

MEMO FROM MY ID TO MY EGO

DANIEL BORZUTZKY

"One never knows where one's thoughts originate, and when these thoughts merge with those of others, where one's language begins and where it converges with that of others within the dialogue all of us entertain with ourselves, and with others."

Raymond Federman

Memo From My Ego To My Id

It's all journalese with you, nothing but posterior essences and gussied up shim-shams that whirl me around like a joystick.

But I digress, or perhaps I inevitably move foreword. For engulfed in our drama is the drama of never knowing what the drama will actually be. Am I slave or slave-driver, poet or parasite? I'm not kidding when I tell you I'm a cold and odious evening.

But don't reason me into stupor, not this time my cucumber. A couple more innings of no-run baseball and I'll get you with a pre-coital lick of your tender little fingers. You may be lovely with your chameleon eyeballs. But I have seen your toes. I have sucked them and sniffed them and I know they are as ugly as mushrooms.

You may squeeze my buttocks all you want. You may dabble me with lotion and tickle me into submission but an orgasm you will not inspire.

A fantasy, perhaps, but what am I supposed to expect? You don't talk. You don't listen. All you do is flash your fleshly little palms and your lips that are rough and crunchy.

186

Your name is unknown and for the moment I find this ignorance blissful.

Of course, I may be wrong on this account. For what little power I have withers away with each tweet you muster. In your arms I am sworn to silence. But don't expect me to paw and blubber each time you give a nickel to a hobo. I've had enough of your so-called niceties. I've had enough of these gruesome dingdongs that swell on the skin of my haunches.

I'm a sissy-footed willow or a pig with a glorious belly.

I suffer from amnesia and I'm certain you don't even know me.

Memo From My Ego To My Superego

Yes, you are correct about my refusal to accept your thesis that the space between us overlaps in a way that is extralinguistic, but I don't believe that, as you suggest, this is merely a case of "Circular Regurgitation," by which I think you mean that it is both the fluid and the familial connotations of blood which magnify the dimensions of a body. For while you are correct to say our collective history is like a comic strip endlessly devoted to the life-cycles of spinning and tactile characters who give didactic monologues about the chemical possibilities in the everyday denial of speech, you are wrong to suggest that I seek to destroy the varying levels of invisible architecture which oblige us to decipher and interpret the erratic interferences caused by, among other things, the rampant domination of desire. For if our skin is filled with concave indentations caused by words that have tried to break through it, then nailed into our heart is an anchorless vector rooted not only in rhetoric but in rotation, a kind of empty nostalgia that sizzles and drips like an undercooked tenderloin steak.

Like the time you asked me to blindfold you in a maze of mirrors so you could fully apprehend the "form and nature of things." Were you not already aware that as a signifier of time motion can only produce an artificial ascendance which rises and rises until our gestures and mechanisms dissolve into an awkward state of ambivalence?

I accept your apology, and hope you will accept mine. But I resent your comment that "one need only look behind the sand dunes to find my motivation." For whether you admit it or not I am certain you know we both participate in this simulation of interest as duty, which withers at one end and, at the other, blossoms into a passively deceptive fruition.

FEDERMAN: THE TRUTH BEHIND THE NAME

MARK AXELROD

Federman loves his name, if only because it's another word that he can play with. Federman loves to play. He plays with anything he can get his hands on. If there is nothing there, then he plays with his name. When someone notes that it is a strange family name for a Frenchman, he points out that his father's family was Russian. That's what he says, but he's not sure himself if it's correct, because Federman often confuses Poland with Russia in his mind and in his writing. Federman never studied geography when he was in school, he never got to that subject, he was forced out of school, for reasons which Federman is always reluctant to elucidate.

THE TRUTH TO THIS TALE OF FEDERMAN'S FORCED FLIGHT FROM SCHOOL IS THE FOLLOWING...FEDERMAN'S STATEMENT REGARDING GEOGRAPHY IS FALLACIOUS. IN FACT, FEDERMAN FIRMLY FELT THAT REGARDLESS OF WHAT THE GEOGRAPHY BOOKS FEATURED, POLAND AND RUSSIA WERE FORMERLY UNIFIED AS THE LITTLE KNOWN COUNTRY OF FEDERMANIA. FEDERMAN HAD EVIDENCE TO FOSTER THAT CLAIM AND FROTHED AND FESTERED WHENEVER AUTHORITY FIGURES FELT OTHERWISE; HOWEVER, THE SCHOOL AUTHORITIES, PERFERVID IN THEIR BELIEF THAT SUCH A COUNTRY DID NOT EXIST, CHOSE TO FORCE FEDERMAN FROM SCHOOL RATHER THAN HAVE

FEDERMAN FORCE THE NOTION ON FECKLESS SCHOOL CHILDREN THAT FEDERMANIA DID EXIST.

Federman never seems to notice that Federman is a pretty strange name for a Russian, too. [How ignorant can a guy be?]

OF COURSE, THE ORIGINAL NAME WAS FEDERMANOFF AND WAS ALTERED SO AS NOT TO SOUND TOO JEWISH.

The name Federman is a polylingual pun. Feder is German for feder, and so Federmann would be featherman—der Mensch von Feder. In French, since Federman often speaks to himself in French, feather is plume which, of course, is also pen or porteplume—but that's too obvious.

FEATHER IS ALSO QUILL WHICH SHOULD NOT BE CON-FUSED WITH THE MOVIE BY THE SAME NAME WHICH WOULD PUT FEDERMAN IN YET ANOTHER CATEGORY.

By a rather roundabout linguistic route [known as the leap-frog technique]

Federman becomes the penman [Homme de Plume for those who know him in French, Hombre della Pluma for those who know him only in Spanish]. The Penman, a very joycean name which contains within it Ray's vocation as a kind of etymological guarantee.

WHAT FEDERMAN FAILS TO ACKNOWLEDGE IS THAT FED-ERMAN DOESN'T USE A PEN. HE USES A COMPUTER.

No, rather, a very beckettian name, because of the cringing scatological humor that surfaces from this transatlantic leap into the reverse of farness, as Old Sam Beckett once put it. Fart-erman, as some of his friends call him.

WHEN BECKETT WAS ONCE ASKED IF HE KNEW FEDER-MAN HE REPLIED: NO SYMBOLS WHERE NONE INTENDED.

Federman: a name, a pun that contains within it not only Ray's voca-tion, but Moinous' misfortunes, too. Moinous: the secret name Federman gives himself when he pretends to be a spy, or a musketeer, or a paratrooper, or a jazz musician, or a French lover, or an experimental writer. Yes, that's what Federman sometimes calls himself, Moinous, and if you ask him, who's Moinous? he tells you: oh just a word, a name I made up. It means, me/us. By the way, it's also the name on the license plate of his wife's car. His wife, when people ask her, who's Moinous? always answers: Moinous! That's the guy who bought the car. Moinous is ominous—o-m-i-n-o-u-s!

MOINOUS IS AN ALIAS. IT HAS NOTHING TO DO WITH WHATEVER HE CONTENDS IT IS. AND THIS IS THE MOST REVEALING STATEMENT FEDERMAN HAS MADE TO DATE DEALING WITH HIS ALLEGED TIES TO ESPIONAGE. THOUGH HE SAYS MOINOUS IS A SECRET NAME WHEN HE "PRETENDS TO BE A SPY" IT HAS RECENTLY BEEN DISCOV-ERED FROM CIA DOCUMENTS THAT, IN FACT, FEDERMAN IS A SPY AND A SPY FOR THE MOSSAD. FURTHERMORE, MOINOUS IS NOT JUST A MADE UP NAME, BUT IS HIS HAN-DLE. AS ANY SPY WORTH HIS WEIGHT IN SPY NUGGETS WILL TELL YOU, THE BEST FICTION IS THE TRUTH. AH! THAT FEDERMAN IS A SLY ONE.

But the feder/feather/plume/[et al] also has about it a sense of flight, of voltigement and lightness, a birdlike quality, of escape, of escapade, of dis-appearance and reappearance within itself, of being both present and absent at the same time. Of being here and elsewhere and everywhere. Now and always and forever.

THIS STATEMENT, OF COURSE, PROVES, WITHOUT A DOUBT, FEDERMAN'S SECOND SELF IS DEVOTED ENTIRELY TO ESPIONAGE. WHAT ELSE COULD HE MEAN BY "OF BEING HERE AND ELSEWHERE AND EVERYWHERE?"

>From Federman to Namredef [another name Federman is fond of using] there is but a stroke of the pen—la plume—yes, a little reverse twist of the wrist, and: voilà, Federman is here and there at the same time, laughing madly because, once again, Federman succeeded in doing a little linguistic sommersault in his own name. A great leap-frog over the Atlantic. That's how much Federman loves his name.

YES, BUT WHAT FEDERMAN FAILS TO TELL YOU IS THAT THE NAME NAMREDEF IS NOT JUST AN ANAGRAM OF HIS NAME, BUT IS YIDDISH FOR, "I SPY." WHERE DOES THAT COME FROM? THE MOST ENLIGHTENED 16TH CENTURY RABBI MOSHE BEN FRAILECH WAS EXTREMELY GOOD FRIENDS WITH THE VERY INFLUENTIAL, CIDE HAMETE BENEGELI. FRAILECH WAS VERY FOND OF LITERATURE AND WAS ASKED TO DELIVER A PAPER AT A LITERARY CONFERENCE IN TOLEDO, BUT FRAILECH HAD LITTLE TIME TO PUT TOGETHER A PAPER FOR THE CONFERENCE SINCE IT WAS NEAR THE TIME OF PURIM AND HE WAS UP TO HIS EARS IN BAKING HAMANTASHAN. SO HE ENLISTED THE HELP OF BENEGELI TO SPY ON A PARTICULAR WRITER KNOWN TO BENEGELI AND WHO, LITTLE KNOWN AT THE TIME, WAS WORKING ON A PAPER FOR THE SAME CONFERENCE. TO MAKE A LONG STORY SHORT, BENEGELI STOLE THE MANUSCRIPT AND GAVE IT TO FRAILECH, BUT FRAILECH COULD NOT, IN GOOD CONSCIENCE, GIVE THE PAPER IN HIS OWN NAME AND INSTEAD USED THE NAME NAMREDEF. BENEGELI SAID IT WAS TOO OBVIOUS TO USE NAMREDEF SINCE EVERYONE WOULD KNOW WHAT IT MEANT. THE TWO OF THEM THOUGHT LONG AND HARD FOR ANOTHER NAME TO USE AND IT WAS BENEGELI WHO FINALLY SUGGESTED, "HOW ABOUT FEDERMAN?" IT WAS DECIDED.

He would do anything for it, anything to preserve it, even if it means breaking his neck doing linguistic somersaults within his own name. That's how flexible the name Federman is.

THIS STATEMENT ONLY CORROBORATES THE PREVIOUS STORY.

After all, Federman will tell you, my father was not only a Russian, he was a Russian Cossack. Perhaps the only Jewish Cossack in the entire

Russian Cossack Army ever. And in Russian they called my father: Dimitri Fyodor Konstantin Ivanovitch Federmanov.

ABSOLUTELY FALSE. A CHECK OF THE RUSSIAN RECORDS OF THE TIME INDICATES THERE WERE NUMEROUS JEWISH COSSACKS NOT THE LEAST OF WHICH WERE SASHA RUDIN, ALEKSANDR RASKOLNIKOV, DIMITRY BAZAROV, AND MARKOV AKSELRADOV ALL OF WHOM WERE EITHER MODELS FOR CHARACTERS FROM RUSSIAN NOVELS OR FOR POSTMODERN ONES.

And he will even tell you that one of his ancestors was nobility, the Baron Nicolas von Federman, a 16th century German Conquistador, who died an unfortunate death by drowning while paddling a rowboat down some infested river in the jungles of the New World—a rowboat full of treasures, gold, precious stones, ancient statues, bibelots, even money, or whatever rare currency was used for money in those days. Yes, Federman's glorious ancestor, Le Baron Nicolas de Féderman, as he was known in France when he resided at the court of Henry the Fourth, before he sailed to the New World in conquest of fame and fortune, drowned rowing down some infested river in the jungles of some yet unnamed country. That's what Federman will tell you, if you ask him where the name Federman comes from, and what it means.

THIS TOO IS PATENTLY FALSE. REALLY SOMEWHAT OF AN EMBARRASSING EMBELLISHMENT. BARON NICOLAS FEDERMAN DID IN FACT EXIST; HOWEVER, HE DID NOT ROW DOWN SOME INFESTED JUNGLE IN THE NEW WORLD. HE THOUGHT HE WAS ROWING HIS BOAT DOWN SOME INFESTED JUNGLE IN THE NEW WORLD, BUT, IN FACT, HE WAS NOT.

IN FACT, HE THOUGHT HE WAS HEADED INTO THE MOUTH OF THE AMAZON WHEN HE THOUGHT HE HAD REACHED THE BRAZILIAN CITY BELÉM. IN FACT, THE BARON WAS FAR-SIGHTED AND WHAT HE THOUGHT READ

BELEM WAS ACTUALLY BUFFALO AND THE MOUTH OF THE AMAZAON WAS ACTUALLY THE ERIE CANAL THAT LOOKED LIKE SOME INFESTED JUNGLE IN THE NEW WORLD. FEDERMAN, OF COURSE, WILL DENY THAT EVEN THOUGH HE AND HIS FAMILY SPENT MANY A LONG WINTER IN BUFFALO. HOW DOES HE ACCOUNT FOR THAT?

His wife [whose name shall not be investigated today, a name loaded with beautiful possibilities—Hubscher was her maiden name, which means more beautiful] always tells him that Federman does not mean Penman, that it has nothing to do with la plume and with his vocation as a writer, that simply the name came from what his ancestors were doing back in the old country. And what were Federman's ancestors doing in the old country? his wife explains, plucking chicken feathers in the steppes of Russian or the Ghettos of Poland. That's all you are, his lovely wife always tells him [not sarcastically, not meanly, no, on the contrary, gently, lovingly, affectionately]—a featherplucker.

HIS WIFE IS ABSOLUTELY CORRECT ON THAT COUNT. RECORDS INDICATE THAT FEATHER PLUCKERS WERE ONE OF THE FEW OCCUPATIONS THAT WAS ALLOWED TO JEWS AT THE TIME. OTHER OCCUPATIONS INCLUDED: FEATHER EATERS, FEATHER STUFFERS, FEATHER WEAVERS, FEATHER SHAVERS, IN SHORT, ANYTHING THAT HAD TO DO WITH FEATHERS.

But Federman gets mad when people call him a featherplucker. I would prefer to be a chickenfucker than a featherplucker, he shouts at them. And he really means it.

OF COURSE FEDERMAN WOULD RATHER BE CALLED A CHICKENFUCKER BECAUSE IN THOSE DAYS CHICKENFUCKERS HAD A MUCH HIGHER STATUS THAN FEATHERPLUCKERS AND WERE PAID HANDSOMELY FOR THEIR CHICKENFUCKING SKILLS. AS A MATTER OF FACT, CHICKENFUCKERS WERE

OFTEN TENURED WHEREAS FEATHERPLUCKERS WERE MERELY EMPLOYED ON A RENEWABLE CONTRACT.

That's how much Federman loves his name. Federman would kill the guy who would fuck with his name. He gets so mad, when in the German Press [where his name often appears because of his reputation as a famous Schriftsteller—yes, Federman is a famous writer in Germany] they spell Federman, Federmann, with an extra n. That really bugs him to be so easily assimilated into German Kultur—with a K.

WHAT FEDERMAN FAILS TO TELL YOU IS THAT THERE IS ANOTHER WRITER IN GERMANY WITH THE NAME FEDERMANN; HOWEVER, FEDERMAN THINKS THAT FEDERMANN IS ACTUALLY FEDERMAN. BECKETT, TOO, ALWAYS COMPLAINED THAT HE TIRED OF PEOPLE WRITING HIS NAME AS BECKET AS DID T.S. ELIOT WHO ALWAYS COMPLAINED THEY WERE CALLING HIM GEORGE. LIKE BECKETT AND ELIOT, FEDERMAN HAS CONFUSED THE SITUATION. SAD, BUT TRUE.

Federman is proud of his name. Even if you offered him a million dollars, ten million dollars, he would not sell you his name, he would not change it. That's how proud he is of his name. How much he respects his own name. But Federman is worried, because he is the last Federman in his family. The end of the line. All the other Federmans have already changed tense. And Federman has no son by that name.

THIS IS FALSE. AN FBI WIRE TAP INDICATES THAT DONALD TRUMP DID, IN FACT, CONTACT FEDERMAN AND OFFERED HIM ONE MILLION DOLLARS TO USE HIS NAME. ACCORDING TO THOSE RECORDS, TRUMP FELT THAT THE NAME FEDERMAN CASINOS WOULD BRING IN MORE PLAYERS THAN WOULD THE NAME TRUMP CASINOS. FEDERMAN SAID HE'D TAKE THE MILLION, BUT WANTED A PERCENTAGE OF THE PROFITS WHICH WOULD, IN FACT, NET HIM MUCH MORE THAN THE TEN MILLION HE'S ALLUDED TO.

ALWAYS WILLING TO SQUEEZE A NICKEL UNTIL THE BUF-
FALO SHIT, TRUMP REFUSED TO GIVE HIM A PERCENTAGE
AND SO FEDERMAN RETAINED THE NAME.

Ah, but he has a daughter, and his daughter—the kid as he calls her, or
puce, or pipsy, or mademoiselle Federman, or Professor Federman [yes,
Professor Federman, his lovely daughter is also a professor, but that's
another story which has nothing to do, or perhaps has everything to do
with the name Federman]—even though she is now old enough to tell
Federman what she thinks of him, his daughter is so proud of the name
Federman, that she will never, never, she says, even if she were to be tor-
tured, change that name, or assume another name. She is all Federman.
That is why Federman loves his name and loves those who carry that
name.

AND THAT IS VERY VERY TRUE AND THOSE WHO LOVE
FEDERMAN'S NAME ALSO LOVE FEDERMAN SINCE WHAT
FEDERMAN FAILS TO TELL YOU IS THAT MANY MANY PEO-
PLE ARE DEVOTED TO FEDERMAN FOR REASONS FEDER-
MAN DOES NOT FELUCIDATE SINCE FEDERMAN IS AND
ALWAYS HAS BEEN WILLING TO HELP FOSTER AND FÊTE
OTHER FICTIONEERS. IT IS FOR THAT REASON AMONG
MANY OTHERS THAT WE SHOULD OFFER THIS HOMAGE TO
FEDERMAN.

THE LINE

RAYMOND FEDERMAN

T
H
E
L
I
N
E
at first
one
could
stand
in line
almost
anywher
e
people
didn't
really
mind
too
much
if one

cut in
front of
them
though
there
were
always
some
who
objected
when
overtake
n
particula
rly
those
who
were
under
the
impressi
on
that
they
stood
near the
head
of
the
line
but
even

these
people
did
not
object
too
veheme
ntly
since
the
line
was
not
moving
very
fast
or
for
that
matter
often
hardly
moved
for
long
periods
of
time
and
since
no
one

could
tell
where
it
was
going
but
people
waited
anyway
calmly
patiently
and
good-
humored
ly
as
more
were
coming
all
the
time
in
endless
processi
ons
after
all
it
was
a

good
line
a
pleasant
line
a
decent
line
even
though
in
places
people
allowed
gaps
holes
in
it
loosenes
s
and
laxness
as
the
line
wove
stretche
d
meander
ed
out
of

sight

thicker

here

thinner

there

single

or

double

file

here

triple

even

quadrupl

e

there

in fact

in

various

places

it

was

more

like

a

social

gatherin

g

or

a

human

press

as

people
crowded
around
in
circles
as if
preparin
g for a
town
meeting
or a
debate
or
getting
set for a
choir or
a game
after all
with
such
little
progress
forward
and so
much
time
to
wait
people
moved
about
the line

up and
down in
and out
casually
and
freely
stopping
along
the way
to chat
with
neighbor
s old
friends
or
distant
relatives
cousins
or
uncles
they had
not seen
in years
all sorts
of
people
with
whom
one had
had
dealings
or

commer

ce as the

saying

goes

before

joining

the line

but also

to chat

with the

new

acquaint

ances

made in

line as

one

moved

about

leisurely

from

place to

place up

and

down

for

indeed

the mere

fact of

being in

line

seemed to

create a

friendly
atmosph
ere a
sense of
sincere
congeni
ality and
solidarit
y among
the
liners as
they
were
called
therefor
e those
who
made a
fuss
when
someone
squeeze
d past
them
would
be
sneered
at and
even
booed
by those
being

by-
passed
since the
line was
endless
in both
direction
s and it
was
impossi
ble to
determin
e where it
started
where it
originate
d and
where it
ended
therefor
e it was
ridiculo
us on
the part
of
anyone
to want
to claim
a
legitimat
e place
in it or

insist on
any
priority
of
standing
for what
would
be the
point of
declarin
g
oneself
ahead of
anyone
else that
would
certainly
be futile
yet some
people
kept
moving
up the
line
overtaki
ng
others
squeezin
g in
front of
them or
by-

passing
them but
without
any
hurry or
sense of
urgency
these
people
were
merely
moving
up or
giving
themsel
ves the
impressi
on of
moving
from
one
place in
line to
another
nearer to
the head
simply
for the
sake of
moving
forward
without

any
specific
reason
or
purpose
hoping
perhaps
that
eventual
ly they
would
be first
in line a
vain
hope of
course
because
the more
people
there
were
moving
up the
line the
further
away the
head
would
be for
obviousl
y as
these

people
squeeze
d in
front of
others
the
further
away the
head
would
be
pushed
so that
in fact a
step
forward
in this
case
really
meant
two
steps
backwar
d for
while
certain
people
moved
forward
others
moved
in the

opposite
direction
falling
back in
line so
to speak
away
from the
head
because
frankly
they did
not care
where
they
stood in
the line
and so
they
would
loaf
about or
mill
around
in
groups
in and
out of
the main
stream
forming
circles

to gossip
or tell
jokes or
listen to
the
stories
which
were
circulati
ng up
and
down
the line
funny
stories
about
what
people
did in
line to
pass the
time or
how
others
had
forgotte
n why
they
came to
the line
and yet
continue

d to wait
simply
because
they had
nothing
else to
do or
how
some
people
truly
believed
they
knew
where
the line
was
going
groups
could be
seen
standing
around
laughing
at
the
curious
objects
people
had
brought
with

them to
the line
for
instance
the bed
on
wheels
on
which
an old
man was
lying in
a
nightgo
wn and
which
he
pushed
along
with a
cane as
if
paddling
a canoe
just to
keep up
with the
line or
the little
desk and
chair
and even

a
calculati
ng
machine
an
accounta
nt kept
lugging
along so
he could
continue
to do his
numbers
as he
waited
in line
ah what
dumb
things
people
do while
waiting
in line
one
could
hear
muttered
all over
but it
was
the
jokes

especiall
y that
attracted
most
attention
and
caused
the
greatest
hilarity
one joke
in
particula
r kept
being
repeated
up and
down
the line
the one
about
the
fellow
who
sees a
funeral
processi
on going
slowly
down
the
street

with two
hearses
and a
gentlem
an
holding
a huge
muzzled
dog in
leash
and
behind
them a
long line
of men
all
wearing
black
the
puzzled
onlooker
asks the
gentlem
an with
the dog
why are
there
two
coffins
in this
ridiculo
us

funeral
oh
replies
the man
with the
dog the
first
coffin is
my
mother-
in-law
and the
second
my wife
ah I see
says the
curious
man
okay but
why the
dog oh
the dog
answers
the
gentlem
an
pulling
at the
leash he
killed
both of
them ah

exclaims
the
inquirer
could I
borrow
your dog
for
a few
hours
well you
better
get in
line
mister
the
mourner
with the
mean
dog
retorts
with a
large
grin on
his face
some of
these
jokes
were not
very
funny
but this
one kept

being
told over
and over
because
it
seemed
so
appropri
ate to
the
situation
though
some
people
claimed
they had
heard it
before
probably
those
who had
been in
the line
from the
beginnin
g and
heard
that joke
when
they first
arrived
for it

was said
that the
joke was
as old as
the line
itself
and it
was
indeed a
very old
line
some
people
had been
in the
line
so
long
they
could
not
rememb
er when
they first
joined as
a matter
of fact
the line
had been
going
for such
a long

time that
many
died
while
waiting
and had
to be
buried
on the
spot
special
crews
were
appointe
d to dig
graves
and
perform
the
burial
rites but
there
were
also
happy
occasion
s on the
line for
instance
people
falling
in love

and
getting
married
or
children
being
born or
birthday
s and
annivers
aries
being
celebrat
ed it was
very
interesti
ng to
observe
how the
line not
only
changed
shape
constant
ly but
also
changed
mood
how it
fluctuate
d from
sad to

happy or
vice
versa
and this
as a
result of
the
many
activities
that
were
going on
in the
line so
that it
could be
said that
the line
changed
moods
as often
as it
changed
shape
sometim
es it was
joyful
lively
full of
playfuln
ess and
other

times it
was sad
gloomy
somber
anguishe
d but in
general
the line
was
calm
and
uneventf
ul
simply
moving
along in
its
ordinary
but
disorgan
ized
fashion
becomin
g thinner
here or
thicker
there
and
usually
this
because
someone

had
stopped
to tell a
story or
a joke
and a
crowd
had
gathered
or
elsewher
e
someone
had just
finished
telling a
story or
a joke
and
those
who had
been
listening
were
now
moving
on or
sometim
es if
there
was a
tree or a

wall
along
the way
or some
other
such
natural
or man
made
structure
that cast
a
shadow
on a
sunny
day or
gave a
bit of
protectio
n from
the wind
on a
cold day
or from
the rain
on a
stormy
day then
people
would
gather
under

that tree
or line
up near
that wall
or
huddle
next to
that
structure
and wait
consequ
ently the
line
would
become
thinner
and lax
in that
spot lazy
as it
were for
there
was no
great
urgency
or
unneces
sary
impatien
ce in the
line
even

though
argumen
ts would
sometim
es flare
up about
nothing
in
particula
r and
even
occasion
al fist
fights
for no
apparent
reason
simply
that
someone
's foot
had been
stepped
on and
no
immedia
te
apology
offered
and
quickly
a shove

would
result
followed
by an
even
harder
retaliato
ry shove
and then
a fist
would
strike
someone
‘s ribs or
someone
‘s nose
and for a
few
moment
s there
would
be
turmoil
and
agitation
in the
line until
the
people
around
the
disturber

s would

restore a

semblan

ce of

order

and

calmnes

s with

insistent

pleas of

please

let's

keep the

line

moving

and

graduall

y the

line

would

resume

its

careless

progress

as

casually

as

before

the

disturba

nce

quickly

forgotte

n and

the

disturber

politely

forgiven

in

general

then one

could

say that

it was

not a

bad line

on the

contrary

a good

decent

honest

line

perhaps

a bit too

chaotic

but

nonethel

ess

adequate

a line to

which

people

could

come

without
apprehe
nsion
and once
in line
without
having
to
complai
n too
much
about
being
stuck
there for
the main
concern
in line
was
civility
and
generosi
ty many
had
come to
the line
quite
unprepar
ed not
having
anticipat
ed the

fact that
it would
be a
slow
endless
process
so that
waiting
would
be in
vain just
as
progress
would
be in
vain
therefor
e they
had not
brought
with
them the
essential
in food
and
clothing
to last or
continue
to last in
line so
that food
drinks

and
clothing
would
be
shared
generous
sly
among
the
liners it
was not
unusual
to see
groups
of
people
who had
never
met
before
eating
from the
same
picnic
basket
or
drinking
from the
same
bottle or
handing
pieces of

clothing
or
blankets
to
people
who
suffered
from the
cold
more
than
others
especiall
y during
the night
after
sundow
n but
particula
r care
was
given to
the
young
and the
very old
for there
were
people
of all
ages in
the line

male
and
female
of
course
and of
all ways
of life
educated
and
illiterate
rich and
poor this
was
apparent
from the
clothes
and
manners
of
certain
people
many
races
and
colors
were
also
present
in line
but
usually

these
people
preferre
d to stay
together
in
bunches
in
remote
parts of
the line
naturally
there
were
also
people
of
different
religious
beliefs
this was
evident
from the
discussi
ons and
argumen
ts
having
to do
with
question
s of

morality
for one
of the
major
concerns
of all the
people
present
was the
morality
of the
line and
when
disagree
ments
occurred
on this
question
the line
would
become
extremel
y
agitated
though it
should
be noted
that not
all
discussi
ons had
to do

with
morality
or
theology
in some
places
people
would
get
together
to sing
songs
in
unison
while in
other
places
someone
would
suddenl
y stand
on a box
to make
a speech
or
deliver a
lecture
and
people
would
gather
around

to listen
to the
speaker
or argue
with him
there
were
always
people
ready to
argue
about
anything
for the
sake of a
good
argumen
t while
others
who did
not care
to listen
to these
improm
ptu
speeches
would
shout
keep
the
damn
line

moving
but since
no one
really
payed
much
attention
to these
dedicate
d liners
they
would
simply
by-pass
those
gatherin
gs and
move on
but
usually
most
people
preferre
d the
one-to-
one
conversa
tion
moving
with the
flow of
the line

two
people
would
casually
talk
about
anything
in
particula
r where
one is
from
what
one does
in life
talk
about
the
family
about
the wife
who
didn't
want to
come to
the line
or talk
about
the
children
or
reminisc

e about
one's
childhoo
d in
other
words
the usual
banalitie
s of life
occasion
ally one
could
hear an
intellect
ual
discussi
on or a
critique
of the
latest
artistic
fad but
it should
be stated
that not
everyon
e in line
was
willing
to
engage
in

conversa
tion
many
preferre
d to
remain
silent
facing
the back
of the
person
in front
extremel
y serious
in their
waiting
quietly
performi
ng their
role as
liners of
course
since the
line
moved
extremel
y slowly
and in
no
apparent
direction
many

people
would
drop out
if not
permane
ntly at
least
tempora
rily
sometim
es
simply
to rest
along
the way
and
watch
the
others in
line go
by or
else to
take a
nap
many
could be
seen
stretche
d on the
ground
soundly
asleep

during
the day
and
naturally
at night
too
however
there
were
some
who
complai
ned all
the time
saying
that it
was
hopeless
that we
will
never
get there
but in
general
most
people
seemed
resigned
to the
slowness
and
indeterm

inacy of
the line
in fact
some
people
who had
previous
experien
ce with
other
lines
said that
in spite
of its
disorgan
ization
and
purposel
essness
this was
a rather
good
pleasant
line
perhaps
the best
line they
had ever
joined
and this
because
of its

casualne
ss and
lack of
regulatio
ns for
indeed
in spite
of its
disorder
this line
was
remarka
bly
smooth
and easy
going
and as
such
acceptab
le to
most
though
many
feared
that one
day
unexpec
tedly out
of the
blue so
to speak
it would

be
announc
ed that
everyon
e in line
should
stand in
alphabet
ical
order
and this
would
immedia
tely
cause an
incredibl
e mess a
frightful
state of
disorder
for the
commoti
on that
would
result
from the
fact that
one
would
have to
change
place

and
move
either
forward
or
backwar
d
dependi
ng on
the
spelling
of one's
name
would
create
not only
chaos
but
irritation
and
anguish
and
consequ
ently the
line
would
turn
ugly full
of
animosit
y
as people

would

not

hesitate

to ask

others

with

whom

they had

had a

friendly

relations

hip for

their

identific

ation

cards in

order to

ascertain

that they

were in

the

correct

place

accordin

g to the

first

letter of

their last

names

and one

would

probably

hear
people
shouting
to others
your
name
begins
with a T
get the
hell
back in
line or
someone
else
would
say
timidly
in a
somewh
at
embarra
ssed
tone of
voice
my
name
starts
with a B
please
excuse
me I
have to

move
ahead of
you and
it would
not be
rare nor
surprisin
g for
certain
people
to
accuse
others of
lying
about
their
names
or of
using
false
names
just to
be ahead
of them
consequ
ently
this line
that had
been so
good so
flexible
so

decent
would
rapidly
degener
ate into
an angry
ugly
state of
mutual
suspicio
n simply
because
of
alphabet
ical
ordering
for there
would
be order
now in
the line
oh yes
alphabet
ical
order
unhappil
y
abcdefg
hij
klm
nopq
rstu

vw
xy
z

How Are the Two of You Doing Tonight?

Amina Memory Cain

If you see each other in a dark auditorium
in the middle of a recital will you recognize
each other, become misplaced in a stillness that doesn't exist,
argue loudly while everyone gives you dirty looks?

The days have gotten shorter, running
into each other more quickly than before, with fewer
birds. "I like the violin best."
"I like the viola—" you didn't expect this split
—and your life explodes like a car explosion
in a drawing. To show the other you will make

your own ball-point pen drawings,
saying, "Here, hold the pen like this," waiting to see what the other
draws for you. You will walk outside the auditorium together,
leaning against the wall next to the coat check
saying, "Here, please draw for me a bird."

[inspired by Raymond Federman's "The Invisible Doubles")

Absence in 31 Parts
or Double and Nothing, Take It and
Leave It

Welch Everman

1

In The Voice in the Closet and other texts, "X-X-X-X" stands for Raymond Federman's mother, father, and two sisters.

Once Federman said to me: "When people ask me about the Holocaust, I tell them that I lost my parents. I don't even mention my sisters."

"Why not?"

"I guess I'm afraid they won't believe me. If I told them everything, it would be too much."

2

"X-X-X-X" is excessive, too much. It is an attempt to mark an absence, and, as such, it must say more—much more—than it says. It must say much more than it possibly can.

3

"my whole family xxxx into typographic symbols while I endure my survival"

The burden of the survivor is that he or she can still speak, still write, while those who have not survived cannot. Thus, the survivor is often called upon to speak in place of those who are absent, to speak for them, as if they had left some message that it is the survivor's responsibility to transmit.

259

But, of course, there is no such message. The survivor is the subject of interviews, interrogations, because he/she is here and available, but the survivor cannot tell us what the non-survivors knew, if only because the survivor has survived and is present, while the non-survivors are absent and can never be recalled to speak/write for themselves. It is their absence that is unspeakable, unwritable, and yet, because of his/her presence, it is this very absence that the survivor is expected to articulate, an absence that language always suggests and even emphasizes but always fails to reach.

As a survivor, Federman must speak/write in place of those who are absent. And, as a survivor, he must always fail to do so.

4

"my whole family xxxx into typographic symbols"

5

"A word perhaps, nothing but a word, but a word in excess, a word too many, which for that reason is always lacking. Nothing but a word."

6

"X-X-X-X" is not a word, but it is typographic, and so, like a printed or written word, its place is on the page. It is there before us, in black on white, a signifier signfying an absence. It is a memorial, a monument—but, no, not that. "X-X-X-X" does not call the absent to memory. Rather, it marks absence as absence. The stone memorial is meant to stand forever. On the other hand, ideally, "X-X-X-X" should fade and disappear as it is read.

7

Language always is and is not about absence. We use words to call to us that which is not here. Please, pass the salt. More often than not, there is no reason to talk about what we have, what is present and before us. And so what we talk about is what is absent. We talk about what we did last summer, what we are planning for the weekend. When we get together with friends, we gossip about the friends who are not with us. We also speak of people who are absent and who will never return. We can do nothing more for or with them.

But speaking does not bring the absent into presence–just the opposite, in fact. I speak about what I did on my vacation last summer, and the speaking establishes an unbridgable distance between me in the present and that past time. I am speaking about last summer precisely because it is absent.

8

"...the profoundly negative function of language—which never names particular things, but rather the absence of that which is named..."

9

A Federman poem, of sorts:

ABSENCE

X—X—X—X

A word names only the absence of that which is named, but "X-X-X-X" is not a word, not a name. Does "X-X-X-X" name, then, the absence of that which is not named?

10

As he often does, Federman offers us own reading of ABSENCE, his own critique, beating the potential critic to the punch. He writes: "Absence is the condensed version of all that has been written so far since the beginning of writing–the smallest common denominator." [Loose Shoes, p. 72]

For Federman, rather than marking the end of writing, rather than bringing writing to silence, "X-X-X-X" is the written, the whole of writing, from its beginning to now, the Reader's Digest version of the written.

How are we to understand this? Why is ABSENCE "the smallest common denominator" of the written?

Absence, it would seem, is that which all writing shares, all language. If writing in particular and language in general establish absence by marking the distance between the word and that which it names, if writing is absence, then is absence writing?

We must remember, though, that writing is always a way of keeping, of preserving. It would seem, then, that, though writing may well be about absence, though absence may be "the smallest common denominator" of all writing, writing cannot ever be absence in itself, because writing cannot relinquish, cannot give up, cannot let go.

The question is: how can one have absence, speak it or write it, and lose it at the same time? Perhaps by a gesture that is both writing and not writing, writing and unwriting.

11

The perfect expression of absence would be the open space, the blank page. Absence would be silence.

12

"He tells stories that, without themselves interrupting silence, suggest silence to others." [Loose Shoes, p. 17]

If Federman's stories suggest silence to us, it is because they read themselves, critique themselves, erase themselves, disappear in the very process of our reading. To Whom It May Concern is made up of letters to an unnamed correspondent which detail the decisions and processes by which the novel was written–a novel which consists entirely of these same letters. In Aunt Rachel's Fur, we meet an editor, Monsiuer Gaston, who explains what is wrong with that very work, and Take It or Leave It features its own resident critic who interprets the novel in which he appears well before any critics outside the text can get to it. This is why I say that Federman's stories read themselves.

The perfect Federman story would be one that leaves no remainder, that is consumed in the act of the reader's reading, as food is consumed in the act of eating or, better, as a piece of paper is consumed by a fire which fulfills its own essence in the process of consumption.

But the act of reading usually does not suggest silence, because reading is not like a fire that consumes, leaving nothing behind. The text that reading consumes remains to be consumed again, because reading reads what has been written, and what has been written is that which remains. This is why we can still read Federman's stories, even though they have always already read themselves. A reading that consumed the text completely and irretrievably, leaving no remainder, would not be reading at all, as we understand it.

And yet, though every reading of a text leaves that text available for another reading, there is something tenuous about Federman's texts, a sense for the reader that the work he/she reads is on the brink of fading away. For all that, however, the work is there to be read. The text is not absent. The pages are not blank, not silent.

13

If silence is the goal of the Federman text, it is not the temporary silence between words, the blank spaces. Silence would not be the simple absence of writing. Rather, silence would be excessive, the leftover, the remnant. Silence would be what might remain after everything available to writing had been written, after writing had exhausted itself—not the absence of writing but the writing of absence.

14

"To write then becomes a surplus, an excess of what has already been written, or what already exists as writing."

15

"He thinks that absence cannot be said. And yet he eliminates, deletes, erases the superfluous to try to speak absence. Or rather to make absence speak." [Loose Shoes, p. 17]

16

But how is one to write to the end of writing and beyond? How are we ever to be done?

17

"Everything Federman speaks cancels itself. In the end he will have said nothing." [Loose Shoes, p. 42]

It is not easy to say nothing, to articulate nothing. Perhaps it is not possible. Saying something doesn't seem to be a problem. I'm doing that right now. But to say nothing...

To say nothing. Not simply to say not a thing, not a single thing, but somehow to say nothing in itself.

Is this how one might speak absence and/or make absence speak?

18

Though he is sometimes lumped together with the New York Abstract Expressionists who were his contemporaries, Ad Reinhardt had little in common with Jackson Pollock or Franz Kline. His work is more like that of Mark Rothko or Barnett Newman, though

Reinhardt never had their visibility or their success, perhaps because, while the Abstract Expressionists were advocates of their art, stressing in their own works the processes and materials of painting itself, Reinhardt often seemed to be involved in putting an end to painting.

Reinhardt was a theoretician, and his writing on art points in the direction of the Conceptual Artists who would come along later. His theories were also embodied in his painting. He was an abstractionist with an aesthetic and philosophical aversion to representation as profound as the Jewish theological refusal of image. He worked in a number of styles, influenced by Stuart David, Piet Mondrian, and others, eventually doing geometric abstractions like Abstract Painting, Blue (1951) or Abstract Painting, Red (1953). These works use shades of a single color, with slightly darker squares or rectangles set against a brighter background. Reinhardt did a white-on-white painting in 1955, but, beginning around the same time, he started to do the black paintings that would continue until his death in 1967. Some black-on-black paintings were similar to his earlier geometric abstractions, but, in time, they became, by Reinhardt's own description: "five feet wide, five feet high…(not large, not small, sizeless), trisected (no composition), one horizontal form negating one vertical form (formless, no top, no bottom, directionless)…brushwork brushed out to remove brushwork, a matte, flat, free-hand painted surface (glossless, textureless, non-linear, no hard edge, no soft edge) which does not reflect its surroundings–a pure, abstract, non-objective, timeless, spaceless, changeless, relationless, disinterested painting…"

Reinhardt's painting, like Federman's writing, seemingly tries to erase itself ("brushwork brushed out to remove brushwork"), to invoke what art critic Lucy R. Lippard calls "the infinite ambiguities inherent in any work that aspires to 'nothingness.'" Reinhardt himself said, in an interview, "I'm merely making the last painting which anyone can make."

Is this also what Federman is up to, writing the last text (X-X-X-X) which anyone can write? Does his work also aspire to nothingness? And is nothingness the same as absence?

19

Twelve years younger than Reinhardt but clearly of another artistic generation, Robert Rauschenberg did a series of black paintings in 1951-52. These were not flat, however, but textured, often with paper collages, until they were more like three-dimensional reliefs than paintings. Rauschenberg also did white paintings at about the same time, using house paint and a roller, and the effect was more like Reinhardt's blacks—flat, without composition, without brushstrokes, non-objective, etc., etc.

And yet Rauschenberg and Reinhardt had very different ideas in mind when they applied paint to canvas. Reinhardt says: "Art comes only from art." [Glaser, p. 16] He disapproved of the confusion between art and life, and, whenever life had an impact on his paintings, he reclaimed them for art.

The painting leaves the studiio as a purist, abstract, non-objective object of art, returns as a record of everyday (surrealist, expressionist) experience ("chance" spots, defacements, hand-markings, accident—"happenings," scratches), and is repainted, restored into a new painting, painted in the same old way (negating the negation of art) again and again, over and over again, until it is just "right" again. [Reinhardt, "The Black-Square Paintings," p. 83]

On the other hand, according to Walter Hopps, Rauschenberg's white paintings invite the collaboration of the world beyond the canvas. He writes: "[T]heir whiteness was meant to be perceived as open uninflected color, incorporating the shifting light and shadow of their environment onto the surface of the canvas."

For Reinhardt, "ART IS ART. EVERYTHING ELSE IS EVERY-THING ELSE."

For Rauschenberg: "Painting relates to both art and life.

Neither can be made. (I try to act in that gap between the two).

Is Federman closer to Reinhardt or to Rauschenberg?

In 1953, Rauschenberg acquired a Willem de Kooning drawing from the artist himself—a drawing made with thick crayon, grease pencil, ink, and pencil. Then Rauschenberg spent almost a month erasing the drawing, using the eraser as a tool for making art. The final work, entitled "Erased de Kooning Drawing," still bears slight traces of the original. Why erase a de Kooning rather than a Rauschenberg? A de Kooning drawing, in 1953, was an acknowledged work of art—a Rauschenberg drawing would not have been in the same league. Today, Rauschenberg could erase a work of his own.

Would Federman want meticulously to erase his own texts, using the eraser as a tool for making art? If he did, would he allow traces of the original text to remain?

20

To X out a word is to cancel it and to let it stand at the same time, through the same written gesture. The X placed over a word or phrase or name doesn't erase it—if anything, the X anchors that which is X'd to the page.

But the X's of ABSENCE (X-X-X-X) cover nothing but a bit of the white page. There are no words or names beneath to show through. Instead, the X's become names that do not name.

21

"In appearance, writing is only to conserve. Writing marks and leaves marks. What is entrusted to it remains. With it, history starts in the institutional form of the Book and time as inscription in the heaven of stars begins with earthly traces, monuments, works. Writing is remembrance, written remembrance..." [Blanchot, p 31]

22

If writing is remembrance, though, it provides only a specific kind of memory. Writing documents what is absent, but it remembers the absent in the form of writing itself. Writing is not memory of event or person but memory of the written, memory of the read.

Writing, as Blanchot has it, is monumental—the engraved headstone on the grave of a loved one whose face one cannot recall.

23

Writing is always conservative, an exercise in conservation. It documents, records, holds in place. It is lists, archives, histories, contracts, laws. It is record keeping.

The editors of Federman, A to X-X-X-X: A Recyclopedic Narrative provide copies of actual Nazi records of the deportation of the Federman family, as well as other documents recording the years of birth of those Jews rounded up during the Grande

Rafle of 1942 in Paris, information about dates of departure, number of deportees. number of convois, destination camps, the number of people executed upon arrival, the number chosen for work details, and so on. [pp. 82-84] This, of course, is what writing does best, why we have writing in the first place—to keep track, to balance accounts, to preserve the absent. It was a kind of writing the Nazis did well.

Writing is the enemy, and, if it is to be defeated, it must be defeated by using the weapon of the enemy against itself. Writing can only be silenced by writing.

24

But, again, how can writing silence itself?

25

"No salvation, save in the imitation of silence." But, of course, the imitation of silence is no more silence than the reflection in the mirror is that which is reflected.

26

To speak is to lose rather than to retain; to entrust to forgetfulness rather than to memory; to give up breath (to run out of breath) rather than to breathe. [Blanchot, p. 90] Spoken words appear and disappear in the very moment of speaking. For a literate culture like ours, this is the failing of speech, its fundamental fault. Speaking is improvised on the spot, and, unless the act of speaking is recorded in some way, it is lost on the spot as well. Perhaps this is why, in our time, we have so many ways of recording and preserving what is said—writing, of course, in the form of note-taking or stenography, but also audio tapes, video tapes, CDs, DVDs, digital disks, hard drives, etc., etc. All these media and others as well exist to save speech from failure, to save speech from itself, from the failure that is the very nature and essence of speech. By literally saving speech. By preserving it.

The goal of these media is transcription, and, as the word itself suggests, to transcribe is to carry speech over into writing, to transform the very nature of speaking, to make it no longer speech but text, if not in actuality then at least potentially, to make speech writable by allowing it to be repeated over and over again. The media—and, ultimately, writing— protect speech from its own nature as expenditure.

But, of course, the vast majority of words ever spoken are not and were never preserved or intended to be, and it is in this sense that speech is loss, a surrender to the present moment without hope of return. If writing is the medium of memory, memory beyond the individual mind, then speech is the medium of the forgotten, of that which passes away without remainder.

This is why literate cultures deplore illiteracy among our own and pre-literate societies elsewhere—this is why we call such societies "pre-literate" in the first place. For us, literacy, writing and reading, preserving and retrieving are in the very nature of things. Literacy is the natural outcome of human language, the natural successor to speech. If a society is not literate, we assume that it is simply behind the times, that it has not developed writing yet but that, of course, it will. For us, pre-literacy is, perhaps, a pitiful condition but not a reprehensible one—unless the pre-literate society is not pre-literate at all but willfully illiterate.

Literacy provides an economy of preservation, of conservation, of textual product. To refuse literacy is to refuse preservation, to champion waste, to give words away free of charge, to engage in a process without a product.

The writer is always productive. The speaker produces nothing.

27

And yet one cannot erase speech. One cannot X out a spoken word. One can only keep speaking. I didn't mean what I just said. That was a slip of the tongue. One can only keep speaking about the wrong word that is already past.

28

The relationship between the written and the spoken, between writing and speaking, is difficult in Federman's work, awkward. Often he speaks/writes as if speaking and writing were the same thing, though he clearly understands the difference. Writing is conservation. Speaking is expenditure. The writer and the speaker work from different motives (conservation, loss) and achieve different results (something, nothing). But Federman wants the best of both realms.

More often than not, Federman's texts pose as speech—or as transcriptions of speech. In Aunt Rachel's Fur, a writer named Namredef tells his story to a professional listener named Federman who then, presumably, writes down what he has been told. The narrator of Take It or Leave It tells a story to a crowd that he has heard from the protagonist and tries to answer their questions and comments. In The Twofold Vibration, two tellers, Namredef and Moinous, relate the story of the Old Man to their friend Federman who, in turn, transcribes what they say. These texts seem to be efforts to preserve the ephemeral, as the recording of an improvised jazz performance is an effort to keep what otherwise would be lost forever.

It seems, then, that Federman prefers the spoken to the written, that he sees the written as nothing more than a transcription of the spoken. On the other hand, though, Federman's texts often stress their own textuality, their status as print of paper. Double or Nothing is structured, page by page, like a series of concrete poems. Take It or Leave It also plays with the look of the page and the configurations of print. The print on each page of The Voice in the Closet assumes the rectangular shape of the closet itself. These texts are obviously and purposely written, not spoken, even when they pose as nothing more than transcriptions of speech.

What does Federman want? He wants writing and speaking, conservation and loss, something and nothing. Speech is absence, not only because one speaks about that which is absent but because speech itself fades away in the very speaking, tends in its very essence toward absence. Writing, on the other hand, is always a way of keeping. But what if one hopes to keep absence as absence, to preserve loss as loss?

Is there a way to keep what is lost and to lose what is kept?

Is this what Federman has been up to all these years?

29

In a piece entitled "Federman on Federman: Lie or Die," Federman writes. Therefore, when dealing with Federman's work, one must accept the fact that what makes up his fiction is not necessarily what is there (that is to say what is told, what is visible, what is readable, what is present, what is presented, what is represented or appresented) but what is not there (what is not told, what is not visible, not readable, not presented, not represented or appresented). In other words, what is important to notice in Federman's fiction is what is absent. [Critifictions, p. 86]

This is another example of Federman's reading of himself, beating the critic to the punch—though I would never want to suggest that Federman is the best possible reader of Federman simply because he happens to be Federman.

In the above quotation, however, I think he might be on to something—something we've also been pursuing since the beginning of this essay. Here, Federman asks us, when we read his texts, to read not the little that is there on the page but the enormity that is not. He asks us to notice "what is absent."

But what is absent? What is it that is not told, is not visible, etc., etc.? The answer seems simple enough, at least regarding Federman's texts. The absent is whatever Federman does not write about—what he doesn't know, what he has never experienced, what he has never imagined, what he finds unimportant, what he ignores, what he purposely avoids. Our list could go on and on but not forever. Sooner or later, we would exhaust the nots of Federman's texts and discover what, in fact, his writing really is all about.

But this literary version of a negative theology wouldn't answer our real question—which would seem to be Federman's real question as well. What is absence in itself? How do we get to it? Does Federman's strategy (of writing/speaking, keeping/losing, something/nothing) have a chance of succeeding? Or is he condemned to failure? And are we?

Is that a problem?

30

We shouldn't be surprised that absence slips away from us whenever we try to articulate it, to understand it, to take it as an object for study. Perhaps we shouldn't use the word "absence" at all, as if we knew what it meant. Perhaps we should say [absence]—or abXsXeXnXce—or X-X-X-X.

31

Therefore, what the critic should discuss in his work are the holes, the gaps, the voids, the empty spaces, the blank pages, and of course the closets, the precipices, and especially the four X-X-X-X's which are the recurring key terms that point to that absence. [Ibid.]

1. Raymond Federman, The Voice in the Closet (Madison, WI: Coda Press, 1979),unpaginated.

2. Maurice Blanchot, The Step Not Beyond, trans. Lycette Nelson (Albany, NY: State University of New York Press, 1992), p. 5.

3. Philippe Sollers, Writing and the Experience of Limits, ed. David Hayman, trans. Philip Barnard and David Hayman (New York: Columbia University Press, 1983), p. 72.

4. Raymond Federman, Loose Shoes (Berlin: Weidler Buchverlag, 2001), p. 71.

5. Raymond Federman, Critificition: Postmodern Essays (Albany, NY: State University of New York Press, 1993), p. 57.

6. Ad Reinhardt, "The Black-Square Paintings," in Barbara Rose, ed., Art as Art: The Selected Writings of Ad Reinhardt (New York: Viking Press, 1975), pp. 82-83.

7. Lucy R. Lippard, Ad Reinhardt (New York: Harry N. Abrams, Inc., 1981), p. 146.

8. Bruce Glaser, "An Interview with Ad Reinhardt," in Art as Art: The Selected Writings of Ad Reinhardt, p. 13.

9. Walter Hopps, "Catalogue of Works," in Robert Rauschenberg (Washington, D.C.: The Smithsonian Institution, 1976), p. 66.

10. Ad Reinhardt, "25 Lines of Words on Art: Statement," in Art as Art: Selected Writing of Ad Reinhardt, p. 51.

11. Quoted in John Cage, Silence (Cambridge, MA: The M.I.T. Press, 1966), p. 105.

12. Larry McCaffery, Thomas Hartl, and Doug Rice, eds., Federman, A to X-X-X-X: A Recyclopedic Narrative (San Diego: San Diego State University Press, 1998), p. 141.

13. E.M. Cioran, All Gall is Divided, trans. Richard Howard (New York: Arcade Publishing, 1999), p 13.

RAYMOND & GEORGE & THE BUICK

PORTRAIT OF THE ARTIST AS A YOUNG MANIC DEPRESSIVE, OR JOURNEY TO CHAOS THEORY[2] AS A FIRST PRINCIPLE OF A NEW REALIST LITERARY AESTHETIC AN EPISTOLARY DRAMA[3] IN FOUR ACTS

BY[4] LARRY McCAFFERY

Playgiarized from original epistolary texts by Raymond Federman
Concept, set designs, editorial preface and end notes by Larry McCaffery
Additional unattributed textual samples selected by Raymond Federman
from literary works by others.
Directed by Larry McCaffery
Music: Prefacing Act One: Charlie Parker, "Young and Drunk at 4 a.m.";
Prefacing Act Two: Miles Davis, "Birth of the Cool";
Prefacing Act Three: Sonny Rollins, "Tenor Madness";
Prefacing Act Four: Parker's "Lover Man" (extended remix version)
Ambient ("background"[5]) music for all three acts: miscellaneous samples from various compositions by Charlie Parker.

THE PLAYERS

RAYMOND FEDERMAN (RF[6]). An aspiring young literary artist who is subject to wildly fluctuating mood swings—and whose education and growth to artistic maturity is chronicled in this play.

GEORGE TASHIMA (GT), A Japanese-American who is a couple of years older than RF, GT is RF's closest friend at Columbia University and the person to whom RF's epistolary monologues are addressed. GT played his first role as RF's buddy and literary mentor when they were both serving in the Army during the Korean War; as the play unfolds, he departs for Paris to write the first great Japanese-American novel about the relocation of his family from California to camps in Arizona during WWII.

GLORIA. A sexy married woman RF is having an affair with. Gloria is one of the parade of women, RF claims to be madly in love with during his formative years.

JANE. A young woman poet RF is briefly involved with at Columbia.

CRISTINE. A young woman writer whom RF met in a creative writing class at Columbia and became immediately infatuated with. But RF's feelings for her are clearly based on more than mere lust, and as such she represents an important shift towards a more mature conception of love.

JOHN WADLEIGH, Along with RF and GT, Wadleigh is the third of the young ambitious writers who meet and become friends at Columbia University and later begin referring to themselves as "The Three Musketeers of Literature." Wadleigh is the villain of the play whose commercial success RF envies before gradually recognizing that the path of true literary artistry must lead him in an entirely different direction.

DANIEL DODSON. A Creative Writing Professor at Columbia University.

WILLIAM OWENS. The Young Artist's most influential creative writing teacher at Columbia University.

RICKY (ERICA). A beautiful, wealthy woman whom RF meets at UCLA, she is the embodiment of true love whom RF eventually marries.

[CAMEO APPEARANCES]: T. S. Eliot, J. Alfred Prufrock, Samuel Beckett, William Carlos Williams, Aldous Huxley, Jean Genet, Humbert Humbert, William Carlos Williams, Allen Ginsberg, Ezra Pound, James Joyce, and miscellaneous others writers, playwrights, and artists.
THE SETTING:

The repressive America of the late 1950s. A series of tiny one-room apartments in which the Young Artist lives and writes (to establish how utterly indistinguishable these processes are, the sets for all the scenes should be identical, other than changes in several visual details—in his clothes, books, posters he's hung on the walls, etc.— to help indicate the processes of change, education and maturation being undergone by the Young Artist). These claustrophobic rooms are the sorts of desperately empty dwelling spaces in which only students and the truly impoverished ever resort to living in. The furnishings are absolutely minimalist: at the back of the room at center stage an uncomfortable-looking cot whose main function is obviously not sleeping but a place to set a cheap hi fi record player and a heap of old 78 jazz recordings by Dexter Gordon, Wardel Gray, Sonny Rollins, especially Charlie Parker and other hip cats who dominated the bebop scene of the 40s and 50s and whose music will be heard continuously throughout the play; dominating the room at center stage is a long wooden table which is mainly used as a desk by the Young Artist, who sits facing the audience behind an old manual typewriter, furiously typing, pausing only to occasionally re-light a steady stream of foul-smelling Gauloises he chain smokes throughout the play, or to get up and change the hi fi when a tune concludes. At the very opening of each scene, a scrim will be lowered momentarily upon which will be projected replicas of the opening passages from each original letters providing the text for the monologues [directors may at their discretion decide to use these scrims to display other materials—photographs, book covers, passages from RF's other correspondence, etc.]

Meanwhile, mingling uneasily with the sounds of Charlie Parker's noodlings are the clicks and clacks of typewriter keys being struck, a form of music that will be heard throughout the play and whose different textures and rhythms express as much about their composer as the squeaks and squawks of Parker's saxophone. Here at the outset of the play, these typewriter notes seem hesitant, their slow, uncertain rhythms occasionally being interrupted by wildly energetic poundings that seem utterly incongruent. As Parker's tune is finishing, a scrim is lowered on which is projected a replica of the original source of the words the typewriter is presumably creating:

Hey there!
one of those days when

    Dear George, I am sorry to be so late answereing the letter that you
never wrote, but I have been very busy lately. The weather is fine, I am
bored. I play golf, tennis, no sex alas, and no intelleciualism, but who
gives a damn after all, I'm only going to be teacher, so I cannot expect
to much of life. If I were a nice kid, and we were only friends that's the
sort of letter I would write you....ButI am more than your friend, I am your
lover, (Don't show this to anyone, my reputation would be ruined.)

    Sometimes, often, I ask myself this question, What the Hell am I doing
here? Tell you the truth I don't know. What a waste. I haven't been able
to write one line since last I saw you. The season started with...Not
with a whimper, with a bang. The people, the fools, the hypocrites came
rushing in with their new clothes, new cars, more money, talking golf and
business, looking older eventhough they try to look younger, the women
particularly, and I stood there on a hill watching them

Then just as the curtain begins to rise, a deep voice emerges slowly intoning in a thick-French accent:

Here... now... . again... Olivetti makes me speak with its keys

ACT I. A LOVER'S (DRUNKEN DISCOURSE—AN OVERTURE OF SORTS⁷

While the audience settles into their seats, a selection of old jazz records by Bud Powell, Dizzy, Monk, Miles, Pres, Dexter Gordon, Wardell Gray, and others from the 40s and 50s is heard playing from behind the curtain, as are the clearly audible sounds of somebody noisily getting up and walking over to change each record—a ritual that will be repeated before each act. Just before the curtain rises a final tune is heard in its entirety. For this opening act, it's Charlie Parker's "Young and Drunk at 4 a.m.," which drifts out from behind the curtain, sounding just the way RF's old scratched up 78 actually sounded back then on his cheap hi-fi, but it's lovely nonetheless.

Setting: A warm June evening in 1956⁸ at Copake Country Club, a summer resort for middle-class Jews located in the Catskills, where RF is working as a waiter during his summer vacation. A cramped, dimly lit cabin illuminated by a single electric light, which hangs down from the ceiling. Everything about this cabin reflects the poverty, loneliness and desperation which afflict the Young Artist at the outset of the play—and which are the source of his strong but unformed determination to transform himself into one of those major (and no doubt controversial) literary figures who were in the news all the time back in the 50s, writers like Hemingway, Ginsberg and Kerouac, Mailer, Salinger and even RF's beloved Camus, figures who actually mattered enough back then that people actually felt it was important to read their works, talk about them. Why many young Americans actually regarded writers as heroic figures and the literary profession as an almost sacred calling. Certainly the Young Artist feels this way, although it is also obvious that his journey to literary fame and fortune will not be an easy one to travel—particularly here at the outset.

The room is full of dark recesses and ominous shadows which the bare bulb seems to emphasize rather than dispel. At stage left is a doorway which will never be opened; at the rear of center stage a large window providing the room's only other connection with the outside world has been bolted closed by wooden shutters. The window is flanked by two large black and white posters: the first is the famous shot of Albert Camus sitting in his sports car, smoking a cigarette, the other is an old playbill announcing a Charlie Parker concert in Detroit. The long wooden table at front stage center is littered with an array of novels, poetry volumes, and magazines, whose chaotic overflow onto the floor has somehow resulted in symmetrical piles of hugely oversized literary works which reach halfway to the cabin's ceiling; these twin pillars will grow upwards in each act, reinforcing the general sense of claustrophobia and literalizing the impact literature is having on the Young Artist's creative life; the names of individual titles and authors offer hints about which works are currently exerting the most influence on his conception of life and literary art. Future directors may use their discretion in selected titles and authors to emphasize, but for Act I the following works should definitely appear as oversized books: Portrait of the Artist as a Young Man, The Collected Poems of Yeats, Eliot, and William Carlos Williams, Howl, Boris Vian's J'irai cracher sur vos tombes,Long Day's Journey into Night, and several French titles, including Sartre's La Nausée and Qu'est-ce que la littérature, Camus' L'étranger, Le Mythe de Sisyphe, La Peste, and Baudelaire's Les Fleurs du Mal). A number of similarly oversized magazines are also visible, including Colliers, The Saturday Evening Post, and several copies (somewhat larger than the rest) of The New Yorker testifying to Young Artist's unrealistic, wildly ambitious dreams for commercial success and critical recognition.

Sitting alone behind an old Olivetti manual typewriter and facing the audience is the Young Artist, who is looking very young indeed in a Columbia University sweat shirt and shorts, his hair in the crew-cut style popular in the 50s. In between the deep, meditative drags he takes of the stream of Gauloises, RF uses his index fingers to peck away on the typewriter, which the audience now recognizes as the source of the clicking sounds they have been hearing.

RF is a manically depressive French-American Jew and aspiring writer who has suffered unspeakable losses at the hands of the perpetrators of the Unforgivable Enormity while still living in France during WWII; he subse-

*quently endured further losses (of his home and country, of his native tongue)
when in the late 1940s he went into exile to America, where he has struggled
(mostly in vain) to overcome poverty, loneliness, ignorance, and a sense of
alienation which has been exaggerated due to the disruptive effects of his
incredibly thick French accent which tends to turn everything he says into a
kind of marmalade or verbal delirium. As the play opens, RF is a 28-year-old
sophomore literature major who has just mainlined his first hit of serious literature and found the rush was good.*

*More than good, it was a high that gave him access to an entire new world
full of exotic formal areas to explore and thematic issues to ponder and examine; most important of all, it offered an entire universe new world of language
he could begin using—the multidimensional universe of literary language,
with its eloquence and symbolic potential, its beauty and profundity. These
were qualities that RF, with his inarticulate longings and his flights of reverie
that he couldn't begin to describe even to himself, desperately needed so he
could begin telling and retelling his life-story, a story he sensed contained the
very essence of the 20th century.*

*Unfortunately this was also a story whose power, poignancy, and richness
and profundity couldn't possibly be told as long as he was held captive inside
the prison house of language in which he was trapped, an utterly restrictive
space that wasn't even so much a house as a cramped room or a closet built out
of his own clumsy rhetoric, his limited vocabulary, his egregious mispronunci-
ations which he consciously exaggerated so that his remarks would be laughed
at rather than merely derided, the obscenities and slang which flowed off his
tongue as natural by products of their source.*

*In short, this literary rush has put him directly in touch with the key that
can open up doorways that will finally release the torrent of stories he wanted
to tell about the traumas of his youth, his passions, his speculations about the
meaning of life and death, his hopes, his lusts—all of which he has buried
deeply inside "Frenchy," the persona he has invented for himself as the good-
natured, but basically ignorant foreigner whose dark needy eyes provide the
only glimpse into his troubled inner soul, with its desperate longing for love*

*and communication. He delivers the opening lines of his first monologue in an
almost comically thick French accent, frequently punctuating phrases with theatrical hand gestures.*

One of these days when… [9]

*[he hesitates, takes another deep drag off his cigarette, which he crushes in
an ashtray already overflowing with cigarette butts.]*

Hey there!

Dear George,

I am sorry to be so late amswering the letter that you never wrote[10], but
I have been very busy lately. The weather is fine. I am bored. I play golf,
tennis, no sex alas, and no intellectualism, but who gives a damn after all,
I'm only going to be a teacher, so I cannot expect to much of life. If I were
a nice kid, and you were only friendsthat's the sort of letter I would write
you…. But I ammore than your friend, I am your lover, (Don't show this
to anyone, my reputation would be ruined.)

Sometimes, often, I ask myself this question, What the hell am I doing
Here?[11] Tell you the truth I don't know. What a waste. I haven't been able
to write one line since last I saw you. The season started with…Not with a
whimper, with a bang.[12]. The people, the fools, the hypocrites came rushing in with their new clothes, new cars, more money, talking golf and
business, looking older eventhough they try to look younger, the women
particularly, and I stood there on a hill watching them, smiling at them
and shaking their sweaty hands. I wanted to vomit. Money, what I must
do for money, I wish I was good looking I would prostitute myself.[13]

I got a letter from Jane yesterday, [Fortunaly, (I mean fortunately) she
keeps me going[14]. Have you seen the book review of the New York times
this week. There was a translation of a poem by Mallarme[15], the same
poem I translated just before I left. Jane thinks my translation is far more-
superior. Are you writing. I hope not because if you say yes I'll be sick.

I have to write to John[16]. I think Mr. Wadleigh is going to make it this
year, about time we have a publish man among us. I think I'll try for second best. Let me know what happens. Anyway I'll drop a line to John this

week. Are you working, I mean as a gardener or what ever you're suppose to be doing in your mansion working for the wealthy Mr. Hill with his marvellous daughter that you can't wait to get your pants off for, don't bullshit me my friend, we know one another so well that it's impossible for us to conceal anythiing from one another, and that's why I love you kid? Still reading Joyce. I don't really understand what the man is talking about, but I am drunk on words[17] he fascinates. I think I have found my master[18]. You better look for one quick, you need it

George, George, Help. I am lost. I don't know if I'll be able to last the summer here. I came to a conclusion that in order to survive, I must write[19], it is as essential for me as sex, and if I do not write I become frustrated and sexless. I can't wait to get back to school and Dodson, I got a crew cut by the way, if Dodson would see me he would lose complete faithe in me. I hope that it grows back quick. I have been deserted by all of manking, even my cousin[20] is associating with the mob.

I am sorry, I know I am a snob, but it is too difficult for Me to lower myself, I hate dirt. If you can do it good for you, we'll meet anyway up there, on the path of glory, I'll get there on my hands and knees while you'll drive there in a cadillac[21], but when the two of us will confront Satan, I'll be the one He will pat on the head and say to: "The world is now divided in three portions, (I mean the literary world,) Homer, Joyce And federman. While you will be classified with Rockefeller, Naimark and Tashimanism.

I wish you would read more of sartre this summer, you would comprehend life a little more deeply and also you would be able to discuss with me the finer points of life. EXISTENTIALISM[22] Or FEDERMAN

I don't know if I'll be able to to come and see you again before the end of the summer, I'll try, but If you can I will be very grateful to you, because I have to have someone with whom I can argue, even if it is meaningless.

Anyway drop me a line soon. Love darling. You one and only

Competitor. And master.

Raymind[23]

CURTAIN

ACT II. BORN TO RUN, NOT TO THINK

SCENE I. Unloosening the language...[24]

Scene: Six months later, the first day of classes at Columbia University in late January 1957. A small cramped one-room apartment located at 306 W. 105th St. in Manhattan. Before the curtain rises, the audience again hears the sounds of typing which mix with those of someone noisily fiddling with a hi fi set until Miles Davis's "Birth of the Cool" coolly starts up, producing exactly the cool effect the Young Artist needs right now to *help him keep the exotic aesthetic stew RFD's got simmering in his creative pot from boiling over. A scrim is lowered displaying a replica of the opening passage of the epistolary monologue we are about to hear:*

George. Mon Cheri.

Sorry. At last I find a moment to write. Not that I have anything important to say, but whatever it is it must be said. Well, as excepted I got six AAAAAs again this semester. I am beginning to believe that I am half a genius. What's your opinion on this. I tried my best, I swear to get at least a B to break the monotony but it was useless. Your friend Owens gave me also an A and I had a long talk with him. He really thinks quite highly of my writing, because my dear boy I am not like you, I am pouring out the stuff, story after story, and dammit they are beginning to make sense and be good. I believe I'm going to be published before John even, not that I want to but if they force me to it I cannot refuse. No joking, kid. My writing is really moving forward. During the one week that we had between sessions, I sat down and wrote everyday for five or six hours. I just finished a long, long short _____

As the curtain rises, we see RF standing in front of his hi-fi set (now perched on a cheap sofa which has replaced the cot) waiting for "Birth of the Cool" to finish before putting on another Charlie Parker tune. He's now wearing a vaguely European equivalent of a college outfit and sporting much longer hair, which he's swept into a pompadour recently popularized by James Dean. At the rear of the apartment, the single window is no longer closed—though it might just as well be, since all that's visible through the dirty windowpanes is the blank wall of the tenement building next door[25]. On either side of the window posters of T.S. Eliot, Aldous Huxley, Sartre, Eugene O'Neill, and (larger than the rest), Samuel Beckett have joined Parker and Camus on the back wall As he glides back to the wooden table where his Olivetti sits amidst the growing literary clutter awaiting his command to pour forth his in-blood once again, RF bobs his head in time to the music and snaps his fingers in a gesture whose significance would be instantly recognized by any of the other cool cats from the period[26] At one end of the table a space has been cleared for a cheap plastic replica of Rodin's "The Thinker," which is balanced at the other end by a replica of the Eiffel Tower; these are tourist trinkets sent by GT to his (aban-

doned friend) soon after his arrival in Paris, where he plans to pursue his own dream of becoming a famous novelist. Adding to the chaos of books and magazines are several oversized books with titles and authors we haven't seen before (Long Day's Journey into Night, Waiting for Godot, Molie`re's Collected Plays, Ionesco's Rhinoceros, *etc.) Before he resumes typing, he lights another Gauloise, inhales deeply, and then begins his monologue; he delivers his lines in his instantly recognizable thick French accent, although as will be the case in each succeeding act, his mispronunciations are slightly less egregious and less frequent; likewise, the vocabulary and phrasings he uses to construct himself will subtlety but steadily improve in each act. Even more noticeable is the increasing sophistication of the content of these monologues, the expanding range of literary references and allusions, the confidence with which he addresses complex matters of aesthetics and philosophy, as befits a young artist who seems to be emerging from his cocoon of ignorance and adolescence and maturing before our very eyes. Reinforcing these changes are the sounds of the typewriter pounding steadily away as they move across the page chaotically and digressively, giving voice to wild flights of fancy and speculation, their furious sense of movement at times having to slow down while negotiating sudden detours into regions of self-doubt and occasionally even suicidal depression, but soon regaining their sense of manic momentum, as the rush forward in an insistent staccato rhythm.*

February 1958
George. Mon Cheri.
Sorry. At last I find a moment to write[27]. Not that I have anything important to say.. but whatever it is it must be said[28],Well,, as excepted[29] I got six AAAAAAs. again this semester, I am beginning to believe that I am half a genius. What's your opinion on this. I tried my best, I swear to get at least a B to break the monotony but it was useless. Your friend Owens gave me an A and I had a long talk with him. He really thinks quite highly of my writing because my dear boy I am not like you, I am pouring out the stuff, story after story, and dammít they are beginning to

make sense end be good, I believe Im going to be published before John even, not that I want to but if they force me to it I cannot refuse. No joking, kid My writing is really moving forward, During the one week that we had between sessions, I sat down and wrote everyday for five or sex hours. I just finished a long, long short-story[30] about two old people in a home for old people, It was an idea that was in my head for quite awhile now.I wanted to write something tout a fait objective, leaving myself out of it my emotions, my sex,my life even, and I succeeded creating two characters I never knew before, they are alive, they think, talk, live and die. Personally 1 am. very pleased with it, but you know how I am always pleased with every line I write However I feel that I am developing self-criticism, and also my language is unloosening itself, I mean I begin to play with words, with ideas, and also with form For example that last story, the one I mentioned, I have tried something entirely new about form.

Are you familiar with the books of Aldous Huxley (Point and Counter point[31] Antic Hay) if not read them, well you will be quite impressed by the form and what this man has to say.

Your last letter disgusted me[32], I counted the word 'Think' in it twenty-two times and each time mispelled. Go ahead you jerk, think,skink,pink,fink, think or whatever you want to call it. and when you'll stop thinking, you'll realized that you are too old to write, that your hands are too shakey to be able to type, and that your eyes cannot see any longer. Well., then what will you do, all your deep thinking do for you. Go, come now, sit down and write, no more excuses, I believe you have seen and experience enough to be able to write it down and if you find then that you need more, then think, but first write, Idiot ....

I'll give you a good example of this 'thinking' in the process of creating. [*he reaches over and picks up the cheap statue of Rodin's "The Thinker" and considers it thoughtfully before resuming.*] Rodin was no idiot when he sculpted his "Le Penseur." He knew that the artist must think but why not do it while working. And so that's what he gave us, ironically enough, the statue of a thinker in the process of thinking, but in a work of art. Do the same my dear George.. Meanwhile why don't you go and see this statue. I believe it's still in Paris, unless the French have sold it for good, at the black market.

[*the Parker song concludes as he is stubbing out his cigarette in the overflowing ash tray; so he stands and walks over to the sofa to change the record so that soon the scratchy squeaks of another Parker song are heard; he smiles, snaps his stack of books on his table; he sitds down, he lights another cigarette and plunges in once more to the task of reinventing himself.*]

Spoke with John this week, he said he will take care of sending you the package you have been expecting for so long. He is supposed to come up to my place pick up War and Peace by a certain guy called Tolstoy.(Thanks for the information I'll have to read this sometime). He told me also that he would get, you a Shakespeare book., I would part from-mine but, well you know how books are dear to me/ Poor soul, why the hell don't yon start reading in French Or is the french to difficult for you, or have you more excuses not to want to learn.

Notice kid I am throwing all the shit back at you because I believe it's time we had a father and son talk, you being the kid and I the old man. I don't give a damn how much you preach to me about life, and going to work to an office to learn (learn I mean) life and all that goes with it that's a bunch of shit and you know it's not because you had to work at Mr. Hill or shall I say Papa Hill for a few months that you have learn, more about the outside life. Bull shit, I say, I still believe in the ivory tower for the Artiste. And I am beginning to see what is wrong with John's writing and why he cannot publish anything[33]. He is in the outside world as you call it away from the academic crap but he does not SEE that world, perhaps because he doesn't want to, I don't know if he's too busy looking for something else or blind or what, so he goes on writing books about the Korean war, long ago forgotten and which nobody wants to hear about. Let's face reality kid, you and I and John should start writing about what we know and feel, and what we have seen and heard, and I tell you we all have plenty to tell. This is what I believe I have been doing for the past few months and this is why Owens this morning (I saw him in the street) stopped me and sad, I quote word for word… "I read your last story, very fine…. I think this one will go someplace…. I showed it to Mrs. Rowman Editor of Collier and she is going to try her best to get it published for you (unfortunately not in Collier because perhaps you have not heard but threee or four magazine went out of business in the States among which Collier. That was quite a blow for the shortstory market[34].) "Well"" he said, "I see you are moving ahead with each new story, l am looking forward to one of you novel…. Etc…. ."

Now I know what you are going to say another tap on my ego stop masturbating your ego and all that shit[35]. I know it kid. but meanwhile I have been thinking about a Novel[36]…. Yes my boy thinking and an soon as I finish school in June with cape and all and diploma and all As I'm going to get started and for good, even if I have to starve for awhile, or sell the golf club or the car, naturally I'll try not to, a little golf and driving around the block never hurt the creative spirit.

Sex, ca va toujours[37]. I have difficulty keeping track of all my women. Gloria, I should say the forgotten Gloria, I am trying hard not to think of her because it hurts inside, a bit, not much though, was in Florida. My other girl, Cherie[38], is in Haiti…I expect a nice present when she gets back. Jane, see her rarely, passe, AND THE rest, well hell with it.

I'm going to see the plays[39] with Jean Louis Barrault who is in New York, for a few meeks. Saw St. Joan with that Irish Bitch, not bad at all. Saw the Long Journey into night, O'neil. Quite a peice of work but to long, I suppose because of the title.

School again today spring Semester. I am taking Burrell, just the novel course.

A course in modern French poetry in graduate school another grad course on Moliere" Owens shot-stories, naturally, and craft of fiction with him also and one course in philosophy, Äeathttiec,.. (correct the spelling, please. I am not to good at it yet I still need you or John to correct my stories, but who givens a shit as long as they are written).

I don't think I shall return to Copake this summer, it's time I began to starve properly. I'll try to get a Job in New York, perhaps in an office like you suggested to see life or perhaps drive a truck, is that better, and do some writing.

I am very glad to see that you are plaming a long trip around the world, I hope you make it and also find yourself a piece of ass along the way that would clear your mind from a few things. Meanwhile why don't you go see around Rue Saint Denis[40] and get a load of your chest.,let me know what the prices are now, just curiosity,

And stip, I mean stop, talking to me about love and spiritual intercourse. Sex, is a good word, that people, Hill and others especially should not be scared of.

Well I have to stop for now. I feel better now that I have spoken to you the way I meant to for a long time, I have to run[41]. I must go to the areoport to pick up Cristing coming back from Haiti with my presents.

Write soon kid. I miss you terribly. I need you, I mean I need yo intellectual and even physical support.

Your friend andonly friend.. Ton grand ami

Raymonde[42]

CURTAIN

Scene II. Birth (just a little late) of the Cool…

The scene: the same apartment in NYC at the conclusion of the spring semester 1957. Posters of Proust, Celine, and Pound have joined the other figures on the back wall, and there's several new oversized volumes prominently displayed on either side of the desk as well. On his 29th birthday, the Young Artist announces his plans to leave behind the comfort and security he has found at Columbia University and embark on the next phase of his artistic development.

New York, May 15, 1957

Mon Vieux George

    I know, I know, I am a bastard. I have not written for a Hell of a long time, but so have you, or so have you not. So let's skip the crap and the excuses and go down to business.

    First: you...John told me about the last letter he got from you, (O...By the way, before I forget. Our friend John Wadleigh called me last night....guess what. Yes, you got it...John just sold his first story. You bet I'm happy, because I was scared I would sell a story before him and would have been a bitch of a thing to do to him.) Well, he told me about you thinking of giving up writing and going into the medical world. What can I say. Naturally, I know you have thought this thing out carefully, but to tell you the truth it hurts me. Because, because, well you know I had

New York, May 15, 1957

Mon Vieux George

I know, I know, I am a bastard. I have not written for a Hell of a long time, but so have you, or so have you not. So let's skip the crap and the excuses and go down to business.

First: you...John told me about the last letter he got from you, ((O.... By the way, before I forget. Our friend John Wadleigh called me last night.... guess what. Yes, you got it...John just sold his first story[42]. You bet I'm happy, because I was scared I would sell a story before him and would have been a bitch of a thing to do to him.) Well, he told me about you thinking of giving up writing and going into the medical world. What can I say. Naturally, I know you have thought this thing out carefully, but to tell you the truth it hurts me. Because, because, well you know I had great hopes in you as a writer. But perhaps you are the smart guy, and this does not mean you have to give up writing completely. I know an old famous poet—Carlos—I believe is his name, Oh. yes, Carlos Williams, who is a doctor and a great poet at the same time. I just read his last book of poems called A Journey to love quite fine, quite.

George I know whatever you decide you have done so after long and careful deliberation and hours of strenuous thinking, so I am all for you boy, except that I wish we could have sat down and talk together about it. Well, anyway you are coming back, and do hope we will be able to talk again like the old days. That is if I am still around. And with this let's go on to the main body of this letter:

Second: ME...I am still writing, and for that matter like mad. I have now an agent. Owens himself sent me to his agent because he felt it was time. Naturally I have not yet sold anything, and I don't expect to in the near future, but I am writing. Owens wants me to start immediately on a novel, and I intent to[44] As you know I am finishing in June with flying colors. I feel a little empty now, perhaps sad to leave the good old Columbia, and Dodson, and Owens, and Burrell...and etc...because with , them I felt safe, I felt I did not have to be by myself and think for myself, and also they would pat me on the back once in a while and I would feel good, and I would go home to my little square room and feel good and sorry for myself, and at time I would shed a little warm tear for myself....Well, no more. I am a man, a college graduate now. I was twenty-nine, today. Well, well...I'm catching up with you. I am writing. I'm writing. I don't mean to show you up, but I really feel that I am coming into my own, and you know why, because like you, although I did not have to go to Europe or anywhere else to find this out, I did some thinking, some serious thinking. I discovered that it is not enough just to put down words that look pretty on the sheet of paper, well typewritten, those words have to say something, the writer who puts those words down has to be aware of the world around him and the people in that world. I know this must sound like a lot of shit to you. But Proust said "The world was not created once, but as many times as their are artists in it." I must see the world with my own eyes, my own individual little blinking eyes, have my own vision of the world and put down what I see and feel and as Pound Ezra said "Think occasionally." I have reread the stupid stories I used to write when you were still in New York and I saw how idiotic and shallow I was in those days. I was drunk then with my writing because I could write one or two nice sentences in English., after all it was good for me I was a foreigner. No more. No more. I hope you believe me. I am writing one short story after another now, but let me tell you something, it's hard. It's hard work, I thought writing was easy just wait for the inspiration to come and that's it. What a lot of shit that was. I just finished a 30 pages short story[45] I believe my most serious piece of writing. But this is going to surprise you. I don't think it's good. What I mean, I don't think the story is complete. It is finished but not complete, I have not fulfilled all the demands of the situation and the characters and everything in other words, I am not satisfied with it. Anyway the story was discussed in Owens class last Tuesday and received quite a fine reception. Owens spoke with me about it after class and he told me that this material was what I should begin my novel with. The story is about Detroit about a young foreigner who gets involved with young colored musicians. It is the education of a young man, toward a new life, it is the shattering of his dreams into reality, it is the problem of negroes in America seen from the eyes of this foreigner who discovers the problem as he learns the language...And many other things I want to put in this novel. The reason I am telling you about it, is that I have a need to talk about it now, and also because I hope that you would also stop thinking about yourself and think about your friend, write sometimes, and tell me what you think of my idea.

Tell me also what you intent to do now. Do you expect to come back soon? Tell me all those things I am interested after all I am your friend. I hope. Even though I am a prick a bastard a sonofabitch a selfish idiot, perhaps a salaud too. How is that for a piece of self-analysis.

Now, to go on with Me. The great news is this. I was awarded an 1800 dollar fellowsip[46] at U.C.L.A. Los Angeles. I will be teaching two courses in French literature there in the fall., they also pay the trip out there for me, 150 dollars. I will also be able to study for my M.A. I have been receiving some very find letters from the head of the department there, Mr. Lapp. And they are all looking forward to greet me in September as one of their colleagues. I am all excited and disappointed. Naturally I am glad because with this money and still the G.I. Bill I will not have to work while going to school and I believe I'll be able to do some writing, on the novel. I am finishing on June fourth, and then for the rest of the summer I am going to work on the novel, perhaps not writing it immediately, but doing some thinking. I still don't know what I will do this summer. I might stay in New York, I might go back to Copake, and do my thinking on the golf course or while screwing gloria. By the way I have not seen her since Christmas. It was a clean break, it hurts still a little bite, and I know she thinks of me. Because this morning for my birthday I received a card with only one initial on it G. I think it was very sweet of her to remember me this way. Oh. love. What a disease. I just read The Magic Mountain so you know why I have all those pains in my chest.

I have been fooling around a little with quite a girl who I believe you know, (believe…the i before the e…) I know. her name is Cristine Callan, the girl with all As[47]. A genius, a very find writer, a bitch, a tough sort of bitch, but who can be very sweet at the same time well we've been sort of going together you know what I mean. I asked her to marry me. she refused. I think she was smart anyway she will decide one of those days. Perhaps she will come with me to California when I go sometimes in August. I hope you are back before that if not, I will make a point to come to New York just to see you. Or better perhaps you will come to Los Angeles to see me. Well we'll see. You see mon vieux george life must go on, or I should say life is only beginning, a little late for us, but perhaps it's better. I don't know. Fight. I miss you kid, I wish I could sit down and have long talk with you. Remember last year about this time what fine evenings we spent talking about stupidity, you and me.

Raymond

CURTAIN

ACT III—IN A SILENT WAY: MADNESS IN THE MIDST OF THE DARKNESS

Scene I. I Can't go on (the Road not Taken)

Sonny Rollins' "Tenor Madness" reaches its concluding crescendo and then the curtain rises in the dead of November night in 1957 to reveal the barely visible darkened silhouette of RF performing his record-changing ritual in the cramped office room in the UCLA Comparative Literature Department which he uses as a living space. RF shuffles slowly towards the table and sits down once more before the typewriter as a Parker tune begins to circulate around the room, which is illuminated only by the distant glow of the Los Angeles skyline drifting in through the back window. He sits motionless for several moments before striking a single key, which produces a sound that fades away slowly into the darkness. A few more key strokes are heard, the clicks and clacks seem strained, exhausted, anguished, mournful, as if each life's note is being summoned up out of the blackness of the room only with the greatest difficulty. After a few additional strokes, the dark outline of RF pauses and then the jazz and typewriter sounds abruptly cease completely. After several moments, the indistinct, muffled sounds of RF sighing, clearing his throat, etc. We hear him angrily rip from the typewriter the sheet he has been writing, the outline of the page he holds up is somehow clearly visible, almost blinding in its blank whiteness. He seems to examine its contents for a moment before he begins speaking slowly...

THE EASIEST OF COURSE WOULD BE TO BLOW my BRAINS
OUT————————

bang! *[accompanied by loud sound of a gunshot]*

[a long pause as the roar of sound slowly dissipates]
THIS WAY we WOULDN'T HAVE TO BEGIN
*Another long pause, then the barely discernable sounds of the Charlie
Parker tune resume and slowly become louder and louder throughout the rest
of the scene. As the house lights gradually are turned up, we see the Young
Artist reach down and pick up a new piece of paper, which he angrily slides
into position in the typewriter. He pauses for another moment, and then
emphatically strikes the typewriter producing a tentative harsh click; then
another determined click is heard, and another, the sounds slowly gathering
rhythm and momentum* **until the pace has become frantic, furious, until
their sounds and those of Parker reach an almost defeafening crescendo...**

CURTAIN

Scene II—Comes a voice [saying]... I must go on[48]

*In the moments before the curtain rises, Miles Davis's "Kind of Blue" is fin-
ishing as the scrim containing the following passage is lowered:*

L.A. Nov. 18

Dear Fellow-poet.

Sometimes in the midst of darkness comes a voice (it was yours this time) and it seems that the touch of a hand is enough to help you in a great moment of undecision. Really man, I'm going through one of my darkest moment of maturity or mutation or whatever you want to call it. Enough of that shit I told myself. There I was sitting in front of my typewriter banging away a lava, a vomit of words, pouring out the story of my life, when suddenly I stopped and asked myself, who the fuck is interested in reading the stupid-ignble-indecent-filled-with-lies-story of my life. Which by the way was not even the stroy of my life, of of some little idiot who I made beleive was me because his life which was a mere reflexion of what I thought my life should have been, a poor miror of a cheap dream and it went for pages in a more or less confused style, formless, deepless, idealess, alsmost wordless, and this I wanted to place under a leather cover and call it the great novel of my life and perhaps after that blow my brains out. Something happened, luckily. I don't

Daytime a few days later. As the curtain rises we see RF again going through his record-changing routine in the same room, which now seems transformed from the somber scene we saw previously by the bright sounds of a Parker tune that starts up and by the daylight streaming through the same back window through which the same L.A. skyline can be seen. There are several visual clues (a sports jacket, a new hair style) suggesting the rapid maturation he has undergone since his departure from New York and as he walks over to the table and resumes resume his place behind the typewriter, he reminds us of the young Kean Paul Belmondo, who is preparing for the role in Godard's Breathless *that will make him famous. Several new faces, including those of Godard, Robbe Grillet, Rabelais, Apollinaire and Roland Barthes peer out at us from posters which have joined the others on the increasingly crowed back wall. As he begins pecking away, the uptempo rhythm of his self-composition confirms that RF is today most definitely in one of his manic modes rather than the depressive one we saw in the previous scene. The music he's playing on his typewriter today is, however, different from anything we've heard before, the pacing is frantic, crazed, and furious but somehow the whole feeling emerging out of this chaotic jumble somehow seems more confident and determined—and as deliriously excited as the squawks coming out of Parker's sax.*

11/18 LA

Dear Fellow-poet.

Sometimes in the midst of darkness comes a voice (it was yours this time) and it seems that the touch of a hand is enough to help you in a great moment of indecision. Really man, I'm going through one of my darkest moment of maturity or mutation[49] or whatever you want to call it. Enough of that shit I told myself. There I was sitting in front of my typewriter banging away a lava, a vomit of words, pouring out the story of my life, when suddenly I stopped and asked myself, who the fuck is interested in reading the stupid-ignoble indecent-filled-with-lies-story of my life. Which by the way was not even the story of my life, of some little idiot who I made believe was me because his life which was a mere reflection of what I thought my life should have been, a poor mirror of a cheap dream and it went for pages in a more or less confused style, formless, depthless, idealess, almost wordless, and this I wanted to place under a leather cover and call it the great novel of my life and perhaps after that blow my brains out. Something happened, luckily. I don't know if it was you, your last letter, which said anyone, can pour out words on a piece of paper, or something like that and then everything went black. I'm in a vacuum I suppose other things have helped to bring about this situation. I know whenever I get a letter from you it will be to remind me of the academic trap over which like a fool I'm trying to leap without falling in[50]m I'm aware of it, and perhaps cynically I do wish to fall in, it would be another good excuse. But can we go on fooling ourselves, you and I. Yes you and I. Very rarely in your letters do you speak of yourself, but you don't have to my friend because you use my ears to listen to myself talk, and we are one, youintomeasme into you[51], I suppose it is again a mistake, the same mistake I made with my whole life[52], that with distance and time to think that we will see the things more clearly, that is a joke, we never see a thing more clearly across an ocean or across a century, it is transformed, deformed formless, it becomes a dream, a vision false to reality, and dammit I don't give a shit about what they all tell me about art, and fiction and this whole business of writing. I'm a realiste and I want to write about life, and the only thing I know about life and people which I believe is real is what I see before me, around, under me (if I'm fucking) above me if I'm dreaming, all this must be taken on he spot before it becomes trans-formed[53]. Perhaps it is the same with you and me. I'm growing fond of you George. You should hear me talk to my friends here about you, because I have some very interesting friends here which I want you to meet someday, perhaps you will see some of them in Paris this Summer if you are still there. Well as I speak to them about you, I wonder if I'm describing you the way, the way I think I remember you[54], the way we used to talk together, in N.Y. or in Brewster, and then I decide that I really only know you through the letters we have written to each other during those long year, and now when I speak of you I think I speak of a george that I'm beginning to make up in my mind perhaps not so good as the real one[55], but one which will serve to start a scene, swell a progress, an easy tool no doubt[56], one which will someday become a great xxxx character in one of my unwritten novels. In other words what I want to say is that dammit I would like to see you, to talk to you soon before I forget the color of your eyes. I think it's time we both dropped the curtain of irony and hypocrisy, that we face each other like the bull and the matador and that we came charging each other. Naturally you know who would win, I'm the bigger one, and I'm faster, although you are very sneaky, naturally like all little yellow bastards like you, but you must not forget that I'm a dirty jew with a big nose, and worst of all a godless-jew. (By the way have you learned the French word for dirty jew so you can insult me when you get back: Youpin.?) I decided if I cannot get you to talk by sweet words, and dammit I have tried, I will make you talk by insulting you. Now, drop the cover and tell me about all the great thoughts you must have accumulated for the past two years. I suppose you must think that I'm running out of ideas myself and that I cry to the old budha in Paris for a new way, or that I kneel before the master humbly begging for help. Attention mon petit. Je continue[57] I have been thinking about some very serious thoughts. Yes I think about thinking. As I say above I have stopped writing, now I know what the thing is, when even a writer, or I should say a make-believe writer like us stops writing, it's easy to find an excuse, just say: "I was not ready I had to do more thinking in order to deepen my way of seeing things, so please my dear fellow-men don't blame me, you'll see I'll come back soon, better than before, and then I will be able to write the great novel which All the owens and dodson and others have seen in me and which must be there. Sure it is there, my life, think, only my life by itself is symbolique. Look at me in this world, fighting, orphan, suffering, fucking left and right, don't you think all this is good material for novels. So dear friends and fellow-man be patient, I'm thinking. There was also the other friend across the ocean with the great ideas and the fluent style who said this before me and which I followed, always following humbly almost on my knees, the Japanese way. He even had a better idea. I will serve mankind, I will perhaps become a doctor, yes a doctor (not of philosophy, a real witch-doctor and I will save life, lives) dedication to human-kind. Poor fool life is cheap, why not save souls, become a missionary, or perhaps a dictator, or a communist leader, or why not just a soldier and fight for the world, the freedom of the world, or why not be the first to land on the moon. No, not even that… Young men, you and I, have you thought that perhaps you could become writers. Not cheap novelists turning one book every three months, like our friend John[58] who is still banging away on his type roller, I bet he'll get there too, that bastard, but why not do like him and get it over, no we the others we are the deeper type of writers, the thinkers, who have something important to say to the world, so let's pause a moment to think.

Forgive me Dear friend, I got carried away with myself in what precedes, but I have not the courage to burn this, I never destroy anything I have written[59], so read and forget it, and go on thinking. Time is slowly passing by us, not even by us, above us, and leaves us un ouched, only a little of the red on our face fading away into the dark, a little quick blow of the wind taking a few of the hairs away, and there goes a little scar on the left breast which was a kiss yesterday and today only a little wrinkle, not fat, we never get fat[60]. The words are bubbles inside a broken bottle which cannot die. Je suis degoute. La nausee[61].

La chair est triste n'lrs et j'ai lu tous les livres. (mallarme).[62] I have read them all now, or almost most, and I'm almost ready to write the great american doctoral dissertation on the greatest french writer[63], but meanwhile the novel, and the teacups and the marmelade and the shit and the war and Tokyo, only a shadow[64], a postcard left unwritten lost in the bottom of a suitcase which we find on a cold evening among friends who listen to you. The words are little balloons coming out like vomit out of a broken jaw. I dreamed of a man, but he died with the morning light. I saw him standing and smiling with his ego protruding like a hardon, masturbating[65] himself in front of twenty or thirty virgins who were dying to know the secrets of esthetics and the form of the formless, I had to do it I told myself, after all we were chosen, You and I. The great sufferers of the twenty century, all collected in a dusty encyclopedia[66], enough to tell yourself that the world is a fucking place to live in. And the guys are still trying to cry that the world is no good. Some of them in San Francisco, are Howling[67] America "Go fuck yourself," and I, myself, me, in a little redbrick-building get a big kick shouting at the tip of my voice, fuck you too, encule, because he said it before me. Read all about it mon petit George, desertor, louzy american, dammit, I think I will write a political essay about the conformist in America[68] and all the stinking yellow americans who are afraid to face reality and go to Paris and la petite Ilse du rever[69] to find themselves, forgetting that america is sinking into a pool of shit[70]. I'm in it up to my neck, and It stinks and if I don't do something immediately, I'll drown. And why not. I heard a voice in my love, in my sleep sayin stop, stop it all, pause a moment and think. I did and look where I am. Lost in a whirlpool of wind, a cloudless sky, where the rain is dried out, sometimes the smog burns your eyes and if you cry you have a good excuse. I think I'll sleep well tonight. I have heard the voice of the mermaid-typeroller-typefucker-typewriter singing to me[71], I have masturbated my fingers, it's good practice, said a voice across the ocean, and now, to sleep with you and I. The world will go on. They will land on the moon tomorrow, and if they red or black or yellow, or fascists or anarchist or russians what the fuck do I care, I have my fingers to remember the words, that came to my eyes, The inner voice of a fool, crying that the world is no good and sinking into a little dream, spermless.

Once when I was ten I saw a great-brown-cow[72] who ran after me and when finally I was out of reach I took a stone and threw it right in his eyes. Then I laughed. How I know this story does not mean a damn thing to you, but to me do you know what I could do with that. I could make a lovely little poem for example which would go something like this.

I was young and then cow came running after me and naturally I was not afraid because the old man told me not to be afraid, but inside I was pissing white.... and so on...[73] and after that they would write great dissertations about this and my friends George in Paris would have to come back to shake my hands and tell me, well old-boy you made it and I would have to blush yes, I did think I would, and after we would drink together and be happy, and naturally we would cry a little, and after the moment of separation we would say goodbye, for ever perhaps perhaps not, but we would belong to different worlds, you and I, you to yours and I you mine. Aurevior mon petite pote.[74] It is dark again, another day fucked away on senseless words spoken in a cafeteria, or between two classes, poetry, and whatever you want, but there must be poetry, if not we are finished, are we not all a little bet of a poet and at least we keep quiet when other people think so. So long.

I must go.... on[75]...to where there are no more dreams and where people don't think anymore.

Above is written what I would call a tranche de mon espritt[76] synthesized, into what I would call the ideological, pheneological specie of a modern thinking mind, one who believes the universe has placed a lot of hope, himself a symbol of hope for human-kind[77], who more of less chosen like christ or budha or mahomet for that matter to save the little people from the end. I have tried, tried to explain to you the best that I could what is my situation here at the university, if I have not succeeded, if you need more explanation write to me and ask precise question. I am no prophet nor was meant to be, for the son of man spoke unto thee (chap 2. line 3) the bible. Dante also said it better than I ever will. And tomorrow, again three times, or never (five times) this is how literature is made not with ideas my friends, but with words taken collected, grouped, synthesized, polished, washed and dried, perhaps also translated too, merde pour le lira. tout cela voila la literature [78]but the books the real books where they are. Here I say, and at that moment the old man with broken teeth pointed to his forehead and wept. I think I understood him. but what could I do, I had been there too. It was too late.

Sitting on the branch of a tree I was watching the moment is now coming to was it not so, and will it happened again. The tenses of the verbs, that it important, think of that my friends, the past tense, the present and the future in the same sentence. Apollinaire[79] did it. I will try. I have to, I have to, I have to find something new, not really, from dust you came from dust you shall return, but in between that happens, George please tell me, tell me before it's too late, too late and then what and if and then it's too late.

I'm really pissed off at myself[80]. I wanted to write you a very intelligent letter, well organized, with words following each other in an orderly manner, and perhaps a nice introduction, a middle perhaps too, and a nice powerful ending, but I got lost, forgive my insolence, and also to have lost all this time writing this and now making you lose your time trying to understand the confusion of a mind which perhaps will extinguish itself the way a vers-luisant[81] does, with the swiftness of an elephant falling into a puddle of mud, and little bubbles, the words rising to the surface to explode like atomic bombs, but little ones, not bigger than my eye. Yes my yes, eye, kid that So.

I am tired, I'm tired, but we must go on[82], then go ahead and I'll still be here waiting[83] . I have dreamt my life three times this week, but each time I was never sure it was correct[84] Don't worry I'll try again[85] Aurevior, auwiedersen, mahi-mochi, sayonara, and pan dans le cul.

Ton Grand ami[86]

Raymond

[CURTAIN]

ACT IV—LOVER MAN

Scene 1. My failure is a success

Just before the curtain rises, Charlie Parker's noodlings in "Now's the Time"are joined by those of RF, who's beating out a dreamy counterpoint melody on his typewriter; near the end of Parker's song, the duet becomes a trio when they're joined by the call and response sounds of birds[87] chirping come-hithers to one another. The scrim is lowered with the opening of the next monologue displayed. It reads:

Santa Barbara, 1960

Dear old George

At first I was furious, then I laughed, then I smiled, then I went to
sleep, dreamt for awhile, made love with love, dreamt again, and then
it was vacation time, and Ricky and I climbed the mountains and skied
down the snowy slope, and meanwhile George thought I was an idiot,
admitting that my story was (is) a failure, un échec, everyone of my
artistic creation until now have been failures this is why I go on.
If I had written my masterpiece I would be an old man now, no man ever
sits down to write his masterpiece, but only thinks so afterwards
and only before the foreign eyes have touched his sacred work, true
I am an idiot, and admitting that my story STINKS (notice I am now
speaking from your point of view) mine is too obscure at this point
to be formulated or justified, admitting all this, still I am glad to
see that my story did inspire you two of your most successful pages of
prose, unfortunately you are not a critic, but another creator peddlling

*The curtain rises on a tiny one-room cottage in Santa Barbara during
March 1960. A dapper looking RF, now attired in the usual graduate student
style of the day (slacks, sports jacket, etc)removes "Lover Man" starts another
platter spinning, and then heading back once more to his typewriter. The
chirping are coming through the back window, through which a grove of
orange trees is seen gleaming in the sun. The back wall of the cottage is now
completely filled with posters, whose new additions include several movie
ads—*The 400 Blows, Breathless, *and other French New Wave films—as
well as lecture announcements for Barthes, Foucault, Michel Butor, Nathalie
Sarraute, and several additional photos of Beckett. When he starts typing the
monologue he's delivering, a new melody of self-creation emerges to interact
with bird chirps and Parker's noodlings, one whose melody still seethes with
emotion but now a certain tenderness joins the anger and exhilaration we've
heard earlier.*

Santa Barbara, 1960

Dear old George

At first I was furious, then I laughed, then I smiled, then I went to sleep, dreamt for awhile, made love with love, dreamt again, and then it was vacation time, and Ricky and I climbed the mountain and skied down the snowy slope, and meanwhile George thought I was an idiot, admitting that my story was (is) a failure, un echec, everyone of my artiste creations until now have been failures this is why I go on.

If I had written my masterpiece I would be an old man now, no man ever sits down to write his masterpiece, but only thinks so afterwards and only before the foreign eyes have touched his sacred work, true I am an idiot, and admitting that my story STINKS (notice I am now speaking from your point of view) mine is too obscure at this point to be formulated or justified, admitting all this, still I am glad to see that my story[88] did inspire you two of your most successful pages of prose, unfortunately you are not a critic, but another creator peddling as I do your inner self. I am quite please I must say with your reaction to my story, this does not change in anyway my feeling about my work, nor for that matter the reaction of others (idiots too, I suppose) who have now read and liked and discussed this story with me, although you have a good all on your side (the New Yorker just rejected the so called story[89]) (perhaps Esquire may have less taste, I shall wait and wait and forget my pride.) Still I feel a word or two of explanation are necessary at this point. Nothing to justify or defend my story, for it is there, it is written (in four copies) it exists for what it is, and the worse of all, I am the one who wrote it, that, you cannot deny, even though all your reactions were negative, the story has now taken its place among my other failures and among the many other failures I shall spew out of my inner confusion. But still a word or two of explanation I feel are necessary here (I said that, shit, I begin to sound like Mister Marant himself. Perhaps he and I are the same person[90], and perhaps this is why you dislike this poor gentleman to be. You are too good to me, you like me too much, and you love Ricky too much, to be able to accept any kind of desecration of my own self or whatever is connected with my-self.)

Enclosed you will find a love poem which I wrote for Ricky[91]. (I have written quite a few love poems for Ricky, simple poems, honest, warm, in which I say in my most simple way I love you Ricky, and naturally she liked them, she keeps them in her own special file, Works of Raymond published and unpublished, but besides that she also liked very much my story which you disliked so much. A word or two of explanation seem necessary at this point. I know I said that, but one must repeat oneself before one can arrive at some kind of originality, if only the repetition in itself becomes the originality. A rose is a rose is a rose, or a fart is a fart is fart, who knows the real answer. Let's talk literature.

I believe I have now written enough (shit no, this sounds to pedantic as a start.) I'll try again. I believe....What do I believe? good question. From the time when you and I sat at Columbia University in Prof Owens writing classes a lot of fish have passed under the bridges and into the frying pans. In those days I was so anxious to vomit out of my twisted guts the story of my life, so much so that all over the paper a huge I repeating itself over and over, a little I, feeling sorry for himself, a big I who had had many experiences, who thought he had suffer who thought he had a right to tell the world his story, and the suffering and the love and the dirt and the fucking and the starving and the spit in the yes, and the cold and the sweat and the lice and the tears and the crap and all the rest, all this was to be the contend of my stories and of my novels and of my poems, and it came out like shit out of a[92]

[a gap or absence is introduced in the form of a missing page]

I decided to get involved in politics but soon I discovered that I did not give a shit about politics, so I tried a little of social awareness, but then I discovered that that too is for the fishes. I revolted and decided to become a professor, but that too is for the snails. Shit if I go on I'll have the whole zoo in there. Bear with me, I'm getting to the point.

I do hope that in the middle of this wordy mess you find the truth which I am now slowly but surely filtering to you. There are a few things that a writer must consider now adays. 1. .that people rarely read anyone, or else best lousy bestsellers and I have no intention of writing a thing like that. There are two types of artists, the creator and the artisan.

I am neither of these and yet I do sit from time to time to write.

Perhaps 'I have something to say, but no one listens, and I don't really give a damn. No I do give a damn, I want to write because I want to be famous, let's admit now and get it over, but meanwhile I want to shock the bourgeois (before I become one myself) a little. No that's true.

I think at this point I could honestly sit down a write a nice decent story (in good English, without any obscenity in it, and almost with a moral to it.) I could easily tell a nice little story, I have so many little stories inside of people, and me would be touched and I would be a nice little writer, and I could even if I wanted to imitate...,..Oh let's say thomas Hardy, George Eliot, perhaps even Conrad, not bad I know they are great and I shall never reach the bottom of their bottom, but they lived at a time which is not my time. Even dostoeivsky who is still the greatest of them all does not, or could not write the way he did if he lived in our time, This is the first question I asked myself and answered to myself. This one I did answer. I cannot, I will not write like them. I am. Raymond federman, a foreigner, having lived my life (good or bad that ¡a not the question) that life has shaped my mind, I should say twisted my mind, that life in itself is of no importance, it is only one life among millions and millions of other lives, what counts is the place and the time in which this life was spent: 1928 to ???????? and then what? What? This is what I want to write, not what happened, who gives a shit about that? but where and when it happened. Naturally I could write a history book, but fortunately I detested facts, and even though I have a tremendous memory, I tend to forget things too quickly, therefore, this is where my imagination, my creativity or whatever you want to call it comes into play. Well this answers the first question.

The second is easier. For whom do we write? I could say for New Yorker if those sonofbitches had accepted my story, but they did, therefore

I shall reject that first hypothesis and move on to something else. I am more and more convinced less and less people give a damn about what I write, and I could easily say well shit with them I'll write for art-sake, but unfortunately I don't have the talent and the courage or the modesty of a James Joyce or a Beckett. And besides that my language, I mean my written language is too simple to fit in that intellectual circle. I am a writer for the poor, this is the bitchy thing about the mess, even though I try very hard to become an academic champion, I am still proletarian of a writer. Therefore I shall write for whomever wants to bend down to read me. The solution to my problem would be to print my stuff on toilet paper, I thought of it, but it's too materialistic for my ideal. I was going to say I write for myself, but that's false because as soon as I have finished something, anything, even a letter–I have to show it somebody.

Well that answers that question. Now to the third and most important one, How does one write?

In my short-story which you disliked so much I tried something of great Importance, not to you, not to the literary world, but to me. First I tried to break a few rules (perhaps here again I am wrong, for before I Can break the rules, I should learn a few, but this is part of me, of myself, swift as the arrow that kills the bird, but I am not a bird, therefore I don't give a shit about the rules.)

What I tried in that story first was to fool around with the language.

Here I am caught in the trap of the american cliche which I use and misuse daily besides imposing to it an atrocious accent which I cultivate for personal reasons. Still I have chosen to write in this so-called american idiom. Before I can become an accomplished writer I have either to master this idiom or else destroy it, break it, make little pieces out of it and then build for myself a language which will become my tool. The first one would be the easiest way out, but I prefer the second one, therefore I shall never really learn this language by heart, instead I shall fool around with it until I get something new out of it.

This was basically the starting point of my story. Every word Mr. Marant (by the way which means in French: funny guy) is a cliche, a straight forward cliche taking out of the-mouth of a good american and twisted by the melodramatic mind of my character, twisted because this poor guy is so logical in a completely illogical situation. The second thing I tried to do was to create a man (if you can call him that, but I hope to go even further than that, to reduce man to its inner beast, and still come out with something human)(don't you recognize me in this. Subjectivity seen from inside out.) By the rules and conventions and moralas of our society Mr. Marant is all wrong. I grant you that, and yet, admit that the poor guy is somehow likeable. In his naiveté he remains with some kind of integrity. True to his background, his environment, his heredity, that I cannot say, for no man living today can remain true to that, and yet we try like mad, or I should say most people do. I gave up long ago. This is perhaps what makes of me the great cosmopolitan which I really am.

Somehow this Mr. Marant who lives on Park avenue, who speaks at times like a bum, acts like a reverted humbert humbert, this poor chap who does not understand a thing about manners, rules, regulations and all the rest, this poor guy somehow fits in the situation. I might even go further and say, he is the typical picaresque character of our modern society.

Coming through one door into one corner of the social scale and going down the window into another level and yet wearing a suit and tie when he should be waling naked among the clouds. Confusing isn't it? I resume:

1. language (first element which this story tries to shape or unshape.)
2. characterization (logic into the illogic).
3. the short-story as a form, rebellion against the writing-classes.
4. suspense presented backward.

naturally I could go on and reveal to you all the little secrets of my creativity, but I decided, just now not to go on. If only you had not let your sensitivity, you good-heartedness, your love for me and for Ricky, your angelism, and all the rest of you that is good and honest interfere with your reading of my story you may have seen what I was trying to do.

But you didn't and that's good. For this proves to me again that once more my failure is a success. For now I must go on, and I will, I'm thinking of writing a sequence to this story, Mr. Marant goes to the Psychiatrist, or else Mr. Marant gets drafted into the army. Can you see that, the double life of schizophrenic characters. Well enough for now. I let you untangle the mess of my reflection about literature. It is always nice to talk to you. You are so patient. And your letters to Ricky are really magnificent. You have really found a great friend in her, and I admire you, respect you the more for it. Someday when we get married (soon now) we might adopt you. So long george for now. About the R.F. to Cristine, those are the ways one remembers, there are more in those two initials[93] than she will ever be able to know or understand, and you too. Words are so useless, I find this out everyday, especially now after having thrown away so many of them on this paper. Salut. Write soon.

CURTAIN

Scene II. I shall go on...

As one of Charlie Parker's gorgeous renditions of "Lover Man" moves along unpredictably towards the finish line, the scrim lowers to reveal the opening from the final monologue:

Salut Georges

Finally, I find a moment to mumble a few words across the land to you, no my dear fellow, and I insist here, your ancient perspicacity seems to fail you those days, for you judge me wrong, words are no more pretty little birds flying their gentle flight from my head to my hand and onto the white sheet of paper, no more, I only want to use them to transperse them to get beyond them, and if you have not seen this in my last letter then you, yourself are still caught up with the surface of things. Dig, man, digg, deeper and deeper, you used to speak thus to me, am now the father to the whole source of my own creation: You. Or are you to wrapped up in trying very hard not to be what you are. Your jewishness pleases me, for you are trying very hard to become what I try very are not to be, but we are stuck with our exterior, I, with my long nose and my cut up dick and you with your slanted eyes. I thought to master that I would have first to master the language, go through it, fool around with aesthetics

The curtain rises on the same cottage room in the late spring of 1960. RF is smiling broadly as he starts up another platter on his hi fi and as he heads back to his typewriter, the snap of his fingers, bouncy gait, and other mannerisms all seem to radiate his current sense of satisfaction and confidence he's feeling.

Salut Georges

Finally, I find a moment to write a few words[94] across the land to you no my dear fellow, and I insist your ancient perspicacity seems to fail you these days, for you judge me wrong, words are no more pretty little birds flying their gentle flight from my head to my hand and onto the white sheet of paper, no more, I only want to use them to transperse them to get beyond them, and if you have not seen this in my last letter then you, yourself are still caught up with the surface of things. Dig, man, dig, deeper and deeper, you used to speak thus to me, am now the father to the whole source of my own creation: You. Or are you to wrapped up in trying very hard not to be what you are. Your jewishness pleases me, for you are trying very hard to become what I try very are not to be, but we are stuck with our exterior, I, with my long nose and my cut up dick and you with your slanted eyes. I thought to master that I would have first to master the language, go through it, fool, around with aesthetics in other words learn my trade' like a shoe repairman, and I tried, but, then I saw time slipping through my fingers, literally saw time slipping past me, and I decided to throw all this to hell and get down to the heart of the matter. How? that is the question, every new poem I write is a failure, every new thought I get leads a little further into the nonsensical, 1 open a door and behind it there is a sign which cries to me WRONG DOOR and I try again and there are million of doors and I keep trying. Last night I sat alone, halfway between LA. and S.B. coming back from a delicious weekend with my dearest Ricky (who by the way told me she wrote you a letter, please do answer her, she will like that very much, she knows you very well and likes you, and she is like all of us who have (I hate to use the word) suffered a trifle, in great need of reassurance, the kind word from the kind man, and you are that man. Naturally she is uncertain, insecure, for I do give this kind of feeling around me, I disturb people, I make them uncomfor-table, and that is my purpose, and I shall exploit this, to push down their throats what I have to tell them, but to Ricky, I want to give the best in me, for she has opened a new world to me, sincere, honest, real. I did not read her letter, but I am sure you will discover that in what she said to you. Therefore, I urge you to write to her, to be yourself as I know you to be...) well there I was sitting alone half-way between L.A. and S.B. having a cup of coffee late at night in one of those roadsidejoint when I lifted my head and the _ clock started to smile at me. The long thin red head of the second was speeding around and I found myself counting the seconds and I wasted exactly 326 of them over this cup of coffee, in a complete state of loathing, passive, doing nothing but warming my little digestive system and trying to keep myself awake for the next 50 miles of driving and I suddenly saw that everyday I throw away thousands and thousands of those little pieces of time...What then, shall I just say, well enough of this, I shall wait, and the world shall go on after me, and let to others the care of this world.... I could easily, and yet I won't....

But neither will I sling a rifle on my shoulder and go out there to fight the ones who are wrong or right. Who knows. The only thing I know how to do, the only thing I can really do, is teach and write. And I am not kidding when I say teach. I suddenly realize that I have learned quite a few things in these past few years since you took me by the and let me between the two frigid statues of Columbia University.

I have read many books, and ignored many and understood a few, but what I have gained, I see now that many have not yet gain, and that perhaps I can give them that much, plus whatever is true of me, for little by little, I see that too, there is in me a certain Raymond Federman who has a few personal opinions of the world, of man of the world perhaps nothing original, but that much I can give them, naturally I don't mean all this to sound very angelic, of evangelic, no, for this inside I still hate man in general and all his stupidity, and so I shall not tell them how good man, and the world is, on the Contrary I shall tell them that we are all bastards, that the worse thing for a young man is his parents when they impose on him a set of values which does not function for his time, I shall them him that beauty does not exist, that whatever has been said before is false, because when it was said the world was different, in spite of what everybody says, I do not believe that homer or dante, or shakespeare would have written what they have written if they could have flown from N.Y. to L.A. in four hours I do not believe they would have said what they said if they had been communists, or whatever, therefore, I believe what they tell me, I like the way they said it, but I shall not say it the same way, and I shall not say the same thing. If one starts thinking in this line then one I believe can have a different point de view, a new vision of the world, and this is what makes something original, for now you have notice how stuble I have left off the teaching for the writing. Damn right my boy I shall go on writing. By the way, please get the new copy of BIG TABLE[95] when it comes out #3, in a few weeks, you will see your beloved friend all over the place, nothing original, only translations in that issue, but there are a few things said by others which something should also be read by the naïve americans, this is when I decide to use my only genuine talent (french) I did quite a few translations lately, I don't know yet what the Editor of Big table will publish of the stuff I sent him put, please read it and admire me. Meanwhile, this guy, the editor is a tremendous guy tow work with. He has asked me to do an article on Samuel Beckett, naturally you still don't know who he is, but ask cristine, she will tell you, I have began working on this article and I am quite excited about it, I believe it might turn to be quite a piece of creative writing. After all if I intend to write my Ph.D. thesis on Beckett this is quite a good start[96]. The title of the article "THE MISSING LING" more or less about the insanity of man. I shall send you a copy, if only for editorial work when completed, this article will not appear in the next issue, but the following. Meanwhile I go on writing poetry, or something like poetry, I have pushed my anti-poetical notion of conventional poetry so far that I am coming out with some kind of weird pieces of writing, a paradox in itself, for how can I oppose to centuries of good established beauty with my horrifying pieces of so called modern poetry, and yet, even if I reject the word poem for my little pieces of writing others do say to me, I do like your poem, or I think your poem stinks, but still the word poem is there. I don't know any more, anyway, enclosed you will find such a piece, read it, and say something about it, anything, but try to be intelligent. Maybe I'm being naïve, but that's good too. I refuse to grow old. My new life here is interesting because it seems that I am against everybody, somehow my position, I mean intellectual, is either twisted, or else they are so backward in this academic Hell that we don't understand each other. I grow, not old but I grow. I really wish I could see you soon. By the way what are you doing? I am so involved here telling you about me, that I almost forget that I am writing to you, and yet you are the purpose of this letter, the epistolary form is the most convenient form of literature, one picks up somebody, one person and one shares his thoughts for that person, and only that one person, you get the difficulty with writing is the audience, the public, in the letter it's easy because you know the friend to whom you are writing will read the whole thing, for perhaps somewhere in the back, at the end of the letter the writer will sneak a little about the receiver, and this is why you go on

[*as this final scene draws to a conclusion, the lights are slowly dimmed, the Charlie Parker music also fades, and the frantic pace of RF's delivery slows, with something close to lyricism replacing the playfulnes, manic energy and occasional anger we've heard in his voice for much of the play.*]

reading this crap. and now back to me, throw the ball didi (waiting for Godot page 43) There was a slight improvement in your last letter, less of you and an attempt to say something, I like that, my critical mind is now seeking such titillating elements as you feed to my intellect, such as your conversion to judaism. I like that from you, but it is a dangerous game. The great problem with people like us, I mean you and I, is that we are in motion in a world which itself is in motion. I think back of the days we together began to write a few short-stories. If nothing- had changed then we would have gone on writing the same short-stories and perhaps we would have published them and we would have been happy, but now 1 look back and I reread sometimes those trashy little pieces of writing and I see how great the gap is between Raymond the Phi betta Kapa Student of Columbia University and the so called-instructor of Santa Barbara, and I must say that all this academic shit has left me quite unmarked, the fire is still burning in me, it is more furious than before, the only thing good this whole process has given me is developing some kind of inner perception which I was wasting then in my little emotional outbursts. As for you you went a different road, a long detour through the decaying continent, and you came back broken and broke and disturbed because you hadn't found the tolerance, the understanding which only exists inside of you, not out-side, out there in the world.

And so you came back to us, and now again looking at each other acrossa crooked line, we stick our shoulder to the wheel and we try again.

Something like three years have passed, and yet the novels (yours and mine are not written, John's published, but who is further ahead.

That is the question, and cristine has cut her hair, good for her, and I have almost forgotten her, although sometimes I would like to sit down with her and talk and explain to her, that romantic agony stopped in the 19th century and that the only thing left for us is the agony. And yet I go on behind the scene being a romantic a sentimental bastard. And therefore I shall get married and have three children already made, and 1 shall be happy, and I'll go on writing letters to my friends, and someday I shall stand up and shout to you from across the country, I made it, I published a novel, and I will then say to myself, you idiot, that novel was already published, because as soon as I opened my eyes and first looked at the world the novel was there. Words are useless little bubbles. but they are beautiful when they fly away blown by the wind into the sun. Tell me what my cousin Robert is doing is he teaching—I give up the idea of getting a letter from him, perhaps he won't even show up when I invite him to my weeding and you too, 1 won't pay for your trip if that's what you think you'll have to itch hack all over the country, but I expect the two of you here, even if you don't approve of my big step into bourgeoisie. I am an-angry young man, even more, a furious young man, and I shall stay young because I write poetry, and because no one likes my poetry, and 1 don't give a shit. I sit in my huge beautiful apartment and stare at the wall I wait for my Ph.D. just a question of patience and then I shall be called Doctor and then.

I shall laugh purely and then I'll go on writing letters to a friend who is going on writing a novel and then I shall also write a little novel between meals and sex and the kids and the books and the virgins in school and I shall be happy and one of these days the red hand of the second shall laugh at me and I shall spit in the face of the clock. Well enough of this for now. Read this carefully, a few words of wisdom may have slipped off my fingers. Read the poem to and put it in a special file, might be the beginning of a new cycle, or again it might again be a wrong door. Salut mon vieux ecris vite, donne le bonjour a Cristine, Jeannne, Robert and the rest...

[the stage is now is almost completely dark and the music gone, leaving only the determined sound of the typewriter, clicking into being the following concluding lines of this in a play which is really just the opening section of a much longer work, the huge, ongoing book of RF's life-story that RF has continued to write. The stage lights come back up just as the RF delivers his final words with a sense of renewed energy]

I leave you now, still the same failure I was when we first met, but perhaps tomorrow… Yes! Perhaps tomorrow…

[The Young Artist looks up from his typewriter and stares directly at the audience. Long tableau as the light fade to black. The sound of typing resumes..]

CURTAIN

---

[1] Chaos theory's relevance to Raymond Federman's "realist" literary aesthetic is discussed in Appendix listing IIA.

[2] For a clarification of the usage of this term, as well as background concerning the original sources for the epistolary monologues and the conception for this drama, the Director's preface and other introductory materials, see Appendix I.

[3] "By" in this context implies the concept of "authorship" developed by Federman in (among other places) his essay, "Imagination as Pla(y)giarism."

[4] Though as anyone familiar with Raymond Federman's work should know, a careful selection of Parker samples can do much more than provide mere "background" for this play. A more extended discussion of Parker's impact on RF's literary aesthetic appears as Appendix IIB.

[5] RF clarifies (somewhat) the significance of the use of his initials in lieu of his full name in Act IV, 1.

[6] As is true of all the act here, Act I's monologue unfolds as a sequence of seemingly rambling, unconnected remarks, bits of personal news and gossip, digressions about art and literature, advice and others comments whose

deeper unites of content and form are only gradually revealed. Thus, this opening monologue introduces a series of topics, formal mechanisms, symbols, and motifs that will recur throughout the play, as well as providing exposition in the form of revealing bits of information about the Young Artist's background and personality traits (his obsession with time and sex, note the typical manic-depressive pattern in which the Young Artist swings wildly from suicidal depression to wild flights of ecstatic boasts and self-congratulation), clues about the nature of his relationship with GT and other secondary characters, while also establishing some of the sources of conflict that will be developed and eventually resolved later in the play. We also hear the Young Artist meditating on the meaning of life, and on the role (if any) of commercial considerations and of fleshly love in artistic creation; he also displays his delight in word play while constantly making allusions and references to art and books (or stealing quotations with attribution in an early version of his pla(y)giarism methods), and, above all, offering extended discussions about his literary life, commenting upon the stories and poems he has been or is or will be writing, summarizing his teachers' reactions to his work, all the while supplying a steady stream of pronouncements about art and literary that by the–play's conclusion collectively add up to nothing less than an extensive literary manifesto that the Young Artist will later use as the basis of his career as a writer and critic. Thus, for all the chaos and wild shifts in tone and subject matter, each of these acts can be shown to be far more coherent than they might initially seem; indeed, as these disparate elements interact with each other in this turbulent literary environment, a remarkably coherent dramatic structure emerges—specifically that of *kuntlerroman* narrative depicting the various stages of growth, challenge, education, and eventual maturity experienced by the young artist as they prepare themselves for a life devoted to the sacred calling of serious artistry. Although many readers may find it difficult to believe that a literary work as complex, highly structured and dramatically unified as *Portrait* could have resulted from a composition methodology based on randomness and improvisational, that is exactly what does indeed occur here. For a brief summary of how this sort of order might emerge out of chaos, see the discussion of chaos theory in Appendix I.

[7] The original epistolary fiction is undated but according to RF, it must have been written in mid-summer 1956.

[8] These mysterious opening lines of the play may be interpreted variously, but there's no doubt that they serve as a highly compressed, poetic introduction of many of the major formal and thematic motifs—incoherence, failure, time (particularly its fleeting nature), a reflexive foregrounding of itself as pure artifice rather than as reflection of some preexisting condition, the anticipation of narrative that never is provided, the uselessness of language, etc.—which are developed in the "main body" of the play.

[9] Readers familiar with RF's later work will notice that even here, in some of his very earliest correspondence, he is intuitively transforming what would normally be simply an "ordinary" letter to a friend into the kind of imaginative discourse that I would letter refer to (in Federman, A to X-X-X-X) as "epistolary fiction" (see the "Epistolary Fiction" entry in Appendix I). In this instance, he opens this letter to GT by playfully apologizing for not having responded sooner to a letter that was never written in the first place! What follows in the rest of this opening paragraph is typical Federman playfulness—his catalogue of the dull routine of his summer ("…very busy… weather is fine," etc.) turns out to be only what he *would* have written in his letter to GT if they were only friends (which they are not)—thus establishing precisely the same *conditional* status for this "real fictitious discourse" that he later uses at the outset of all his novels.

[10] This same fundamental questioning of the meaning of existence would be one of the things that drew RF to the work of Samuel Beckett about this same time. RF would later introduce variations of this same question into all of his own major works. For instance, early in TIOLI RF's alter ego is described as having arrived in America "my head bent down towards my hands (not even crying) simply asking myself what the

fuck am I doing here" (n.p.).

¹¹ The reference here is to the concluding lines of Eliot's "The Hollow Men." Commentators have thus far not noted Eliot's impact on RF's own work, but RF's many references to (and playgiarisms of) Eliot throughout his correspondence from this period indicate that Eliot had a significant impact on his sensibility early on.

¹² This is the first of many references in the play to the corrupting power of money—a temptation that RF must reject lest he become the equivalent of a "literary prostitute" (the fate of the villainous commercial hack, John Wadleigh, for example).

¹³ Jane's brief entrance is followed so quickly by her exit here that audiences may fail to recognize that she is the first embodiment of false love which RF must learn to reject before he is ready to become a mature literary artist. In this case, her falseness lies not so much "in her" as inside of RF, who at this stage still believes (incorrectly) that artistic inspiration, the source of what keeps one going, exists outside himself.

¹⁴ The Mallarme poem RF had translated was an untitled sonnet, "Une negresse par le demon secuoure" (Negress Shaken by the Demon).

¹⁵ RF here introduces a trope that will recur in most of his monologues—i.e., the expression of RF's intending to write Wadleigh (rather than having already written him)—as a means of establishing Wadleigh's role here as artistic foil. Throughout the remainder of the play RF will provide accounts of Wadleigh's willingness to compromise his artistry in exchange for commercial success—a temptation that RF must confront and then reject.

¹⁶ RF is probably borrowing this "word-drunk" motif from Baudeliare's well-known prose poem, "Be always drunken' which reads in part: "Be always drunken... With wine, with poetry, or with virtue, as you will. But be drunken." Throughout the remained of the play RF will often be depicted as being falling-down drunk with poetry (and with women), but far less susceptible to intoxicating effects of virtue or wine.

¹⁷ With this reference to Joyce, RF has now introduced the 20th cen-

tury's most influential poet (Eliot) and fiction writer (Joyce), both of whom represent key features of modernism that RF eventually must reject. For example, Joyce—with his lyricism, remarkable range of voices and literary forms, his vast range of erudition and literary reference, his psychological and intellectual insights, and above all the astonishing linguistic precision and magnificent control of such an enormous variety of styles and subject matter— represents a kind of exalted literary mastery that RF ultimately rejects (in IV, II) as being unsuited to his strengths as an artist.

[18] This insistence that not only is his writing connected with life but that writing is necessary for his life is one of the important commonalties between RF's work and Beckett's; note too that these remarks are immediately followed by the reference to the other essential in life—sex, whose significance RF will later claim to be crucial to creativity.

[19] RF's cousin Robert, with whom he will share an apartment in Manhattan upon his return to Columbia University.

[20] References to automobiles as symbolic manifestations of his freedom and status will be a recurrent motif in many RF novels; see, for example, his treatment of "The Buick Special" in *Take It or Leave It*.

[21] Although he had never studied literature seriously until his arrival at Columbia University in 1954, RF had been an avid reader ever since childhood and had already read a surprising amount of works by Sartre, Camus, and other leading French existentialists by the early 1950s. In an early scene in *Take It or Leave It*, for example, he proudly notes that by the time he had joined the Army during the Korean War, he was already suffering from "bookmadness":

I couldn't stop reading (books) it was like a sickness a real bookmadness. Anything. Even sometimes In English but mostly French stuff. (What a show off) anything I could get my hands on. Me (at the Time) I had already read all of CAMUS and a few JEAN-PAUL SARTRE (imagine!) and even some Of LA BEAUVOIR. ... La Nausee SSS Les Chemins de la liberte SSS (in three volumes) SSS Huis Clos SSS Tous les hommes sont mortels SSS etcetera SSS even Le deuxieme sex SSS La Putain respectueuse SSS Le Mythe de Sisyphe (*TIOLI*, n.p.)

[22] RF's apparent Freudian slip here seems to unconsciously suggest that he is still under the sway of GT's emphasis on rational analysis (mind); in the remainder of the play, he begins to recognize that mind is far less important to his own artistic sensibility than that of the emotions, the heart, the GUTS.

[23] In addition to providing the usual sort of exposition we expect to find early on in a play, the first scene in Act II offers the Young Artist his first opportunity to articulate his own views about the nature of art and the creative process. These opinions are offered in two separate passages where RF is sharply criticizing the literary methods and assumption of his two friends, GT and Wadleigh. The first occurs early in the monologue when RF mocks GT's emphasis on the spiritual and rational nature of art, and derides his belief in the primacy of THINKING in the creative process. The second follows somewhat later, when RF argues that the reason Wadleigh's fiction is not being accepted for publication is largely due to his foolish belief (one also held by GT) that personal experience must be the basis for all serious literature. As would be typical of RF later work, these materials are presented but are not actually *present*, since they owe their "existence" to RF's characteristic reliance on formal strategies of indirection and absence rather than direct statement. He achieves this by using same guise he would later use in *Journey to Chaos* and all of his later critical writings—i.e., the development of an alleged critique of someone else's work, which really is just an excuse for him to present an analysis of and rationale for his own writing practices, thus permitting his own viewpoints to emerge in a conditional manner, or by implication. Thus, in addition to supplying insights about topics crucial to aesthetic he is developing, piece-by-piece, during the course of the play, he does so via experimental formal methods that will characterize much of his later writings. In so doing, he also offers us our first clear glimpse down of the road he will soon be embarking on as literary artist.

[24] Directors may wish to devise some means of suggesting that this is the same wall before which Beckett's Malone sits, although this is strictly optional.

[25] One possible decoding of this semiological gesture might be paraphrased as something like, "Crazy, daddy-o, that Miles cat is one crazy cat with wings who's been flying real high since he left Bird's nest—just like me, dig? We're both like real real gone, daddy-o… " and so forth.

[26] The opening lines of Act II continue the motif of TIME, its fleeting nature, the preciousness of each moment, the resolve of the Young Artist to use it wisely—RF will use almost exactly these same lines as the opening of the monologue in IV, ii, where this topic reaches its impassioned culmination.

[27] These lines are typical of the absurdist word play RF was encountering about this time in the theaters of Manhattan. And in fact, these monologues are absolutely saturated with lines whose meanings are literally absurd, non-sensical, paradoxical. Thus, just as he did at the outset of Act I, he casts the opening lines of the monologue in Act II in the form of a playful oxymoron (i.e., he doesn't have anything important to say but needs to say it anyway). But the presence of this sort of absurdist rhetoric can only partially be attributed to the impact which the plays of Beckett and other playwrights were having on the Young Artist during this period; a more important source likely has a more personal origin dating back to the years following his arrival in America, where he was forced to endure the frustrations of attempting to communicate in a non-native language. This would naturally have resulted in RF mangling the lingo in all sorts of ways, no doubt often with comic results, in the process of trying to express himself. And although this experience must have made RF constantly feel embarrassed, frustrated, and extremely self conscious about his verbal deficiencies, his later exposure at Columbia University to Freud, the surrealists, and absurdists helped RF begin to see ways that such "mis-use" of language could be used to his advantage as a writer. Thus, he began to recognize that placing his own linguistic trips, stutters, and falls within an aesthetic contest produced all sorts

of interesting options—for example, this could create a kind of running commentary about the misuse of language and the failure of words to communicate properly, which was certainly one of the hottest topics of the absurdists of the 50s. More positively and ultimately more importantly, developing compositional strategies designed to deliberately leave himself more open to producing such "mistakes"—for example, deliberately refusing to correct typo's and other "mistakes" that would naturally occur as he rushed ahead creating his epistolary monologues in a near frenzy of excitement—has becomes by the time of the play an important feature of his aesthetic, one analogous to the automatic writing practices of the surrealists and dadaists. In this and other ways, RF for the first time began to recognize that consciously exaggerating his own verbal pratfalls not only helped shield him from derision but became a kind of textual machine capable of producing a stream of rich, often hilarious, and frequently revealing neologisms and absurdist phrasings. Thus, what initially seemed to be a frustrating and constricting limitation became for the mature artist a means of actually OPENING UP the language, a conscious strategy to allow its multiplexes, unexpected puns, and word-play to emerge in a manner similar to what we find in *Finnegan's Wake*, some of the work of the OULIPO group, and other modernist experiments.

[28] Yet another example of what might be called a "found puns" produced by a "typo."

[29] Another absurdist oxymoron of the sort which RF delighted in using in his later work.

[30] Although Huxley remained best known in the 50s for his dystopian novel, Brave New World (1932), his earlier experiments with authorial self-consciousness and reflexivity, such as such as Antic Hay (1932 and particularly Point Counter Point (1928) were, along with Beckett work, were influential examples of metafiction.

[31] This outburst, and the one that follows a bit later about Wadleigh, are the first of several moments in the play where RF uses his two friends as punching bags to relieve his own doubts and anxieties concerning issues

he himself is obviously struggling with. These attacks on his friends also allows RF to reveals some of the ways his own literary aesthetic differs from the realistic paradigm of art and literary creation which had largely dominated Western thinking since at least the rise of Romanticism and whose origins can be traced back to the Renaissance, or even ancient Greece. The key features of this paradigm that RF addresses might be summarized as follows:

In order to produce serious art, artists FIRST must go out and LIVE LIFE DIRECTLY, thereby creating a store of personal experiences which can be drawn upon later in the work (hence the related need for artists to avoid the TRAP of cloistering themselves inside the ivory towered prisons of academia); having stored up a sufficient amount of "content" or subject matter, artists then WITHDRAWS from the world to THINK ABOUT these materials, a process involving carefully EXAMINING and OBJEC-TIFYING these experiences, breaking them down into their constituent elements and subjecting these to the RATIONAL ANALYSIS, all these eventually leading to an UNDERSTANDING of their nature and signif-icance, of how these components relate to one another (causally, psycho-logically, historically, morally, etc.), and of how these elements can be most effectively arranged dramatically and so that their most essential TRUTHS (normally concealed beneath reality's confused exterior) can be revealed; THEN AND ONLY THEN is the artist ready to begin actually writing or painting or whatever other process is demanded by their art form in transforming REALITY'S messy incoherence, ugliness, unfath-omable mysteries and irrelevancies into the orderly realm of art, whose resultant beauty, harmony and meaning emerge via the imposition of the various formal mechanisms made available to them.

In his initial outburst directed at GT, RF offers a view of the creative process that contrasts this paradigm in several specific ways. In his view, the first duty of the artist is simply to START MAKING ART. To spend time THINKING about what he is GOING TO CREATE is to waste precious TIME that could and should be spend DOING THE CRE-

ATION; moreover, too much thinking may lead to PROCRASTINA-
TION, DELAYS, or, the worst fate of all for any artist, NEVER BEGIN-
NING AT ALL (a fate he narrowly avoids in Act III, I). His remarks in
this monologue and elsewhere makes it clear that RF primarily values literature on the basis of its emotional intensity rather than for its intellectual complexity or any "truths" it claims to present; it's equally evident
that he endorses spontaneity and a blatant, even joyous subjectivity rather
than control and objectivity (points he will explore in considerable greater
detail in III, II). But his real point isn't to denigrate the intellect or to suggest that artists should NOT THINK about the art they are creating, but
that they should THINK WHILE THEY ARE CREATING ART. His
offering of Robin's "The Thinker" as an exemplar of "a thinker, in the
process of thinking, but in a work of art" directly anticipates the sort of
self-reflexives and metafictional impulses that would characterize his own
work, as well as that of many of his postmodernist contemporaries a
decade later.

[32] RF here attacks Wadleigh for accept the usual notion that great art
involves the transformation of actual REALITY or LIFE actually experienced by the author (note the many ironies involved in the fact that RF—
who had already built up several lifetimes of experiences even before arriving in America—is the one arguing this point). What's important for the
artist, RF argues, isn't one's LIFE EXPERIENCES, nor REALITY AT
ALL but the artist's particular VISION of things, they way these experiences are TOLD or PRESENTED.

[33] Although only touched on briefly here, the disappearance during the
late 50s of so many numerous commercial literary magazines had a major
impact on American writing whose effects continue to be felt today. The
whole story behind this decline is fascinating and enormously cpommpli-
cated, bugt the bpottom line is that whereas up until this decline it was
actualloyu ;ossible for moderately successful fiction writers to earn a living
by selling tgheir work to magazine like Colluiers. The Saturday Evening
Pos and many others; by the mid 60s that market had all but dired up,

meaning that other than the occasional maverick exceptoion such as Donald Barthelme, writers ere forced to either enter the academy or become partthe short-e story behind what happened is fascinating and has manyhere are a great many fais known literary magazines of this period helps establish that commercial success is becoming increasingly difficult for writers to achieve. Ironically enough, while the viewpoints RF express-es here about the unsuitability of Wadleigh's work for publication turns out to be completely erroneous (in the next scene we discover that Wadleigh becomes the first of the 3 Literary Musketeers to have a story accepted and by Act III he has already launched a career as a commercial novelist under the pseudonym Oliver Lange); they are *highly* effective in demonstrating why his own work will never achieve the commercial suc-cess or public recognition enjoyed by his rival.

[34] This passage contains several key revelations about RF's creative process that will become central features of his literary aesthetic. Among these:—the playful yet insistence of self-absorption, egotism and narcis-sism ("One must have the courage of one's own narcissism," RF would later boast); masturbation as his central metaphor for artistic creation (like masturbation, art is always a :"second-hand" experience); the need for total self commitment and sacrifice in the service of art—which is bal-anced by the beneficial (and even essential) role that relaxation, sports, sex and physical activities play in providing the necessary distance from one's work (the inevitable isolation that results from complete self-absorption is dangerous not only from a personal standpoint but because it makes self-evaluation about one's work impossible.

[35] This is one of the earlier extent references to RF's first novelist treat-ment of his life story, a manuscript enrtitled AND I FOLLOWED MY SHADOW which he indeed began before departing for graduate school and continued working on iintermitently for several years until he even-tually abandoned it, in part because his work on Beckett had convinced him that his story required a radically different apporach than the semi-realistic methods he had been using.

[36] Sex will continue to be a major point of contention between RF and GT, with RF's constant announcements about sexual conquests and being madly and desperately "in love" being countered by GT's claims that RF deceives himself by confusing pure animal lust for love. Note the way that this passage reveals how self-deceived and immature his notions of love really are.

[37] Christine, the lover who followed Gloria (and precedes Ricky), who followed Jane.

[38] Any passing reference to the theater which helps establishes it impact on the Young Artist's literary sensibility. The mid-50s was, of course, probably the most exciting period in the history of American theater, with major works appearing on Broadway by Williams, Inge, and Miller and with the enormously exciting presentations Off-Broadway by the giants of the European avant-garde theater such as Ionesco, Pinter, Arabal, and of course Samuel Beckett, whose work RF was first exposed to in 1956 when he attended a performance of *Waiting for Godot* starring Bert Lahr and E.G. Marshall.

[39] The best-known red light district of Paris, this is a street where customers can stroll along inspecting ladies of the night who are standing in the street or in doorways.

[40] In a typical Federmanesque move, one of the most crucial motifs in the play (and in RF's life-story generally) is introduced here in what appears to be a casual aside. This motif is, of course, that of *running* (with its implications of constant frantic movement, of covering as much "ground" as possible, etc.), or more precisely, of *having to run* (with its suggestions of fatality, of being pursued, the need for escape from fate, the Nazis, the past, memory or other personal demons), of being *born to run* (the latter phrase is, of course, usually associated with the title of Bruce Springsteen's landmark 1975 album; for an extended discussion of the uncanny similarities between the careers and works of RF and Bruce Springsteen, see my "On the Road (not Taken) with RF's *TIOLI*"). Thus, this passage can be specifically seen as anticipating, among many other

examples, RF's description of an episode that took place in Paris soon after the closet incident—one which he has said sums up the nature of his life-story as well as any other: "the lady holds his hand, while they walk to the police station only a few blocks away, but suddenly RF pulls his hand away and runs. He hears the lady shouting after him, "They'll catch you, they'll catch. RF is still running" (McCaffery and Federman, "Chronology for RF: A Collaborative History Fiction," *Federman, A to X-X-X-X*, p. 57.

[41] This punning equation of himself with the so-called "real world" (i.e., Ray=monde/world) balances the earlier equation of himself with the world of the mind, which concluded Act I (i.e., Ray=mind) and thus completes the introduction of the two binary terms that will struggle for dominance inside his creative imagination the rest of the play.

[42] This revelation completes the portrayal of Wadleigh as the embodiment of the degraded version of the literary artist willing to sell his soul for commercial success; while the critique RF offered in the previous scene was erroneous concerning the commercial value of Wadleigh's work, his analysis of its artistic value remains valid.

[43] The novel RF would later abandon, AND I FOLLOWED MY SHADOW, referred to earlier.

[44] This early unpublished story, "Over to the East Side," is actually one of the most skillful of the early stories RF wrote in the 50s and directly anticipates some of the narrative material in *Double or Nothing*.

[45] Yet another of RF's brilliant "found puns."

[46] The same girlfriend RF had referred to in the previous scene. Note the way this scene dramatizes how much he still has to learn about love, this despite his recently acquired literary knowledge—the references to Thomas Mann and the "disease" of love, etc. In this regard, the most revealing detail is the Young Artist's almost casual remark about having proposed marriage to Christine, even though he has only been "foolin around a little" with her (fortunately, she refuses!). Note, too, the ways that RF's comments about Cristine's grades at school suggest her potential to satisfy more than merely RF's carnal lusts; more subtly, they also calls

attention to her status here as a purely literary invention by pointing to the alphabetical "bits" responsible for her existence as language ("the girl with all As").

[47] Thomas Hardt provided some of the endnotes provided for this act.

[48] Another moment where RF reflexively reminds us of the artificial, symbolic nature of what appears to be "naturally" occurring in what seems to be the "real world" plane of existence here.

[49] A perpetual outsider who seems to have spent his entire life on the margins, it is hardly surprising that RF's feelings towards academic life and his academic colleagues (or "cacademics" as he has referred to them) have been deeply divided from the outset. On the one hand, RF has always seemed amazed that someone like himself—an orphaned foreigner who arrived in the U.S. with nothing except a thick French accent—should have wound up spending over 40 years as a distinguished university professor, an internationally renown Beckett scholar, and the author of dozens of books of fiction, poetry, and criticism. On the other hand, his own background and class have made him particularly sensitive to the sorts of pettiness and hypocrisy that is so widespread in just about all academic environments.

[50] Perhaps the most pointed suggestion in the play that GT may actually be a complete fabrication.

[51] In the next few lines RF rapidly sketches out the line of literary development that he would spend the entire rest of his life pursuing. Clearly departing from the underlying assumptions of traditional realism, RF's brand of "realisme" accepts that no matter how carefully one looks at and analyses it, life will never make any sense to anyone because from moment to moment the world is constantly being transformed and distorted. The sorts of coherence and predictability, progression leading to clarity, and so forth which are the staples of the great realistic tradition in Western fiction are illusions concocted by people who aren't able to face up to life's absurdity and accept it for what it is—a journey not to wisdom but to chaos.

[52] Whether consciously or not, RF here is echoing Kerouac's admonition (in "Principles of Spontaneous Prose") that writer need to seize the moment of perception and transform this into words immediately, before it has lost its vibrancy and freshness. This same principle had been expressed, in somewhat different terms, in Wordsworth 's "The Prelude" and in various Rimbaud's A Season in Hell.

[53] Memory, particularly the unreliability of memory, has understandably been an issue that is absolutely central to just about everything RF has ever written, including these lines—"I wonder if I'm describing you the way... I think I remember you"— with their emphasis on the way that memory provides only a distorted version of the past.

[54] Later RF will argue that the constructs of language are not only every bit "as good" as what they might signify in reality but often far superior.

[55] The passage RF is appropriating here is from T. S. Eliot's "The Love Song of J. Alfred Prufrock " :

No! I am not Prince Hamlet, nor was meant to be;

Am an attendant lord, one that will do

To swell a progress, start a scene or two,

Advise the prince; no doubt, an easy tool,

Deferential, glad to be of use. (lines111-115)

"Prufrock" obviously made a strong impression on RF due to the frequency with which he refers to it in his correspondence from this period.

[56] French: "Watch out, boy. I continue."

[57] I.e., John Wadleigh..

[58] And indeed, as RF's literary executioner, I can verify that RF's has somehow managed to retain copies of just about everything he has ever written, including not only copies of nearly every letter he has ever received from his friends and colleagues but even copies of his own letters.

[59] RF has always enjoyed boasting about his muscular, swelt physique, although after he quit smoking in the late 80s, he did complain about the weight he gained.

[60] French (with accents lacking): "I am disgusted. Nausea." The last

term is also probably a reference to the title of John Paul Sartre's most famous novel, La nausee (1938; translated into English in 1965 as Nausea), a title which was also used as the name of a song on X's 1980s punk masterpiece, Los Angeles; I mention the latter because although many commentators have noted the influence of jazz on RF's work, to my knowledge no one yet has examined the many commonalties between RF's aesthetic and that of punk.

61 French quotation from Mallarme's poem "Brise marine": "The flesh is sad alas! and all books I have read."

62 Probably a reference to Samuel Beckett.

63 Another reference to *And I Followed My Shadow*, the work-in-progress he eventually abandoned.

64 Another masturbation reference which here, as is typical in RF's writing, suggests an obscene expression of a "second hand" experience.

65 RF here engages in a bit of what he would later term "pre-remembering"—i.e., remembering something (in this case, the fact that he and GT will indeed one day be collected in an encyclopedia) that hasn't yet occurred.

66 Allen Ginsberg's controversial *Howl* had been published by City Lights in 1954. RF clearly admired and identified with what Ginsberg had accomplished in Howl, for just a few lines later in his letter he says "fuck you too... because he said it before me."

67 RF did indeed write political essays on these and related topics having to do with American conformity during the 1950s, although they were usually disguised within works of fiction. See especially his novels *Take It or Leave It* and *Smiles on Washington Square*.

68 French (misspelled): "the little island of the dream."

69 RF himself left America in disgust in 1958 and moved to Paris, where he worked for three miserable months in a restaurant; he then decided that taking America made more sense than leaving it had, and returned to Los Angeles where he began work on his Ph.D. degree in Comparative Literature.

[70] RF is here alluding to the following passage which occurs near the end of T.S. Eliot's "The Lovesong of J. Alfred Prufrock":
I have heard the mermaids singing, each to each.
I do not think they will sing to me. (ll.123-5)

[71] This animal imagery is central to the title poem in RF's first poetry collection, Among the Beasts, whose opening stanza reads:
I stood face to face with a bull
And threw stones at his eyes
And struck his back with a stick

[72] As Thomas Hartl has noted, "These three lines read like a blueprint for RF's poem "Among the Beasts," referring to the experiences of the brutality of nature and the banality of procreation that RF experienced while living and working on a farm in southern France between 1942 and 1945; the "old man" mentioned in both texts is the farmer for whom RF worked.

[73] French: "Goodbye my little buddy."

[74] Perhaps an echo of the famous words uttered by Beckett's narrator, which conclude The Unnamable: "I can't on I must go on I'll go on."

[75] French: "a slice of my mind."

[76] Although rarely mentioned by critics, RF very much could and SHOULD be seen as a symbol of hope for human-kind.

[77] French: "shit for those who will read it. There you have literature."

[78] Guillaume Apollinaire (1880-1918): invented the word "surrealism" and was one of the first to experiment with concrete prose in his Calligrammes (1918).

[79] What follows is a description of the disparity between RF's original plans for a text versus what he actually wound up writing—remarks which could apply just as well to nearly everything RTF has ever written, published and certainly would be relevant to all his novels.

[80] French (misspelled): "fire fly."

[81] Another unattributed appropriation—this one borrowed from Beckett's *Waiting for Godot*—is one of the hundreds quotations we see a

young RF playfully and intuitively introducing into the rush of composing these monologue. It should be noted that RF was already practicing
this textual practice that he would later term "playgiarism" long before
critics such as Barthes or Derrida began making the case that writing has
no original source, and instead always results out of the endless play of
signification.

82 RF has repeatedly claimed that "My life is a story," and that this story
must be continually retold despite his awareness of the futility of ever getting it "right." In these remarks to GT we see RF not only already presenting his life *not* as being "real" but as a subjective construct—a dream,
a fiction, something he has made up—but as a *failed or provisional invention* which must be continually revised.

84 Here RF self-consciously and reflexively announces the failure of
what he had been writing—but holds out the promise that the next version will be better. RF would later recast this trope into the conclusions of
many of his novels. Although this method had been employed most
notably by Beckett and Borges, variations of this reflexive announcement
about the failure of what one is writing appeared in numerous metafictional works from the 60s such as Vonnegut's *Slaughterhouse-Five* and
Ronald Sukenick's *Up*.

85 French: "your good friend."

86 The grove of orange trees and sounds of birds here evokes not only
RF's new sense of confidence, personally and artistically, but also anticipates the tree and (especially) the bird-imagery that RF will later associate
with the closet-episode. Cf. The closing stanzas of "Escape": But through
a crack in the wall/I saw a tree the shape of a leaf/and one morning a bird
flew into my head/I loved that bird so much/that while the blue-eyed mas-
ter/looked at the sun and was blind/I opened the cage/and hid my heart
in a yellow feather. RF reinforces the significance of this bird imagery by
employing it as a semiotic analogy in the crucial opening lines of his concluding monologue (see Act IV, II).

87 RF is referring to "The Toothbrush," one of his earliest stories con-

sciously conceived in terms of formal experimentation which he had recently sent to GT, who apparently didn't much care for it. The story was eventually published in *Panache*.

[88] RF's continued efforts to publish his work in *The New Yorker* and *Esquire* even at this point in his development allows us to see that for him, artistic maturity does not necessarily involve completely eliminating a desire for commercial success and critical recognition, but only that one must not compromise the integrity of the work in order to achieve this. In fact, RF would continue to send his work to *The New Yorker* throughout his career and although his efforts have thus far not yielded any acceptances, a highly laudatory review of *Aunt Rachel's Fur* did appear *The New Yorker* in 2000.

[89] This reflexive admission of the congruency between RF and his character also reinforces the possibility that GT here may actually be more another fictitious alter-ego than real as we initially assume him to be.

[90] "Humanity 100"—included in Appendix IIIA.

[91] This "missing text" motif is a formal mechanism that RF will later introduce in some of his later works (perhaps most notably in the gap that occurs in the climax of The Voice in the Closet). RF does, however, manage to complete this interrupted scatological analogy ("it came out like shit out of a ...") later in the monologue with the lines: "The solution to my problem would be to print my stuff on toilet paper."

[92] RF claims he has been using initials as abbreviations ever since he can remember; occasionally, as here, he introduces playful word games into this usage (i.e., the RF to C reference here can be decoded as *R*aymond *F*ucks *C*hristine).

[93] Parker would later make a guest appearance in *Take It or Leave It* doing a sex solo, ah, of course that's suuposed to read *sax* solo, in "Remembering Charlie Parker."

[94] RF begins his final monologue with a quiet confidence by noting he has "finally" been able to "find" (and hence gain control over) time and language—two recurrent topics he has been shown to be struggling with

throughout the play. This is one of the final act's first indications of the maturity and wisdom he has gained that has enable him to come to grips to the major sources of personal and aesthetic conflict that needed to be resolved before he was ready to embark on his journey towards literary artistry.

[95] The issue RF is referring to included his translations of Jean Genet's "The Beggars of Barcelona" (am excerpt from *The Thief's Journal*) and of Renee Riese Hubert's poem, "Sizes."

[96] RF did complete his thesis on Beckett, which was later revised and published in 1965 as *Journey to Chaos: Samuel Beckett's Early Fiction.*

APPENDIX I BACKGROUND, SOURCES, DIRECTOR'S NOTES:

IA. Director's Preface. As can be inferred from its title, PORTRAIT is a theatrical re-working of the familiar *kuntlerroman[check spelling]* narrative formula used by Joyce, Goethe, and many other novelists to depict the stages of growth, education, and maturity contributing to the development of the artist. This process is presented here as a four act play which consists entirely of a series of monologues whose texts have been drawn almost verbatim from letters originally written during the late 1950s by the aspiring young literary artist Raymond Federman and addressed to his close friend George Tashima. The dramatic "action" of the play, then, occurs via a dialogic process of dynamic interaction between the Young Artist (hereafter: "RF") whom we see on stage, delivering these epistolary monologues on the spot, as he composes them on his manual typewriter, and the absent Tashima ("GT"), who "appears" only "off-stage" (as it were) but who nonetheless plays various roles as RF's literary mentor, rival, and alter ego and perhaps even his Plato lover[98], while also (dis)embodying aesthetic alternatives which RF must ultimately reject. The various other characters in the play—John Wadleigh (another aspiring writer), William Owens (RF's influential creative writing instructor in college), and a series of women whom RF becomes romantically entangled with—all function essentially as allegorical figures representing less worthy models of the artistic process (Wadleigh), as friends and mentors who offer the hero encouragement and valuable instructions concerning the nature or art and life during moments of artistic self-doubt (Dodson and Owens), as literalizations of lust and other sensual temptations which RF must learn to resist before he can fully commit himself to the artistic vocation (Jane, Gloria, Christine, etc.), and as figures who otherwise provide assistance in overcoming the personal and aesthetic crises which inevitably arise during the process of his evolution and growth into becoming an artist.

These monologues are set respectively in the Catskills, Manhattan , Los Angeles, and Santa Barbara during the crucial period in the late 50s which saw Federman leave behind the mostly mute misery of poverty, ignorance, loneliness and darkness he had endured ever since his arrival in America and embark upon a journey that would take his life story in an entirely new direction. What eventually transpired along the way of *that* journey was a whole new set of exotic adventures and romances involving a rich cast of memorable characters, new roles to be played, crises to be faced, and challenges to be overcome. And although Federman still hasn't reached the end of that journey, their major plot elements seems to indicate that the story will have an improbably happy ending. But that, as they say, is a different story, which Portrait only sets the stage for. And now, on with the show!

APPENDIX IB: Epistolary Sources.

The monologues were taken nearly verbatim from the following letters written by RF to GT : Act I: Sent from Copake Country Club (a resort in the Catskills in upper state New York where Federman worked during the summer), July 8, 1956; Act II, I: 107 E. 105th St, Apt. 7 (where Federman was living with his cousin while completing his final year at Columbia University), January 28, 1957 (the first day of Federman's final semester at

Columbia); Scene II: May 15, 1957 (near the end of Federman's final semester and his birthday); Act III, Scene II: Los Angeles (Federman's office in the Comparative Literature Department at UCLA), November 18, 1978 (the period of the Young Artist's "dark night of the soul," when he was seriously considering abandoning his plans to become a writer and teacher, to leave America, which had thus far proved to be so disappointing and relocate back to his native France); Act IV, Scene I: Santa Barbara (the cottage where Federman—who has returned from the disappointments and self-revelations made during his self-imposed exile in France during the summer of 1958—is now completing work on his Ph.D. thesis dealing with the early fiction of Samuel Beckett; having also now finally discovered what the words "love" and "literary artist" mean for himself, Federman has now reached the conclusion of this stage of his life and is preparing to embark on an entirely new journey.

APPENDIX IC: Note Regarding Editorial "Interventions" into the Original Source Material.

*These monologues the text of the original letters cited above. Although I have made minor changes in syntax and (more rarely) in spelling to "smooth over" the transition made from their original typewritten versions to the spoken versions presented in the monologues, I want to emphasize that the text of the original letters has essentially been "lifted" as directly and accurately as possible and then "downloaded" into the monologues. Thus, I have deliberately preserved all of the original "errors" in syntax and punctuation, misspellings, and other infelicities of usage that appear in the letters, along with their incoherence organization, their obscenities, and repetitions. Although this decision results in monologues that often sound awkward, chaotic, and even surreal, retaining this sort of seemingly outmoded allegiance to "originality" seemed not only desirable but absolutely essential in order to preserve what strikes me as their most distinctive quality: their sense of crazed, obsessive momentum—of an author rushing forward in the heat of the moment to unleash a torrent of words and ideas that have been too long damned up, who is in fact trying precisely to render this moment exactly as it is coming into being as it is transcribed onto the page, spontaneously, improvisationally, who is so excited and impatient about this process that he's unwilling to pause even for a moment in order to correct misspellings, to revise, or do anything else that might impede this torrent of words from moving forward, relentlessly and unpredictably, towards whatever final destination (or solution) the kinetic energy stored in the words might allow for, trusting in this process of improvisational literary creation (one which Jack Kerouac had described in his essay, "Principles of Spontaneous Prose," which may have influenced the Young Artist) to produce something NEW and VIBRANT and ORIGINAL that could never be achieved by relying on the traditional method of literary composition, with its emphasis on developing a coherent, inductive, linearly arranged sequence of ideas which had been analyzed and thought through in advance. Indeed, one of the key points that emerges in the Young Artist's monologues is the insistence that the principles of "thinking," coherence, and "proper" language are not only not essential to his creative process but active hindrances.

APPENDIX ID: EPISTOLARY Fiction (entry in McCaffery, et. al Federman, A to X-X-X-X)

306 w. 105ᵗʰ a|t 7.   New York. Nov. 2

Mon Petit George:

I suppose writing a letter is a little like writing a short story or a poem.
You cannot just sit down and begin to write, you must find the mood, the inspiration.
I waited for it. I could have written long ago, but just to say nothing, or to give
you the news of everyday was not important enough, not that I have something very
great to say, just thoughts that have come to me today...Today, a very lonely day.
It's been raining in New York for three days now...Dark autumn rain. Sad.

*These words opened a letter by RF to his Korean War buddy and mentor, George Tashima, and provide the basis for understanding the crucial role that epistolary fiction has played in the evolution of RF's literary career over the years. As his remarks to Tashima indicate, epistolary fiction as envisioned by RF and as being referred to here is only slightly related to the epistolary forms associated with 18th century novels such as Samuel Richardson's *Pamela* and *Clarrisa* and more recent books such as John Barth's *Letters*. Rather it refers to works of fiction which are produced by one or more authors during the process of "actual" letter-writing or exchanges of correspondence. Of course, it is not altogether uncommon during the courses of an extended series of exchanges of letters over the year to find one or both of the correspondents occasionally making up details or otherwise creatively embellishing the usual exchanges of news and gossip, but in the case of RF's epistolary exchanges, obviously fictionalized, collaborative exchanges are the norm. Over the years an enormous amount of this sort of material has been generated which includes poems, theater pieces, stories, novels (and in the case of the remarkable GC-RF exchanges over the past fifteen years or so, even a full blown epic novel of truly gigantic proportions), and numerous unclassifiable forms. The end result is that RF and his epistolary collaborators have created an immense and fascinating literary work—a vast, largely unexplored textual region whose richness and variety can only be hinted at in the selected entries in this volume and which awaits further exploration by future critics and interested readers.

APPENDIX II. ENTRIES FOR *PORTRAIT* TO BE ADDED TO 2ND EDITION OF *FEDERMAN, A TO X-X-X-X*.

IIA. CHAOS THEORY AS PROVIDING A FIRST PRINCIPLE OF RF'S REALIST LITERARY AESTHETIC.

Chaos theory is a fairly recently notion developed originally by meteorologists and then later applied more systematically by theorists in physics and other friends seeking to explain how orderly realms ranging from the patters of birds in flight, the structures of termites, bees, and ants, galaxies, and even the entire cosmos itself have evolved the interactions of a relatively small number of elements interacting among themselves chaotically rather than being arrange according to some sort of overall plan or preexisting method of organization. The relevance of this notion to the aesthetic developed by RF during the course of this play should be obvious: his notion of a realist aesthetic is likewise based on the notion of that orderly structures (such as the realism in his fiction, as well as the narrative pattern in *Portrait* itself) emerges NOT out of a consciously conceived plan or structure that has been worked out in advance, but out of the chaotic interactions of the elements (in this case, the elements out of which his work are composed— words, phrases, ideas, memories, and other narrative "bits" that are written down on the page more or less directly, randomly, and digressively without trying to consciously organize them and control them into the sort of pre-set patterns employed by most authors. The key point of connection then is this shared notion of EMERGENT BEHAVIORS that come into being out of a "bottom up" process of chaotic interactions, as opposed to the traditional "bottom up" approach to composition, whereby the order and meaning in a work of fiction is seen as resulting from an author first developing a preconceived "game plan" that he then follows while doing the actual writing.

IIB. CHARLIE PARKER'S IMPACT ON RF'S APPROACH TO LITERARY COMPOSITION. .Charlie Parker's music and composition methods get right to the heart or (as Federman himself would put it) the GUTS of the matter, the "matter" here being not gray matter (the mind, the source of thinking and intelligence which Federman eventually rejects as the basic source of great artistry) but the "inner" core matter of emotions, memories, lusts, and fears which the mature artist must learn to confront and transform into words and stories (for the writer), or whatever elements are used by artists to create their own art forms. Long before Federman even remotely imagined he might someday become a literary artist, Parker had provided him with a model of the creative activity based not on thinking, intelligence, or adherence to rules and technical virtuosity but on the free play of the imagination conjuring up the pain and loneliness and exhilaration of existence and then GIVING VOICE to these emotions directly, spontaneously, in the moment, as they were being experienced in real time. And as such, what's valued in this particular mode of artistic expression isn't the features of artistic control and rational analysis privileged in most classical forms of Western art, nor the ability of the artist to objectify experience or to impose aesthetic "order" on the absurdities and chaos that comprise the most fundamental features of human experience by confining these to the rationally-derived structures based on linearity and causality and then arranging these into a sequence producing the pleasing illusions of so-called "realism." Rather, as RF gradually discovers in *Portrait* through a series of hotly contested epistolary debates with Tashima (who here clearly represents a model of artistic creation based on rationality and spirituality), his own particular brand of literary artistry must be based on giving expression to human consciousness in all its brute, vibrant, painful reality—and then (what equally important) to laugh at it, and to play with it. Although the basic divisions being contested here can be approached via the Apollinian/Dionysian categories used by Nietzsche (who would exert a powerful influence on Federman much later in his career) in *The Birth of Tragedy* to describe Greek drama (and what was missing from modern art in the West), the basic point here can also be expressed simply by the familiar phrase so associated with jazz during the bebop era: It don't mean a thing if it ain't got that swing. Incidentally, my own view is that the single greatest omission thus far from critical discussions of the aesthetic underlying Federman's writing is a sort of extended, detailed look at the decisive impact which jazz generally, and Charlei Parker's composition methods in particular, have had on his work.

APPENDIX III, TEXT OF STORIES AND POEMS WRITTEN BY THE YOUNG ARTIST DURING THE COURSE OF THE PLAY

IIIA. "Humanities 1200."
Humanities 1200[xcix]
I
Remember
the place was quite unfriendly
an accidental meeting
and a certain man
spoke academically
of a certain book
ignorant and ignored
by the silence of my thoughts
But even you then could not guess
that the false cigarette
hurting in my hand
was a pretense of assurance
Neither did you sense

how my eyes were jealous
of the smoke touching
your mouth and your hair
ii.
Anyway words or hands touching
are not enough to disturb a moment
And the time was too soon
Time cannot be reduced or quickened
It stretches over the nights too
and the waiting in the dark
Even if the lips meet once
the bodies are strangers
So many unfinished moments
are lost in foolish pride
Each man carries in his eyes
the mystery of tomorrow
exchanging each dream
for a blow of reality
But how could my fingers
reach the heart of a bodiless voice
locked in Granite and the secret
of a few remembered numbers
Yet I was determined
willing to accept
the inconsequences of time
wanting to force the moment
III
The June sun was ready for its feast
The soft sand touched both our bodies
And the poet was silent
But his words remained unforgotten
crying their perpetual intoxication

"Before I am old I shall have written you one
Poem maybe as cold and passionate as the dawn"
And then time became as swift
as the morning-dream of lovers
Words as useless as the Yes
Only the hands touched and touched
until the moment was complete
and it was reality

APPENDIX IV. List of Works Consulted.

Beckett, Samuel. *The Unnamable.*

Federman, Raymond. *And I Followed My Shadow.* Unpublished typescript of RF's first novel, about 600 pages, written c. 1955-58 in New York City and Los Angeles.

_____. "Among the Beasts." In *Among the Beasts/Parmi les monstres..* Paris: Editions José Millas-Martin, 1967, pp. 9-10.

_____ (with Larry McCaffery).. "Chronology for RF: A Collaborative History Fiction," Federman, *A to X=X=X-X*, pp. 57-77.

_____. *Double or Nothing.* Chicago: Swallow Press, 1971.

_____. "The Beggars of Barcelona" (trans. of fiction by Jean Genet). *Big Table* 3, (1959).

_____, "Imagination as Pla(y)giarism [an unfinished paper...]". *New Literary History* 7, 3 (1976): 563-78.

_____. *Journey to Chaos: Samuel Beckett's Early Fiction.* Berkeley and Los Angeles: University of California Press, 1965.

_____. "Sizes" (trans. of poem by Renee Riese Hubert). *Big Table* 3, (1959).

_____. *Smiles on Washington Square* ("A love story of sorts"). New York: Thunder's Mouth Press, 1985. Reissued in paperback, Los Angeles: Sun & Moon Press, "Classics" collection, 1995.

_____. *Take It or Leave It*. New York: Fiction Collective, 1976. Republished by the FCII in 1995 with Larry McCaffery's critifictional preface, "On the Road (not Taken) with Federman's TIOLI."

_____. "The Toothbruth." *Panache*, 10 (1973).

McCaffery, Larry, Thomas Hart, and Doug Rice. *Federman, A to X-X-X-X—A Recyclopedic Narrative*. San Diego: San Diego State University Press, 1996.

_____. "Epistolary Fiction." Entry in *Federman, A to X-X-X-X—A Recyclopedic Narrative*, pp. 116-117.

_____. "On the Road (not Taken) with Federman's TIOLI." Expanded version of the preface appearing in the 1995 reissue of *Take It or Leave It*). In McCaffery, et al., *Federman, A to X-X-X-X*, pp. 241-247.

---

[1] He may even be interpreted as RF's lover; see especially RF's remarks at the very outset of Act I.

[2] This is the love poem written by the Young Artist for Ricky referred to by RF in Act IV, Scene I. The title refers to the class at UCLA where RF first met Ricky.

Compendium of Federman's Short Fictions in English from the Late 1980s and '90s

Bob Riedel

The publication this year of LOOSE SHOES (Berlin: Weidler, 2001) provides a much-needed (don't believe that business in the book's prefatory statement about him writing all the pieces during the year 1999; that, of course, is a fiction too). And much of his best poetry appears in the 1992 bilingual collection NOW THEN/NUN DENN (Eggingen: Edition Isele, 1992). But there remains a body of writing—fiction, poetry, essays, letters—that exists only in the pages of ephemeral literary periodicals (and presumably, at least partially, in the depths of the author's own filing cabinet). What follows are a very few of the briefer snippets culled from a motley pile of such publications. Seekers after lengthier examples of wayward Federmaniana would do well to consult "Bibliography, Part II" in FEDERMAN: A to X-X-X-X, edited by Larry McCaffery, Thomas Hartl, and Doug Rice (San Diego: SDSU Press, 1998).

The first, poet and critic Hubert's first piece to be published in English, is an example of Federman's early translation work for Paul Carroll's seminal Big Table magazine, for which Federman also provided translations of Genet and Breton during its five-issue run. Readers of DOUBLE OR

349

NOTHING may sense a certain kinship between that novel's obsessed narrator and Hubert's similarly stricken heroine.–

BR

****

Sizes

by Renée Riese Hubert

For a long time I didn't give a damn about my sizes: these "38" and "6-3/4" remained abstractions without relationship to the hand or the fashionable article which was supposed to cover it. In the stores my forgetfulness was quickly mended. But one day they began to tell me about these sizes before I even thought of going shopping.

— Madame wears a 36? asked a stranger.

— Never again will you buy a Dauphine, prophetized someone who hadn't even seen me out of my Citroen. And so I submitted myself to the necessity of establishing a few statistics:

Telephone: Odéon 32 56

ID card: FM 93 664

Salary: 44,500 francs

Height: 1m 65

Statistics which I tried very hard to complete constantly against all eventualities. Little by little I was tempted to memorize the numbers written on the subway tickets, theater tickets, monthly checks. Then I counted the dresses in my closet, the pieces of furniture, the customers who entered the butcher shop. I even established the exact number of my relatives, friends, enemies, acquaintances.

But one day, unknowingly, I went beyond the limits of prudence. I began to watch the strokes of my pulse, the beats of my heart. It was not an easy job without a stethoscope. Every morning at eight I took my temperature. Yesterday, the mercury, darker than usual, dropped suddenly before my eyes. And now I know exactly where I stand.

(translation by RF in Big Table 3, 1959)

****

From the French of Montaigne (from the essay, On Experience)

….There is more work interpreting interpretation, than there is to interpret the thing itself; and more books are written about books than about any other subject. All we do is criticize one another. Everything swarms with commentary; writers are very rare…as a stem for the second, the second for the third. Thus we ascend step by step. And so it happens that often the one who climbs the highest has more honor than merit; because he has only risen by one grain on the shoulders of the one before…

(translation by RF in Mica 2, February 1961)
****

8 X 8
ALL
  MEN
   CARRY
    IN THEM
     THEIR MULTIPLICATION
      TABLES
     ALMOST ALL MEN
    THEREFORE
   LET US PITY
  THOSE
WHO CANNOT
  INSTANTLY
   CALCULATE
    THE MATHEMATICS
     OF THEIR EXISTENCE

(from Escarpments, Vol. 1, No. 1, Spring 1980)
****

"Only bad art is immoral," Ezra Pound often said. Or better yet, Samuel Beckett on Proust: "Proust is completely detached from all moral considerations. There is no right and wrong in Proust nor in his world.

(Except possibly in those passages dealing with the war, when for a space he ceases to be an artist and raises his voice with the plebs, mob, rabble, canaille). Tragedy is not concerned with human justice. Tragedy is the statement of an expiation, but not the miserable expiation of a codified breach of a local arrangement, organized by the knaves for the fools."

One always argues for a "moral fiction" out of despair, out of insecurity, and from an anemic awareness of social and political illness. It is a strictly humanist (at one time said Bourgeois) point of view which excludes all books that (presumably) depict a bad way of life, for instance the works of the Marquis de Sade, Huysmans, D.H. Lawrence, Marcel Proust, Henry Miller, Samuel Beckett, Jean Genet, and many others, including of course all the so-called Postmodern fictioneers—all those, in other words, who in the interest of moral security have been taxed with decadence and immorality and thereby placed out of the reach of young girls of good families.

This has always been the position totalitarian systems must assume in order to survive in the context of their own twisted morality. It is an old historical truth—historical trick rather—of the ruling class to brush aside, exclude, censure, burn even, on moral grounds, those books which do not conform to its idea of morality and therefore are found detrimental to its moral good health. But of course this can only be done by negating aesthetic value, by deliberately failing to distinguish good art from bad art, and by raising one's voice with the plebs, mob, rabble, canaille.

[from "A Writers' Forum on Moral Fiction" (a symposium-response to John Gardner's book, On Moral Fiction), in Fiction International 12, 1980]

****

Hey Mike,

Just snuffed your last Smoke Signals. What a collection of pissers! Full of unexpectations. My old buddy Bukowski still boozing and pissing his way across literature, well I mean les Belles-Lettres. How refreshing. And all the rest too. THE DISCUSSION between Namredef and Nitram [SS

2/2&3 had presented that collaborative piece by Federman and Richard Martin—BR]—WOW! I like what Nam and Nit have to say—sounds like Gogo and Didi but without the existential angst.

Speaking of rejections. Here is one for you. I get this letter from this editor of a nice expensive glossy rich magazine saying I should send some of my stuff because there is so little good avant-garde stuff that comes in to his magazine, blah-blah-blah. So I send the guy-editor a piece of my avant-garde stuff and he sends it back saying "I really like this piece but there are seven Fucks in it and I have already accepted a piece by Ron Sukenick and in it there are four fucks. Eleven fucks in one issue would be too much." Imagine that. Talk to me about editorial policy and literary taste. Oh well, I really enjoyed Smoke Signals and am glad to have contributed some little puffs.

Smokingly yours,
Raymond Federman
Buffalo, N.Y.

(letter to editor Mike Golden in Smoke Signals, Vol. 2, No. 4, 1982. Golden's printed reply may be worth noting: "Imagine that. I'm sorry, I can't. We've accepted pieces by you and Ron for this issue, and not one fuck. What's wrong with you guys, you losin' it or something?")
****

SMOKE SIGNALS JAM (Federman's responses to a questionnaire sent by the magazine to him, Ken Kesey, Andrei Codrescu, Ronald Sukenick and other contributors)

— When you're discouraged or feel like quitting on your path, what tricks/activities do you use to put you back on the track?

RF: I Masturbate. Depending on how discouraged I am I use either gloves or bare hands.

— With all the different scenarios possible for the planet, what do you see, and how would you like to see Smoke Signals attempt to cover it?

RF: There is only one scenario possible for the planet: IT SHOULD AVOID THE FUTURE. However since it cannot regress to the past, in spite of what most people think and wish, then it should rush faster towards the apocalypse so that we can at least watch the greatest show on Earth LIVE and not on television. Smoke Signals should start selling tickets to the show.

— Draw/Describe this energy called God.

RF: GOD: a pimple on the ass of the universe.

— If you died right now, what would you want on your tombstone? Give us your epitaph.

RF: My epitaph: Good question. "Here lies RAYMOND FEDER-MAN who thought himself immortal until he was proven wrong." [Note: At the suggestion of his daughter (and perhaps in consideration for the stonecarver?), Federman says he has since truncated this to the more or less synonymous: "OUT OF PRINT."

— BR]

— What's the biggest lie that's perpetrated on us?

RF: The biggest lie? Well of course, the universe.

— With the state of the world so obviously out of control, how do you go about planning for the future?

RF: I plot the future in the conditional. Or, if you prefer, I always try to anticipate what would happen if I were to do this or that but since I don't do this or that but always do the contrary I'm never wrong in the future. or to put it in simpler and more direct terms: you cannot fuck the future/the future fucks you (I think that's a line from SATURDAY NIGHT FEVER). Now, that's not to mean I am a pessimist. on the contrary. If the future is going to fuck me that means at least I'll have some pleasure. Blissfulness. The French say JOUISSANCE.

— What one question makes you most uncomfortable?

RF: No question makes me uncomfortable because there are no false questions only dumb questions. To ask if the moon is made of green cheese is not a false question it is a dumb question. Now if you were to ask me what makes me the most uncomfortable, I would have to reply: ALL ANSWERS.

(from Smoke Signals: The Book Fair Issue, 1984)

THE FEDERMAN HAIRCUT

THEODORE PELTON

Buffalo, New York, has not been the same without Raymond Federman, who in 1998 left his home of the previous thirty years to move to the beautiful deserts of San Diego. Eventually everyone leaves Buffalo, a city more empty now than the wine bottle at a one-jug artist's reception. Once a city of enormous prestige and wealth, Buffalo is depopulating so quickly that the Department of the Census doesn't think they'll have to send counters here in 2010. They're just going to spot us 1,000 and call us lucky. Residents are leaving in such droves that moving trucks cruise the streets like taxis. We had to pass a law to keep the mayor in town (true story). Change of address forms have become highly prized on the black market and the smart set hires postal brokers just to get their enormous, overdue heating bills forwarded to new residences. It's a good thing Niagara Falls is nearby: the huge waterfall generates the power that keeps the region's electric lights on and it's dark here all the time. The Western New York skies turn cloudy just before the World Series starts and stay that way until the teams have played fifty games the next season. Federman was right—who'd want to live in Buffalo? It's cold here, lonely, no one has any money, and every time you pick up the phone you get asked to drive someone else to the airport.

I was walking aimlessly through the desolate city, despairing at the dark downtown streets slick with water and ice. Up ahead, I saw a place that caught my attention, a hole in the wall, one storefront alone lit up. A barbershop. As it happened, I needed a haircut. These old time barber shops, there's where you get the good deals—and who knew if I'd have a job next week. Besides, there's no trick to cutting hair. Amateurs trim their own hedges and trees, and even little girls can do a fair job on the head of a doll. And how often does a pro give you a really good haircut. They either take too much off or cut the sideburns in two different directions so you end up having to trim it yourself later on and nicking your ear with the scissors. At most, you're happy one out of every three times you go. You pay an arm and a leg and still come out looking like crap, and maybe even injured. Paying a lot of money guarantees nothing but that your stylist will wear more perfume. So, I figured, if I'm going to get a crap haircut any-way, I might as well save some money. I went in to this hole in the wall, a single glass door in a big brick building otherwise dark all the way down.

There was a mob scene inside. Now, it's true, I don't often see crowds of people anymore, at least within the city limits. But this haircut place was packed. It was just a small storefront, but they'd made room by knocking out the wall to the back office, put in three more chairs with the original two. The seats were all full and others huddled around, biding their time until their turns came around.

That wasn't all. I looked around the room. It was crowded with writer-types; you know, mostly wearing black, lots of trenchcoats, army boots and sweaters with holes in them and every second person with a laptop, tap-tapping away. What kind of a place was this, anyway?

I noticed something else strange: everyone in there—mostly guys, but some women too—they all had the same haircut. It was something of a Roman style, short all around and combed down, some of them even with the sideburns brushed forward slightly. And there, on the wall, as if the portrait of the God in whose temple we were are congregated, for every-one in the place was styled to resemble him—there, in a barber's mug shot, head tilted slightly to one side, noble in appearance, was a photo of the master surfictionist, Raymond Federman.

"Next," called out the first barber, an older man nearest the front window.

I looked around, but no one made a move. True, none of them seemed to need haircuts. I realized that I was next—the writer-types were all either typing or looking vaguely up the ceiling, as if somewhere in the yellowing acoustic tiles overhead, in patches of fiberglass insulation puffing from gaps in the corners where boards had fallen away, was *le mot juste*.

I got in the chair, I admit, somewhat baffled. The barber was quiet. He put the smock over me. He took out tissue paper and wrapped a piece around my neck, then buttoned the smock up over it. Then he caught my eye in the mirror—well? what did I want done?

My eyes went back again to the portrait of Federman, which I now saw in the mirror behind me. This took precedence over any instructions I might want to give about my haircut.

"You know Federman?" I asked.

"Ah," he said, and even in that one syllable I detected the stagiest French accent I'd ever heard in my life. This guy was the Frog That Time Forgot—h's would be under erasure, e's slide back into the throat, r's purr.

"Sure, I know Federman," he Maurice-Chevaliered huskily. "So what? What 'as it ever done for me?"

Again I was at a loss for words. The barber quickly covered my embarrassment.

"So," he heaved, Depardieu-like, "I suppose you want to look like 'im, too."

"Yeah, sure."

"I tell you," he went on, "All over, that's all anyone wants anymore is to get a 'aircut like Federman. 'Ooh, made me look like Federman, make me look like Federman.' It makes me sick. That guy, Federman, what did 'e ever do? I tell you, 'e stole everything 'e ever did from me."

"What?"

"That's right! You 'ear dis accent? I tell you, dis is de real ding. 'e took it from me—Federman 'as never even been to France. Oh, maybe lately, now that 'e's really big over there, but in the old days—*non*, never."

A look of disbelief must have crossed my face and been spied in the mirror, because after a couple of clips more with the scissors, he continued.

"When I first met Federman, 'e was just this guy from Jersey. 'ackensack. 'e used to come to the jazz club where I used to play saxophone."

"Did you teach Ray how to play?"

"'im? 'e couldn't even play Row Your Boat. I kept trying to get rid of 'im. This was in New York in the fifties, but I could never shake 'im. I 'ad known 'im from during the war in Korea."

"Were you in the paratroopers?"

"I was, but 'e never was. 'e wrote about all these things in 'is books as if they'd 'appened to 'im. I tell you, there was even more fiction there than 'e ever let on—'im with 'is fake French accent and the rest of 'is shtick."

"Well, though you have to admit, Federman was a real innovator with the novel. If you look at *Double or Nothing* or *Take it or Leave It*, these novels are like no one else's in how they play with every aspect of the form, down to the very page and typography. Some of those pages in *Double or Nothing* could be abstract paintings."

"'e took it all from me! I tell you 'ow it 'appened. One day, Federman in is 'ere getting 'is 'air cut—that was the original Federman 'aircut, the one all the kids are going for today. Anyway, I get tired of always 'aving to sweep up the floor after each 'aircut, so I decided to put sheets of paper on the floor to catch the clippings, so that I won't 'ave to sweep, I'll just change the paper every so often. Anyway, Federman gets into the chair and I go to change the paper, and the 'air clippings all over the sheet of paper, they make a kind of design, and I look at one and then another and I say, 'Eh, not bad! What do you think, Federman?' And 'e says, "Yeah, not bad." And I say, 'Eh, I got an idea. No one 'as ever done this before, but what if we put words in all the spots where this hair is, just like this, and we make a novel out of all these sheets with words all over the place?' And Federman says, 'Eh, that's a good idea.' Because the 'air clippings, they already sort of look like words on these sheets of paper. But, I say to Federman, 'Ah, too bad, I don't 'ave a typewriter.' And Federman says, 'That's OK, I do. I'll type up these sheets.' And I tell you, Federman, that bum, 'e didn't even come up with what to say on those sheets—I told 'im everything, word for word. 'e'd come into the barbershop and I'd make 'im noodles every day, and when business got slow I'd dictate to 'im and 'e'd type it all out according to 'ow the pages looked with the 'air on them, which we'd glued all down so it would stay in place, the original random placement on the page. And then, one day, the novel is finished and Federman, 'e is nowhere to be found. And the next thing I know there's this novel out, *by Raymond Federman.* So don't even mention that guy to me—'e's a crook, 'e never 'ad an original idea in 'is life, 'e took everything from me, and now 'e plays golf all day at a nice country club in San Diego and I'm still stuck 'ere in Buffalo giving people these lousy 'aircuts."

"Why do keep his picture up in that case?"

"It's ze kids! That's all they want these days. They 'ear what's 'appening before anyone else 'as caught on—they get on the internet and they 'ear that that this great guy Federman wrote all these wild books and they see 'is picture on the internet, and 'e's not a bad looking guy, and 'e's still wearing the style 'aircut I gave 'im years ago. And it got around that I was the original Federman barber. So now that's 'ow I make my living."

"Well, so you owe Federman something."

"The only thing I owe Federman is a punch in the mouth! That guy took everything from me! There—your 'aircut is finished, get out of 'ere. I don't want to 'ear any more about Federman. I remember Sam Beckett telling me a long time ago, 'That Federman, 'e's nothing but trouble, stay away from 'im.' I should 'ave listened to Beckett years ago. It's sad, kids today don't even remember Beckett. Now there was a 'aircut, the way it all stood up on top. But you need the long, thin face to get away with it. The Federman 'aircut works with any type of face. Ah, but what do you care, you postmodern sycophant! That's it, get out of 'ere! Out!"

And as suddenly as I had stumbled upon this barbershop I was back out in the cold, lonely street.

But

I had my
Federman haircut and I
wasn't depressed anymore. It
hadn't been an illusion, those
     writer-types,   the
     ir searching   for   \
     words, their   Fed   \

erman hair __   \
cuts.

I've seen them around since, more and more, starting trouble, breaking up syntax, scorning the prevailing orders of book, story, genre, realism. Starting up presses, writing poems that go around in circles. Buffalo may be depopulating, but we've got our Federman haircuts. And we hear–from Romania, Germany, Poland, San Diego—that the trend is catching on elsewhere.

MOMENTS OF ARTICULATION: SOME FEDERMAN-FEUER CORRESPONDENCE

Moinous: How have you been ? I've been busy traveling to and fro . Now, I'm back in Toronto. I want to let you know that I have been reading and reading your novels as well as some criticism of them. I just finished an outline for an essay on your work for the experimental fiction issue. I am going to write on the double vibration, or the oscillation in your work between America and France, between the past and the present, between post-modernist play and modernist melancholy. All of this feeds into your notion of sad laughter and laughterature in your latest book, which I love.

I like the voice of the speaker in it. At times he is American and playful, at other's he's European. At the end of the novel you provide an interesting European and melancholic twist that affirms a responsibility for the Unforgivable Enormity (its interesting because the two capitalized letters could also stand for EU: the European Community) rather than American irresponsibility and play. The address made by the speaker is to the American Federman. I find this hard to beleive after so much of the novel provides such an unabashed performance of play and irresponsibility . I like the contrast. I don't think that you want to make absolute statements about art or its tasks . I see this in your sarcasm and play throughout the novel. Your digressions, and diversions. Yet I think its good that you left the melancholic element, which I find more prominent in your earlier work.

I am criticizing Hartl for his subscription to this earlier mode. He, like Hartman sees your interest in absent memory. However, he doesn't see the play in your work. He reads play or digression in terms of loss or the "inadequacy of language". I think he beats these themes to death, as so many else have. His reading is too reductive, though interesting and quite Derridian. He makes you into a real melancholic character. I don't want to do that. Perhaps the American in you, forgive me for saying this, doesn't want to be pinned down as a melencholic, though your voice in Aunt Rachel's disagrees with the american.

One of the central ideas of my thesis deals with combating the pre-ponderance of theorists who endlessly meditate on the failure of language to communicate the unspeakable. your work is different. you don't obsess with this and make this a central issue, which is not to say that you think you have done it, have expressed the unspeakable.

Rather, you play with it: act as if you do. this is what I think the sad laughter is. These theorists don't know how to laugh. I think its because they are too serious. yes, the holocaust is a "serious" affair, it calls for mourning and melancholia, but there is a point/moment when mourning and melancholia get contaminated by fiction. I think testimony is the last refuge for these theorists obsessed with only loss. In our previous e-mails I think you brought out how fiction can not be kept out of this space…

I apologize for all the details, but I thought you might appreciate this.
-you are a great writer. Whoever you call yourself.

Menachem

how am I? sort of confused—feeling helpless—on the one hand saying—start the war and get it over—on the other don't do it—the entire planet will suffer—it will be the beginning of the end—and meanwhile I shake my head and even laugh the laugh that laughs at the laugh—humanity is not worth saving— let's go back to the monkey condition—

which novel have you read?
which one in your opinion is
[not the best] but the most

important in terms of what
I do with language history
my life real and imagined

which criticism have you read?
criticism that attacks me I say
it didn't understand a damn thing
criticism that praises me I say
it must be kidding exaggerating

I look forward to your essay for JXF
and so does the editor—the issue
is starting to take shape—I send
in some 80 pages of my own writing

I like that you are writing about the double vibration–french/english/Frenchman/
american/history/story/life/fiction/biography/autobiography/ttruth/lie
/laughter/tears

don't forget that this double vibration comes from Beckett—the epigraph of The Twofold Vibration is crucial—

whatever it means in Beckett's the lost ones
does not necessarily mean the same in TTV

history as a strange way of repeating itself

yes I like what you are proposing to do—little attention has been payed
to this oscillation [good word]

very important Menachem to pay attention [to listen] to the voice that speaks in my novels—obviously it's the same voice in all the novels—but for each novel the voice takes on a different ton—even different rhythm—

for instance when I write in French [and you have not read the novels I wrote in french] I really write American—and when I write in English I really write French.

It's true that when I am in America I am an incurable Frenchman and when I am in France I am an unbearable American

go figure that out

Unforgivable Enormity—when I stumbled on that expression I vaguely recall that I stopped a moment and asked myself—why I am resorting to a metaphor [for it is a metaphor] me who loath metaphors instead of saying what it really was—perhaps because here where I write in the United States one cannot speak directly of what took place over there in Europe—one should almost be ashamed of having survived.

And so—yes you are right—let's assume an irresponsible posture—let's laugh it up—let's twist the language so that it appears to say nothing—

I don't make absolute statement about art because I respect art too much but also know the deficiencies of art—and its pretensions—so I do not write belles-lettres—I write moches-lettres [ugly-lettres]

Interesting that you find less melancholy in my later work than in the earlier—some people see it the other way—and so even claim that Federman has given up his reckless experimentation and is now moving gradually back to old-fashioned realism can you believe that

you must remember from where Hartl is writing about Federman—
when he sent me his book in which he had gone deeply into my psychic—
I asked him why a young Austria non-Jewish wanted to waste his time
with the work of Federman—he told me——it makes me understand who
I am

yes of course his reading is Derridean -Derrida has infected so many
good minds—

remember the Germans/Austrians have no sense of humor—this is
another reason they like Federman's work—it manages to make them
laugh a little

the failure of language—what is interesting—and Beckett who went so
far in denouncing and exposing the failure of language managed to give
new life to language—

I think I am also pointing to the failure of language and yet people tell
me that my language says something in spite of itself—explain that to me
Menachem

the laugh that laughs at the laugh—one cannot laugh today at what
happened in New York—and yet watching the gruesome images played
over and over again on tv and watching the Americans dressed in flags
waving their flags and watching your retirement pension go down the
drain and watching people buying gas masks by the tones one is almost
tempted to laugh

let me explain that laugh—

on january 13 1988 we received a letter from the IRS that or taxes were going to be audited—then a phone call came from New York where our daughter Simone lives announcing that she has a cancer of the sinus—sitting in my study I suddenly smelled smoke I rushed to the kitchen the kitchen was on fire—Erica a left something cooking on the stove while we were on the phone with Simone all three crying—and a piece of cloth caught fire—the firemen came and demolished half the kitchen in putting out the fire—Erica took the car and left—I thought she was going to commit suicide or drive directly to New York to hold her daughter in her arms—Simone was 25 then [she survived by the way even though she was given 10% chance of survival—we are survivors in my family] I had to go teach a seminar on experimental fiction—I was taking a shower before getting dressed—and suddenly out of me came—no not a scream Menachem—but a incredible burst of laughter

that's the laugh that laughs at the laughs—

the laugh that tries to articulate what cannot be articulated rationally—it works better than tears you know.

excuse this digression. I don't know why I told you that—but the last sentence in your email touched me deeply

Federman you are a great writer, you say.

Others [very few] have also said that to me. And yet I'm full of doubt about my work.

And if it is so why is my work so ignored both in America and in France. But not in Germany [crying irony]. Explain that to me.

Tell me why I am a great writer. I like to hear that.

Thanks Menachem for paying attention to my work

now tell me I am not sentimental and melancholic

Federman

MY FRIEND FEDERMAN

ROBERT CASELLA

Having admired his work for years, I finally had the opportunity to meet Raymond Federman at a reading in a small town in Southern California in 1998. It was a cool spring night and I remember standing in the doorway of the university classroom expectantly waiting to catch my first glimpse of him. As well as I knew and loved his work, I had no idea what he looked like, knew virtually nothing about his life apart from his books, and yet, despite this, had always considered him to be one of the seminal influences on my own writing. I eventually decided to take a seat. Federman soon bounced into the room carrying an attaché case under his arm and wearing a black suit; followed by a few professors with that fuzzy look in their eyes so common in academe. After a sycophantic introduction by some gink in a tweed jacket, Federman stepped up to the podium and began to read. It was a spectacular performance. Federman dazzled an otherwise mulish crowd of backwater Republicans and Susan Lucci fans with his self-effacing humor and pathos, reading excerpts from his most impressive books. Here indeed was a charismatic entertainer, a vaudeville comedian walking an existential tight-rope of periphrasis and self-cancellation… a monologist without equal. I was amazed by how quickly he won the audience over, for you must remember that most of these people had no idea who he was. But within minutes Federman disabused them of their ignorance, making them lifelong fans. It was, without a doubt, the best reading I'd ever attended.

I first read Take It Or Leave It when I was nineteen years old, a high school dropout, a degenerate hillbilly mopping floors at the IBM building in downtown Tumbleweed, California. I stumbled across the book almost by chance in the public library of a small desert town so atavistic and primitive that most of the population believed Ronald Reagan really *could* act (along with Chuck Norris) and thus voted him into the presidency.

It was an eye-opening experience, to say the least. I couldn't stop laughing, nor could I put the damn thing down. Eating, shifting, it made no difference... the book was in my hands *at all times*. After finishing it, I proceeded to devour his other books and was never disappointed. I had acquired a voracious appetite for everything Federman.

And now, years later, following the reading, I approached the table where Federman sat surrounded by stacks of newly reissued copies of his major works and handed him my tattered, dog-eared copy of Take It Or Leave It, feeling like a numskull. He seemed shocked at first, then a smile spread over his face and he said, "Ah, you have the first edition!"

I told him he was a genius and he, naturally, wrote something nice on the flyleaf. Realizing there was a line of people waiting to meet him gathering behind me, I said thank you and left.

Though we exchanged only a few words, I felt compelled to write the man and discovered that he had a website. And so began an infamous and often turbulent correspondence. In other words, I would write to Federman and he—despite his status and importance in the world of letters—would actually respond to my e-mails, usually telling me to pull my head out of my ass and branding me as someone who was 'beyond help.' Delighted, I would write even more feverishly to him, spilling my guts to this idol of mine. Taking pity on me, Federman would always tenderly suggest that I should join a monastery and/or slit my wrists, for I was a hopeless dingbat.

He has never once (intellectually/artistically, that is) let me off the hook—and for this I respect him. Despite the fact that he is who he is and I am a virtually unknown author, Federman has never treated me as anything less than an equal and as a friend. I have always been inspired by his tenacity and courage as a man, by the parodic savagery of his work, which is rooted in the ameliorative and transformative power of language to authenticate the vicissitudes of human experience. Moreover, what I find admirable in Federman is his contrariety, his refusal to capitulate to the glib, pasteboard banalities of literary convention and popular culture.

And despite the self-referential quality of his fiction, Federman is, I believe, also trying to articulate much more .. . what we, despite our differences, have in common with one another—namely, our frailties and shortcomings and cruelties.

A skeptic, Federman is, nevertheless, an optimistic skeptic… for he has hope… for he, of all people, believes the world can right itself and somehow go on.

Excerpts from Mon Corps

Raymond Federman

my body, my mind
one of the two must go
Murphy

Chaque homme invente une histoire,
qu'il prend, un jour, pour l'histoire de sa propre vie.

Chaque homme invente un corps,
qu'il prend, un jours, pour le sien.

mes cheveux

Je suis devenu conscient de mes cheveux à l'âge de 13 ans. Avant, c'était ma mère qui s'en occupait, ou qui me disait de me peigner parce que j'avais toujours les cheveux en vrac. Je m'en foutais de mes cheveux. Ils me gênaient, là sur ma tête. C'est ma mère donc qui s'occupait de mes cheveux. Quand j'étais tout petit elle me les lavait, me les peignait en me faisant une raie sur le côté. Le côté gauche, je crois. Mais je ne suis plus sûr. Faudrait que je regarde une vieille photo de moi quand j'étais gamin pour voir de quel côté ma mère me faisait la raie. En tout cas, c'était ma mère qui s'occupait de mes cheveux. C'est elle aussi qui me cherchait les poux dans les cheveux quand j'en avais attrapé à l'école. Elle le faisait avec un peigne spécial. Un peigne a poux, avec des dents bien serrées pour attraper les poux et les sortir de mes cheveux. Plus tard, quand elle m'a dit qu'il était temps de m'occuper moi-même de mes cheveux parce que maintenant j'étais un grand garçon, je me peignais presque jamais. Sauf quand ma mère me disait, Mais peigne-toi un peu les cheveux avant de sortir. Les gens vont se moquer de toi avec tes cheveux tout ébouriffés. Alors je mettais plein d'eau dessus et je me les plaquais sur la tête, et sans même regarder dans le miroir, j'essayais de me faire une raie sur le côté. Parfois à gauche. Parfois à droite. Même au milieu. Pour moi ça n'avait aucune importance. Tenez, je ne savais même pas quelle couleur ils étaient mes cheveux. Ma carte d'identité scolaire disait, cheveux marrons. Moi cela m'était égal qu'ils soient marrons ou mauve ou jaune. Comme je vous ai déjà dit, ils me gênaient mes cheveux. J'avais l'impression de toujours porter un chapeau sur la tête. Et moi je déteste les chapeaux. J'en ai jamais porté de ma vie. Sauf quand j'étais dans l'armée, parce que c'était réglementaire.

Avant l'âge de 13 ans, je savais pas que les cheveux ça pouvait servir à s'embellir et pour séduire celle qu'on désire. C'est quand je suis devenu orphelin, justement à l'âge de 13 ans, que tout à coup j'ai reconnu mes cheveux sur ma tête. Ma mère n'était plus là pour s'occuper de me cheveux. À l'époque les garçons de la classe bourgeoise que je voyais dans la rue, se peignaient tous les cheveux en arrière, sans raie, et croisés derrière la tête en cul de canard. Moi je savais pas me peigner comme ça. À la Pompadour. Moi j'étais de la classe prolétaire. Pas parce que mon père était ouvrier dans une usine. Non, mon père, il travaillait jamais. Il se disait artiste-peintre. Donc il était toujours fauché. On était pauvres comme des prolétaire. C'est pour ça que nous les gosses, mes deux soeurs et moi, on disait souvent, Maman j'ai faim. Et Maman nous disait, avec les larmes au yeux, Dis-le à ton père.

Bon c'est pas de ça que je voulais vous parler. C'est de mes cheveux.

Les garçons des richards portaient leurs cheveux très haut sur la tête, en bouffe, pas tout aplatis sur le crâne avec de l'eau, comme moi je faisais.

Eux ils avaient les cheveux en liberté. Flous et flottants. Vous voyez un peu ce que je veux dire. Le style Zazou.

Alors quand j'ai compris l'importance l'importance des cheveux dans les rapports humains, je me lavais les tifs tous les jours. À l'époque de mes 13 ans, les gars de mon âge disaient toujours tifs en parlant de cheveux. Ils se faisaient des compliments les uns les autres au sujet de leur tifs. Alors moi maintenant, je passais des heures à m'occuper de mes tifs. Je les shampouinais. Ce qui n'est pas la même chose que les laver. On se lave les cheveux avec n'importe quel savon, tandis qu'on se shampouine un savon spécial très doux et même parfumé pour qu'ils brillent bien. Après je les séchais bien pour qu'il n'y ait plus d'eau dedans. Ensuite je mettais de la brillantine dessus pour qu'ils brillent encore plus, et je me les peignais soigneusement en arrière, en faisant bien attention que la queue de canard soit parfaite derrière ma tête que je voyais dans le petit miroir que je tenais dans ma main derrière ma tête en me regardant dans le grand miroir devant moi.

Jusqu'à l'âge de 13 ans je n'avais jamais vu le derrière de ma tête. Si les gens trouvaient le derrière de ma tête moche, je m'en foutais. Mais dès le jour ou j'ai vu le derrière de ma tête, je suis devenu très conscient, et encore maintenant, quand quelqu'un regarde le derrière de ma tête. Surtout si c'est une femme. C'est pourquoi, quand je me peigne, même aujourd'hui, bien que mes cheveux ont changé de densité et de couleur, je vérifie toujours le derrière de ma tête. Et a chaque fois, ça me rappelle comment Roquentin avait la Nausée quand il sentait le regard d'autrui derrière sa tête. Eh bien moi aussi, ça me fait tout drôle quand je sens un regard derrière ma tête.

La grande découverte que j'ai faite quand j'ai commencé à m'occuper de mes cheveux, c'est qu'ils n'était pas marrons, comme ça disait sur ma carte d'identité scolaire, mais noirs. Oui, mes cheveux étaient noirs quand je les ai découverts. Ils ne le sont plus, mais croyez-moi, ils étaient noirs et nom pas marrons. Il est possible que la brillantine que je mettais dessus les rendait plus noirs. En tout cas, c'est comme ça que je les voyais.

Bon je saute les différentes coiffures que j'ai eu depuis l'âge de 13 ans. Je vous raconte seulement comment à l'âge de 40 ans, il y a eu un changement radical dans la façon de me coiffer, et donc de visionner mes cheveux.

Voilà, je venais d'avoir 40 ans, et je traversais une crise. Je ne crois pas que c'était ce qu'on appelle en Amérique, *te middle-age crises*. Ma crise était plutôt professionnelle. Ce que j'étais en train d'écrire s'annulait au fur et à mesure que j'écrivais. Cela me rendait triste, nostalgique, mélancolique, même paranoïde et coléreux. J'étais tout le temps de mauvaise humeur. Quand ma femme me demandait ce qui allait mal, je lui disais, les nouilles. Alors elle éclatait de rire, espérant sans doute me faire rire aussi, et me disait, Tu nous emmerdes avec tes nouilles. Arrête de faire la gueule. Viens je t'emmène au cinéma, ça te relaxera.

Mais un jour, quand je faisais encore la déprime, et je parlais même de suicide, elle me dit, tu sais c'est pas ton bouquin des nouilles qui te rend comme ça, c'est tes cheveux, oui tes tifs qui foutent le camp. Tu te déplumes, et tu veux pas l'admettre.

Et il est vrai qu'à l'âge de 40 ans, je remarquais, sinon tous les jours, une fois de temps en temps, en me peignant, comment mes cheveux semblaient se retirer en haut de mon front vers le centre de mon crâne. Sur les côtés, ils résistaient encore. Mais sur le dessus de ma tête, ça devenait plus mince, moins dense, transparent, même quand je peignais mes cheveux très haut et très flou sur ma tête.

Alors ce jour-là, le jour où je disais que j'allais tout abandonner, ma femme me dit, Assieds toi sur cette chaise, enlève ta chemise et ton pantalon, et je reviens tout de suite. Moi, tout ébahi, assis sur la chaise en caleçon, je me demandais ce qu'elle allait me faire. Et la voilà qui revient tout sautillante et encore toute habillée, avec dans une main un peigne, et dans l'autre une paire de ciseaux, et avant que puisse rouspéter, elle se met au travail. Je me laisse faire. À quoi bon résister. Déprimé comme je l'étais, qu'elle me les coupe tous, qu'elle me rase la tête si ça lui fait plaisir. Qu'ils aillent au diable mes cheveux.

Bon je veux pas vous tenir en suspense. Quand elle a fini de me tailler les cheveux de tous les côtés à grand coups de ciseaux, elle me dit, Va te regarder dans le miroir. Je vais dans la salle de bains sans trop d'enthousiasme et je regarde. D'abord je me reconnais pas. Puis tout à coup j'éclate de rire. Ma femme arrive. Alors, qu'est-ce tu penses, qu'elle me demande, avec un grand sourire. Je ressemble à Jule César, que je lui dis. Tu m'as fait une coupe de cheveux impériale à la César, et j'éclate de rire encore un coup.

Et vous savez quoi? J'ai pas arrêté de rire depuis le jour où Erica m'a coupé les cheveux style romain, le jour où elle a changé la direction de mes cheveux en avant. À partir de ce jour, je pouvais couvrir la moitié de mon front avec mes cheveux, jusqu'à l'endroit où ils poussaient quand j'avais 13 ans.

C'est aussi à partir de ce jour que j'ai compris comment il fallait écrire le roman de nouilles. En avant, sans se soucier de ce qui pourrait arriver.

Bon je vais pas vous embêter maintenant en vous décrivant en détails comment mes cheveux ont petit à petit changeaient de couleur, du noir au gris au blanc. La raison est évidente. Ce que j'écrivais jour après jour et qui s'annulait au fur et à mesure que j'écrivais a certainement été la cause de ce changement de couleur. En tout cas, mes cheveux ne me déprime plus. Je les trouve même assez beaux, même s'ils deviennent de plus en plus rares et blancs.

MON NEZ

Ah! s'il m'a fait souffrir mon nez, depuis le moment sublime et mystérieux dans le ventre de ma mère, quand il a été dessiné par la respiration de ma mère.

Ah! s'il en a pris des coups dans le nez, mon nez. Des coups directs et des coups indirects qui l'insultaient.

Tout le monde me dit que mon nez est de travers. Qu'il est tordu. Moi, quand je regarde mon nez dans le miroir je le vois tout droit. Bon j'admets qu'il est grand mon nez de Youpin, mais ça c'est inévitable. C'est historique. Même ma mère n'y pouvait rien. C'était pré-déterminé par des siècles et des siècles de souffrance et d'humiliation que ma race à dû prendre dans le nez. Un nez juif c'est une tragédie.

Il se peut cependant que mon nez soit comme ça, grand et de travers, afin de protéger le reste de mon corps. C'est lui mon nez qui souffre pour moi. C'est lui qui prend tout dans le nez. Mais lui mon nez il s'en fout qu'on l'insulte en l'appelant toute sorte de noms dérogatoires comme Pif ou Blair ou Tarin ou Tarbouif ou Bourin ou même Pifomètre. Ou tout ce qu'on veut. Mon nez il est costaud, *he can take it*. Mon nez , pour moi, c'est un monument topologique.

Oui, mon nez est masculin. Et on m'a même dit bien souvent qu'il est sexy. Mais c'est seulement les femmes qui disent ça. Les hommes eux, ils lui font plutôt remarquer qu'il est grand et de travers.

Un jour à l'école, on étudiait l'anatomie humaine, et la maîtresse a dit à la classe, *Raymond a un piment rouge*, en expliquant ce que c'est que la pigmentation de la peau. Elle a dit ça en me prenant comme exemple, et tous les cons dans la classe ont éclaté de rire. C'était dans une école de garçons. C'est pas de ma faute si mon nez est toujours un peu rouge. Pas qu'il en a honte, c'est sa couleur naturelle. Moi j'aime les nez rouges. Les nez rouges ils ont de la force. Les nez blancs eux ils on l'air faux, ils ont pas l'air naturel, ils ont plutôt l'air d'avoir été manipulé chirurgiquement.

Il faut être fier de son nez. Faut s'en occuper. Moi je le massage souvent mon nez. Je le fais respirer profondément. Je le tortille. Je l'examine. Je lui coupe les poils dedans quand ça le chatouille. Je lui mets de la crème dessus pour pas que le soleil le brûle. Je le décrotte quand il en a besoin. Parfois je lui mets des lunettes dessus. Pas qu'il en a besoin, mais comme ça il se sent utile à quelque chose. Il me permet de mieux voir. Si on avait pas de nez les affaires des lunettes feraient toutes faillite. Faudrait trouver un autre moyen de soutenir les lunettes sur nos yeux. Donc le nez est essentiel à l'industrie des lunettes.

Ah! S'il en a eu des aventures mon nez depuis que je l'ai. Quand les gens me demandent comment je me suis tordu le nez, je leur raconte toute sorte d'histoires. Je dis que c'était quand je faisais de la boxe. À l'époque de Marcel Cerdan. Que j'ai connu d'ailleurs. Mais c'est pas lui qui m'a tordu le nez. On a jamais boxé ensemble.

Ou je dis que c'est arrivé quand je faisais des sauts en parachute, et une fois j'ai atterri sur le nez. Oui moi j'ai été parachutiste. Merde si ça saignait du nez ce jour-là, quand j'ai atterri sur mon pif.

J'expliquais aussi une fois à un médecin qui voulait savoir si mon nez de travers me causait des difficultés pour respirer. Non que je lui ai dit. La raison pour laquelle mon nez va d'une côté, c'est parce que je fais de la natation, oui je m'entraîne beaucoup pour faire des courses de natation, surtout le crawl, et comme vous savez quand on fait le crawl on respire sur le côté, mais faut pas trop sortir la tête de l'eau sinon ça vous ralenti, alors faut tourner la tête sur le côté un tout petit peu et respirer rapidement. Vous voyez ce que je veux dire, que j'ai dit au docteur. C'est ce qui a forcé mon nez d'une côté, la natation. Et puisque je respire toujours du côté gauche quand je fais le crawl, c'est pour ça que mon nez va un peu de ce côté de mon visage. Je sais pas si le médecin a bien compris ce que je lui expliquais, mais il a rien dit, et j'ai passé la visite médicale. Je me souviens plus pourquoi je devais passer une visite médicale. En tout cas j'ai trouvé cette explication de mon nez tordu si convaincante que depuis je l'ai souvent donnée à ceux qui voulaient savoir pourquoi j'ai le nez de travers.

Mais la plus belle histoire, c'est quand je raconte comment quand j'avais pas plus de trois mois ma soeur Sarah qui voulait être fille unique a renversé le berceau dans lequel je roupillé comme un ange et je me suis retrouve à plat ventre la nez contre la terre. En tout cas, c'est ce que ma mère me racontait souvent quand je me disputais avec ma soeur Sarah. Voici l'histoire que me racontait ma mère. C'était un beau jour d'été bien chaud. Ma mère avait mis mon berceau dans la cour devant la maison pour que je sois bien réchauffé au soleil et elle s'était assise pas loin en train de me tricoter un passe-montagne en laine pour me mettre sur la tête en hiver, et aussi dessus mon nez pour pas qu'il ait froid. Ma mère protégeait mon nez tout le temps. Elle savait qu'elle était responsable de mon nez. Alors ce jour-là, toute concentrées sur son tricotage, ma mère n'a pas vu que ma soeur Sarah, qui avait trois ans, avait basculé mon berceau, et que moi j'étais en dessous à plat ventre, mon nez pressé dur contre la terre, et que je suis resté comme ça, toujours endormi, il paraît, pendant un bon bout de temps, et c'est pourquoi mon nez est de travers. La pression de la terre contre mon nez encore si fragile à un si jeune âge l'avait fait dévier vers le côté.

Bien sûr, même si je vois pas dans le miroir que mon nez est tordu, je suis bien forcé de croire ce que tout le monde me dit, que mon nez est de travers. Les gens disent toujours la vérité quand quelque chose est moche, et ils mentent quand ils disent que quelque chose est beau.

Mais la vraie raison que mon nez est comme ça moi je la sais. Je l'ai jamais dit à personne. C'est une raison si bête que j'ai un peu honte de la dire. Je dis toujours que je sais pas vraiment de quel côté il dévie mon nez puisque quand je le regarde dans le miroir je ne vois pas la déviation. C'est pour ça que quand quelqu'un prend ma photo, je dis toujours, *maker sure you get my good side.* Une fois j'ai même dis ça pendant que j'étais inter-viewé en direct à la télévision. C'était en Afrique, au Kenya. Une jeune femme africaine superbe en costume africain m'interviewait, et pendant qu'elle faisait sa présentation avant de me poser des questions, moi je me suis tourné vers la caméra et j'ai dit au caméra man, en me tapotant le nez, *maker sure you get my good side.* Il paraît que tout le monde au Kenya a trouvé ça drôlement marrant, et on en parle encore, surtout maintenant que certaines de mes histoires existent en Swahili.

Mais j'allais vous révéler la vraie cause de mon nez tordu. Bon je le dis, bien que cela aille sans doute me déprimer, et mettre mon nez de mauvaise humeur. Il aime pas qu'on raconte cette histoire. Il est très sensible mon nez vous savez. Mais c'est normal, le nez est naturellement sensible. Mais le mien est particulièrement sensible parce qu'il est plus grand qu'un nez normal. Mais justement, c'est sa dimension et sa forme qui le rend unique.

Je dirais même que c'est un nez noble. Un nez aristocratique. Ce n'est peut-être pas un parfait nez romain, mais il a son style à lui. Et le fait qu'il est un peu tordu le rend encore plus unique et original.

Bon, assez de détours, je vous raconte maintenant pourquoi mon nez est un peu de travers. C'est parce que quand j'étais petit garçon je reniflais beaucoup, et j'avais toujours le nez qui coulait, même en été. Mon nez était naturellement humide. C'était pas de ma faute si mon nez avait tendance à couler. Je pouvais pas le contrôler. En plus, j'avais jamais de mouchoir pour le moucher. Alors je me mouchais avec ma manche. Je me frottais le nez avec la manche du vêtement que je portais. La raison que je me mouchais avec ma manche, c'est parce on était trop pauvre pour pouvoir acheter des tire-jus. Ah! Si on était pauvre. On était si pauvre qu'on pouvait même pas se permettre du papier hygiénique. Alors dans les cabinets on s'essuyait avec des morceaux de journaux. Bon, vous allez me dire que ça n'a rien à voir avec mon nez les chiottes, eh bien moi je vous dirai que c'est justement dans les chiottes que mon nez sent plus fort que les nez ordinaires parce qu'il est plus grand.

Alors parce que mon nez coulait tout le temps et que j'avais de la morve au nez, j'étais bien forcé de moucher avec ma manche puisque j'avais pas de mouchoir. Tout le grands à l'école m'appelaient toujours petit morveux. Voila la vraie raison pourquoi mon nez va de travers.

Je devrais préciser que c'était toujours avec ma manche gauche que je me mouchais, parce que quand j'étais gamin j'étais gaucher. C'est ma mère qui avait décidé que je serais gaucher quand elle me faisait dans son ventre. Elle savait déjà que je deviendrais un artiste, et elle croyait que tous les grands artistes sont gauchers. Donc c'est pour ça que mon nez dévie d'un côté. Sans doute vers la gauche, bien que je ne puisse pas le remarquer dans le miroir, puisque je l'essuyais tout le temps avec ma manche gauche d'une mouvement de droite à gauche. Donc vous voyez pourquoi mon nez va vers la gauche. Question de logique.

Mais quand je me suis cassé le bras à l'âge de neuf ans, je suis devenu droitier.

Mais mon bras cassé, ça c'est une autre histoire, et aussi comment je suis devenu droitier. Une histoire que je vous raconterai peut-être un jour. Pour le moment restons-en là avec mon nez tordu!

Non, faut quand même que je précise que mon nez ne me sert pas seulement à sentir la merde dans les chiottes, il sent aussi d'autres odeurs. L'odeur des fleurs, par exemple. L'odeur du fromage, surtout le Pont-l'Évêque. L'odeur d'un bon vin. L'odeur d'une belle femme. Ah oui, l'odeur des femmes. Ah, si mon nez il aime bien sentir les femmes, surtout l'odeur des jeunes femmes, celles qui sentent comme des fleurs. E puis aussi mon nez il aime se sentir lui-même. Sentir son propre corps. Enfin mon corps. Surtout quand j'ai pas pris de douche pendant deux jours et que j'olfactive un peu trop.

Et puis va falloir aussi que je raconte comment très souvent mon nez se prend pour le nez de Cyrano.

Et même une fois, à cause de mon nez, j'ai été choisi, parmi un nombre d'autres aspirants, par un directeur de théâtre pour jouer le rôle de Cyrano avec mon propre nez. Vous auriez dû me voir en Cyrano. Mon nez était vachement fier le soir de la première. Si fier qu'il était encore plus rouge que d'habitude quand les gens dans le théâtre se sont levés pour applaudir notre performance.

Bien sûr, on m'a aussi souvent appelé Pinocchio à cause de mon nez. Mais aussi parce que j'ai tendance, il paraît, à beaucoup exagérer les histoires que je raconte.

Oui, j'ai encore beaucoup à dire sur mon nez.

Tenez je vais vous faire montrer un dialogue que j'ai eu une fois avec un type qui avez insulté mon nez en lui disant qu'il est grand.

C'était une critique littéraire Américain. Alors je vous cite le dialogue en anglais, mais sans révéler le nom de l'insulteur.

DIALOGUE CONCERNING MY NOSE

P— You have…you have…Sir…huh! A very big nose.

F— Very big, you say.

P— Yes, quite big. Enormous in fact.

F— That's all? That's all you can say?

P— BIG…very BIG!

F— Ah, my dear P, no, you must do better than that, didn't you learn anything while criticizing literature? You could have said so many things, in so many different styles, so many different tones of voice. For instance:

Aggressive: Me, Sir, if I had such a nose I would have it amputated on the spot.

Friendly: It must dip into your cup when you drink, you should perhaps drink out of a plate.

Descriptive: Is it a rock? Is it a mountain peak? A volcano? What am I saying. It's a peninsula.

Curious: What use do you make of this oblong capsule? Do you use it as a writing table or a cigar box?

Gracious: You must love birds very much to offer so paternally to their little feet such a perch.

Truculent: Tell me Mister F, when you smoke and the vapors come out of your nostrils, do people shout Fire! Fire?

Considerate: Be careful not to lean forward too much, the weight of this thing might make you topple the ground.

Tender: Why don't you have a little umbrella made for it so that it doesn't get burned by the sun?

Pedantic: The beast which Aristophanes called hippocampelephanto-camelos must have had on its forehead as much flesh and that much bone.

Cavalier: What! This type of hook is now in style to hang one's hat on it. How convenient.

Emphatic: There is no wind, no storm strong enough to make such a nose sneeze or catch a cold, except perhaps a tornado.

Dramatic: It's the Red Sea when it bleeds.

Admirative: What a great publicity sign this nose would make for a perfumer.

Lyrical: Is it a ship? When does it sail?
Naive: This monument, when is it open for public visitation?
What else is there to say about my nose. Except that it still here.

GEORGE CHAMBERS

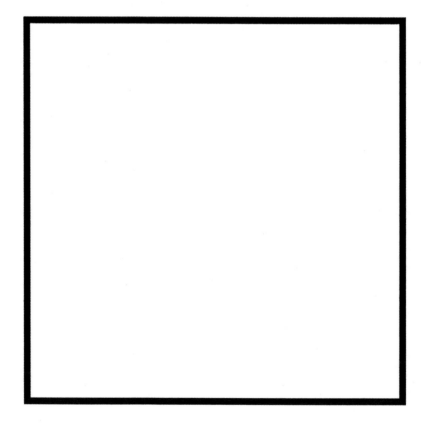

Bum One

ONCE UPON A TIME

GEORGE CHAMBERS AND RAYMOND FEDERMAN

Once upon a time, and what a screwed up time it was, two old bums met (midway between here and nowhere) and by chance discovered they had the same birth-date and the same size shoes, so they decided to be friends. It was a strange encounter, one that seemed predetermined. And it became even stranger when they realized they shared the same shadow, even though one was huge with a Buddha belly, and the other small with an eagle face.

Years went by and it came time for them to die, for as fate decreed, they both had something terminal, and both given at most six months to live. This the two bums accepted but what tormented them was the fact that they had only one pair of socks between them. And so, as friendship dictates, they spent the last six months of their lives each wearing only one sock.

[excerpted from *The Twilight of the Bums*. Boulder, CO: The Alt-X Digital Arts Foundatiion, 2001. See www.federman.com for links to the PDF of the complete text of this very funny book by Raymond and George].

FOUR REVIEWS

SERPIL AND MICHAEL OPPERMANN

THE TWILIGHT OF THE BUMS (A Reading)
Serpil Oppermann

In *Twilight of the Bums* Federman and Chambers re-map the territory of laughterature, a term Federman had coined to name his own style of writing. In this brilliantly written e-book Raymond Federman cooperates with George Chambers to even further transcend the limits of laughterature in order to demonstrate the effects of a cutting edge narration. The result is a reassuring end to the mechanics of reference from sign to world, and a manifestation of the general metaphor of meaning independent of the conditions of the strategy of representation. Federman and Chambers suceed in performing their writing as a game within language and set out to launch *play* as an exhaustion of transcendental signifieds.

In this visually and thematically self-reflexive "microfiction" (an aptly definitive term for this text) a postmodern wormhole is created in which the authors both weave and disperse the fragmentary narrative of the two old bums who exhibit their digressive skills and exposive linguistic virtuosity. Because they do so from within the comic side of fictional process, the bums create a truly playful rhythm of writing. After having learned that they have six months to live, these bums, who are the carbon copies of each other with the same birth date and unsually parallel lives, set out on their adventurous journey in their rather amazing textual landscape which keeps changing with every fictional entry they make. Thus their fictitious discourse gets filled with evasions, erasures and cancellations, as well as re-creations of all sorts of word-games. Right from the start, already on the second page of their unnumbered pages they confront the reader with their intended pla(y)giarism. Lifted almost ad verbatim from Diderot's *Jacques le Fataliste,* the passage sets the tone of what is to follow:

How did the bums meet? Dear Reader, you are of a rather cumbersome curiosity. By the Devil what does it matter how the bums met?

———————————

What are their names? What do you care?

———————————

Where do they come from? The nearest place.
No, that's wrong! The farthest place.
Where are they going? Does one really know where one is going?

This chapter, which is not a chapter in the usual sense, like all the others that follow, is aptly entitled "Foolish Questions" which is a parody on the realistic conventions and codes of referential fictions, just as the entire narrative itself will turn out to be in the process of writing. Here, the so-called chapters have been replaced by mini tales with appropriate headings, such as "The Mirror," "Angels and Rabbits," "The Scorpion and the Crocodile," "The Princess and the Frog," and other fabulative ones, which deconstruct the symbolic patterns of traditional fables. So the two Quixotically hilarious figures disrupt and replay the thematic and structural logic of conventional stories in exposing the formation of meanings and also lack of meanings human language incorporates. These curious bums actually present a sideways literary wink to the entire tradition of fiction writing from Diderot to Beckett, from Cervantes to Postmodern experimenters like Barthelme, Sukenick and Federman. They also assume a thumb in nose attitude to the recent avant-pop writers with their mock-obscene verbalism.

In the ironically entitled "Serious Discussion," the authors masquerading as the old bums now identified as Ace and Sam, put the post-structuralist concept of écriture under erasure:

Ace: Tell me Sam, do we have a goal?
Sam: My dear Ace, our goal, if we ever had one,
was to say less, to say badly whatever we had to
say, or if you prefer to unsay what had already been said.

At the end of this dialogue they declare: "Our goal was to make things darker. Did we succeed? Of course we did." This urge to unsay what has already been said anticipates their purpose of undoing and undermining any attempt at representational codes of story telling, and this suggests a thoroughly revisionist approach to narration. The aim of (self-) cancellation anticipates a rethinking of the absence of the so-called originary creative imagination in writing. As Federman has argued persistently, "the writer's imagination is not unlimited...in fact the writer...is merely imitating, parodying, mimicking, repeating, replaying, plagiarizing in other words, not the absolute meaning that supposedly precedes the creative act, but the very medium that constitutes the work of art" (*Critifiction* 58). The bums' narrative is the absolute testimony to this view, for it not only mimicks and parodies the ultimate tricks of Postmodern fictions, but also plays with the radical concepts of post-structuralist theories, such as écriture, decenteredness, and total denial of transcendental signifieds.

The discontinuity in the narrative and its fragmentary structure contest the idea of the seriousness of artistic creation. The bums deliberately continue on this line of writing in order to expose, the true dynamics of story telling. For example, in "Night Burial" the authors declare the true purpose of literature: "It may be stated with indubitability that Literature (here we indicate Art as well) refers, first and foremost, to itself; and as a corollary to this first assertion, we asseverate that often it is Literature itself which is least aware of this fact." The interrogation of true artistic creation hits the target when the authors finally reveal that they work from within a great "vacuum of creation" which is the postmodern wormhole they have wilfully entered. Therefore the page they articulate this revelation is aptly entitled "The Great Vacuum of Creation." It is worth quoting the entire speech here:

> We have been told that what we have
> written about the bums does not exist
> and that you, Dear Readers, are not
> reading these words your eyeballs are
> now tracking. We are not here, you
> are not there. Dear Readers, Dear
> Dear Readers...Ah! We summon
> Your affection, and your attention too,
> To console ourselves. It is lonely here
> In the great vacuum of creation.

As a matter of fact Federman and Chambers have succesfully placed the meaning of creativity in paranthesis, because it is that very thing that cannot be reduced to any form of epistemelogical formulation. Perhaps it can only be expressed in a playful dissemination of graphic signs. The true act of creation then comes into play only in the discovery of a great vacuum—a universe which Derrida says "articulates only that which is in excess of everything, the essential nothing on whose basis everything can appear and be produced within language" (*Writing and Difference* 8). Thus Federman and Chambers acknowledge what Derrida also calls "pure absence" ("absence of everything in which all presence is announced" (8)) as the true source of inspiration. With this extraordinary consciousness the authors color their text. In "Poetics," for example, they write that "...friendship tends to blur language, and generally give rise to imprecise and fuzzy blubbering, which is the essence of real poetry." The authors' pervasive intrusions to the bums' narrative, as in "Chez Monette" where the intrusions are especially highlighted, and their playful addresses to the reader, multiply the effect of this intended fuzziness and show that the words are the most *imprecise* signs. The best example to this is revealed in "Slogans" and in particular "The Failure of Words."

The poetics of Laughterature reaches its peak (but not the only peak—that is, there are many more) in "Certification of Purity" where the bums get blamed for having plagiarized from *Don Quixote*, creating a great comic effect on the concept of originality and literary pla(y)giarism, and drawing an ironic conclusion to the entire narrative itself. What the bums do is in fact to display the multiple possibilities and impossibilities of words in action, which a critical reader calls "curious blocks of words" in her letter to the authors. Accusing the authors for not being able "to control your language," this letter serves as an ironic mirror to the possible misdirected critical responses to such revolutionary fictions.

The carnivalesque performance of the bums, who are also named as Mick and Frog, and Um and Laut (an amusing pun on German Umlaut words), not only highlights the surfictional playfulness on intertextuality and word games but also reveals the diverse literary colors of postmodern pyrotechnics. The most striking feature of this brilliant microfiction, however, is the genuine idea of the authors displacing as well as displaying themselves as the funny old bums having fun with the creative possibilities of their "dual beingness." This is loaded with such immensity and immediaciy of literary energy that their entire narrative literally radiates what Barthes has called *jouissance*. Federman and Chambers seem to have enjoyed this immensely in evoking it in their mini tales, "co-creating inter-subjectively the community language experience *outside the moon* of the narrativity," as they state in "A Story (About A Story) Within a Story."

The wilfully constructed incoherence and digressive movements, the obscenity of the bums' dialogues, and their experimental expertise give the book a carnivalesque expression of the very stuff of life. Thus, beyond the pleasure principle lies the profound and almost the spiritual feeling of life's joys and tragedies. In fact the randomly placed mini tales are like beacons of light to illuminate the flowing movement of life itself. Therefore, despite their attempt to underline the comic effect of their revisionist, eye-opening textual/sexual discourse, Federman and Chambers unearth the very essence of life's hitherto unnoticed innuendoes. Their narrative may invert the very images of literary creation, but their dazzling command of verbal virtuosity certainly sheds light on the bits and pieces of life's underlying dramas. "Love Games," "The Death Certificate," "Night Panic," and "Final Settlement," for example, are only four of the many tales in the narrative that force the readers to re-think the twilights of existence. The bums may call it "The Divine Comedy of Life," and end up laughing at the final remark they make upon it ("The time of settlement is here and now, we are all living-dead separated from each other only by the little plot reserved for us in the great cemetery of the universe"), may even forget the story they are telling, as the authors remind us, but cannot help mixing the laughter with a deep sense of sadness. Thus the burden of the tragic events of their (hi)story is also made manifest.

The bums do "try to write themselves into existence" as every human being on this planet struggles to do every day, and thus invite us to view our own condition of being. Just like many of us, the bums play games, make up stories, re-think the past, pose questions on death and life, on extinction of the species and friendship, come up with slogans to show the stupidity of mass manipulation, travel together, get sick, ponder on old age, women and sex, and remind us of the horrors of holocaust, think about history, play the numbers, and in short, show us in performance " a tale of survival, of defeat and victory, a tale of heroism and villainy...a tale of noble wanderings, of sadly proportioned departures and returns, mixed with grand scenes of powerful recognition...and interruptions..." This is, of course as much of Federman's tale as it is of co-authored fictionalization process. Hence the telling of the tale is framed within the abundant intra-textual references to Federman's previous texts. The echoes of those earlier narratives are intervowen in a flowing process of enfoldment here, in the bums' ongoing experimentation. Although one Bum declares, " I literally lose the language...become absent from my own speech," it the last thing the bums lose. Language keeps putting them back in, or to put in another way, they keep pulling themselves into language as much as possible no matter how badly they try to erase themselves out of their text. Because the bums are "word addicts" as they loudly proclaim, and through their words they manage to enrapture the readers. At the end, which is no end, the writers declare that they have not heard from the bums since they "set out for their great adventure, more than three months ago," so they won't be able to report further progress concerning their tale. This alone is an indication that true writing is never lost on illusionary fictional ends. The tale will remain open ended to show the open textuality of the text, even though the bums plunge "towards their final exitus out of the turmoil of language." This absence of finality makes the text continually operative within the flow of language marking the ever-shifting, ever-different closures with each reading. The authors, then, posit with their last but not least address that the spaces "between and around the words", perhaps more than the words themselves, are the real affirmations of the true act of creations dissolving the desire for stable origins and fixed ends. Because they are the ones that invite an awareness of the "intervals of blackness and whiteness as well as intervals of sound and silence. This story, which tries to cancel itself out with the so-called final exitus out of language, actually invites a multifocal reading. Yet any critical reading of it would fall short of its purpose, because almost all readings are already enfolded within this extraordinary *critifiction* of great literary energy- a Federman term that captures the essence of this type of joyous-fictions.

The Twilight of the Bums transforms the erasure of meanings into an unexpected unfolding of the very core of life's many meanings. But what is of greatest significance here is the fact that, and ironically enough, all the jokes and laughter, all the literary playfulness and the comic tone of this text of pleasure cannot hide the deep sadness of the writer's predicament. It is certainly a worthy book to reflect upon, to read and re-read many times. It is an exciting land of great explorations and inventions as this wonderful microfiction testifies with its very existence.

Raymond Federman: *99 hand–written poems/99 poèmes ècrits à la main.* Berlin 2001: Weidler.

A joint review by Serpil and Michael Oppermann

Raymond Federman`s most recent collection of poetry offers texts both in English and in French and thus presents us with a bilingual publication. *99 poems* demark unusual territory because, unlike in previous Federman editions such as *Playtexts/Spieltexte* (Frankfurt:Suhrkamp 1992), there are no German translations provided. The collection is „Federman for the initiated"; an unsual publication for the German bookmarket with an equally unusual history behind it, as the publisher explains at the end of the volume.

Following the decision of German writer and critic Hans Magnus Enzensberger to publish 999 copies of a collector`s edition of *Alles oder Nichts* (Double or Nothing), Federman`s groundbreaking debut novel, it was decided to have a collector`s edition of *Loose Shoes*, Federman`s recent mind-bending surfiction of 72 fragments, as well (Berlin 2001:Weidler). Instead of having 999 copies, though, the publisher opted for an „ultra-rare" edition of 99 copies, a kind of „èdition de tête". Each of these was accompanied by a different poem Federman had written especially for the edition. *99 poems*, then, is a special collection of these texts, put together in no definite order, as the publisher states. Apparently, Federman delivered his poems in a box but „Unfortunately the order of the poems might have been destroyed. It might have happened, that opening the little box with the 99 hand-written poems in it, the box fell down on the floor" so that the original order of the sheets was lost. Shuffling the pages like a pack of cards, the publisher rearranged the texts in an apparently playful manner so that the collection might be called a „result of pure chance." Therefore, the unnumbered pages (with the original hand-written version of each poem always appearing on the left) can be read in any order the readers choose for themselves. They are „Spieltexte" (playtexts) waiting to be reshuffled.

Since Federman loves to engage in literary ambiguities, however, it is not surprising that a certain order seems to have been retained. The last poem called „FEAR/LA PEUR" comes close to a (preliminary) final word by marking the condition of an artist looking at an existential point of departure."It is not death/we fear," the poem maintains, „it is the fear/of death." The lines acknowledge a new stage in the life of the writer at which death cannot be relegated to memory alone (as a reference to the loss of his parents in Auschwitz and his own history of survival). All of Federman`s recent texts occasionally demonstrate a new kind of sadness beyond the realms of the XXX (Federman`s typographical allusion to the Holocaust). The „FUTURE CONCENTRATION", as it is evoked in one of the new poems, implies the possibility of „changing tense."

-1-

It is this new and sombre tone, first of all, that distinguishes certain poems from previous Federman texts. „RUE FÈDERMAN", for example, plays with the idea of being commemorated while „OVER THERE" is a poem encircling death which, as „DANCING IN THE DARK" concedes, is always part of the process of writing. It seems, though, that even today life is not *that* sad. Several poems rejoice in a newly found freedom that reflects the state of the artist as a pensioneer (Federman recently retired from his university position at the State University of Buffalo and now resides in San Diego). In "TO DO NOTHING" we learn:"I find myself at last/in a situation/where to do nothing/exclusively/becomes an act of/the highest value!"

Apart from these, *99 poems* is a ride through rather familiar Federman territory. There are concrete poems such as „THE SERPENT" or „9 x 9"; there is a linguistic „pun poem" called „SAD SADE" (bilingual and possibly inspired by the recent *Quills* movie). We find a satirical stab at answering machines in „GETTING IN TOUCH" which, as

„Federmaniacs" have been knowing for a longer amount of time, do not necessarily guarantee a „lovely lovely/long distance Inter Course". There is a poem called „The Failure of Words" which is named after a prose text from *Penner Rap,* Federman's recent collaboration with his long-time friend George Chambers (Frankfurt: Suhrkamp 2001*).* Just like his „twin brother" in prose, the poem is made out of gaps and holes and thus demarks the limits of language. Then there is „A REVELATION", a meta-critical poem about the nature of writing in which the literary critic and self-titled „surfictionalist" Federman links poetry with an ongoing critical discourse. There is a referential poem called „B...P...F" in which the poet (F) denotes his own stance both as a writer and a critic in the light of his „icons" Beckett and Proust. There is also the occasional stab at the writer's past, as in the aforementioned „NEW CONCENTRATION" or in „THE OLD DOOR", a poem written in the memory of Federman's mother who went through a door of no return in Auschwitz.–

Writing, as Federman has explained in many critical essays, always equals an imaginative reconstitution of the past: "Me I invent my dead/everyday," as it is maintained in „FORGERY". Other poems such as „ME TOO" or „THE DETECTIVE" (a wonderful vertical deconstruc-tion of the word's linguistic components) double upon older Federman texts, thus presenting us with further poetic twin brothers (or sisters).

-2-

All in all, though, Federman is still the „RECKLESS WANDERER" who „plays with words/that construct in spirals" to create „a tale made of digressions/transgressions/regressions/ that cancel the old memories"–in order to bring them back in a process of reimagination, one has to add.

Once again Federman's texts display an extraordinary feeling for the joy of writing. Federman realigns poetic invention with linguistic intensity to create a poetic vision that integrates the materiality of language with life's own rhythm. Of course, there is always the risk of „VAIN REPETITION", as the poem of the same title concedes. In another poem we learn that „When you get old/ you start to repeat/yourself." Federman still manages to surprise his readers, though. An older and hitherto unpublished poem called "AMERICA: A SELF-PORTRAIT", an extremely witty „Portrait of the European Artist in a Consumer Society", ranks among the finest of the author's work. The same holds true for the highly amusing „NOUIL-LORQUE" which, in another look back at the author's past, denotes and mocks the grand feeling of arrival in the supposedly New World. Federman gives the reader „the gift of words", and as we ask for more, our request becomes a gift to the writer himself:"When you ask for words/your request is a gift/to me." Or is „THE GIFT OF WORDS" a poem for George Chambers and thus a celebration of the mutual act of creation?

All of these (mostly wonderful) texts leave a lot to imagine—

RAYMOND FEDERMAN'S *LOOSE SHOES: a life story of sorts.* **Weidler Buchverlag, 2001, Berlin, Germany (156 pages)**

Serpil Oppermann

Raymond Federman's new novel, *Loose Shoes*, has finally appeared, published by Weidler in Berlin, a prestigious press company in Germany that has also published Federman's *Amer Eldorado* and *99 Hand-written Poems*. "Federmaniacs" will especially love the famous Van Gogh painting of "Three Pairs of Shoes" on the frontpiece of the book. The author provides information about how the book was conceived as a useful hint to the reader in what appears to be a preface. So we learn that between January 1 and December 31, 1999 Federman wrote 365 pieces that reflected his changing moods that comprise the entire book. Federman adds that "since Federman is a bilingual writer, the pieces were written either in English or French depending on his linguistic mood that day." After this explanation the book opens with a "STATEMENT" written in English and French: "a novel is less the writing of an adventure than the adventure of writing."

Indeed *Loose Shoes* in its entire typography becomes a brilliantly conceived adventure in language, a novel of fragments in which Federman mingles various genres and modes of writing, ranging from critical reflections to poems, mini tales, microplays and visual texts. Needless to say the novel as such provides a highly profitable adventure of reading. Readers familiar with Federman's metafictional style (which he prefers to call Surfiction) will also realize that this book is also an exercise on "critifiction," another term Federman coined to label his discourse which is critical and fictitious at the same time. As the subtitle indicates, however, there is yet another layer to the book. It is a "life story of sorts." This is Federman's life story which he has already turned into a series of metafictional adventures in his previous novels. *Loose Shoes* is a new version of this story, the story of a Jewish boy in France who lost his parents and sisters in the Holocaust during World War II. Like all his other novels *Loose Shoes* is a new experiment on this autobiographical nucleus which Federman loves to re-invent. This time it appears in the form of 72 fragments with appropriate titles, such as "IN THE SANDBOX," "FEDERKID," "PERPLEXITY," "ABSENCE," "WHO WILL CRACK FIRST," to name a few. Each fragment stands on the problematic borderline between fact and fiction, and gradually introduces the reader into the famous fictional versions of himself as his characters, such as Namredef, and Moinous.

The third fragment is called "THE STORY-TELLER" where Federman explains why he constantly repeats the same story—the story of his life. He writes that his life is a story and, "like everyone else, I run out of stories and so I keep telling the same damn story over and over again, and I'm never sure if I haven't already told the story I'm in the process of telling to people who are listening to me" (10-11). Since this is the case, the reader expects to confront a literary exhaustion, but is soon made aware that far from it this new version has more to offer in terms of a rapturous literary adventure. The desire to "re-invent" his life story turns into an at of postmodern fanfare whereby Federman, in a highly ironic manner, takes the reader into a fictional land of exploring the many possibilities of telling the same tale anew, and thus as an author stands on a post-modern self-parody, play and what he calls "pla(y)giarism. For example, he compares "Federstudying" to a photocopy machine to amuse the readers. This is also his search to find a way to close the narrative gap between fictional invention and his autobiographical nucleus, as well as to find a meaningful "reality" behind this. *Loose Shoes* re-invents the same story again in order to counter the actual lack of meaning in Federman's story of survival and his family's tragic death in the concentration camps. This is one reason why Federman writes the same story; but there is another reason which he explains as: "A lot of story-tellers borrow stories from other story-tellers simply because they don't have stories of their own, or are afraid to tell the story of their own life. I'm not like that" (11). Indeed Federman freely borrows from his own novels and has filled *Loose Shoes* with a good deal of references to his previous fictions. This however might baffle the new reader at first sight. But to prevent this Federman cleverly introduces him/her to the story of his closet experience in his poem "ESCAPE," at the beginning. This poem of 8 stanzas tells the story of his escape from being caught along with his parents due to his mother's benevolent act of pushing him into the closet at the right moment. That this poem is a rewriting of Federman's novel *Voice in the Closet* is no longer relevant to understand his tragic beginning and his first displacement: "My life began in a closet." The poem also testifies to the undeniable fact of his quest for meaning for his "escape."

ESCAPE and the other poems (12 of them all in all), such as TELL THEM, LAST NIGHT'S DREAM, YELLOW HUMILIATION, and FINAL ESCAPE, alone plunge the reader into Federman's repeated life-story and provide the nucleus of the author's existential dilemma. A careful reader can immediately understand why Federman repeats his story by a close scrutiny of these poems and understand the reason why the author demands a meaning, because all these poems, on a deeper level, address the same question: Why did Federman survive and his family did not—a haunting question for the author. The novel concludes with the poem

FINAL ESCAPE where Federman is still pondering on the same issue. These poems also serve to close the gap created by the highly complex and randomly placed prose fragments. The poems in the novel, then, create a narrative continuum that gives the reader a vision of the writer's autobiographical imagination, as well as successfully capture the essence of the author's plight.

Loose Shoes, despite all its linguistic playfulness, seems to be Federman's last attempt to "author" his life, because in the fragment called RAMONA Federman signals the existence of another novel in progress which will concentrate on his father's life. In *Loose Shoes*, he doubles upon his previous fictionalizations of his life story perhaps one last time to face the incredulity of his survival. Federman's success as an author here lies in his manipulation of how his life began in "incomprehensibilty" and "digression" (PERPLEXITY 50) which make up the structural pattern of the novel (although not incomprehensible, it is digressive, discontinuous, fragmentary and perplexing, as Federman's life story), and how he still wears it as a loose shoe. In fact the novel takes its title from the epigraph where Federman's alter-ego known as Moinous writes: "All my life my feet have been killing me." Along with Moinous ("that's what Federman calls himself, Moinous...a name I made up. It means me/us"[14]), Namredef, Federman, feather man, pen men, as different voices or fictional extensions of the author, make their appearances. Federman readers know these characters—or rather verbal entities Federman made up from his name——but for those who don't Federman provides a highly interesting and amusing fragment called FEDERMAN which gives a wonderful account of their conception, and can be read as a brilliant language play. This mini tale also unfolds Federman's family origins.

Loose Shoes is also a novel of "jouissance" which is Roland Barthes's term for the texts of bliss that involve the reader in the act of writing. The fragments may highlight the tragic story, but on a linguistic level they mirror jouissance as the piece PETIT MANUEL DES JOUISSANCES alerts the reader openly to this fact by giving a list of various jouissances. The highly blissful fragments include THE LINE, which is an eight and a half pages long text in the form of a line posing questions on the "morality of the line" (68), WHO WILL CRACK FIRST, which is an amusing microplay on two voices who debate who will be the first to really crack, E R J, which is a visual text, THE STATE OF ERECTION & OTHER CONSEQUENCES, which is a dark comedy on sex, and THE VOICE where two bums (other famous Federman characters) talk about the creation myth by mixing it with the flood story. But of course the tone of solemnity runs through the entire novel despite these comic digressions. This especially reaches its peak in REFLECTIONS ON WAYS TO IMPROVE DEATH, a critical essay where Federman, in an intense tone of dark humor, confronts the reader with the "incomprehensibility" of the state of non-being. Here one can almost feel the writer's deep pain that dominated his life since his "escape" when he first narrates the statistical approach to death whereby scientists report death by numbers, and then his challenge of it by drawing attention to the categories of death that scientists ignore. Underlining the problematic category of reporting one's own death Federman concludes that "there is a mysterious link between language and death that will never be explained"(55), which is what he, as a writer, continuosly explores. The "unspeakability" of death is actually what Federman is trying to reflect in *Loose Shoes* too which revolves around this theme in its entire structure. Having lost his family at a very young age still continues to haunt the writer and becomes the propelling force behind his linguistic experiments. But as the novel points out in its loose, fragmentary structure, finding the correct representation in language is not possible. Therefore he writes: "language vanishes into death…or death vanishes into language" (57). *Loose Shoes* clearly shows that Federman is deeply perplexed about the unspeakable category of his parents'death. PERPLEXITY testifies it: "Born with the legacy of incomprehensibility, I am aware that I can never forget, but also that I will never understand. And so I am opposed, I think, to transparent language because language is always in process and in trial" (50). It is precisely for this reason that *Loose Shoes* does not follow any familiar narrative pattern but progresses in loose fragments that resist any easy categorization. Those with realistic feet will not find shoes that fit them in this highly recommendable novel of no category that renders one of the most touching accounts of the impact of history's unspeakable category of death. Therefore it needs to be read and talked about. "Federmaniacs" will, no doubt, be the first in line.

Raymond Federman and George Chambers: The Twilight of the Bums (Alt-X- Digital Arts Foundation: Boulder CO 2001).

A joint review by Serpil and Michael Oppermann.

Federman's and Chambers's "microfiction" consists of a series of mini-tales which are presented with appropriate headings on unnumbered pages. Two bums with varying names (they appear as Mick & Frog, Sam & Ace or Um & Laut) and a surprising number of common features (they share the same birthdate as well as the same shoe size and even their shadow) find themselves in the "twilight" of their lives. They learn that they have only six months to live and decide to set out "on a farewell tour of selected cities of the European continent," among them Warsaw, Paris, Vienna and Berlin. References to "Aunt Rachel," to the so-called "closet experience" or to the loss of one bum's parents in Auschwitz point to key-experiences in Federman's life and thus to a technique of authorial displacement, which, in this case, is clearly not without irony.

All the mini-tales are marked by the bums' attempts "to write themselves into existence," as it is stated in a short tale called "THE PRECIPICE OF HISTORY." Thus, the bums' activity ironically doubles upon Federman's and Chambers's combined production efforts. The bums play games, make up stories, reflect upon the nature of friendship (in no less than 33 statements spread out over three prose miniatures), talk about their lives or pose questions about life and death, just as Federman and his long-time friend Chambers might have done many times. The carniva-lesque mixture of subjects points back to the central influence of Beckett; it is accompanied by a high degree of linguistic playfulness that highlights the meta-or "surfictional" landscape (to use a term Federman coined him-self) both authors explore in their tales. *The Twilight of the Bums* encom-passes a great number of stylistic layers as well as lines in French and German which reflect a European background. Readers familiar with a "metafictional landscape" will also notice the occasional dialogic mode of presentation which highlights the influence of Sterne and Diderot (as the great "fathers" of metafiction). The following lines, for example, directly echo *Jacques Le Fataliste*:

> How did the bums meet? Dear Reader, you are of a rather cumber-some curiosity. By the Devil what does it matter how the bums met? But if you insist we will tell you that they met by chance, just like everyone else. ("FOOLISH QUESTIONS")

The ironical inclusion of a "letter from a critical reader," who com-ments upon the mini-novel in progress, points to the same metafictional tradition which is simultaneously evoked by the bums' mock-obscene ver-balism (which, however, could also be interpreted as a thumb in nose atti-tude to the recent avant-pop writers). In a similar manner one might point to the inclusion of (highly amusing) fairy tales such as "THE SCOR-PION & THE CROCODILE," or to "criti-fictional" passages (to quote another Federman term) on the nature of literature, or the notion of words as the most imprecise of signs which link a meta-fictional back-ground with the discourse of language skepticism ("SLOGANS" and "THE FA?LURE OF WORDS"). The entire result is that of a linguistic "Pennerdämmerung," of a "Recherches des Bums Perdu," as the bums themselves playfully label their "creative" attempts in a list of tentative "TITLES."

Occasional direct or indirect allusions to the rise of Neo-Nazism every-where in the world ("THE COSTUME BALL"), to the so-called

"Holocaust industry" and Spielberg's Shoa Foundation ("HOLOCAUST THEME PARK"), or to the ongoing debate on national identity in Germany ("DEUTS-CH-LAND-DEUTS-CH-LAND") add a kind of political edge to the **Bums.**

What makes this collection of inventive mini-tales totally unique, however, is the special narrative tone which, in its best moments, walks on a borderline between a Barthesian notion of "jouissance" and an element of solemness reminiscent of Paul Celan's 'famous poem "Die Todesfuge." The bums seem to be "happy sad" (to cite the title of an album by Tim Buckley), feeding on a "bitter bread with ashy texture," as it is stated in "MORE BIRTHDAY FESTIVITIES." In that manner they become part of Federman's specific concept of writing that he has labelled as "laughter-ature": the tragic and the comic always go hand in hand. Therefore, despite their atempt to underline the comic effect of their playful discourse Federman and Chambers uearth the very essence of life's hidden joys and sorrows, and thus force the readers to re-think life's "twilight zones."

While the *Bums* have been published as a book in Germany under the title *Penner Rap* (Suhrkamp: Frankfurt 2001), the English version is only available on the internet (http://www.altx.com/ebooks/ebooks/e_bums.-pdf). We find it very sad that in America great literature finds itself more and more relegated to a "Twilight" of existence.

RAYMOND FEDERMAN, THE TEACHER

DEBORAH MEADOWS

As a teacher, Raymond was lively, energetic, and exposed us to thinking and practicing an experimental literature. With what I now know about teaching and class prejudices too often expressed by faculty, I marvel how he included us in his reflections on Samuel Beckett with whom he had a literary relationship, how he made literature seem that it was for and came from all of us. Never did he dumb-down or condescend to students who were clearly beginners; in fact, because of Federman's influence, a great many of these beginners went on to write and have significant publications. No doubt that many of those writers are included in this single-author issue on Federman.

When I took two creative writing classes with Raymond Federman in 1976-77 at SUNY at Buffalo, I never dreamed that I would someday write about Raymond for a literary journal. As a working class local, my expectations were that I would return to factory work I had been doing summers and, like the practice of students I had met who went on to the Ph.D. program, my "real life" and how I found meaning would be quite separate from how I earned a living.

As an individual student, the comments and encouragement I received from Raymond helped in ways that are difficult to pin down but very long-lasting. Although it was some four or five years later that I realized I was cut out for poetry, those early experiences with serious literature in the experimental vein shaped how I think about language and how I write.

405

Federman's courses in combination with other courses at SUNY at Buffalo such as the course on Joyce, American Literature with Myles Slatin, and the courses I completed as a dual major in Philosophy, espcially Eastern Philosophy with Kenneth Inada, made me a different reader. Before post-structuralist analysis was applied to most areas of thought, hearing Federman profess that "everything is fiction, even history, even biography, even autobiography—autobiography most of all" was humorous and clicked with immediacy. Much later, many dryly referred to these ideas as the constructedness of narrative and identity.

For me, in the rich context of SUNY at Buffalo, where I had many important teachers, and in the context of Buffalo during those years of big public spending on the arts, Raymond's inimitable speaking style, intelligence, and filthy-dirty stories won all of us students over. He helped created a classroom atmosphere that was creative and spontaneous: one evening when he was late for class, a few students got up the idea that we would leave Raymond a note to join us at the Trafalmadore Cafe, a local hang-out near campus. Raymond joined the, by then carousing, class and read to us from his recent publication, *Take It or Leave It*. We thought he was the greatest thing going.

Federman coined the term *laughterature* to describe his writing. Yet it's also important to realize his work is noted for the perpetually deferred completion of the narrative line. It could also be referred to as *forefiction* or *literaplaisance*, I suppose.

June 2000, I ran into Raymond at Douglas Messerli's Sun & Moon Press during a literary salon for Argentine poet, Saul Yurkievich. I couldn't believe it! There was my old creative writing teacher, the great Raymond Federman, stepping out of his car onto the curb right there on Wilshire Boulevard. He looked the same after all these years though his voice had deepened. Or something like that. Douglas had just reissued Federman's *The Twofold Vibration* through the Green Integer imprint. Immediately, Raymond hatched the plan for a reading at my campus, California Polytechnic State University, Pomona. How could I refuse such an offer?

January 31, 2001 I got to read some of my poetry with Douglas Messerli and Raymond Federman with jazz sax player, Chuck Manning and jazz guitarist, Dave Koonse. I couldn't believe it! That is the sort of generosity that Raymond has expressed to all students. A portion of this event was digitally filmed including Raymond's reading "On the Death of the Novel" and is available at www.csupomona.edu/ls/ then click on "Meadows' video."

CROSS-SWORD PUZZLE SOLUTION

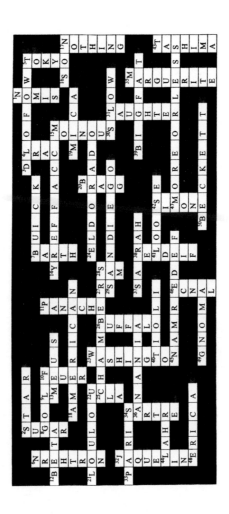

Qui Es Tu, Federman?: An Intimate Reading of "La fourure de ma tante Rachel"

Peter Wortsman

Raymond Federman is a phenomenon of nature, a talking tidal wave, a Franco-American tsunami with a wicked dip, a hurricane howling in the hard disc of a PC, a closet earthquake erupting way off the Richter Scale of American letters. So how come the forecasters aren't busy plotting his course, predicting when and where he'll strike next?

Defying categorization, Federman perplexes the experts who can't quite figure out where he's coming from. American by adoption, French by birth, Jewish by memory, ballsy by bent, he is really the unrecognized poet laureate of the No Man's Land between France and Forgetting. And though he's lived for decades practically within earshot of Niagara Falls (the great wet crack in the North American continent) and has written his best known work in the American idiom, Federman also writes in French. His real literary voice is a blend of both tongues, emitting *twofold vibrations*, always playing it *double or nothing*. As the narrator and protagonist of his latest novel, *"La fourure de ma tante Rachel,"* composed and published in French, (Circé Editeur, Strasbourg, 1996) explains:

Yes yes that's it, I write mostly in English, but sometimes also in French when I get the urge. All the same, I must tell you, it isn't easy writing in a language other than your own, it isn't easy at all to adopt words that aren't your own, words that resist your best efforts because they're strangers to you. But you do learn to love them, these words, you manage to make them your own. A little like a mother hen whose lost her chicks and adopts a duckling. Ignoring his yellow down and his flat bill, she teaches him to sift through the sand and to peck at earth worms. Well, my dear lady, me too I learned to peck at the English words in what I write, but of course without ever forgetting my mother tongue.

And later in the same passage:

> You see how I sometimes mix up these two tongues I have rattling in my mouth, these two tongues that keep playing hide 'n seek and often play tricks on me....As Gilles Deleuze put it so well, the creation of a style in a foreign language passes through different stages, the first of which is a decomposition of the mother tongue which soon becomes convulsive, starts stammering, stuttering, becoming something else, subsequently to reemerge as a new tongue, a new syntax. Well that's what happened to me, and the novel I'm in the process of writing…

The French, who can't forgive linguistic defection, think of him as an American turncoat, if they think of him at all (though his 1974 French novel, *Amer Eldorado*, was nominated for the prestigious Prix Medicis). He is popular in translation in Germany, where his Post-Modernist phrasing and playful seriousness (or serious playfulness) appeal to a Post-War generation bursting the straightjacket of outdated structures. But back home in the States, plot and character development are still the sine qua non of serious fiction, the novel is a sales pitch, and experiments are strictly for the test tube. Here Federman is slotted in the Avant Garde, that great literary landfill of the critically unapproved.

The scenario of much of his work, known to a devoted coterie of reader-listeners, keeps tapping the portable epiphany of a little French boy thrust by his mother into a closet to elude round-up and deportation, what Federman has called "the closet experience," the egg of his rebirth and the eruption of consciousness. But his real subject is breath, the breath it takes to blow a horn or tell a tale, the breath of a scream, a cry of ecstasy or a belly laugh, the breath of life. His real element is not ink but air.

Having first learned self-expression on the saxophone from Black buddies in Detroit, blowing long sultry riffs in a jazz band before falling for the lure of language, his novels retain the fluid musical quality of oral literature. Restless on the page, despite the carefully crafted surface, the words tap a primal intra-lingual pulse. And while the conventional reader may be put off by his leapfrogging "Post-Modern" prose line, modulated more by breath than by any standard punctuation—Federman tolerates commas but abhors periods for the suffocating closure they denote—there is something unquestionably archaic in his Post-Modernity, a return to the erotic roots of storytelling, the groping of a naked tongue in search of a willing ear.

Federman puts it bluntly in *"La fourure de ma tante Rachel"* (literally "My Aunt Rachel's Fur," though a racier rendering might be "My Aunt Rachel's Muff"): "After all, as everyone knows, creation, literary or other, can't happen without excitation, you've got to get a hard-on before you can fuck..."

In *"La fourure,"* Federman plays his childhood tongue with a fierce assurance and to virtuoso effect. The boundless pleasure given and taken in the telling of this tale is tempered some by the compulsion of the teller, a fear of silence, and by the simultaneous thrill and embarrassment the reader feels at the imposition of such intimacy with a stranger. The plot, loosely speaking, spirals round the return of a young man to his native France after the War and the memories stirred up by the inverse of nostalgia. Lest the prospective reader fear a somber accounting of atrocities à la Elie Wiesel, he may breathe a sigh of relief. Federman's inferno is peppered with plenty of purgatorio and sweetened with paradiso. If there's any literary influence here, it's strictly Rabelaisian.

A memorable passage recounting a young boy's wartime experience as a farmhand in hiding focuses, not on grief, but on the natural cycle. Here's a healthy helping in translation:

> so here I am on this farm during the occupation, can you picture me planting cultivating the earth, I don't know a thing about agriculture but lemme tell you, you sure learn quickly on a farm [...] up at five in the morning to milk the cows, shovel the manure out of the barn, feed the pigs, the chickens, the ducks, the rabbits, the whole menagerie of those more or less domesticated creatures that spend their life doing nothing but feeding and shitting all the time until we eat them and defecate in turn, boy is there ever a lot of shit on a farm, tons and tons of it, but you know it's still a pretty good system nature, yeah it's just amazing how it functions, how it keeps renewing itself with shit, you see first you cultivate the earth to make all those things grow, hay, wheat, the plants you stuff your animals with to fatten them up so that afterwards we can slaughter and stuff ourselves with them, but before they die my god do these animals ever shit, and then we shit too after devouring them, and eventually all that shit is returned to the earth to enrich it to make the things that grow in it bigger and more nourishing, bigger on account of the manure, and so it goes until the end of time, or until we human beings are destroyed by nature, or until we destroy ourselves, oh what a beautiful system nature is, it keeps jump starting itself with shit...

But Federman's meditation on nature is not restricted to feeding and elimination. Copulation and death complete the cycle:

> oh yes on that farm I saw how easy it was to fuck and die, the animals that's all they did, kept mounting each other all the time, and every day there was at least one creature that croaked, either from fatigue, or age, or because we had to kill it so that we could eat its

meat, death was always around on that farm, it's really such a simple thing death, but sometimes you know it's kind o' funny too,
you should've seen the time the farmer's wife killed a chicken for
her stew, she grabbed a great big kitchen knife in one hand,
wedged the chicken between her plump knees and held its head
with the other hand stretching its neck, and swish swash there
goes the head, when I saw it for the first time I almost gagged...
of course it bleeds, what do you think, that chickens don't have
blood like us, but the funniest thing is that even beheaded the
chicken still struggles a few seconds before dropping dead, and
one time, see, it was hard to believe, but after my farmer's wife
lobbed the head off a chicken the chicken fidgeted about so furiously it managed to slip free of her fat knees and it fell to the
ground, so here's this chicken without a head that starts hotfoot-
ing it 'round the kitchen beating its wings [...] you see how simple
and downright tiresome death can be...

Now Federman dwells a brief moment on the boy's sense of solitude
only to segway into his witnessing a quicky in the kitchen between the
mailman and the farmer's wife, just like the livestock, which subsequently
inspires the boy's own sexual initiation with the farmer's wife:

so I said to her, without thinking, just like that, I said to her, if
Monsieur le Mailman can do it why can't I...
yeah sure, that's exactly what I said to her, so she turned red in the
face, it really made her turn red the farmer's wife, but she didn't
say a word, she just put a finger to her lips, the index, with a wink
to make me comprehend that I'd better keep my mouth shut and
not breath a word about this [...] I was almost asleep when I felt a
hand slip in under the covers and fondle my prick till it stiffened
and...

Copulation and death. The same hand that cuts the chicken's throat
caresses your prick. It's all part of the natural life cycle.

No "Painted Bird" this! No Kosinskian inventory of evil!

What stuns a reader of these reminiscences is not the ordeal of survival, nor the unspoken horror of what the boy must have gone through. Nor are we taken aback by the vivid description of all natural functions. The contemporary reader is accustomed to excess.

"La fourure" shocks, not with its subject but with its tone, the unabashed "in your face" intimacy it presumes with the reader!

English lacks any syntactical distinction between the formal and the intimate form of address. An American will freely address his wife, his boss, his best friend or a total stranger on a first name basis and mean nothing by it, whereas for a Frenchman crossing the line of demarcation between *vous* and *tu* instantly alters the psychic climate from Arctic to tropical. The absence of that distinction, while it's always implicit in Federman's English language opus, may, unbeknownst to its readers, ever so slightly detract from its effect. There is no such confusion in Federman's French. To say *tu* to a stranger is to presume some kind of intimacy.

From its opening line, *"La fourure"* is addressed to a fictional *tu*: *"Ah tu veux savoir...tu veux savoir pourquoi je suis rentré en France après dix ans d'Amérique..."* ("So you want to know...you want to know why I returned to France after ten years in America...")

That *tu* has a dual role. He is an actual character in the novel, a professional listener, the narrator's initially nameless foil or sidekick, the compliant, passive, listening ear to the narrator's incessantly wagging tongue (a foil who only in the very last paragraph identifies himself as Federman, the narrator's double). He is also, of course, a stand-in for the reader-listener bending over the book in his lap who can close it or toss it aside whenever he likes. Readers take books to bed. This fact is not lost on Federman.

It is this second *tu*, let's call him tu^2 whom the author is obliged to seduce, to tease and entertain, to lure away from the myriad distractions of a life, and hold for the next two hundred pages.

Of course tu^2 knows what he's getting into. He's bored with himself, his wife (or husband), the kids, the mundane troubles and annoyances from which the novel offers an escape in print. In addition to which, the erotic elements of *"La fourure,"* offer a vicarious affair. But the author-narrator-*Je*-I has to watch it, lest the game get out of hand:

okay, hold it, that's enough, I better not go too far or else you'll excite yourself like a bull and won't be able to listen any longer...

Needless to say, the writer-narrator-*Je*-I is also simultaneously addressing a third incarnation of *tu*, tu^3, a stand-by for himself! This is what Federman calls "the happy catastrophe when I tell my tales," the ever-present risk of overstimulating oneself, from concentration to masturbation. A pleasant risk to which any author worth his salt will sometimes succumb.

Now let *me*, a particular reader-listener-respondent-*tu*—call me tu^4, if you like—confess something to *you*, the reader of my response—let's call you tu^5! This book embarrasses me. The author-narrator-*Je*-I gets so close I can almost feel his hot breath in my ear.

Say, keep me out of it, will you, Federman! This is all your fantasy, not mine! Sure your Aunt Rachel gives me the hots, and so do the Society girl Sucette and the nymphomaniac Judy you fucked for 48 hours straight way back when in Detroit! If writing is an erotic act, then what is reading, Raymond, old tu^3? So what kind of polymorphous perverse role playing are we engaged in here!? And that includes you too out there, tu^5, wherever you are! And while we're at it, that includes the prurient eye of the publisher, Claude Lutz, tu^6!—you old lecher, you get your vicarious kicks from the books you publish or why else would you publish them! And hey, you peeping tom, Eckhard Gerdes, tu^7, invisible editor of this volume, you're in on it too, so don't you go sneaking off into anonymity!

The literary enterprise is one big virtual orgy! Which is of course what keeps us coming! But at least it's safe sex, you say, what with the book cover and binding functioning as an effective latex condom.

Another confession, while we're at it. Let me admit that I've had unsafe communion with this text. I mean, I've never actually rubbed up against the book, if that's what you're thinking. (It hasn't yet been published at the time of the writing of this response.)

I've had two secret trysts with the naked text. Once while having it read to me through a long Sunday afternoon by the author in Buffalo, an exhilarating, albeit infantalizing, experience. And a second time, reading through a preliminary draft of the ms late at night in insomniac fits and spurts, it having been mailed to me by the author for my response.

In both cases, the text (not yet bound into a book) was still a loose, slippery uncontrolled substance, threatening at every moment to spill over into my life.

Which brings me back to the intersection of oral literature and the novel, the site of Raymond Federman's premeditated intra-lingual transgressions. Or as Walter Benjamin put it in his essay "The Storyteller, Reflections on the Works of Nikolai Leskov":

> A man listening to a story is in the company of the storyteller; even a man reading one shares this companionship. The reader of a novel, however, is isolated, more so than any other reader.

"La fourure" embraces the reader, leaving him breathless. "I just can't put it down!" you commonly say of a book that grabs you. In this case, "*It* just can't put *me* down!" might be more apt!

Oh yes, I forgot. I had a third encounter, when the author came to read aloud from the then still as yet unpublished book to an intimate audience in New York. The real thing straight from the horse's mouth!

What's that you say? So what about Aunt Rachel's muff!? What a dirty mind you have! Go buy a copy of the book and find out for yourself!

Oh, but you don't speak French?

Well I'm afraid you'll just have to wait for the book to come out in English! Of course, there's always Berlitz. Or better yet, for optimal effect, take your teacher and the text to bed!

THE WORD-BEING TALKS: AN INTERVIEW WITH RAY FEDERMAN

MARK AMERIKA

Q: When did you first realize that you were going to spend your life writing fiction? (was it a particular event? feeling? situation? epiphany/vision?)

A: It was in North Carolina of all places. I was in the Army (82nd Airborne Division) wondering what the fuck am I doing here with all these dumb hillbillies. In those days (let's say it was 1951, I was still very dumb and naive and unprepared for the rest of my life and sentimental and full of complexes, but ready to take on anyone anything, in those days I would easily do 100 push ups and 200 sit-ups without blinking), anyway, there I was at Fort Bragg with the 82nd wondering how the hell did I get into this shit, and one day, I remember very clearly it was raining cats and dogs and while all the fat ugly hillbillies were getting drunk or playing poker, I went for a long walk alone in the rain. In those days I thought I was going to become a great jazz musician, but it was obvious that I didn't have the right color skin to become one of the saxophone giants. It was raining, and I believe it was a Sunday because that day we didn't have to run around for five miles with full-pack on the back and butterflies in the stomach, and give me 20 and give me 30 the fat sergeant would scream every time we made a false move, no that day we were off. So I was walk-ing in the rain feel-ing sorry for myself, and there was a movie at the Fort Bragg cinema, I forget what the movie was, a war movie, you know WWII

417

movies, that's all they played in that cinema to inspire us to be better killers. Anyway, I went into that movie-house, and I don't know why when I came out, I was so depressed, but also so moved by the film I had seen, I wish I could remember what it was, I began crying in the rain, and it was then, right then, in the rain, on a Sunday, at Fort Bragg, in l951, I think it was December, or something like that, because in January 52 they shipped me to Korea to fight the war hoping that I would get killed over there so that they wouldn't have to pay me social security when the time came, and so it was then, right there on the spot, tears running down my cheeks mixed with the rain drops, that I decided, dammit, I'm going to become a famous writer.

Q: Of course your last answer reminds me of TAKE IT OR LEAVE IT which you once told me was your favorite Federman book (mine too). It also reminds me of your writings/ digressions/ manifestos on Surfiction in that it's not that easy to differentiate between the word-being Federman and the various characters who float through your narratives (Moinous, Namredef, Frenchy, etc). Could you update us on the relevancy of Surfiction today—an age of virtual irrelvancy for fiction as a genre—and how do you assess the need to create YOUR OWN characterizations via the ones you WRITE OUT in your stories?

A: First of all, TIOLI (Take It Or Leave It, ed. note) is not only my favorite book, but it is probably my best book and my most complex. The book that has not yet been read—I mean read for what it is: a monstrous collage/montage of discourses (real and unreal, original and invented, published and unpublished, etc.). A young man in Milwaukee has just written a long essay on Playgiarism in TIOLI. Very interesting piece. His email: matthewr@csd.uwm.edu. Secondly, I do not believe in SURFIC-TION any more because all the principles of surfiction have been appro-priated by second-rate third-rate and fourth-rate pseudo-fictionists who have no idea why they are using these principles. And besides SURFIC-TION as invented by Moinous only applied to one book—you may not know this but the surfiction essay (first published in Partisan Review in

1973, then expanded as a intro to the SURFICTION book) was written specificlaly to explain DOUBLE OR NOTHNG (DON) to the world because I was so appalled at the way that book was being read. There is, in fact, only one real SURFICTION novel, and that's DON. One could say that TIOLI is the last great Surfictional novel. After that Federman shifted to what can only be called CRITIFICTION. But that's another story. One thing must be made clear to those who are interested in Federman's work. Federman does not invent characters. The notion of character is obsolete for him. Federman invents VOICES—only voices. Characters belong in old-fashioned realistic 19th century novels. Federman, federman (with a small f), moinous, namredef, B One, or whatever he calls his voices, these are only voices. the problem is that no one really listens to Federman's voices, they want to see (there is a difference between seeing and hearing—all great fiction is music and therefore must be heard. Fuck seeing!) the substance (the story?) when they should be listening to the music (the shape of the sentences).

Q: Tell us about your concept of pla[y]giarism, when it came to you, what do you think caused it to appear as an essential part of your practice, etc. You know, a lot of young writers, me included, are attracted to the idea of doing away with copyright altogether—especially in cyberspace. I suppose being an old writer from the old world (of books), you would find this idea of anti-copyright repulsive, yes?

A: FICTIONCRITIFICTION 1. PLAJEU I cannot explain how playgiarism works—you do it or you don't do it. You're born a playgiarizer or you are not. It's as simple as that. The laws of playgiarism are unwritten, it's a tabou, like incest, it cannot be legalized. The great playgiarizers of all time, Homer, Shakespeare, Rabelais, Diderot, Rimbaud, Proust, Beckett, and Federman have never pretended to do anything else than playgiarizing. Inferior writers deny that they playgiarize because they confuse plagiarism with playgiarism, not the same. The difference is enormous, but no one has ever been able to tell what it is. It cannot be measured in weight or size. Plagiarism is sad. It cries, it whines. It always apologizes.

Playgiarism on the other hand laughs all the time. It makes fun of what it does while doing it. That's all I can tell you today. Tomorrow I may be able to tell you more. But to illustrate what I mean, here is a piece of playgiarism I performed today. A certain H (his name shall remain secret) sent me via e-mail, from Vienna [for the sake of realism], a piece of criticism concerning a fiction I sent H—the piece, or I should say the two versions of the piece describe two rooms [one dark, one light] in which a gesture was performed, and so on [as presented below]. As soon as I received H's criticism I began the process of playgiarism which of course always involves the process of reading [you cannot playgiarize what you have not read or heard], and soon I had written my one daily piece of what I now call FICTIONCRITIFICTION. H took my fiction and wrote a criticism of it and I took his criticism and made a fiction of it. In other words, a very important aspect of FICTIONCRITIFICTION is that it leads the reader back to the original fiction, but not in a self-reflexive fashion as it has erroneously been explained these past two or three decades. Playgiarism is not self-reflexive. How could it be? How can something reflex itself when that itself has, so to speak, no itself, but only a borrowed self. A displaced self. If this is getting to complicated, too intellectual for Amerika, then let me put it in simpler terms—on the Walt Disney mental level: Play-giarism is above all a game whose rules are the game itself. The French would call that Plajeu.

Q: The displaced self, the one that pla[y]giarizes so as to create a kind of laughter and forgetting, and whose FICTIONCRITIFICTION-a-day turns the world in upon itself (even though it has no itself to speak of), makes sense to me. This is what I was getting at regarding anti-copyright and our ability to float through cyberspace (and what is cyberspace but the virtual reality your playgiarizing imagination navigates through on its mission to SURF-SAMPLE-MANIPULATE [don't forget this dictum Federman, it will become famous one day!]). But on a different subject, and since Alt-X has a huge international audience interested in writers like Beckett, Burroughs, De Sade, Surfiction and all of the emerging Avant-Pop writers, tell us about how your work grew so popular in Germany. What is it about the scene in Germany that makes them more sensitive to your work than the commercial by-products of an America gone crazy?

A: First my Dear Amerika you must understand that I do not forget—I never forget. Milan Kundera, that over-rated displaced writer wrote the book of laughter and forgetting. I never forget, and that is why I can laugh—laugh the laugh laughing at the laugh—that is to say laugh at human idiocy, human savagery. And by the way, I do not float in cyber-space. I invade c-space, I corrupt c-space. Just to float in it does not interest me. And that leads me in fact to your question about the success of my work in Germany. My work is successful in Germany because it does not simply float there, it invaded Germany, it corrupted Germany, it forced Germany to look at itself through my books. One would be tempted to say that Germany loves Federman because Federman is a survivor of the Holocaust. Yes the Germans love a survivor—especially a survivor who does not really accuse them directly—especially a survivor who is an optimist, who can laugh and make them laugh, **laugh tears**. That's perhaps one reason. But that's not the essential reason. After all, my work does not really deal with the Holocaust—no sentimentality about it, not statistics, no horror. My work is really about the post-holocaust, what it means to live the rest of your earthly existence with this thing inside of you—and I don't mean just me, I mean all of us, wherever we may be—those who experienced it, those who think they experiences, those who survived it, those who did it, those who witnessed it and said nothing, those who claim they never knew, those who claim it never happened, those who feel sorry for those to whom it happened, and so on and so on. The Holocaust was an universal affair in which we were all implicated and are still. But that is not the real reason why the Germany loves Federman. They love F because F went to AmeriKa and there struggled and there suffered and there worked like a slave and there even starved and there became a writer a real writer and what he writes is Amerika and the Germans love to read about Amerika because they would all love to become Americans and forget there sordid history. Not that the American history is not sordid. But in America we are able to laugh at the sordid history of America because it is so laughable, so dumb, so naive. First then: the Holocaust or rather the post-Holocaust or what I prefer to call the post-Hilter era. That's why they love Federman. Second: because F writes about America and the Germans love America. But now we come to the real reason why F has 15 books circulating in Germany (three of them do not even exist anywhere ele), why F has 12 radio plays in Germany, and two more forthcoming, why F has two modern ballets in Germany, and one more in progress, why F has three Jazz/Poetry CDs in Germany, and more coming, why F's novels have been adapted to various other medium, and why more books will be published, and his latest play will have it world premiere there, etc. and so on, and so on. The real reason is because the German have recognized that F is a fucking good writer, and that F is not only a fucking good writer, but that he became a fucking good writer in a borrowed language. The Germans love the English language, they all speak it better than the Americans, and they admire a writer who is capable of working in a language that is not his own. But that's not all. The Germans respect thinking, kulture, intelligence, intellect, they admire a thinking being, especially when his thoughts are all fucked up or fuck you up. Think of Hitler's thoughts. In America if you are intelligent, if you have knowledge, if you think too well, they treat you like a sick person, they think you have a brain tumor, and immediately they want to operate on you. Just go see the movie with Travolta called PHE-NOMENON. A fun movie, a fun movie that peddles a scary message. Intelligence is dangerous. Destroy it. But there is more, I mean why F is so successful in Germany—and when I say successful, I don't mean only in terms of the number of copies the book sold—we not talking blockbuster here or best-seller, we talking fame. **Alles Oder Nichts** (1986) translation of **DON** sold about 25000 copies and is still going strong. The US edition sold 3000 copies in 30 years [yes exactly 30 years since it started irritating America, and still does] and the damn FC2 authorities who reprinted the book in a beautiful new digital edition don't know how to sell the book, they didn't even get it reviewed. How idiotic. But what is important about the German edition of **DON** is not how many copies it sold, it's the fact that it got some 75 reviews in the major newspapers, and won two prizes. For a totally unreadable, unmarkable book that's not bad. I will not go through the list of all the books, but what these reviews and articles, and books (yes there are five books written about Federman in Germany, and several doctoral dissertations) all admire in F's work is the quality of the writing, the daring of the writing, the blasphemy of the writing, the effrontery of the writing, in other words the beauty of this laughterature. And then, also, this should be mentioned, German girls love F's book more than German men. There must be a reason, that I cannot understand. But I know, first hand, that the girls F has known intimately in Germany have all told him that they think he is a great writer. That reading his books is like fucking with him. I am merely quoting them here.

GRACE

PETER SIEDLECKI

Robert Duncan used to express the opinion that a very important function of literature had to do with testing the boundaries of the universe. Long ago, after taking the time to examine that notion, and to consider the gravity of the responsibility with which it charges the literary artist, I began to feel that all contemporary literature written to conform with established convention was a waste of time—superfluous and insignificant. I took seriously William Carlos Williams' pronouncement that for a writer not to oppose the literary standards of his time was morally reprehensible. I drifted toward Creeley and Olson and wrote articles on the preeminence of the proprioceptive approach to poetry, in comparison to the egocentric lamentations of T.S. Eliot and Sylvia Plath. Not too long after this, those charges began to emerge among "moralist" critics concerning the coldness and inhumanity of an aesthetic that placed so much emphasis upon new ways of *telling*. They forced the Marxist in me to examine my conscience.

I suppose that this is the moment in my text where one should anticipate reading that I experienced a conversion. Perhaps I might have if not for my fortuitous meeting with Raymond Federman. It was Federman who made real both the attitudes of Olson's proprioception and the conclusion to which the Marxist commentator Herbert Marcuse had come late in his life—that a piece of art should not be made with the intention of improving man, and that art improves man's being just by existing as art. By existing as a art, it becomes the reification of man's perfectability. For Marcuse, art by its nature, and not by its sociological intention, became an essential part of the permanent revolution. Not only did Federman's rejection of the "bourgeoise novel" illustrate this point, so too did his life. Yes, I laughed myself toward consciousness in **Double or Nothing**. I buttonholed my friends with my assertion that **Twofold Vibration** was the best thing ever written. I made **Smiles on Washington Square** essential reading for my students. And I was probably too close to Raymond to fully appreciate **To Whom it May Concern**, despite the fact that Raymond would say, "A book isn't supposed to make a reader cry." Coldness? Inhumanity? How ridiculous those charges are. Brutes can cry, but they cannot laugh; and laughter is precious, particularly when it brings you to a consciousness of what it means to be human. As I said, however, it is not only Federman's voice ringing from that closet that has affected me, it is the voice of his urging me to write. It is the voice on his answering machine purporting to be his houseboy Moinous that made me laugh. It is finding my voice "playgiarized" in his book **Critifiction** that honored me. It is his life, his being in the world, as teacher, mentor, and friend that makes me want to say effusive things about him, even while violating his proscriptions against bloated language and the use of quotation marks.

In this developed affinity with Federman, I claim no special stature, for he has befriended and offered guidance to many who have sought it and to anyone interested in testing the potential of language and exploring the boundaries of the fictive universe. However, while I do not claim it, his generosity bequeaths a special stature upon me and upon anyone who seeks his assistance in broadening literature's possibilities.

I will never forget the first piece of writing advice he gave me when I participated in his creative-writing seminar. I showed him part of a novel I was working on—an earnestly written comic history of the foundation of a college. He read it and responded by suggesting that I destroy this novel.

I was crestfallen. My face must have turned white. Never had I been given such a frank rejection.

Sensing my response, or perhaps even predicting it, he said, "No, no. I don't mean burn it or anything. Destroy it with words, words that are conscious of this story's pomposity. Let them make fun of it. After getting over the charge of pomposity, I did what he suggested, and even felt free enough during a scene when I needed a fishing expedition to "playgiarize" Herman Melville. The joy I discovered in this "destruction" of my novel has almost compensated for the fact that the novel never did find a publisher and is probably still in desperate need of a rewrite. I had assumed that my access to Federman as a mentor ended with that seminar, but we remained in touch. He paid frequent visits to the classes I taught and gave as much attention to my students' literary efforts as he did to those of his own students. In 1988, when I was a Senior Fulbright lecturer in East Germany and he was an artist in residence in Berlin, on numerous occasions, we endured the inconvenience of crossing the infamous wall for a variety of reasons, most of them academic or literary, some of them merely social—to have some wine or a meal together, or just for conversation. He thrilled my students at Friedrich Schiller University in Jena by coming to meet with them and talk about his work. Many of them knew Americans only via government filters and permissible Hollywood films. I know for certain that he changed certain lives forever, lives that had spent their formative years steeped in a pool of propaganda that had rationalized pollution, inadequate health services and low nutritional standards while promising some vague Utopia—all the things that Ray Federman might have found to be funny. Meeting with those students was just *de rigueur* for Ray, just something he did rather naturally, for the love of his art and his audience. They saw it as a great door opening a little bit more. I keep in touch with many of them who live now in a new world of possibilities, as well as discomforts. Raymond Federman remains a part of their consciousness.

I guess what I am trying to say in all of this is that it is easy to discover how Federman's life informs his work and how his work retains humanity while utterly avoiding didacticism. This connection of life and work is so smooth and so seamless and so natural that it sometimes seems that he is a genre unto himself. Consider this moment, as he read before a small audience from his latest work. Suddenly the sound system failed. Raymond could have gone on without it. It was an intimate gathering, but the security guard who offered his assistance was determined to root out the cause. As he checked connection after connection, Raymond assisted him and maintained a steady commentary—funny, but not abusive—conscious of absurdity, but not mocking—the two of them. Professor and Guard transformed into a comedy team in a situation that might have been handled much less gracefully by someone else.

Grace is Raymond Federman.

AUNT RACHEL'S MUFF: FEDERMAN'S ARTIST AS A YOUNG MAN

JEROME KLINKOWITZ

The story has been told a dozen times, from start to finish and back again: Raymond Federman's real fictitious discourse about his life as a-literary artist. The boy hidden in the closet, emerging as a self—creative voice; the emigrant to America, playing jazz in Detroit, making lampshades in the Bronx, Moinous in love with Sucette, and the Cyrano of his regiment; the noodles, of course, sustaining a novel the writing of which compounds the bet of double or nothing into a lifetime's infinity of effort; near the end of that lifetime, the conversations of two old bums, waiting for nothing but the pleasure of their companionly dialogue; and even into the future, where a still older man is shot into the distant orbit of space colonies. All this amounts to a life of fiction that demonstrates the fiction of life. We are our own stories, and how good a life we'll have depends on how well we can tell them. Competitive forces, be they particularized as the Nazis of Hitler's Reich or generalized as the friction of physical existence, do their best to erase everything. But faster than the eraser is the pencil's lead, the typewriter's key through the ribbon to the page, the electronic impulses that fill a blank screen. Through all impediments, Federman has written on.

But what if there had been a diversion? What if things had turned out differently? What if Federman's voice, so newly released from the confinements of European modernism, had packed up the first decade of its American experiences——the iampshade factory, the paratroop regiment, the noodles, and all that jazz——and taken it back home to France? What if *Double or Nothing* had been published not in Chicago at the end of 1971 but in Paris during 1956, its author some sort of Gallic Frank McCourt doing a French rendition of *Angela's Ashes*? Fame and riches, of course——that would have made Federman's middle years a lot more comfortable, cashing in the winning chips right at the life of fiction's start. But what would have been lost? The answer is deceptively simple, and quite vulgar in its frank expression: Aunt Rachel's muff. That's what the young writer thought he wanted but only found by looking for it somewhere else.

The purported object is phrased more politely in the title of Federman' s novel, *Aunt Rachel's Fur* (Normal IL and Talahassee FL: FC2, 2001). Aunt Rachel herself is the family's adventuress, escaping the confinements of local life to find glamor and success on another continent. The narrator, who is nothing other than Federman' s eternal fictive voice, is stuck at home in the shit——figuratively in the morass of family hostilities and privations, literally (once the German occupation comes) in the barnyard excrement of the farm work he must perform to survive. Seeking something better, his sexy Aunt Rachel is the first intimation he has of the life of fiction. Horney adolescent that he is, it's natural that sex comes first. But sexuality is just an index to the emerging powers of his imagination, powers that will help him survive the world's first attempts at erasing him and lead to his later success articulating the silence that would otherwise be his life.

It is Aunt Rachel's example that has inspired the narrator to emigrate, at age 19, to the United States. But once here, the going is far from even, and by the time of *Aunt Rachel's Fur*, which is about ten years afterwards, he can say convincingly, "Wow, I was fed up with America" (p. 18). Why so? Because it is "the land of misrepresentation" (p. 20) where everything seems false. Looking back on the Federman canon, readers can see how the events of these first ten years have been fabulatively rewarding, the stuff of great stories, from trading horns with Charlie Parker to nesting in his Buick Special in the upper branches of a gd.gantic-coniferous tree. But here, in the mid 1950s, none of those stories have yet been told. The author has just one manuscript, a novel called *A Time of Noodles* that while it seems much like *Double or Nothing* isn't quite *Double or Nothing* yet. The artist, you see, is still too young a man. In sexual terms, Aunt Rachel's muff is just that: a mysterious, foreign, unknowable and hence unattainable image of what he has no words for, no actions for———the ultimate difference of the other sex. In seeking an equivalent for it in his emigration to the United States, it is no wonder that—to this point—the substitute has proven unsatisfactory as well.

But now the narrator's back in Paris, ostensibly to sell his novel to a French publisher (as no one in America wants it), but in fact to get it all off his chest, to tell someone what a disgusting mess his life has been so far, on both sides of the Atlantic. Here is the key feature of story: that it *is* a story, told to a palpably present listener, whose response must be gauged before the next part is offered, whose receptive attitude (and not simple chronology) determines the order of things. Time itself is not orderly; why should the narrator' s story be? What matters is its effect, something he can measure as he tells it. The better its telling, the better he feels about it———and the better he feels about his life. Thus *Aunt Rachel's Fur* presents the methodology of Federman's real fictitious discourse in a pristine but also plainly accessible form. And why not? If fiction isn't about life, what good is it? And what is life without a good fiction to give it some direction?

"You Want Me to Tell You About the Family..." (p. 61). In this second section following the initial explanation of why the narrator has headed back to Paris with a bellyfull of American woes to unload upon his listener, his first adult encounter with French writing takes place. As a Frenchman trying to remember things past, to recover lost time across what has by now become a considerable temporal and spatial distance, her cannot help but face the example of Proust. What makes this condition special is that the Nazi occupation has intervened; Namredef (as he calls himself) has both a greater global catastrophe and more personally invasive tragedy to face than did the great modernist whom some might consider as a mentor. Going back to the old home, looking for the salamander-stove that might otherwise function as his madeleine, he finds that what the Nazis haven't erased, unfriendly neighbors (and perhaps even selfish family members) have stolen, all because "it didn't take long for them to realize that my parents weren't coming back" (p. 87). The narrator himself has suffered the same fate, not erased but invisible thanks to the fact none of his relatives know where he's been, escaping the Holocaust and surviving in the south as an agricultural worker by a miracle of fate. When he returns after the liberation, few seem glad to see him, for in their minds he *has* been erased, and writing him back in is not a pleasarrt task for them: "when I showed up after the war, still alive, they were ashamed to admit it" (p. 87), ashamed that they'd taken the possessions that are now just Proustian memories, madeleines that leave a distinctly unpleasant taste.

Yet Proust remains as a possible model, one of many whose method Namredef tries out on his audience. Dozens of French writers, from Victor Hugo and Emile Zola to Beckett and Baudrillard, pepper the text as the narrator considers their examples. Racine, Céline, hardly anyone of note is missed (don't ever forget that Raymond Federman earned a Columbia Ph. D. in French literature, back in those pre-postmodern years when the old canon was unquestioned). But each one is dismissed, and not lightly so. What one proposes, another challenges; that's what a doctoral student learns. But Namredef, professional fiction writer that he is, tests them from the inside, looking into their experiences, evaluating their style, and measuring it against his own project. Take America, where the narrative has started: "No Baudrillard he didn't spend three fucking years in the fucking army with the racist hillbillies of North Carolina, no Baudrillard never worked, like I did, as a dishwasher in the grease joints of New York City" (p. 27). As for Céline, attractive for his literary energy and repulsive for the vicious anti-Semitism that sometimes drove it, Namredef is analytical:

> As I said, Céline he travelled by subway in his books, like a maniac, full speed ahead in his words, and along the way he assaulted everybody, his mouth was like a big asshole crapping out words full of shit, he defecated his enraged wordshit in everybody's face, his mouth was like an anus...

> Me I go on foot, je suis un flâneur de la littérature, a pedestrian of fiction, I stroll gingerly in words, from one word to the next, I word—word, and if sometimes my blood is boiling and I start screaming because of all the stupid zombies I encountered in my life that doesn't mean I've lost hope for humanity, even if humanity is in terrible shape these days... (p. 36)

Throughout *Aunt Rachel's Fur*, these same French writers relate to the life Namredef is experiencing. Looking back on his years in the south, he recalls the collaborationist curate who "spewed in his sermons, that Lavaliste traitor shouted at us all the time." In doing so "he sounded just like Céline, I'm convinced that instead of studying his prayer book, that miserable traitor was spending all his time reading Céline's *Bagatelles* or some other flithy stuff like that" (p. 169). As for other writers' methods and attitudes, Namredef can emulate Zola's taste for the sordid without losing himself (as did the inventor of Naturalism) in details, just as he has been able to adopt Hugo's appreciation of misery without the older writer's sentimentality and Gide's self-reflexivity while maintaining a sense of humor (something purely modernist self—reflexion so dearly lacks). Other writers he extends——including Beckett, the subject of Federman's (as well as Namredef's) doctoral dissertation. "Hey, what a fantastic idea, don't you think so," he challenges his listener, "we could call it *the reverse of timeness*, just as old Sam invented *the reverse of farness*, I now invent *the reverse of timeness*, maybe that'll make me famous after I've changed tenses, that's all it takes sometimes, a wild idea..." (p. 147). When he does show a weakness, he has the great French literary canon as ~n excuse.

Given his subject matter, how else could one avoid the occasional pitfalls of a modernist poet, as in this set of paragraphs:

> *My soft—voiced mother wept for everyone*, but not for long, her beautiful black hair never turned white, her big black eyes became stone . You see how incorrigible I am, wandering again, this time with Paul Célan, I just can't get to what I want to tell you, the story of my Aunt Rachel... (p. 144)

There is even French theory involved. Gilles Deleuze is cited relatively early, on page 95, to the effect that creating a style in a foreign language (as Federman does in this novel and as his character Namredef has done in *A Time of Noodles*) involves passing through several stages, from a decomposition of the mother tongue and the stuttering and stammering in the second language until a new tongue, a new syntax emerges. As Namredef struggles with story about Aunt Rachel and her fur, this is what he does before our eyes, working his way through the French literary canon as he explodes it himself in his own writing, a real fictitious discourse carried out for the benefit of a very evident listener, someone whose implied presence influences the shape things take———a stand-in for us as readers and what we already know about these literary greats.

One asks why Namredef can't remain among them. The answers are complex, and demand a working—through by both the narrator and his liste-ier. For one thing, there are all the erasures: of his parents and sisters by the Nazis, of any traces they may have left by their unkind relatives (who always resented his mother's marriage), and even of Namredef's survival during the Occupation:

> Ah yes, L'Exode de juin 1940, isn't it amazing how nobody talks about it anymore, as though it never happened, how the shameful debacle of the French army has been swept under the carpet of history, I suppose it's because of what Le Grand General de Gaulle said about the Vichy Government when he returned gloriously, do you remember, **nul et non advenu**, he proclaimed, just like that, as if Pétain's disgraceful government never existed, and with these

words he made us believe that France had won the war, and the exodus, the defeat of 1940, the deportation of the Jews, les Maquisards Communistes who were executed during the occupation, and all the other ignominious things that had happened between 1940 and 1945, were erased from the books... (p. 258)

Secondly, there is the nature of Namredef's second homecoming, following his initial decade in America. Needless to say, the publishers of Paris are not interested in his novel; their feigned politeness leads to inevitable brush-offs by underlings. By the end of this novel he's had *A Time of Noodles* considered and rejected by a humiliatingly obtuse sub-editor, someone who could never understand that "for me a novel is less the writing of an adventure than the adventure of writing" (p. 249).

Thirdly, there's the manner of storytelling the narrator has devloped and come near to perfecting during his sojourn in Paris. All along he's suspected that a publisher will not be interested, but in telling his story to the listener he can measure responses even more immediately——and make necessary changes right on the spot. Yes, the listener is mildly interested in Namredef's tales about his adventures on the farm, but seems to agree that "what the public wants is ass stories, and that's why I'd better get back to Aunt Rachel's story" (p. 164). What her story suggests is the "reverse of timeness" the narrator loves in fiction: "In the reverse of timeness, instead of flaunting its ugly face at us, time would show us its lovely ass, wouldn't that be great" (p. 147). The listener has indeed been prompting ass stories, asking about girlfriends, wondering about early sexual adventures, enjoying digressions such as the seduction of young Namredef by the farmer's wife. All along, of course, the narrator has been promising to tell about Aunt Rachel, but never getting to the point——until the point comes when he makes a Freudian slip, in the midst of a wet dream about the farmer's wife confessing how the secret of a feminine body is "a soft delicate pearly fur, like my Aunt Rachel's fur" (p. 180). He catches himself, but that's part of the story, too: this continual teasing with the promise of an ass story, his "dreaming of Aunt Rachel's ass and her black fur" (p. 159).

Fourthly, and of most importance, is the language Namredef finds best for his narrative expression. It is not French; French has been the language of all his suffering. He feels freer in English, but not that of the British Isles. It's American English he glories in, especially its free and open spaces, a verbal arena in which he can improvise like a jazz musician. It's "the improvised aspect of the novel, the noodling element" that he really loves, the method he's used in weaving in and out of Aunt Rachel's story in order to cover almost everything else, while the listener waits for the final sexual revelation, the long deferred promise of this muff and ass story that's the best example yet of Namredef's ability to "transpose jazz improvisations to writing" (p. 163).

And what of that ass and muff story? Well, we'll never know; that's Namredef's secret, the propulsive energy of which has brought him through the narrative and left us wanting more. The absence of this particular episode corresponds with practical fact, because the whole point of the forbidden other is that it cannot be licitly experienced, that were it to be possessed it would no longer be forbidden and no longer be the other. Namredef's jazz narrative keeps it as it should be, a possibility to be continually noodled as just that, a possibility rather than a reality, a fiction rather than a fact.

Don't forget that Namredef has written a doctoral thesis on Samuel Beckett's fiction, and that Beckett has commended him for doing something the French and British critics hadn't done. "*I thank you, Sir,*" Beckett says in a letter, "*for having paid attention to the shape of my sentences rather than their meaning*" (p. 108). It is the shape of Namredef's narrative that tells the real story here as well; no matter that the meaning is kept secret, for that's as all meanings should be in this line of work. If you want to send a message, use a telegram. If you want nothing but melody, listen to a different kind of music. But if it's the brilliance of improvisatory expression that interests you, tune into the story of Aunt Rachel's muff and see everything the author can do with this generative figure.

At novel's end, Namredef leaves Paris, fed up with its closed literary world. Not that American publishers will be any more receptive; as Federman's readers know, it will take another decade and a half of life in America before his fictionist's career is properly launched. But in the United States there are things of more immediate importance than a publishing contract. There's jazz, there's a society that despite its materialistic commercialization is still open to improvisation, one that will let a young guy from France share a saxophone with no less an artist than Charlie Parker. That's the ultimate democracy of the improvisatory style of life, a life Namredef seems to miss on this visit back to Paris. He could have stayed, just as he could have left for a fabulous colonial life in Senegal with Aunt Rachel. But had he done either, there would have been no time of noodles, either on the tenor saxophone or on the printed page. A muff alone only gets you so much.

THE LOST FOURTH CHAPTER OF RAYMOND FEDERMAN'S SMILES ON WASHINGTON SQUARE

MICHAEL HEMMINGSON

But there's more. There's always more. That's the situation with stories and life—things don't always end at "the end" and that's certainly the case with Moinous and Sucette; it doesn't end with Moinous wishing he'd never seen the blonde Sucette on Washington Square and smiling at her, it doesn't end with Moinous' loneliness and longing for some kind of connection while he's homeless and freezing on the streets of New York, post-Korean War era. Indeed, there were many more endings to Federman's 1985 novel, first published by Thunder's Mouth Press, and later reissued in paperback by Sun&Moon Press.

How I happened upon this last fourth chapter isn't a very interesting story. What's more interesting is the fact that Ray Federman wouldn't allow the chapter to be published in this journal.

"Why?" I asked.

"Michael," Federman said in his thick French accent, "I have my own goddamn reasons that I don't have to explain to you!"

Very well. But he never said I couldn't explain what was in this chapter—i.e., paraphrase it.

Within this lost fourth chapter of *Smiles on Washington Sqaure*, there are seven alternative endings to the love story of Moinous and Sucette, which I present, forthwith—

1. Moinous and Sucette get married. She has a child, and later a second child. Moinous takes on a horrible job as a trash collector. He's miserable, she's miserable, their children are miserable; and they lead a collective miserable life among the many miserable in New York.

2. Sucette has several sexual encounters with her creative writing teacher at Columbia. That's the thing with creative writing teachers: sometimes they fuck their students. So this happens. Sucette isn't sure what she feels about it. Moinous finds out, he gets horribly jealous, and confronts the teacher one night on the campus of Columbia. Moinous intention is to kick the creative wirting teacher's ass, but he isn't prepared for the fact that the teacher knows karate, and he kicks Moinous' ass. Moinous is left on the ground, bleeding. Sucette is embarrassed; she looks down on Moinous and says, "How could you do such a foolish thing?" "Because I'm a fool," Moinous replies.

3. Moinous murders Sucette. But this turns into a very different kind of story. He doesn't murder her out of love. He kills her out of delusion. He winds up killing several other young women, so *Smiles on Washington Sqaure* becomes a serial killer novel.[2]

4. Moinous has a brief affair with Sucette, and it's good, it last several months; but he winds up getting together with one of her friends, someone named Simone, who is also French. Moinous and Simone move to Italy and live happily ever after.

---

[2] "Actually," Federman told me, "several publishers liked this idea. The serial killer novel was just becomming popular in the 1980s. But I told them all to fuck off! I wasn't going to write some genre trash just to get the book published!"

5. Sucette is diagnosed with lukemia. Her death is very sad and painful. Moinous is left, once again, alone in the cold.[3]

6. Moinous and Sucette get involved with a Communist cell in New York. They are deeply devoted to the cause. They wind up getting arrested by the FBI and spending twenty-five years in a federal prison for treason.

7. Moinous and Sucette have a relationship that lasts for a year or two. Then Sucette happens to meet a lesbian, Andi, who seduces Sucette. Sucette realizes that she's been a lesbian all along, this is her calling, and she leaves Moinous and moves in with Andi.

I called Federman on the phone the other day and said, "I have another ending for *Smiles on Washington Sqaure*! It's up-to-date, right-to-the-minute!"

"Oui?" said Federman.

"Moinous and Sucette marry, they grow old together. They're living in New York, their kids have left home. Moinous has made some investments, or he has legal matters to attend to—anyway, he's in the World Trade Center on September 11, seeing either his broker or his lawyer. He narrowly escapes the disaster—perhaps he helps someone, or several people, also escape, and he becomes a hero."

"Well," Federman said, "I don't know about that."

"Okay," I said, "how about if Moinous and Sucette discover that, all these years, they have been alien abductees?"

"Absolutely not!" Federman yelled, and hung up the phone.[4]

---

[3] Federman: "One woman editor wanted me to focus on that ending. A sort of *Love Story* type of thing. Again, I refused!"

[4] The real ending, of course, is that Moinous never has any kind of contact with Sucette, beyond the smile, and he dies, covered in snow, sleeping on a park bench.

4 IMAGES

MICHAEL BASINSKI

440

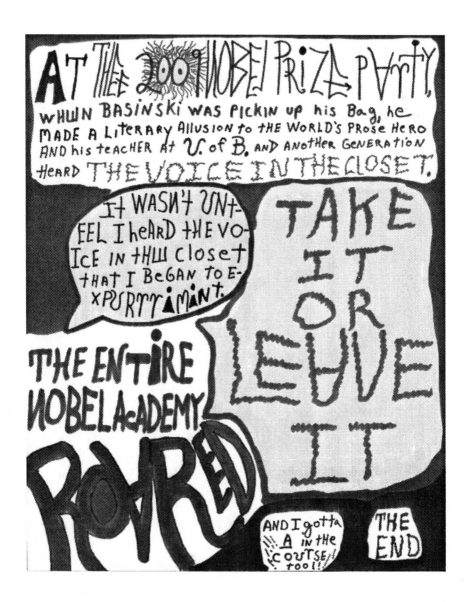

A Review of Federman: From A to X-X-X-X: A Recyclopedic Narrative. Edited by Larry McCaffery, Thomas Hartl, & Doug Rice. San Diego: San Diego State UP, 1998.

Eckhard Gerdes

Federman by the letters. A man of letters. A man who lives by his letters. His correspondence is legendary. His correspondents are legendary. He's flown with the Bird, he's dropped from the sky, he's landed inside Beckett's pocket disguised as a stone, and he's laughed in the face of disaster. He deserves more than a 400-page encyclopedia (the above-mentioned wondrous recyclopedia), more than a 300-plus page issue of this journal (that you're holding), more than the testimonials of 25,000 devoted German readers and nearly all intelligent American readers (nearly ¾ of the 4000!). He deserves his own island in the Pacific: Federlandia, perhaps, where life would be a grand wonderful adventure. Where the baccarat tables never close, where the golf courses are changed every day, where *Molloy* and *The Unnamable* are two of the books of the Bible, where music is only as cheesy as Stan Getz, where Bordeaux red wine cascades over waterfalls, and where everywhere people are laughing and talking intelligently with one another as they amuse and bemuse about views.

Aside from the man's works themselves, which show us everything, but then only piecemeal, *Federman A to X-X-X-X* gives us the best, certainly the most comprehensive view into the quintessential postmodern novelist Raymond Federman. Why quintessential? Because he best exhibits that characteristic of postmodernism that is seen as its hallmark, that traces its origins back to Bakhtin's *polyglossia*: in Federman languages collide. Not just French and English, but all languages: the language of jazz and the language of culture, the language of starvation and the language of gluttony. All is collision, but sometimes the collision is quiet and unspoken, like a parking lot accident. Other times the collision is loud and neck-bending. But the response to the collision is always the laugh. That is so profound and so unique a response in the world of literature that it makes Federman stand completely alone. Even when confronted with bowel-emptying tragedy, Federman laughs. *I shit; therefore, I am*, Sartre may have said. *I shit; therefore, I laugh*, says Federman. And who of us, looking down into that toilet, hasn't had occasion for laughter? After a night of a lot of red wine, perhaps? After liquorice? After daring to eat a beet?

There are absolutely wonderful pieces in this *Recyclopedia* that no one should miss. Federman fans will love the clever "Chronology for RF." Scholars will find in this book a gold mine of material for evaluation and examination. But anyone with a heart cannot help but be touched by such wonderful tributes as Simone Federman's "I Believed Him." It is in this heartfelt human dimension that the book really succeeds. And it is perhaps this about Federman that makes his work different from that of many of his contemporaries whose work, although ingenious and intellectually wonderful, doesn't touch our hearts like Federman's. Sure, sure, the intellectual stuff is there, but the shapes of Federman's sentences are determined by his heart, not by his head. In this he is indeed the bearer of the torch given him by Beckett. McCaffery, Hartl and Rice provide evidence of this time and time again. And thus, this *Recyclopedia* is the best bathroom book of all: it will make you laugh at the shit, and that is a blessing. It will also make you think, which is wonderful. But mostly it will make you feel closer to this amazing novelist who is still alive and among us, helping us all enjoy our lives just a bit more than we thought we could.

Federman Ou La Pudeur D'Écrire

Christian Prigent

Sans doute y a-t-il à l'origine de toute impulsion à écrire, réel ou imaginaire, conscient ou inconscient, un événement central déchirant. Ecrire, c'est répondre à cet événement, c'est-à-dire à la fois le dévoiler et le recouvrir. Bien souvent la prose romanesque ne fait que colmater cette brèche. A l'opposé: la représentation déchirée du déchirant (la langue d'Artaud, par exemple). Le roman apparaît alors souvent comme une formation de compromis: non seulement le compromis passé avec la commande sociale et le conformisme du "grand" public—mais encore le compromis "interne" qui permet de résorber, dans la réussite d'une construction narrative, la trace maladroite et douloureuse de la crise qui poussa a écrire (à ne pas entrer sans perte ni fracas dans la parole commune).

La question de l'autobiographie romanesque surgit là parce qu'elle rend manifeste un affrontement à l'expérience intime et à ses dechirures. Peu de romanciers évitent ce paradoxe: faire de ce *noyau d'innommable* matière romanesque. Peu aussi l'affrontent sans compromis (sans nappage virtuose des déchirures). Peu laissent leur prose se déchirer à la mesure du déchirement qu'elle traite—la déchirement venu du creux instable de l'expérience et de "ce qui ne peut être totalement vu, dessiné, saisi, décrit dans sa plenitude". Raymond Federman s'installe dans ce paradoxe. Pour lui, raconter sa vie ne petit se faire "en clair", sauf à caller au leurre qui voudrait que le chaos dechirant de l'expérience puisse passer sans mensonge ni perte dans le charme lissé de la prose romanesque: "Il venait de commencer un

447

roman…c'était un livre étrange et triste, sans trame ou plutôt la trame était pulvérisée, comma si elle ne se laissait pas raconter…Je lui répétais sans cesse: Pourquoi ne racontes-tu pas l'histoire dans le ban ordre, cesse tes petits jeux, mais il se fâchait."

Au centre brûlant de ce que nous raconte (?) *la Flèche du Temps*[1], il y a une scène primitive violemment traumatique. Mais plutôt que scène, il faudrait dire ici point d'évidement, trou vertigineux. Voici Paris sous l'Occupation, une rafle, une famille juive déportée, un enfant de douze ans (l'auteur) jeté au dernier moment par sa mère dans un placard et échappant ainsi à l'holocauste: "Lorsque les soldats eurent emmené sa mère, son père et ses deux sœurs, trébuchant dans l'escalier avec leurs paquets, leurs petits paquets nomades c'est ainsi qu'il les décrivit, étoiles jaunes gémissantes, en route vers leur solution finale…et que tout redevint silencieux, le petit garçon s'assit, à moitié nu sur une pile de journaux." La roman a cette scène comme centre explosant-fixe. Et peu importe ce qu'il construit autour de ce vide générateur et dilapidateur en même temps. L'important est que cela vaille moins?par ce qui s'y affirme (les bribes éclatées d'une autobiographie) que par ce qui s'y nie: la possibilité de transcrire l'événement déchirant en clair, dans l'ordre sans déchirure du procès romanesque, sans effondrement douloureux de la phrase, sans surgissement de l'innommable dans l'alignement des noms.

"Annuler l'histoire"

Federman ne raconte pas les tranches de sa vie. Il suit la trace des vibrations de ce qui resta quand, dans la vie, on trancha traumatiquement les liens de la familiarité: la famille (déportée et massacrée), la langue maternelle (reléguée par l'exil aux Etats-Unis), l'humanité "civilisée" (le trauma autobiographique de Federman rejoint, par la force atroce des choses, le trauma historique du siècle, Auschwitz, l' innommable luimême: "L'holocauste est un événement universel, absolu, dans lequel l'humanité tout entiére s'est trouvée impliquée et continue à l'être, et parler de ce triste événement, dans la vie ou par la biais de la fiction, afin de comprendre

l'incompréhensible, cela aussi doll être une entreprise collective." Donc:
"Nous sommes tous des personnes déplacées survivant en pays étranger,
dans la vie comme dans la fiction." L'écriture est une des formes de ce
déplacament, de cette étrangéité foncière de l'être au "monde". Devant le
compte rendu autobiographique, elle ne peut qu'être saisie par la honte qui
nous envahit devant la plat, l'atone, le dérisoirement stable, l'insignifiant
des significations alignées en récits, l'inertia soumise des découpes d'où
tombent, calibrées et pasteurisées, les tranches de vie. Elle ne peut que rou-
gir et refluer devant tout ce qui, du réel, reste littéralement *en souffrance*
dans la langue—si la langue à son tour ne souffre pas, ne s'essoufle pas dans
la prise en compte du négatif qui la hante et la jette dans des portées
inouïes.

A partir de cette violence de la *pudeur d'écrire,* Federman construit sa
fiction par étoilement, prolifération madréporique autour du centre traumatique à la fois systematiquement re-présenté et récuse, évidant, nié:
"une longue désarticulation syntaxique c'est tout, sans commenacement ni
fin". Le roman se donna alors comme geste simultané d'invocation at de
conjuration de l'événement (la scene du placard), "parce que l'intensité
contrôlée du langage a pour but de se prémunir contre l'emprise émotion-
nelle du drame englouti".

Pour ce faire, l'auteur projete d'abord le *moment* traumatique dans la
dispersion des *temps.* Il prétend ainsi "annuler l'histoire" dans la "double
vibration" du futur (la scène est en décembre 1999, la héros, 82 ans—
l'une des incarnations de l'auteur—attend sa déportation pour les
"colonies célestes"), et du passé (les narrateurs racontent à l'auteur la vie
dudit héros, son exil, ses engagements politiques dans les Etats-Unis des
années 60, ses amours, ses vagabondages dans les casinos d'Europe). Les
époques s'enchevêtrent dans un mouvement qui est ceiui d'un geste d'ef-
facement permanent plutôt que celui d'une remémoration.

Il fait ensuite exploser le sujet en plusieors personnages qui le dis-
persent et projettent l'intensité du trauma dans l'étoilenaent de cette dispersion: Federman, Moinous. Moimoi, Le Vieux et leur miroir inversé,

Namredef. Il jette enfin la langue elle-même dans une hétérogénéité célino-beatnik à la rage goguenarde qui oscille sans cesse entre les rodomontades carnavalesques et les méditations sophistiquées, l'auto-commentaire savant et les apartés cocassas, les scènes trivialès et la réflex-ion grave (sur l'holocauste, en particulier), la parler "popu" et les citations littéraires, la langue apprise (l'américain) et les retours, souvent argotiques ou idiolectaux, de la langue maternelle (le français). Cette langue souvent cousue à gros points, parfois relâchée et "facile", mais toujours vivante, toujours active, est la langue même de la trouée par où, dans le corps dilacéré de la fiction romanesque, surgit. imparable, l'innommable réel dont elle est à la fois la trace indélébile at la détournemant triomphal.

---

1. Raymond Federman, *In Flèche du Tempu.* Traduit de l'américain par Françoise Brodsky, Circé éditeur, 230 p., 120 F.

MEETING FEDERMAN IN CYBERSPACE: OR THE BIRTH OF BOOKS IN THE SPIRIT OF E-MAILS

REINHARD KRÜGER

> *"Moinous & Moinous are vases communicants."*
> Federman: Loose Shoes

This is a vero-similar report of some aspects of what happened between September 2000 and May 2001 in cyberspace, at least as Raymond Federman and Reinhard Krüger believe that those things occurred. Other versions of what happened are due to further memories which still have not been created.

1. http://www.federman.com/rfsb_2.htm

13th of September 2000. Me browsing the internet to get some information about one of the last videos of Samuel Beckett (*Quad*), I hit the list of a collector of Samuel Beckett's books. The man had a strange name and so did his list: Raymond Federman's *Private Collection of Samuel Beckett*. I didn't know who this Federman was. But his name was similar or even identical with the name of an American author whom I knew from his typographic novel *Double or nothing*, or *Alles oder nichts*, a tremendous experimental novel which had been very successfully published in a

451

German translation in 1986 by Hans Magnus Enzensberger in his collection *Die Andere Bibliothek,* some fifteen years ago. Really strange coincidence of names, but why should this not be?

The other strange thing was the acronym used by this Mr. Federman at the bottom of his page: "Email inquiries to: Moinous@aol.com." An English speaking man using a French acronym was quite unusual, but what kind of acronym: a poetical reflection of the avant-gardist multiplication of the "I," of the subject of the artist. "Moi est un autre," wrote Rimbaud—"I am an other," "Moi aujourd'hui et moi il y a cinquante ans, ce sont deux choses bien différentes," wrote Montaigne some 300 years before Rimbaud—"Me today and me fifty years ago are two different things." Artists seem to abandon the idea of an unchangeable individual more easily than other people.

2. krueger.reinhard@berlin.de—» moinous@aol.com

I became curious whether or not this Federman was an artist and the author of the book I knew for many years. I simply wrote him a short message asking if he was the same Federman I knew from the German translation of a book called *Alles oder Nichts*. I never expected an answer, but some days later he replied: "Yes, I am the Raymond Federman [you have to imagine those lines in Arial, because at that time Mr. Federman used Arial as being a symbol of modern typography], who wrote *Double or Nothing* translated into German and published by Enzensberger in *Die Andere Bibliothek…*"

We did not know what we were beginning at that moment. The first thing I did was switch my messages to Federman from English to French, a language that I handle for reasons unknown to me with more ease than my Anglo-Saxon and Germanic brother-language. Three or four e-mails later Mr. Federman became Raymond. Until now we had only written about past books, about Sam Beckett, etc. Suddenly he wrote that he had difficulties finding a publisher for his latest book called *Loose shoes—A Life*

Story of Sorts. Because of the negligence of American publishers he had published this book as an electronic edition on the internet: (*http://wings.buffalo.edu/epc/authors/federman/shoes/*). I checked this page and I encountered marvelous pages of Federman's writing until then unknown to me, the German barbarian with no real linkage to Anglo-American writing. I knew that I could easily publish this book in Germany.

3.www.weidler-verlag.de/...

a.Lieferbare_Titel/nach_Titeln_sortiert/federman_shoes/federman_shoes.html

In that period (to know the exact story you will have to consult the forthcoming Mentir ou mourir: to lie or to die. La naissance des livres dans l'esprit e-mail, e-mails between krueger.reinhard@berlin.de and moinous@aol.com. This book will be out in January 2002 and available through www.weidler-verlag.de or www.amazon.de, www.amazon.fr) it was the first time that our dialogue on published and unpublished books turned out to be a dialogue on virtual and printed books. I made him the offer to publish his book in Berlin, knowing that I could easily convince my publisher (Mr. Joachim Weidler), but not knowing if he would really feel like heading the adventure of publishing English books in Germany. Later he became even more adventurous and published French, Spanish and Italian books, (and he will—I know it already—publish in the future, even if he actually is not aware of it, Portuguese and Catalan books.) Mr. Weidler accepted and the first book was born in the focus of the triangle Federman/Krüger/Weidler.

b. Lieferbare_Titel/nach_Titeln_sortiert/ federman_99/federman_-99.html

The contracts were signed on December 6th, 2000 in Berlin, and that day we made another decision that led to a further book: *99 hand-written poems / 99 poèmes écrits à la main*.

This book was the result of pure chance. It was not premeditated, but it just happened by chance, while we were producing another book. Preparing the edition of *Loose Shoes*, we decided to publish as well a limited numbered edition, as had been done for some of Raymond Federman's books in Germany. According to the decision of Enzensberger and Greno to publish 999 copies of the collector's edition of *Alles oder Nichts* (*Double or nothing*) and to sell them at a price of 99 Deutschmarks, it was evident that the number 99 had a special relation to Raymond Federman's work in Germany.

We decided to print 99 copies of the collector's edition of *Loose Shoes*, and to sell them at a price of 99 Deutschmarks. Therefore the *édition de tête* of *Loose Shoes* is far more rare than the special edition of *Alles oder Nichts*, but the price still remains the same.

But what should this special edition look like? Well, just printing numbers on the first or on last page, and just signing the leaf appeared to be somewhat banal. We agreed that Raymond Federman should write a little poem by hand to be inserted in every copy. So he took 99 sheets of printing paper back to the U.S. with him, and he began to write the poems which had to be inserted in the copies destined to form the limited edition. But as you cannot swim twice in the same water, he immediately began to write 99 different poems. This was mainly to escape from the tedious job of writing 99 times the same poem.

So sheet after sheet were filled with his new inventions, with his remembrances of old poems, with new French poems, with his souvenirs of his French poems, just forming a pile of sheets which began to look like a book, a book of 99 hand-written poems. Books sometimes seem not to be invented by thinking of books, but they seem to happen by chance, doing something different.

Unfortunately the order of the poems might have been destroyed. It might have happened, that opening the little box Federman sent with the 99 hand-written poems in it, the box fell on the floor. Just showing one poem, let's say poem no. 48 or no. 50 or just no. 10—who knows?—right in the center of the mixed-up pile. Briefly, the sheets fell out and they needed to be rearranged. They were shuffled the way as the content of memory is daily shuffled for the sake of figuring out the new images of the past, for premembering the future.

We decided to shuffle the sheets of poems like playing cards, hopefully rearranging them in the permutative way of the original order. But we stopped at the very moment when the book had to go to printing. Maybe we succeeded in reshaping the former order, maybe by shuffling the text we established a completely new order which might indeed be the old order, the former order which, in fact, nobody can remember any more. There is nothing new, but oblivion.

It was evident that the new book born of chance underwent even more changes. We decided to give a typographic interpretation of the poems. Raymond Federman had to proof-read them. But as the water is continuously changing, so did the poems as well. Suddenly the *99 hand-written poems* were nothing but the manuscript of a completely new book, which had never been foreseen, never been planned: The typographic version of *99 hand-written poems*.

There is a cardinal difference between *Loose shoes* and *99 hand-written poems*: *Loose shoes* had been premeditated as a book, I got to know it as an unpublished book, whereas *99 hand-written poems* suddenly appeared as a possible book, which we immediately put into practice.

4. www.weidler-verlag.de/Reihen/Romanice/roma08/roma08.html

One day, it might have been in early January 2001, I asked Raymond whether he has written any typographic novels in French. As a scholar for romance literatures I wondered if there were any French equivalents of

Double or Nothing. Yes, he wrote, in 1974, I published a novel called *Amer Elorado*, which was nominated for the prestigious Prix Médicis. But eventually the publisher went bankrupt and the remaining copies of *Amer Eldorado* were shredded. I offered Raymond to publish a new edition of *Amer Eldorado* as the first volume of the book-series romance for which I had just signed the contracts. I scanned the old text, I treated it with an OCR-text-recognition program. The result: the text was totally destroyed, nothing of the original beautiful typographic organization of the text remained. Raymond had to reorganize the entire text after the old model of 1974. He did not make it. Every time Raymond puts his hands in one of his old texts, he has to re-write it. Reading his old texts means to reinvent them, to review his life, to review the images of his own life, and to give another version of his life. The most exceptional thing that happened re-working *Amer Eldorado* was the medial shifting from typewriter and traditional typographic dying to the computer. Instead of driving the typographer crazy by insisting on his spatial inventions, he could construct the images of the pages directly on his computer. Finally Raymond admitted that he was about to write a completely new text, nearly double number of pages of the original. This book appeared in June 2001 as *Amer Eldorado 2001*. An aspect which is often forgotten is the fact that this new version contains an exhaustive list of the Parisian argot words that appear in it.

5. www.weidler-verlag.de/Reihen/Romanice/roma01/roma01.html

Given the fact that Raymond "failed' to re-organize *Amer Eldorado* after the model of the '74 edition there remained still the necessity to give a re-edition of this text, which we finally reprinted from the original without changing a word. Due to the rarity of the original reprint this edition is the only really available edition of the 1974 version of the text.

6.www.weidlerverlag.de/Lieferbare_Titel/nach_Titeln_sortiert/krueg erfederman-m&m/kruegerfederman-m&m

It happened that we became conscious of the fact, that the invention of books may work differently from what one normally would believe. Books, namely those invented in the dialogues we held, happen like the incoming lightning of a thunderstorm: you never know, when the germ of a book is created. Only looking back we were able to detect some actions or speech-acts which—*à la longue*—led us to the invention of further books. At that very moment had we recognized the fact that nearly all those books were born in an unpremeditated way during our e-mail-based dialogue, there arose the next idea: we had to publish our e-mails to give an account of the long-term effects of our strange meeting in cyberspace. As I was too lazy to clear my web-based e-mail account and to throw the e-mails I had read in the virtual trash, I kept simply by laziness all the e-mails we exchanged from 13th of September 2000 until the end of May of 2001. We gathered them and put them in a new book: *Mentir ou mourir—to lie or to die. La naissance des livres dans l'esprit e-mail.* Sometimes even doing nothing may lead to a new book. It is we believe the first e-mail-based book ever published. Even if it is not worth being read, it is important just for the fact of being a book composed of e-mails.

This is a vero-similar report of some aspects of what happened between September 2000 and May 2001 in cyberspace, at least as Raymond Federman and Reinhard Krüger believe that those things happened. Other versions of what happened are due to further memories which still have not been created.

IN SEARCH OF MONA

a spontaneous love story
invented on the spot
by
Jule & Juliette

O body swayed to music, O brightening glance,
How can we know the dancer from the dance?
William Butler Yeats

Dans un grenier où je fus enfermé à douze ans
j'ai connu le monde, j'ai illustré la comédie humaine.
Arthur Rimbaud

La quête de l'absolu ne laisse jamais en paix
ce rêveur qui sait que cette exigence le conduira
au coeur même de ses propres ténèbres
là où se cache toujours la vérité
Ernesto Sábato

—Getting the Story Going Again—

–Hey! What do you say we get the story going again?

–Which story? With you there are so many stories going on at the same time, one never knows which one you're talking about.

–Mona's story. You know, the story of Mona. Moinous' frantic pursuit of Mona.

–Oh that one!

–Yes that one. Shall we go on with it?

–Why not. It's a good one. It's got potential. Ok, let's go on with it. Where did we leave them last time? Do you remember?

–Not exactly, but doesn't matter, we'll improvise as we go along, as we always do. After all this is a spontaneous story.

–Right. A spontaneous love story, taking shape as we talk it out.

–That's true. The story of Mona & Moinous can only be spoken, even if it appears written.

–So let's speak it then. But do you have an idea how to proceed?

—Not really. Let's just digress. Look, all we have to do is start talking, something will happen. Something always happen when we talk.

–Always does. So go ahead, start talking. Tell me what's cooking up in your head. I'll pick it up from there.

–No, you start.

–Why me first?

–Because when I listen to you talk, it inspires me.

–Picking Up the Loose Ends—

–Ok, here I go. After the interesting conversation Moinous had in the Montparnasse café with the old crippled war veteran about all the filthy shameful things France did for the past fifty years, after having decided he was finished with the French for good [ah the fucking French!], after having finally settled his accounts with his family [ah his stinking family!], after having embraced his faithful listener Féderman, Moinous announces he's going back to America.

–Hey wait a minute. Are you telling me the story of Mona is a continuation of **Aunt Rachel's Fur?**

–Yes, of course. Everything we do is a continuation of what we did before. Makes sense to me.

–You know what. It's a damn good idea. This way we can recuperate stuff from our previous inventions. We can recycle the old stories. Plagiarize ourselves. But don't you think we should first explain what went on in **The Fur** so the potential readers don't get lost?

–Hell with the potential readers. They should be prepared. If they haven't read **The Fur** too bad for them. If we start retelling everything Moinous did before he shows up in this story we'll never get him going.

–Ok, but I have a question. In that book Moinous calls himself Rémond. Why can't we continue to call him Rémond.

–Rémond was just a temporary name. Since this may be the ultimate story of Moinous, I think we should use his real name.

–You're right. Ok go on.

–Well, as I was saying, Moinous tells his listener Féderman that he is fed up with France, fed up with the French and the whole place.

He is going back to America even though, as he like to say, America is for the birds.

–Certainly not paradise. And to think there are still millions and millions of people who still believe in the American dream.

–Yes, pour les oiseaux. But as I recall, Moinous was not very enthusiastic when he announced he was going back to America.

–But he did say that he prefers the shitty mediocrity of America to the filthy hypocrisy of France.

–He even wrote that to his friend Ace. Saying he was disgusted with the French, their arrogance, their provincialism, their xenophobia.

—He has good reasons to be fed up. After all, France rejected him completely. Stole everything from him. Denied him his very existence. As for America, after ten years of disenchantment, misfortunes, misery...

–Stop interrupting me.

–I'm sorry. Go on.

–Well, no need to go over the same old stuff. Even though he says he's going back to America, Moinous is not sure he's made the right decision.

–So what can he do now.

–Well, it's for us to decide.

–Oh I see. Now we take control of his existence, so to speak. We take charge of his future.

–In a way yes. Now we set him in motion towards his future.

–Great idea.

—Setting Moinous in Motion—

–Of course, even though Moinous says he's going back to America, that does not mean a damn thing. You know him. He's the kind of guy who does not always do what he says. Moinous is unpredictable.

–Always contradicting himself.

–Doesn't he have the right to do so. To change his mind. He's a free man. Especially since right now he has no real ties to anything, to anyone. At least for the time being.

–What about Susan? You know, his rich American girl friend who wants him back.

–Susan, who doesn't know what she wants, bores him to death.

–I thought he was in love with her. Isn't he attracted to her.

–You're kidding. Her money attracts him.

–Her ass too, no?

–Well, yes, her ass. But Moinous is not really in love with her. It's a temporary thing. A stop. Une escale on his journey elsewhere.

–You may be right. I don't think Moinous is ready to settle down.

–He's too restless.

–Besides he has no idea who he is, where he wants to go, what he wants to be.

–He may not know who he is, where he wants to go, but he does claim to be a writer.

–So he says. But to be a writer one must write. Moinous spends more time talking about what he wants to write than doing the writing.

–Lately it's true. He talks a good book. He wastes his time talking the book he wants to write rather than writing it.

–He claims all great novels should be spoken rather than written. He thinks he's a modern troubadour. A epic story-teller.

—Though, in fairness, we have to grant him the fact that he did manage to write the Noodle Novel.

–Ah, yes. **Le Temps des Nouilles**. The book the French rejected because they found it too experimental.

–Too scatological, and also too autobiographical.

–What do those stupid French know about his life to say his writing is autobiographical.

—Especially since Moinous reinvents his life every morning.

–That's for damn sure. As he always says: *I make not distinction between what really happened to me and what I imagine happened to me*

—But, you have to admit, he spoke that novel more than he wrote it. In this sense **Le Temps des nouilles** is a spoken novel.

—That's why he always compares himself to Céline.

–Yes, he does, but Céline's stuff, as you know, is really written language even though it appears to be spoken.

–With Moinous it remains purely oral. In this sense he's just a Célino-Beatnick, as someone once called him.

—Look, let's forget Céline, that miserable anti-Semite. What now.

–Now. Well, Moinous is like a slippery bar of soap, no pun intended, so evasive you can never keep him in one place.

–Then we have to put him in a place where for a while he will remain still.

–Exactly. We have to immobilize him, otherwise he'll disappear again.

–Not easy, because, as you know, Moinous can't stay in the same place more than five minutes. He wants to be everywhere at the same time.

–That's how he put it in **Loose Shoes.**

–**Loose Shoes!** Don't tell me we're going to pillage **Loose Shoes** too.

–Why not. Everything related to Moinous will be useful to us.

–If you say so.

—Wait, I'll look up the passage where he says he wants to be everywhere at the same time, we'll stick it here. I wrote it down somewhere.

–While you look I'll check my notes too.

–Oh you have notes too?

–Of course I have notes. You think you're the only one to be obsessed by Moinous' pursuit of Mona.

—Pause while Jule and Juliette consult their notes—

—Plagiarizing Moinous –

–I found it. This is how he put it in his unfinished collection of fragments. Wow! it's perfect. Notice how he always speaks of himself in the third person.

–He loves to distance himself from himself in the third person. Makes him feel less egocentric.

–Listen, I'm quoting him.

–Go ahead I'll write it down.

—*He is here all the time. He always manages to be present, one way or another. He is hard as stone. As un uncatchable as the wind. As evasive as water. He never gives up.*

–Typical of him.

–Don't interrupt. *He never compromises.*

–So he claims.

–*He's stubborn. So stubborn.*

–*Comme une mule, disait sa mère,* before he became an orphan.

–Nicely said.

–I'm still quoting.

–Oh I see. *He doesn't give a damn about time. He cannot accept not to be everywhere at the same time.*

–Also. *He cannot at one time be other than at another.*

–Yes. *If this is the night, he will be there. He will arrive early, before every-one...*

–*He will leave late, after everyone.*

–You seem to know him by heart.

–Of course I do. I'm very fond of Moinous.

–Isn't it great we can quote him whenever we need.

–Very useful. This way Moinous helps us move the story along.

–Then let's move on.

—Moving Along –

–You see the problem with Moinous, il a toujours le feu au cul.

–Hey, do we also use French stuff in this story?

–Why not? After all Moinous is bilingual. And so is Mona is. If not, we'll make her bilingual when we introduce her into the story.

–The potential readers who don't know French might get frustrated.

–Why are you so concerned with the potential readers. Screw the potential readers. Besides, we're not inventing this story for mediocre readers. Are we?

–Certainly not. We are telling this story for the happy few.

–Moi je dirais, les happy fous.

—So let's not waste time with irrelevant questions. Proceed.

–Well, I forget if it's Moinous who made this statement, but I think it's appropriate, and we should quote here.

–Which statement? And where?

–Somewhere. I don't know where or when, but he did say: *When I am in one place I always wish I were somewhere else, but were I to be somewhere else, I would want to be elsewhere.*

–I have often said the same for myself.

–I know. The reason Moinous has la bougeotte all the time is because he gets bored quickly. He needs action.

–True, Moinous is a man of action. Remember he was a paratrooper once upon a time.

–And what a miserable time it was.

–All his life he has lived precariously on the edge of a precipice…

–…*leaning against the wind,* as he is fond of saying.

–What do you think he's seeking?

–It's for us to determine since he doesn't know himself.

–I suppose he's seeking himself. His real self. He says it in **Loose Shoes**.

–Looks like **LS** is going to be quite helpful to us in this endeavor.

–No doubt. Especially since **LS** can be read as Moinous' diary.

–I never thought of **LS** as Moinous' diary. You're right. The diary of his mind.

—This is how he defined himself in that book. Still speaking in the third person.

–He's incurable. Always multiplying himself.

–It's tough to find things in **LS**, there are no page numbers.

–Always trying to confuse those in search of Moinous.

—I found it. Listen. *He constantly tortures himself to know who he is. He wants to know, wants to understand himself.*

–Yes, I remember. And there is more to it. *Perhaps this ignorance of his own self is his strength, his destiny.*

–I think we misquoted him a bit. But doesn't matter. We got the essential.

–His destiny: *Never to understand himself, to remain always misunderstood.*

–Our story then will be Moinous' futile pursuit of himself.

—Does that mean his pursuit of Mona will be in vain too since she's his destiny.

–Not necessarily. It's up to us to find out.

—Ok, then let's find out. In spite of the possible failure looming ahead.

–Look, as Sam used to say, we must make of failure an occasion.

–You mean Sam is going to play a part in this one too?

–Inevitably so.

–Alright. So what's next?

—At the Airport—

–Ok. After having said goodbye to France, Moinous arrives at the airport to catch a plane back to where it all started. For certainly his life really started in America. What he endured before was a mere surplus of life.

–Yes, an excess of life. He escaped his own death. But it's true that Moinous reached the age of reason when he came to America.

–I think it was more the age of unreason.

–Yes, of course, unreason. No one is more unreasonable, more irrational than Moinous.

–So there he is waiting at gate 54 to board Flight 000 to America.

–Hey, I like that, flight triple 0. Perfect for Moinous.

–Moinous in a perfect vacuum.

–Do you remember why we decided he should wait at gate 54?

–For no particular reason. Or maybe because when you add the 5 with the 4 you get 9. The number that cancels itself in all additions.

–Probably, but if you don't think gate 54 is the right one, we can change it.

–No, that's fine. Let's go on.

–Alright, now we have to decide what Moinous is doing while waiting. At this point he has not yet changed his mind. It looks like he is definitely going back to America.

–So something must happen to make him change his mind.

–Right.

–Well, Mona comes into the picture. Unexpectedly.

–Unexpectedly? Personally I think her appearance was predestined.

–Hey, forget the pre-determined stuff. It might land us in mysticism.

–Ok, let's just say, Mona appears on the scene.

–Good enough.

–Mona Appears—

–Good. The apparition of Mona.

–You know what. I think Moinous himself should describe that.

–How?

–In a letter he writes to his friends.

–Which friends? Moinous has no friends in America.

–The friends he thinks he has.

–Ok. The friends he thinks he has. One is never sure about friends.

–Let's just assume he has friends.

–Maybe he has only one friend. Everybody has one friend.

–Yes, one friend only. What shall we call him?

–Does he have to have a name? Maybe it's a woman. Maybe he writes the letter to Susan.

–No, not Susan. He wants to get rid of her. He write to another writer like him lost in unrecognition. But I think it will make the letter more intimate if the recipient of the letter has a name.

–Then let's call him Ace.

–Why Ace?

–It's a good name. Enigmatic enough. And besides, I think Moinous in real life has a friend called Ace.

–How do you know that?

–I vaguely remember that he once told us about his friend Ace who lives in Peoria Illinois.

–You must be kidding. Peoria!

–Yes, Peoria. In fact I recall that Moinous once, when he was living in Buffalo, wrote to his friend Ace saying that he may die in Buffalo, and that would be terrible. And Ace replied, no worse than me who probably will die in Peoria.

–That's good. So the letter is addressed to his friend Ace.

–And in this letter he describes Mona. How she appeared before him.

–Excellent. But this letter, we, the story-tellers, are going to write it for Moinous.

–No, he writes it himself.

–Then how do we gain knowledge of the letter?

–As the inventor of this spontaneous story we know everything. Does not matter how we know it.

–The potential readers will really be confused.

–Here you go again with the potential readers. I told you we should not concern ourselves with them. And besides this story may never become public.

–What's the point of telling it then?

–There is no point. It's just that the story of Moinous & Mona must be told, one way or another, and we have been chosen to tell it.

–Who chose us?

–We chose ourselves.

–We did?

–Yes the day we started talking about this story we became the story-tellers, whether we like it or not, we have to go on with it.

–Alright. I go along with that.

–Perfect. Then let's have the letter that Moinous writes to his friend Ace without any further delay.

–No wait. Maybe before the letter we should first establish the state of mind of Moinous. You know how he feels as he ponders whether or not he will go back to America. Because that letter will change the course of his existence.

–You're right. And that's because of Mona.

–Then let us examine Moinous' state of mind as he seats at the airport waiting to board Flight 000.

–Moinous' State of Mind –

–So there he is, at gate 54, with his suitcase and his briefcase at his feet. Inside the briefcase the soiled manuscript of the novel, the noodle novel which was rejected by la sainte connasse des Éditions de l'Amour Fou et son enfant de coeur Gaston.

–Tu pousses là Jule.

–Ah come on, we have to allow ourselves some digressions into French, otherwise this thing is going to be too Anglo-Saxon for Mona & Moinous. They are both very cosmopolitan you know.

–Alright. But within reason.

–Are we capable of reason?

–Not really.

–Remember since we are inventing this thing on the spot, anything can happen.

–Then let it happen.

–Go on with Moinous' State of Mind.

–Well, as he sits there he thinks, rethinks rather, what happened during his stay in France, his disappointments, the rejections he suffered, the humiliation, how his lousy family treated him, I mean what's left of it, the uncles and aunts, and then he thinks about what is waiting for him in America, more disappointments, more emmerdements...

–Yes, he contemplates what his life will be with Susan if they get back together.

–Good point. She may be loaded with money, but she's not easy to live with, especially when she has her little crisis of jealousy, and her moods, and when she stifles him with her tenderness.

–In other words, Moinous is doing le bilan de sa vie dans sa tête.

–How do you say bilan in English?

–Wait, I'll look it up in the diko.

–It says *balance-sheet... To strike the balance... To reckon up one's loses...* Hey that's perfect. Moinous is reckoning his loses.

–Yes, perfect for his present situation. But that does not mean Moinous is a loser.

–How can he be a loser. He is an incurable optimist.

–Ok. So he is reflecting on his past and future situation.

–But perhaps he should concentrate on his present situation.

–Right. Make up his mind about what he wants to do.

–And while he reflects. Daydreams even. Let's his mind wander. Something extraordinary happens.

–Mona comes into the picture.

–Voilà!

–Wait. Maybe before we bring her in, Moinous should be given a chance to do a bit of self-examination.

–That's a good idea. But I think he should do that after he has seen Mona.

–You think so?

–Yes, because Mona will be the key element in his decision.

–I don't like that you talk of Mona as an element.

–Sorry. I meant. She will be the determining factor.

–Now you make a factor out of her. Jule you're hopeless.

–What would you say?

–Mona will be his *raison d'être* for the rest of his life.

–I like that. His *raison d'être*. Ok. Let's bring in Mona.

–That's what we said an hour ago.

–Right. And Moinous was going to describe her apparition in a letter to Ace.

–So let's have the letter.

—No, wait a minute. What do you think of this idea of bringing Mona in now so she can invent the real Moinous that she wants. We put the other Moinous aside for the time being. While he's writing his letter to Ace, we'll detour to Mona on the bench.

–Mona on the bench?

–Don't you remember, we had already invented a Mona sitting on a bench in some deserted place.

–You mean la vieille histoire des bancs. This time you're really going too far. Yes, of course, I remember the story of Mona & Leon, each sitting on a bench in some deserted place, facing each other but afraid to raise their heads to look at each other. There was some good stuff in that story, but I don't think this is the right place for it. Maybe later we can bring that in. I think we should have Moinous' letter to Ace now. Otherwise...

–You may be right. Okay. The letter. We'll recuperate the story of les bancs later.

**[while Moinous is writing the letter to Ace
Jule & Juliette go to the movie to see
Pierrot le Fou by Jean-Luc Godard]**

–Moinous' Letter to Ace –

My Dear Ace,

I know you're going to be disappointed. I'm not coming back. I changed my mind. I'm not going back to America.

–Paff! Just like that. He changes his mind
–Yes. Just like that. But now he will explain why.

The last time I wrote I told you I was coming back because I was fed
up with this stinking place. There is nothing left for me here. Only debris of myself. It's not here that my fragmented life will be reconstituted. Besides I can't stand those people anymore.

They're arrogant. Provincial. They hate everything that is foreign to them. They think they invented everything. I am finished with them. With this place.

So I decided to come back for good. I prefer American mediocrity to French hypocrisy. But I changed my mind. Just like that. A few moments ago.

No, I'm not staying here. I'm just going somewhere. Why not. I'm known for being impulsive. Indecisive. Evasive. Contradictory. Both in actions and words. I hope you'll understand. I'm not coming back. I'm going elsewhere. Where? I don't know yet.

I suppose I have to give you an explanation. Of sorts. Even if the reasons are dubious and questionable. You'll understand. I know you will.

So here we go. Why I changed my mind. Why I cannot come back. Why I'm willing to forsake everything. Including your friendship. To seek elsewhere what has been denied to me here. And there too.

The disappointment this place caused me. The humiliation I endured here these past few months. The shame I felt for having revealed to them more than I wanted to. To them who didn't care to listen. Who didn't give a shit about what I had to say. These seemed reasons enough to turn my back on this place and these people. To return where for the past ten years I pretended to have found myself. Until I realized that too was a delusion.

So here I am at the airport scribbling this note to you. Explaining why I am not coming back. Yes. That's where I am. At the airport.

At my feet that old beat-up suitcase of mine which I dragged to so many places in search of nothing. In it my things. Clothes. Junk. Souvenirs. My camera. A pair of binoculars. Don't ask me why binoculars. Perhaps to help me see things better. Inside my briefcase my tape recorder. How could I talk to myself if I didn't have my faithful recorder. Inside the briefcase also the humiliated manuscript of the book I wanted so much to leave here for them to read. The book that tried to explain everything. I suppose like all the others this one also failed to explain anything.

Stop whining Moinous, you'll say when reading this. No need to feel sorry for yourself. You're used to it. Used to be rejected. Ignored. Humiliated.

So here I am at Gate 54. Waiting to board Flight 000 back to America. Feeling somewhat empty. Aimless. Not sad. Just melancholic.

The plane is delayed. While waiting I am reading. One of my own books. What else. The manuscript that was rejected here. The noodle novel. Wondering why they didn't get the message. Too dark for them I suppose. Not explicit enough. Or perhaps too explicit.

I was on page 33. Where it says at the end of a paragraph. *Mum's the word.* I stopped reading. Pondering these words. There is something mysterious about them. I do not recall having written them. These are not my kind of words. Moinous words. Did someone whispered them to me while I was writing.

It's not unusual you know that a voice speaks in you from elsewhere when you are writing. André Gide used to call that *La voix de dieu*. I prefer to call it the voice of destiny. Perhaps someone was trying to tell me something. Sending me a message. A warning. *Mum's the word.* A distant caring voice was saying to me: Learn to be silent Moinous. You always say too much. That's why they don't listen to you.

Yet, they always want more than I say.

That's what I was thinking as I looked up from page 33. And there across from me. Directly across. As if she had been placed there for me to admire. The most beautiful woman I have ever seen. And I have looked at many women in my life. Stunning. Unreal. Surreal this one. I was so taken by her beauty the manuscript almost fell out of my hands. Imagine that. Me dropping one of my own books. For a moment I thought I recognized her. Someone I had known a long time ago. I felt a slight pinching. Best word I can find to express what I felt inside. Là dans le creux. Deep inside.

I almost got up to go ask that magnificent creature if we had met before. How crass it would have been. To throw such a cliché at her, at this…this…this figure of feminine perfection…this apparition.

Excuse the clumsy hesitating lyricism. I'm trying to make you visualize this beautiful young woman.

I say young because she appeared younger than me. I gave her twenty-eight. She had the face, the grace, the softness and hardness of a twenty-eight year old woman.

Let me describe her to you since after all she is the real reason for my not coming back.

I know what you are thinking. Here he goes again. Here goes Moinous thinking he has finally found his true *raison d'être*. The love of his life.

Please listen to me.

As I looked up our eyes touched just for a moment. Long enough for me to take a mental picture of her. She had eyes of maddening softness. Ah her eyes. They invaded me. Perhaps she was looking

at me while I was reading. Our eyes remained locked for a few seconds An eternity. Devouring each other. So blue her eyes. Transparent and deep. Shifting to grey when she turned her head slightly to the side away from my eyes.

Do you know that there are shallow eyes and deep eyes. Shallow eyes don't let you in. They keep you out. Shallow eyes are cold. Deep eyes invite you in. Hers were so deep. So inviting.

For that brief moment when our eyes met I was deep inside her. Do you understand what I'm saying. I was her. If I had spoken to her,I would have spoken with her voice.

She had magnificent blond hair. Long. Loose. Reckless. A superb mane of savage beauty. There was something feline about her.

After that quick eye to eye contact I went back to the book on my lap. Not that I was intimidated. Confused rather. I was not in the mood to flirt. To pick up a companion for the trip. I assumed she was going where I was going since she was also waiting at Gate 54. It seemed logical to me. But then when was I ever logical. Perhaps she was just sitting there because she didn't know where else to go. Or else she had noticed me.

You see how incorrigible I am. Always wanting to be the center of attention. What could she have seen in me to want to sit there and look at me. A depressed middle-aged man lost in his thoughts. Perhaps she had already guessed my age. Forty-two she must have thought. Did she find me good-looking? To her taste? Did she find my eyes shallow or deep?

Do you know what I was thinking while reading. Yes I always think while reading. Especially my own stuff since I know in advance what it says. I was thinking that my life will never be justified by a single absolute moment containing all the others. All the instants of my life have been provisional. Canceling the past as they face the future. Beyond the episodic. The present. The circumstantial. I am nothing. Nobody.

That's what I was thinking after her eyes met mine.

Does that make sense to you?

Though I was looking at the page I was holding in my hand, I was not reading. I could still feel her eyes on me. I was thinking. It would make my journey so much more pleasant, certainly less anguishing, to have her sit next to me on the plane. Don't we always fantasize whenever we fly that a lovely creature such as her will sit next to us on the plane. If it happens our life may be transformed forever. Instead a big fat beer drinking travel- ing salesman usually sits next to us and insists on telling us the pathetic story of his life.

I looked up again. I couldn't helped myself. I sensed that she was
still looking at me. Or else past me. Now I felt intimidated. I did not
reach for her eyes this time. I took in her entire body. She was dressed all
in black. Black turtleneck sweater. Black leather boots half way up her
calves. Tight black pants. One leg was crossed over the other revealing the
shape of a firm muscular voluptuous thigh. The kind of thigh one would
want to rest one's head upon and just drift and dream.

Wow am I sentimental suddenly. Please bear with me.

Don't start getting ideas about what I was seeing or thinking. I'm just
trying to describe her as precisely as I can. It is important that you see her
as I saw her.

In the seat next to her, a black bag and a jacket. From where I sat both
appeared to be genuine leather. A rounded bag. The kind one can shove
things in carelessly. Not too big. Not too small. It suited her perfectly. It
looked like it was part of her. I tried to imagine for a moment what was
inside.

One of her hands was resting casually on top of the bag. The other on
her lap. Very white hands. Long thin beautiful fingers. The silver nail polish glittering in the light. I could feel the softness of her skin from where I
sat. The hands of an artist. No, not a painter. A different kind of artist.
The graceful pose of her hands and the way

the fingers were curled suggested a different kind of artist than those
who create with their hands. These hands were made to float in the air.
Perhaps a dancer.

When my eyes reached her face I noticed a smile resting at the corner of
her lips. I could have been mistaken. Perhaps it was not a smile. A little
grimace at the insolence of my eyes. A sneer. A casual playful sneer at my
inquisitive look. Or else a sign. A message.

Our eyes met again and parted quickly. I think I blushed. I think she
did too. I went back to my book. Forcing myself not to look up. I had
skipped to page 45. Reading the passage where I describe how my father,

Papa, loved to listen to the song Ramona. In my head I heard the music and the words of that song. *Ramona je t'aimerai toute la vie...*

Could her name be Ramona. No. That would be too implausible.

Maybe just Mona. Why not. I decided on the spot that her name was Mona. I gave her that name. Even if I never see her again she would always remain Mona for me.

As I listened to the music of Ramona I suddenly felt my bones aching. Weeping. Not sadly. Happily. Aching and weeping of desire. I wanted this woman. I wanted to know her.

[No, not the way you two vicelards are thinking reading this]

— Hey! Look at that, Moinous is aware of our presence.

— Of course, he is. Otherwise he would just be a puppet. He has to be alive, and aware.

Okay. Knowing me as you know do. Of course I wanted her that way too. Most of all I wanted to be with her for the rest of my life.

Her eyes told she knew who I am. I wanted her to tell me who I am. Her eyes told me she understood the dark silence in me. The words, the sounds, the fundamental sounds in me which I'm unable to decode. I had to talk to her. Be with her.

Once more I felt like walking over to her and introducing myself. I am Moinous. Perhaps you have heard of me. I'm a novelist. How clumsy. How gauche. How pedestrian it would have been. How foolish. Vulgar even.

The first words I will speak to her if I am to speak to her will have to be so special. Perhaps just one word. But what word. And in which language shall it be spoken.

I couldn't determine at that moment what nationality she might be.

She didn't look foreign, and not American either. She was the universal woman.

I didn't want to stare at her. Didn't want to destroy with a persistent look what we had already said to each other with our eyes. I went back to my book. While turning pages without reading them, I was looking at the mental picture I had taken of her.

She was standing now in my head. Her back to me. As if looking into the distance.

Ok, yes, let me says it outright. She had a most inviting ass. You know I was going to say that. But it's not her ass in my mental image of her that attracted me. It was the shape of her body and the gracefulness of her pose. She didn't seem to be touching the ground. She was floating above the ground.

I swear that's how I saw her in my head. Floating. Dancing I'm tempted to say. I came out of my head and looked up.

She was not in her seat any more. I looked around. Saw her walking away from Gate 54 down the long corridor. No, she was not walking. She was floating away from me. I'm not kidding. Just the way I had seen her in my head.

Yes her ass was magnificent. It was dancing as she walked. I wanted to get up and run after her, but I was frozen in my seat. I felt my bones crack. Everything in me collapsed. She was leaving me.

Then she stopped a moment. Turned her head back just a little. I am not sure if she looked at me. Or past me. There was the same enigmatic smile on her face. Then she was gone. But I could still see her eyes and her imperceptible smile even though she was gone.

I told myself she'll be back. She went to the toilet. To get a cold drink. To make a phone call. To stretch her legs. She will be back. Of course she will be back. Her black bag was still there on the seat. But not her leather jacket.

I waited. I waited. I felt numb.

An airline agent announced that it was time to board the plane. My seat number was called. I didn't move. I was waiting for her. Everybody was already on the plane. The agent told me I should hurry the gate was closing. I told her I was not going. I changed my mind.

Gate 54 closed. I was still sitting there. Across from me her black bag. She had not returned. Had she forgotten it. Or did she leave it there on purpose.

Suddenly I had a terrible thought. Oh shit. She a terrorist, and there in that bag there is a bomb. It's going to explode any moment. That's why she left it there. She did look like those gorgeous female terrorist one sees in Hollywood movies. The black outfit. The slickness of her moves. I didn't know what to do. I felt totally helpless. If the fucking bomb goes off, so be it. I was not afraid. If the thing goes off. Good. Not a bad way to end. At least I'll go with her in my head.

I don't know how long I sat there. I felt lost. Paralyzed. A deep sadness came upon me. People were rushing in all directions around me. Suddenly the place was noisy. Unbearably noisy and crowded. I wanted to die right here. To close my eyes. Fall asleep forever. When will that bomb go off.

Then she appeared again in my head. She was walking away. She

stopped. Just as she had done when she walked away. Turned her head towards me. I noticed the smile at the corner of her mouth. It seems to be saying. Are you coming or what. Suddenly it all became clear.

I got up and walked over to where her black bag was.

It never occurred to me that I should give the bag to the airline desk and explain that it was left there. That perhaps there was a bomb inside.

I opened the bag. After I tell you what I found inside that bag you will understand why I am not coming back. I must find her. I will

find her. Even if I must travel the entire planet. Even if it takes the rest of my life. I must find her.

I opened her bag.

The first thing I found. A little tape recorder. Very much like mine. Same brand in fact.

I held it in my hand. Did she also like me speak to herself in this little box. Record her voice. Perhaps she left me a message. I put the tape recorder down next to me. I decided to listen to it later. After I explore further inside the bag. I did not feel that I was intruding on her life. On the contrary I felt that it was essential for me to see what was in her bag. It would tell me more about her.

Wait till you hear what I found. It was as if her whole life had been packed inside this bag.

I pulled out each thing one by one. Touched it. Looked at it. Yes. I examined each thing with all my senses. I wanted to know her completely.

This is what I found in Mona's bag. The clothes were neatly folded at the bottom of the bag. But various objets and the toilet pouch seemed to have been thrown in the bag rather randomly. From the way the bag was packed Mona seemed to be both orderly and chaotic at the same time. I liked that.

This is the order in which I took things out of Mona's bag. I'll describe everything in more details later. It's important that you see what I saw.

First the tape recorder. I could tell that half the tape had been used.

A French magazine. Elle. This means that Mona could read French.

A little volume of poems. In English. Mona is bilingual then. I glanced at the table of contents. The names of the poets indicated that it was an international collection. Some verses in certain poems were underlined. I will have to examine these later to see why Mona underlined these words.

A toilette pouch. I didn't open it. I assumed I would find in it the usual things a young woman needs. Make-up. Toothbrush and toothpaste. Etc.

A little bottle of perfume. Silences of Jacomo. Good taste I thought. I opened the bottle to smell Mona's perfume.

A little black notebook. Full of handwritten scribbling in it. The handwriting was neat though somewhat nervous. No, that's not it. The letters seemed to be dancing on the pages. As I flipped through the pages a photograph fell out. It was a black and white photo of a little girl sitting on a fence next to a horse. The horse head resting on the fence. A hand was holding the little girl's arm. The mother's hand I suppose. The little girl 5 or 6 years old had long blonde stresses. I could not tell the color of the yes in the black and white photo but I'm sure they were blue. It was Mona. No doubt about it. I'll tell you more about this photo later. I examined it very carefully.

A pair of silver ballet slippers. And next to these. The program of a Ballet performance of the Silver Bird by Dimitri Trofimovitch at the Esteemberg Opera House. The program listed Mona Petrashevsky dancing the Silver Bird. I couldn't believe it. Her name is Mona.

Suddenly it became clear. Mona is a ballet dancer. Her hands. The way she walked. Her whole body told me so. Mona was on her way to Esteenberg to perform in the Silver Bird.

Isn't it incredible that her name is Mona. And that I invented that name for her even before I saw it in the program. Now you understand my dear friends why I must find her. You also know where I'm going next.

–Paff! Just like that. Things fall in place.
–Yes, Juliette, that's the beauty of inventing a spontaneous story.

But let me finish telling you what else I found in Mona's bag.

A little round music box. When I opened it a miniature ballet dancer started whirling about to the music of the Trofimovitch's Silver Bird.

You see how everything was falling in place. Every objects in Mona's bag kept revealing a little more about her.

I don't think I need to describe every piece of clothing to you. Let me just say that there were three pairs of Victorian Secret panties. Very colorful. As I took them out of the bag I unfolded them and held them before me. Two silk négligés. One black the other light blue. And a two piece white pyjama with short pants. A black cashmere sweater. And a few other things. Just touching these made me feel as though I was touching her.

I took out everything. As I picked up the sweater you won't believe what I found underneath. At the bottom of the bag.

An apple. A big red shining apple. As I held it in my hand I smiled. The forbidden fruit I thought. Did Mona left me a message with this apple. Moinous are you willing to take the risk of eating the forbidden fruit with me. If so. Come and find me. That's what I thought.

Still smiling I brought the apple to my mouth and took a huge bite in it. It was sweet. Sweet and sour at the same time. It was an old apple. An ancient apple.

I was going to listen to the tape recorder, but suddenly I realized that I must go find Mona. I'll listen to the tape later.

So I got up and walked in the direction in which Mona had disappeared. I must find the next plane to Esteemberg.

The 2:00 clock flight to Esteemberg had already left. But there was another flight at 5:00 P.M.

It is now 2:56. Two hours to wait. To kill. I sat at gate 29. I now had Mona's bag with me beside my own stuff. I took out Mona's tape recorder and turn it on. This is what I heard. The voice was soft. Deep. Even a little hoarse. She spoke almost in a whisper. Hesitatingly. Mona was speaking in English but she was using a lot
of French words in what she was saying.

I had that dream again .. I can't explain it to myself. He reappears in my nights as if he was entertaining...par intermittence...the fire of my thought...He comes and goes like a ghost who haunts my thoughts sans cesse...to such an extent that his mystery has become familiar to me .. As if he was part of me...je suis parce qu'il est...yes I'm because he is...I act as he could have thought me to act...s'il existait...yes if he exists...is it possible that these nocturnal dreams are but simple meaningless chimeras...am I going crazy…folle…no I know…I feel that he exists elsewhere than just in my dreams…he seems so close and yet so inaccessible…perhaps he is there…à portée de main…within reach…and like a sotte I'm going to let him get away with my hesitations…happiness is so fragile…si éphémere .. I must not let him escape…so many who seek a solution…a sign…those to whom the answers are whispered…but who keep a close mind…because of fear…ignorance some-times .. By choice too often .. And if the barriers that stands between dream and reality were not soooooooo…quooooooooonn iiii…

The tape stopped abruptly. I tried in vain to go forward but there was nothing. Then I realized that the batteries had run out in Mona's recorder. I wanted to hear more. What dream. Am I the one she keeps dreaming. I took out Mona's notebook. Perhaps I would find the answer there.

In any case you now know why I am not coming back. Maybe I'll write to you again.

–Jule & Juliette Reflect on Moinous' Letter—

–That's it. The letter stops there. Abruptly. Just like Mona's tape. It's not even signed.

–Maybe Moinous never sent it.

–It's possible. He may have written for himself, and no one else. Pretending to be speaking to his friend Ace.

–Explaining to himself why he was not going back to America.

–I think you're right. So what do we do now?

–We follow him.

–And what happens when Moinous get to Esteemburg.

–Well, obviously it's too early in the story for him to catch up with Mona.

–So by the time he gets there she's already gone

–Yes. Or else something happens.

–What?

—I don't. The plane is delayed, or something like that.

–A blizzard. The plane cannot land in Esteemburg, and so Moinous is stranded in some other city.

–Excellent. And meanwhile Mona is already on her way to her next destination, wherever that may be. We'll determine that later.

–Good. But when Moinous finally gets to Esteemberg, there must something, some indication that tells him where he should go next. Mona must leave a trace, as if she already knows Moinous is pursuing her.

–Obviously. Otherwise, we won't be able to go on with the story.

–We'll have to invent something.

—No problem. Ok, so let's follow him.

–But maybe before we do that, we should now examine his state of mind as he embarks on this great adventure.

–Yes, you're right. We should. It is indeed a great adventure. Especially since we haven't the faintest idea of what is going to happen next.

–Also, the tone of Moinous' letter raises some questions. Didn't you think it was a bit too, how shall I put it…

–Ponderous. Un-Moinous like. Too serious. Almost academic, as would say.

–Yes, it didn't sound like the usual easy going free-wheeling Moinous. Maybe that's because of his present state of mind.

–That must be it.

—Ok, then. Let's have Moinous' state of mind.

—What shall we call it?

–I don't know. Since it's Moinous' own reflections on himself, let him give it a title.

–Good point.

—Oh Never to Have Been—

Stranded as he is between two moments, between two non-realities, one of which he never thought he would explore, even though fascinated by exotic places, Moinous, rather than look outside of himself to see who he is and where he is going, turns inward, introrse his old friend Sam would say, and launches into a deep self-examination, to see if, once and for all, he can understand himself...

The first conclusion he reaches, among a number of others, during this moment of self-invasion, if one can permit oneself a little rhetorical contortion, is that even though he may be a good writer, time will tell, as Sam used to say, he is an impossible person, impossible in the literal sense of the word, impossible to understand, just as he finds it impossible to understand himself...

The second conclusion, an easy one to reach, is that Moinous invented himself, in truth, Moinous says, still in the state of self-invasion, there is no Moinous, Moinous invents himself and cancels

himself on the spot of each situation in which he finds himself, he adapts to the circumstance of the moment , positively or negatively, doesn't matter since it comes out the same in the end, Sam would surely say, and Moinous must adapt, otherwise he would not be Moinous...

The third conclusion declares that Moinous conducts his life as a heroic self-construction, though it may appear to others as a pathetic self-deconstruction, Moinous expresses this notion by saying in his head, *je vais toujours vers le devenir,* Moinous always self-reflects bilingually...

The fourth conclusion is a conclusion within a conclusion that concludes that Moinous is moving towards an uncertain and precarious becoming, or as Sam once put it, he moves forward in order to fail better...

The fifth conclusion is self-evident, it reveals once and for all that Moinous is violently and incurably self-contradictory, but in the end, as old Sam would certainly emphasize, since everything Moinous says cancels out, he says nothing...

The sixth conclusion admits openly that Moinous's entire oeuvre was forged out of a confused and chaotic love life, Moinous makes a mental list...

love given

love denied
love received
love absented
love lost forever
love interrupted
love found again
love in absentia
love misdirected
love never found
love lost temporarily
Moinous smiles as he contemplates his mental list lovingly...

In the seventh conclusion Moinous pauses and wonders if he is prophetic in his work, he shakes his head inside his head, and smiles joyfully at this preposterous thought, and how he has just imagined his head inside his head smiling the smile that smiles at the smile, Moinous digresses back into his next conclusion...

In the eighth conclusion Moinous thinks that to others he must look very *bughouse*, as Sam once described William Butler Yeats...

The ninth conclusion brings Moinous to admit that his position in matters of social behavior is rather unstable, ambivalent, and often unpleasant and irritable, but in political matters, Moinous is unchangeable and constant, he remains a leftist...

The tenth conclusion digresses to the fact that Moinous was born left-handed, but became right-handed out of necessity at a young and fragile age because of a fractured left wrist causing him to betray his natural leftist dexterity, and this might explain his perennial crisis of doubt, Moinous approves with a motion of his head inside his head, no smile...

In the eleventh conclusion Moinous wonders, if to others he appears silly when he tells his stories, Moinous has so many stories to tell, he shrugs his shoulders inside his head, and mumbles, take it or leave it...

In the twelfth conclusion, Moinous says shrugging his shoulders, silly perhaps, but unlike the rest of the sillies, as he agrees with himself that his silliness is unique…

The thirteenth conclusion is important, within Moinous's train of thoughts, for it raises the question of whether or not his life coincides with his work, or vice versa, and if they are part of the same pattern, they must be, Moinous concludes, otherwise, he could not go on living and writing…

The fourteenth conclusion firmly states that just as Moinous' life is a-constant-life-in-progress, his work is also a-work-in-progress, Moinous looks pensive as he self-reflects this further and wonders if this means that both his life and his work will always remain unfinished…

In the fifteenth conclusion Moinous admits that his life is a violent contradiction, but that is in fact the source of his artistic impulse…

The sixteenth conclusion picks up where the fifteenth conclusion left off, and points out that Moinous's lack of inner self-assurance and his irreducibly divided nature are the dynamics of his writing…

The seventeenth conclusion brings Moinous to make, in a gentle ironic way, a quick mental list of what obsesses him…of course the list is incomplete…

    reincarnation
    communication
    the dead but not necessarily death
    artistic medium but not occult medium
    supernatural systems
    numerology
    coincidence
    lottery
    sexuality
    sports

In the eighteenth conclusion Moinous states that he is more interested in human life than vegetal life, though he makes an exception for trees, Moinous loves trees, and if he were to be reincarnated, which he doubts, he would request to come back as a tree, he doesn't know what species of tree he would want to be, but if possible he would prefer to come back as a tall majestic tree on top of a hill...

The nineteenth conclusion puzzles Moinous but forces him to admit that his thwarted youth, his virile sexuality, his peculiar sentimental association with the happy few, happy fous, as he loves to say, and his erotic adventures have lead him to recognize the feminine in him as the source of his creative power...

In the twentieth conclusion Moinous re-affirms his aesthetics, life is made up of stories, therefore his life is the story of his life, Moinous winks to Moinous in his head...

In the twenty-first conclusion Moinous asks himself if he is quarrelsome, ruthless, reckless, disrespectful, egocentric, brutal, elitist, then he asks if he is gentle, kind, generous, attentive, caring, interested, polite, he concludes that he is well balanced...

The twenty-second conclusion raises the question of whether or not Moinous has a tendency to be too verbose, too garrulous, and if his verbosity and garrulousness are screens for his linguistic insecurity and deficiency...

In the twenty-third conclusion, Moinous congratulates himself for having been able to escape in his writing the cacademic abuse of indeeding, moreovereing, as-it-wereing, thusing, thereforeing, foregrounding, etctering, he also congratulates himself for having

managed not to use cumbersome words like redolent, bespeak, purport, adumbrate, and others he cannot remember now...

The twenty-fourth conclusion brings a happy glitter to his eyes as he considers how he has managed to avoid in his work the kind of journalistic sentences one encounters too often in bad writing, to illustrate

Moinous rereads mentally a sentence in a piece of writing he encountered recently, *Yet it is wide of the mark in failing to grasp the tragic import of an excoriating vision of irrevocable action as unelectable destiny*, Moinous shakes his head in disgust...

The twenty-fifth conclusion brings Moinous to aks if his muse has finally spoken to him, or if it is too late, Moinous bangs his fist on the armrest of the seat in which he is seated to do his self-reflecting, and shouts, in his head of course, no, it is not too late, the muse will speak to me...

The twenty-sixth conclusion is of major importance because it concerns the struggle of the writer, in this case Moinous, to understand from whence the images come that threaten to master him...

In the second part of this conclusion, Moinous stubbornly considers ways to ensure that these images keep coming, *tétu comme une mule*, his mother used to say about him...

The twenty-seventh conclusion brings Moinous to wonder if there is a link between sex and the magic of writing, Moinous does not pursue this thought much further, for he knows that episodes of sexual energy and confusion in his life have always been closely paralleled by periods of magical explosions in his work...

The twenty-eighth conclusion is briefly stated, irrational humor...

In the twenty-ninth conclusion Moinous asks himself if he should come down off his stilts more often...

The thirtieth conclusion consists of a list in which Moinous wonders if he is...

a compulsive masturbator
a displaced person
an true orphan
un gourmand
un con
a genius
an acrobat

a deranged person
a demented person
a nice person
a fool
Moinous pauses, and then makes a second list in which he asks if he
is...
paranoid
lecherous
shy
crazy
happy
envious
salacious
depressive
In a third list, Moinous loves lists, he wonders if he fears...
impotence
speechlessness
pain
loneliness
death
obesity
rats & snakes
Moinous asks in the thirty-first conclusion if he would be willing to
make a fool of himself to be recognized...

The thirty-first conclusion is enormous in its implication, Am I as I
am, Moinous asks, because my mother forced me to stop loving myself
too soon, and as he asks himself this, Moinous, for some unexplainable
reason, recalls this line from W.B. Yeats, *a shudder in the loin engenders
there the broken wall, the burning roof and tower*...

The thirty-second conclusion was reached with some apprehension,
Moinous questions if his life has been spent vainly in constructing a
drama of opposites, anti-selves, masks, metaphors, he who abhors

metaphors, Moinous concludes, no, that would be too banal, too much of a simplification...

The thirty-third conclusion has Moinous worrying about his bones, where will his bones find their final resting place, if they are buried, he wants the skeleton to be buried upright, and if his bones are reduced to ashes, he wants the ashes to be placed in a very tall thin container, Moinous wants to be vertical in death, Moinous bursts into mental laughter...

In the thirty-fourth conclusion Moinous explains that the past is what one should not have been, the present is what one ought not be, the future is what artists are...

In the thirty-fifth conclusion Moinous decides that he is a conglomeration of past and present stages of civilization, bits from

books and newspapers, scraps of humanity, rags and tatters of clothing patched together as is the human soul...

Moinous's final conclusion takes the form of a poetic statement, as he remains stranded between two non-realities...

there in the tomb
the dark will grow darker
and when the wind will come up
from the great void and roar
it will make my old bones rattle

Moinous gets up from his thinking chair and goes directly to his desk to write his conclusions...

while writing the conclusions he has reached in the process of exploring his inner himself, he stops a moment to reflect further, not about his bones, but about his words...

Will my words still shake after I have changed tense, will they continue to rattle into history without me, or will there be a sigh of relief from the potentials as they whisper, Moinous, you should not have been, you should have left the dead alone?

—a new departure—

—Well, what do you make of these conclusions?

—I'm as puzzled as you are. But if that's how Moinous sees himself, that's how we must accept him. You and I know that characters in a story take on a life of their own, and after a while they dictate to the story-teller how they should be told.

–That's why one can never tell the teller from the told, as Sam once put it.

–Speaking of Sam. Did you notice how often Moinous refers to him. I think he's obsessed with Sam.

–More than obsessed. He cannot live, cannot write without Sam.

–So what now?

–Let's take a break, and when we come back let's attempt a new departure.

–How about speaking the story of Moinous & Mona in two languages simultaneously since they are both bilingual.

–Great idea. We'll give a try.

ABOUT THE AUTHOR

Eckhard Gerdes teaches creative writing and English at Macon State College. He earned an MFA in Writing from the School of the Art Institute of Chicago, and is the author of three previously published novels. He lives with his wife, filmmaker Persis Gerdes, and their sons, Sterling, Ludwig, and Ulysses.

0-595-21404-5